TANGLED IN WATER

A NOVEL

The costume could hide her scars
but not the truth.

PAM RECORDS

Award-winning Author of *Trapped in Glass*

HISTORIUM PRESS

U.S.A.

First Edition published by Historium Press

Images by Shutterstock, Imagine, Promeai, & Public Domain
Cover designed by White Rabbit Arts at The Historical Fiction Company

Visit the author's page at
www.historiumpress.com/pam-records

Library of Congress Cataloging-in-Publication Data on file

Hardcover ISBN: 978-1-962465-92-2
Paperback ISBN: 978-1-962465-91-5
E-Book ISBN: 978-1-962465-90-8

Historium Press, a subsidiary of
The Historical Fiction Company
New York, NY / Macon, GA
2025

Pam Records,

award-winning author of the novels

"Trapped in Glass" & "Tied with Twine"

PART ONE
CHICAGO, 1932

CHAPTER 1

NATTIE maneuvered her rollie chair across the mezzanine, zig-zagging around cardboard birthday hats and paper streamers scattered around the floor, remnants from last night's hullabaloo.

What a mess.

She rolled up to the railing so she could peer over, see how close they were to departure. There was a four-foot gap where the railing was busted, the pieces hanging, precariously suspended over the deck below. Tempting.

Her chair fit right through the gap. She rolled out to the edge. Her bare toes hung over. Two stories below, deckhands hustled, loading inventory, hauling crates, hoisting cables, chasing rats, swatting at bloodthirsty mayflies, and spewing rants of rancid jokes, both blasphemous and raunchy. She only heard bits. But she knew. It was the usual rigamarole before they left port.

She thought about spitting, seeing if she could hit one of the oafs on the head, but then she'd have to hide. Some of those gorillas could run and wouldn't think twice about tossing the ship's star attraction overboard, sequins and all. It was too early in the morning for so much fun.

And no one needed another incident.

Buster went through the railing four nights ago, took a dive. Headfirst. Or maybe a cannonball. No one saw what happened. Could have just tumbled. Just drunker than a skunk, again. The jerk.

Words from the five-minute funeral still hovered over the scene. Made her teeth itch with the creepies. A red carnation smeared on the floor didn't help matters. Must have fallen from the mortuary man's lapel. Icing on the nightmare cake.

The busted railing looked chewed. Little rat teeth? Or a switchblade, the kind the sailors used for picking their teeth? Did someone sabotage the railing? Why didn't Captain-Father send someone with a toolbox to fix the mess? It was just a stone's throw from her station, the spotlight making the jagged wood tears seem more grotesque, rude and vulnerable at once. She shivered.

She closed her eyes. She scootched her chair back, safer. The wooden wheels made crunching sounds, carnation crumbs, dead gnats, Buster slobbers, and a preserved scream or two.

She rolled out again.

Then back.

Out further.

B a c k.

Out.

Back.

She teetered, sensing the edge of the deck under the wheels. Was this how Buster fell? He leaned too far? Did he hear the railing snap? It was a long way down, knowing you were going to splat on the deck.

She had liked the old coot. He musta been sixty, maybe seventy years old, overcome with nose hair and earwax, eyebrows like beasts. He had worked in the boiler room, came topside for a smoke and a look-see over the water when the partying was packed up and put to bed, a whisper short of dawn.

He used to call her Fish-Girl, which was stupid. But, coming from him, it wasn't so bad. When he went ashore, he brought back taffy and always shared some. When she was a kid they played Pocket Hunt. She got to keep whatever she found. Pocket lint, strings, quarters, or taffy. "Don't break a fish tooth," he used to say with a goofy wink.

"Mermaids aren't fish," she always mumbled back around mouthfuls of cherry-lemon, her favorite. He always laughed at that.

She was smarter now, all grown up. Sixteen candles were on the cake last night. Sometimes Captain-Father said something different, older or younger, depending on the yarn he was spinning and who was listening or why.

She just played along with the game, wore the costume, sat in the tank, hid her ugly legs in the sequined get-up, daydreamed about being a sea critter able to swim far far away. But she had limits.

"Right, Buster?"

Laughter rippled over the metal floor, over rivets and rust and over the ledge, a waterfall of old man gut-chuckles and sputters. She heard it. She could touch it. She reached—

A wind current rushed up from the lake below. A gull swooped so close that she could feel the air movement on her cheek and smell traces of fish guts and lake foam. Her costume tail dangled over the edge, the fabric cascading into a silhouette, a famous shape, curves with two points, alluring and childish at once. Loose sequins flittered all the way down. Bits of pinks and violets caught light flickers. All. The. Way. Down. Almost pretty.

No one noticed. No one said, "Hey, mermaid, don't get so close. That's not safe. You could fall."

It was just as well. She wouldn't listen anyway. She could do what she wanted.

She stretched her neck, looking down to the main deck of the *Lake Maiden.*

Jakub was supposed to be on the deck. She was just going to wave to him, that's all. Maybe smile. She had practiced in the mirror and had a little half smirk picked out. She didn't want to appear too eager. Men prefer subtle, Viola said. With her boas and fancy fringe, Viola was far from subtle.

On Saturdays, Jakub manned the ticket booth, collecting fares. Most voyages were short, day trips. Once a month they made a three-day excursion, Chicago to New York with a stop in Canada to take on inventory, the good stuff, not bathtub swill. That's what 'Tender called the moonshine that came from copper stills. Swill. Or chicken piss.

Jakub should be setting up the ticket booth by now. There were posters and flags for the gangway where passengers boarded, the hoity-toities of Chicago's Gold Coast, plus various distributors and aldermen and prosecutors with poor eyesight and large palms joined them for the excursions. Entertainment, food, and beverages were included. No one came on board for a boat ride.

A few came to see the Polish mermaid. *Natalia.*

She watched the deck below. And waited.

Still no sign of Jakub, the goofy boy. He had promised to visit her Mermaid Lagoon before they left port. He liked to tease, though. Maybe he'd pop up out from behind a rack of lifeboats or a bolted-down deck chair and say, "Ha! I surprised you! Now give me a kiss."

She had been waiting for that kiss for an awful long time. She was starting to think it might never happen. She would die an old maid, her sickly bones too weak to carry her own weight, her legs withering away to nothing but sawdust and mush, maybe some fishing line and glue to hold the make-believe in place. Her rollie chair and mermaid costume were her only defenses. And her lovely wit, of course. And that smile she had practiced.

Where is he?

She watched the clock, the big one on the main deck. Minutes tippy-toed over the mezzanine's dance floor, dainty-like.

Tick Tock.

The invisible band warmed up. She yawned.

A few leftover fog wisps sulked around the grand staircase, conniving in corners, plotting mildew and other mayhem. Conspirators invited her to join them. Mutiny at midnight, they promised. The pirates looked mischievous.

Maybe she dosed.

Old spirits sang sea shanties and told wayfaring tales no one sane could believe. She saw them hobnobbing behind the lifeboats, uninvited guests swarming together. There were native fishermen and French fur traders and British soldiers who made navigation charts. Their bones were buried on the lake bottom, 150 fathoms below the surface.

They invited her to join them on the deck, the ill-fated mermaid, jilted by a boy, a lousy land lubber. She could splat right there. That spot.

"C'mon, honey," one of them called.

Hmm. Not today.

"I've got taffy in my pocket," called bloody Buster.

Where —

She jumped. Startled awake.

A large ship sailed past, too close, too fast, creating a wake. Furrowed waves hit the *Lake Maiden's* stern.

Kabumb. Kabumb-bup.

The paddlewheel bounced.

Nattie's chair lurched forward, the front wheels spinning in air, over nothing.

Her stomach dropped. Arms flailed for something to grab. Her costume tail billowed out like a sail. Flicks of color bit her face. She slid—

She screamed.

Her costume caught on a floor bolt—jerking the chair to a stop.

Frozen. One wheel on the edge.

She reached behind her and found the railing stumps. She grabbed. Using her arms, she rolled herself back, away from the edge. Far enough.

Whew.

She sat motionless, waiting for her heart to slow down.

I'm fine. Fine. Just fine. No trouble here. Just another death-defying mermaid stunt, folks. No harm done.

She sighed. She realized her hands were trembling.

How silly.

She looked around to make sure no one had witnessed her near demise. Or heard her scream. She almost went over, just like Buster.

Just like poor Buster

Nattie rolled to her station, a glass tank with plaster rocks, some sand and a couple buckets of water, not even enough to cover her knees, if mermaids had knees. NATALIA, THE GREAT LAKES MERMAID was etched in a brass plaque at the base.

She sniffled, wiping her nose on her arm. Her eyes got all watery for some reason. She didn't have a sleeve. Couldn't use her fancy top— there'd be hell to pay if she got snot all over her sequins and shells. Why test her luck?

Daredevil tail dangling was enough danger for one day.

She took a big whiff of lake air, trying to steady herself. Morning was still heavy with fog, dampness, and lingering moon vapors. The boat settled into small bobbles, up and down. No more big waves, for now.

A cricket carried on in some corner, not caring one bit that night had expired and dawn had taken over. The alarm in the crew's quarters had sounded hours ago, calling the deck hands and boiler rooms boys to report to their stations. The clanking of metal hatches and feet on gangways always woke her. Every. Single. Morning.

Her nest was on the same level as the galley. She loved the smell of coffee brewing and morning biscuits baking. She wasn't allowed to eat with the deckhands anymore, though. She had outgrown sitting on laps and lucky belly rubs and hair petting, like she was puppy.

She was a distraction that hungry men didn't need, Mabella, the cook, had told her in a hushed tone with raised eyebrows and winks Nattie was supposed to understand but she didn't. She should eat at her station, where she belonged, Mabella had said.

Where I belong? Where's that?

PAM RECORDS

She sniffed again. And again. Maybe she could get a hint of biscuit goodness through the air vent. Nope.

A strange, flowery scent came through the vents instead, overly sweet. Overwhelming. Why would some funeral-grade gardenia smell suddenly be slinking around the mezzanine? Buster didn't have any fancy florist wreath. Perfume? Couldn't be. Passengers hadn't boarded yet, and it was far too early for the chorus girls to be up and flouncing about. They'd still be recovering from last night's shindig. So, who—

> *"Young lady! Put that bottle down immediately. Don't you dare spill it."*

She shivered, dread tickling at the back of her throat, like a cold coming on. Something wasn't right.

Her stomach gurgled. Maybe it was her almost-fall that had riled her up. Or thinking about Buster. Or maybe she'd eaten too many green olives. She'd scarfed down a handful when she first rolled across the mezzanine this morning. She had scavenged them from the martini glasses that were still scattered about on the tables, leftovers from last night's party. Jedidiah hadn't been by for his sweep-through yet. He wasn't himself these days. It was understandable, Buster being a friend of his and all.

Seagulls circled overhead, crying too, looking for their breakfast. Nattie waved and tossed them the last of the olive pimentos she'd been saving for them. They made cawing screeches, some kind of thanks. They preferred biscuits. Tough titty.

> *"You can't always get what you want."*

Her stomach churned, gurgling louder, uneasy. This perfume smell was doing it. Its flowery stink was downright creepy, out of place against the regular port smells: rotting fish, galley scraps, oily bilge.

> *"That's not for you, I've told you a million times. Don't touch my gloves. Not my perfume. Not my pearls. Do you want me to smack you?"*

Nattie's hand went to the pearls around her neck, yesterday's birthday present from Captain-Father. It was a small miracle that the busy ship's captain had remembered his daughter's birthday at all. He usually left such parenting obligations to the crew. Maybe Mimi, the seamstress, had nudged him to buy a gift. She'd arranged for the celebration after the second show. Or maybe she bought it herself, all for the act.

"Every girl deserves a birthday party when she turns sixteen," the seamstress had declared, her French accent making the idea seem overly dramatic, more farce on a boat built of hooey.

> *"We'll bring a cake out on stage with candles. We'll sing to you. You'll pretend to be humble and grateful. You can do that cute pucker-up thing you do. The audience will eat it up."*

Mimi had been right. The men in the audience got a kick out of the cake bit, even the stupid paper hats. The Detroit distributors in the front row had hooted it up big then promised to show her a real celebration, until the captain waltzed on stage, all somber and dead serious, scowling like he was posing for a museum exhibit of great seafarers. He took the microphone and blubbered some nonsense to the audience, his usual made-up mermaid story. A mysterious sea creature washed up on the beach of Lake Michigan, and it was his great luck to find her and adopt her as his own daughter. It was the old malarky he'd come up with years ago, when it became clear the leg braces weren't doing much good.

At least the costume hid the scars. Too bad it couldn't cover up the other pains from the Before days, when their little family had lived on land. She remembered the apartment, the yelling, the slamming, being told to shut up. And that she had ruined everything. It was all her fault. Who wants a sick kid? No one.

She remembered the carpet with giant red flowers on green. She remembered crawling, because she fell, face first into the rug. She had pulled herself over the vibrant colors, crying, wool fibers in her mouth, slobbers falling on the rug. The smell of wet wool. And perfume.

On the stage last night, Captain-Father told a different story, complete with an eye-dab and throat-catch on cue to commemorate the magical mermaid's birthday. Then he had handed her a wrapped box with a big bow and whispered to her, "These were your mother's. You're so much like her. Every day I see more of her in you."

The words had shot straight to her brain and burst into sparks of red. She'd wanted to yell that she didn't want to be like her mother at all, but the air was knocked out of her. She couldn't say a word, not alone open the box. So, Margret, Miss Theater, had jumped out from behind the curtain and tore open the wrapping paper like Nattie was too stupid to do it herself.

"Smile, will you? Just smile," Margret had hissed in her ear, always the stage director and dictator. She was also Captain-Father's special friend.

Nattie had felt her face blush; heat climbing to her scalp. That was when things went from bad to worse. Her stupid, warped, good-for-nothing legs—hidden in her costume—had buckled under her. Captain-Father had scooped her up and carried her off stage.

Last night's gift box had contained a pearl necklace. The glossy pearls looked real, with a warm swirly glimmer that could make you feel dreamy, safe and snug, wanted. Nothing like the pretend pearls that were sewn onto her costume along with the sequins and plaster shells Mimi bought at Woolworth.

She wore the pearls all night. Even to bed, mostly because there was no one to properly undo the clasp and she knew she shouldn't yank and bust the string, making little pearls bounce all over the prop room floor. It wasn't easy to sleep in pearls. They had kept her awake all night, telling her she was useless, had half a brain and a paper spine, and snowball's chance in hell of amounting to anything much. For being a present, those pearls had a vicious side.

No wonder she was awake so early and so tired and mad about a stupid boiler room boy and curious about edges and falling and thinking about Buster.

"Come fly with me," sang a woman in the dream, wearing nothing but a boa, chicken feathers dyed pink and strung on fishing line.

Nattie covered her ears.

Enough.

She fumbled for the necklace clasp at the back of her neck but couldn't find it. Her fingers tore at the beads and the strings and the glossy finish that coated—

My mother's necklace.

My mother's voice.

My mother's perfume.

14

That was it! She sucked in a snootful of the flower scent just to be sure. Yep. That was the smell. She recognized it now—the same perfume her mother had worn back when Nattie would watch her get ready for her stage shows. Perched in front of a mirror framed with lightbulbs, Queenie would dab eau de cologne from a pint-size bottle, almost enough to hide the cigarette stink that clung to her pale skin. She then applied layers of rouge and painted her lips with a tiny brush she dipped in a small pot of lip paint. Her mother was a star at the kind of theater where stars, even the Queen of Opera, tossed their long white gloves into the audience.

Bada boom.

Who else would wear that God-awful perfume? Nattie looked around, half expecting to see Queenie in all her regal glory climbing the curved staircase, her auburn hair flowing behind her like a flag rallying troops through a battlefield. Perhaps the famed vaudeville star had decided to drop in for a mother-daughter chat. Maybe she wanted to give her mermaid daughter some performance tips.

Wouldn't that be a real hoot? *Where have you been all these years, mother?*

Queenie wouldn't have encouraging words. She'd nitpick. Hem-haw, nag, and stew. Find something to complain about because that was her way. Nattie, in her sequined costume, was almost as famous as Queenie had been in her day, before the incident.

Facedown in the sand, red lips open . . .

CHAPTER 2

JAKUB jumped down from his bunk, his boots making a loud thud as he landed on the metal deck. The ringing metal masked his grunting and groaning. He was mad and wasn't worried about keeping his grumbles to himself. He even kicked at the hatchway as he stormed out of the bunk room. No one noticed. At least no one said a thing. It wasn't like he had buddies among the crew.

He had been ordered to work the boiler room this morning. The last-minute change was flaming his temper. He was used to being shoved around, pushed around, yelled at, kicked at and slugged, threatened, and harassed, up one side and down another. He had been taking it, like a man. But it was getting old.

He was supposed to meet Nattie before they left port. He had promised her. He was going to give her rides in that wheelchair of hers, fast-sailing down the mezzanine before the dance floor got all filled up with passengers. She deserved to have some fun.

Now Nattie would think he was a jerk for not showing up, as promised.

Maybe he was a jerk. A stupid one to boot. He had no idea how to sweet-talk a girl like Natalia. She was a mystery. And it just wasn't that costume she had to wear. She was something else. All serious but with a funny streak. Innocent, but with an ornery side that was gonna get her in trouble one of these days. She had a way of stirring up the embers. Even old Buster could get hooked, with his drooling, flapping jowls, gumming that taffy.

He got what he deserved.

Jakub quick-raced to the boiler room, taking the rat-run and the ladder down to the ship's belly. Maybe he could help get the boilers steamed up and squared away then they would let him go back topside to sell tickets. He liked selling tickets, especially on Saturdays. That was when fellas brought their doll faces with them for some romancing and dancing. And even the respectable, married ones, the bankers and businessmen in wool suits, sometimes brought their missus in tow, as if they might like to watch dancing girls strut on stage in pirate outfits.

16

Sometimes when he sold them a ticket, the women licked their lips and pinched his cheek, ruffled his hair, and gave him a tip. They liked his red hair and freckles, especially if he wore his overalls, rolled up to his shins and did lots of aww-shucking and grinning the way they expected hick boys to do. He wasn't no hick. Was born and raised in the back of a saloon in a Polish corner of the southside. He knew alley hustling. Hell, as a kid he had rented his cot in the storeroom to an enterprising waitress, named Margret, for a dime. Spent most of his youth sleeping in a wet spot, cans of peas and mason jars of pickles looming over him, judging.

Knowing Margret was proving useful. She gave him fluff jobs on the boat, like selling tickets, when she could. As long as he kept quiet about the old days when she had to take all those ten-minute naps.

He didn't like the women pinching. But he liked the tipping. Only sometimes the womenfolk had other ideas too, it seemed. And he wasn't interested in none of that. But he was saving his dollars. He knew just as well as any fella that courting a young lady required cash, even if she lived on a boat.

He had a lot of saving up to do. A lot of planning. A lot of proving himself. That's why he was here. Antonio had arranged it. He was being watched, he knew. Antonio had people on board the boat, just didn't know who exactly. So, Jakub stayed wary. Alert. Look at what happened to Buster.

The boiler room was past the galley. He could smell the biscuits. Then as he got closer to the boiler room, it was only coal and flames and heat and Godawfulinferno that could melt the skin off your face before you thought to back up a step or two. The fire scared him. The heat scared him more.

The other men scared him the most. They were mostly big men with blubber bellies that poured out sweat like leaking dams. There were a few scrawny ones, too, sacks of bones, the meat already cooked off them like they had been stewing for years. They were the dangerous ones, the decency cooked off long ago, too.

Big John, the man in charge, was from the big boy camp. Three hundred pounds on him, at least.

"What took you so long? Putty-boy? You fill in where we need you. Filler. That's you," yelled Big John over the roar of coal burning.

Jakub shrugged and picked up a shovel.

"Yeah, well, I came when I got the word. Saturday is usually ticket

17

day. Today's Saturday. Miss Margret likes me to sell tickets."

"Oh, really? Did you hear that, boys? Putty here wants to be topside to sell tickets. He says it's Saturday. Ticket day." Then Big John cocked a fat hip and put his hands on his waist, sticking his bulbus chest out, mimicking the woman. "Miss Margret says so," he squealed in a falsetto that was strange coming from the man's fat face.

The other fellas paused shoveling to yuck it up.

Don't get worked up. Ignore them.

Milton, one of the scrawnies, fluffed at Jakub's hair, making it stand up. "He likes selling tickets, like this here is the County Fair and we're selling rides to the kiddies."

"You mean the Ferris Wheel? Fairy wheel? I think the fairy boy must like the fairy wheels," answered Rocko, one of the big fellas, his face bright red and shiny with sweat.

"Yeah, he likes the fairytales. He's sweet on a mermaid, you know," said Lamont, joining in the razzing.

Let it go. Let it go.

"Where do you want me, Boss?" Jakub asked, trying to stay calm.

Big John patted him on the back and pointed at the second boiler. A scrawny Black man was there. He looked new. He leaned on his shovel, like he was weak kneed, his eyes wide open like he was taking in a wonderous sight. Or maybe he was wondering if this was the burning hellfire he heard about in church.

The new guy was quick to jump in, like he was curious. "There's really a mermaid on board? Is she all fish? She's got a fancy tail? Does it come off? What's underneath?"

Jakub tried to ignore him. The man sounded incredulous like he believed the story. Nobody could be that dumb, could they? Maybe he was just teasing. Maybe he ought to get to work.

"I thought she was too good for working lads like us. Only took a shine to the distributor boys?" piped in one of the scrawny fellas, wiping his face.

"Naw, she'll fish wiggle her little shiny fish ass for anyone that feeds her. Just offer her a biscuit and see what she does."

"She'll pucker up those lips in a little fish face like this," said Ronald, imitating fish lips opening and closing. Then he added a wiggle to his ass.

The men roared with laughter. The new guy slapped him on the back like they were best buddies sharing a joke. The imbecilic hee-hawed, carrying on like he was a mule, his big buck teeth sticking out crooked, a picket fence after a storm.

Jakub had enough.

His damaged heart thumbed in erratic beats, skipping the usual rhythm. He felt the pangs. Breath came in spurts. He dropped his shovel. It clanged like an alarm.

Jakub patted his pocket. He found his jackknife. Just in case.

"Maybe she sucks on him with those fish lips. You think?" asked Ronald

"Only if he brings taffy!" said Milton

New man laughed. It was the laughing that made Jakub furious.

"All right," shouted Big John coming between the men. "Enough. Get to work all of you. Putty, get your shovel. Haul coal. Ronald, shovel. Now. Silas, get to work."

Ronald wasn't done. He mumbled, sneering out the side of his mouth, loud enough for Jakub to hear.

"Look what it got old Buster. Now he's swimming with the fishes."

"He deserved *better,*" added Milton.

"Ought to have *known better,*" said Jakub and he went to work, heart thumping fast, but steady. Steady as she goes. Out to deep water.

And laugher rippled over the metal floor.

CHAPTER 3

NATTIE tried to ignore the odd perfume scent, although she had no idea where it could be coming from. And it was downright creepy.

Don't think about it.

She tried lounging back in her rollie chair like a servant should be fanning her and feeding her peeled grapes. She fumbled in her hair for a bobby pin and used it to pick olive pieces out of her teeth. It was something to do, killed a minute or two.

A snail race! How about that? She rooted around in the rocks of her tank for Billie and Millie, the current champions of Mermaid Downs, the most famous snail racetrack on Lake Michigan. She found the shells—but Billie and Millie were nothing but shriveled gray boogers stuck in the shells. Seemed they had both expired overnight.

So rude of them.

She flicked them over the railing. They didn't scream the long way down. No one shed a tear. No point in boo-hoo-hooing over the dead.

Right, Buster? Right Queenie?

She sat back and watched and waited as the crew carried on, plodding through the steps for departure. Nattie was impatient to get out on the lake. The further from land, the better. The wind was always much cleaner and fresher—after Chicago and the haze from the East Chicago mills and the stockyard run-off. Such stink.

In the open lake, the *Lake Maiden* sailed better too, free of the land tethers that made her rivets and welds strain. The boat was old, showing signs of neglect. No one pampered her or promised her fresh paint or other gifts. No pearls for this has-been lady. Nattie patted the metal wall beside her tank. The engines purred like a giant cat.

"We'll be going soon, friend. I'm sure. Don't worry. Not much longer, now," she said.

The wind was picking up, she noticed. A storm was coming, probably. She felt the ache in her legs. It might be a good one, with thunder and lightning and the crew battening down the hatches so no one washed overboard. Losing a passenger wasn't good for business, especially if it was one of Chicago's all-powerful politicians, businessmen, or bankers. Captain-Father had been courting a whole slew of bankers.

She wasn't too worried about a storm. Mermaids were nearly one hundred percent waterproof. The cardboard crown she wore, though, wouldn't survive a sneeze.

She opened the clamshell case, the child-size suitcase next to her tank, so she could stash the crown for safekeeping. She moved the sequined brush and comb, mermaid props, to the side, then shifted the prized possessions. There were six hatpins, one diamond bracelet, two gold watches, an ornate brass key, and a collection of fountain pens. Toward the bottom there were the beach treasures she had collected as a kid: dandelion fluff in an old mustard jar, rocks with fossils, brittle dragonfly wings, a milkweed pod, and heads of wheatgrass that never got a chance to drop their seeds and propagate next generations as they should.

She was too old for such silly treasures now, but she kept them anyway. At the bottom was a postcard of Queenie on the opera house stage, fully dressed. Underneath that was the real treasure, one that was truly useful.

Sharp. How sharp? Sharp enough.

She ran a finger over the mother of pearl handle, lovely, like it was made for her, not some pushy sailor. She wondered if the first mate realized yet it was missing from his pocket. Probably not. He always had his nose too far up someone's ass to see what was happening in front of him. That's what Viola always said.

Nattie put the paper crown on top of the treasures and tucked the whole case away, safe from the storm that was coming—and from prying eyes. Some secrets were best stored in the dark, out of reach.

Roberto, the banjo player, walked past in a hurry, his white shoes clacking on the metal floor. He whistled appreciatively and shimmied his chest, trying to get her to shimmy her shells back at him. She pretended she didn't know what he wanted and stuck out her tongue instead. He laughed and turned the corner, not even pausing. She wasn't worth the time, it seemed. She wasn't keen on the banjo man, but still, he could have stopped and talked—or something.

Maybe she should have rattled her shells.

Nattie listened for engine sounds and looked over the railing. On the main deck, passengers were finally arriving. In small clusters they strolled up to the ticket counter and boarded, carrying small valises for the three-day trip. Some had porters carrying a travel trunk. Some men had nothing. They didn't plan to sleep, it seemed.

The onslaught of passenger voices was sharp-edged against the metal hull, ricocheting from rust patches and layers of paint over iron bones. Teeth-hurting noises, metal scraping on metal, came in bursts. Tugs in the harbor made big hoot-hoot bellows, like jumbo-sized mama owls calling their owlets for dinner. The owl babies never answered. Maybe they had deformed legs, too, and were ashamed. Maybe they were waiting for the mutiny at midnight.

She thought about slipping away before passengers had a chance to stroll up to the Mermaid Lagoon. She could use some quiet time in the rat-runs, the crew-only passageways and secret-door vaults that crisscrossed the ship, places to hide bootleg barrels in case of a raid. They were also a good hiding place for a mermaid sick of being on display.

The water was choppy, the wind gusting in haphazard whooshes and wails. The up-and-down motion of the boat was making her gastric abnormalities act up. Being sickly was inconvenient.

Margret would be by soon, making sure she was ready for passengers. Nattie checked the ink on her arms. Some scales were forever ink under her skin. Other rows were added with a fountain pen as needed. Drawn with water-blue ink and a very unsteady hand, the scales looked like ivy groping on wind. Perhaps she'd had too many dribbles and maraschino cherries from discarded Polynesian Passions when she did the last touch-up.

Nattie rubbed some spit polish on her bare shoulders, making the mix of old and new ink scales glisten like she was fresh out of the lake. Men liked her to look slippery like that, or so they said. Then she adjusted the shells hanging around her neck to make sure all her right parts were covered. No point in giving away the goods, Mimi always said.

She finger-combed her hair, tucking the big tangles behind her ears, letting the ribbons knotted with pearls and strings of sequins skim her neck and bare shoulders. She hoped she looked at least a little bit lovely. Jakub had promised he would come by. He still might.

On each side of Nattie's tank, hanging blue and green scarves draped off a small dressing room for her. She wheeled her rollie chair through the silk curtains for one more check of how she looked.

A mirror, bolted to a metal beam, was cracked so her face looked sliced and spliced, put together by a blind man. Bangs fell over her eyes.

Her hair was a dirty blond color, ordinary. But her eyes were vibrant, turquoise, like still lagoons at twilight. A saxophone player had told her that once. He smelled like BO and she told him so. He didn't make her sit on his lap after that.

She could see the new pearls in the mirror. Maybe they weren't so bad after all. She could wear them for Jakub to see. They were silky and warm to touch, like they were absorbing her body heat. Actually, she was feeling warm all over. And wanting . . . something. Maybe this was what being grown up was about.

Jakub could still show up, she told herself.

"Maybe we'll go sailing Saturday," Jakub had said. That was Thursday, backstage during the late-night show, while they were waiting in the curtains for their cue. He was supposed to push her and the Rocky Shore platform out onto the stage at the second thunderclap.

"That would be fun," she had answered. Or did she just think it and forget to open her mouth so the words could come out? Her tongue got fat and stupid when he was around; her brain was all mushy too, racing in circles, full of static like the wireless when they were too far from shore.

> *Thunderclap one.*
> *"We'll sail down the mezzanine, you and me. I bet those*
> *wooden wheels could get going plenty fast with a good shove.*
> *That's what I'll do. Give you a big shove and jump on the back*
> *and we'll go a-flying off into the blue."*
> *Thunderclap two.*

The dangling scarves of her dressing room made a refuge. No one could see in. She wrapped the silky fabrics around her face. They smelled like wind off the lake. She saw only blues and greens and she was underwater, where it was quiet and safe, no pirates, no saxophone players, no old men bearing taffy gifts.

Voices interrupted, jerking her up for air. She peeked out.

It was only Quin and Jinks, two waiters, making grating noises, bickering. Their waiter-aprons tied at their waists looked flat, no stashed-away biscuits to toss her. They were clearing the leftover martini glasses and setting up more round tables at the far end of the mezzanine, with chairs and red tablecloths, the VIP ones with fuzzy fringe along the hem, tassels that were tickle-torture in the hands of that saxophone man.

Maybe she should wave. Maybe she could coax a snack from them. Maybe something else to eat would hush the olives churning in her stomach. And make her forget Buster. And perfume. And a boiler room boy who lied.

Quin and Jinks didn't see her, it seemed. She could hear them talking. Their voices rippled over the water, amplified in the storm-heavy air.

"Mermaids are supposed to be little," said Quin, head waiter and top jerk.

"Either that or voluptuous," said Jinks, eyes big. "She's almost there."

"I don't think she has 'voluptuous' written on that flat chest."

"She's still a girl," said Jinks, sounding hopeful.

"Not hardly. She's too big for this nonsense now," Quin said.

"She's in between, that's all. Outgrown cute. Not quite the seductress. She's got some developing to do."

"Some of the Polacks like 'em young. And the WOPs. They marry girls when they're fourteen in the Old Country. They like 'em young." Quin sneered like he had a bad taste in his mouth. "Some of Cappie's sleazy friends like 'em young, too."

"She's old enough. She knows how to play along. She knows the whiskey racket, knows her place, too. Don't you worry none."

"Just wrong, if you ask me."

"No one asked you, Quin, old fogey."

She came out of the dressing room, not wanting to hear more. She wasn't sure if she was embarrassed or mad. Quin thought she was nonsense. Jinks thought she was almost voluptuous, whatever that meant. Then he'd said she wasn't a seductress—yet? She didn't know if that was a good thing or not, either. Seemed like it might have shameful strings attached, like being a floozy.

"What are you two talking about?" she asked, just to see if they would fess up, knowing they wouldn't. They were low on gumption.

"Oh, hello there, Miss Mermaid, no time to chat. We have tables to set up," Jinks called back to her while he locked table legs into place. "Going to be a combo playing up here tonight. For some of Cappie's friends, I heard talk—"

"Why are you telling her, numb-nuts?" Quin interrupted. "She's probably invited. Probably knows all about it. Probably going to do some mermaid smooches for luck on the cards, for the fellas. Right, Nattie?" He sounded like he was still arguing about her and didn't think she ought to be at the parties with Captain-Father.

She thought they were both numb-nuts.

She glanced toward their crotches, but their aprons blocked the view. She knew what nuts were but not why they would be numb. Men were stupid. And mysterious.

"Of course. Sure, Cappie told me all about tonight's party," she lied, feeling her cheeks blush.

"I hear this combo is pretty good," Jinks added. "They were playing at Dukes Downstairs on Rush Street—you know, where the cool cats jam." He snapped his fingers like he was about to step on the dance floor, jitterbugging. The Negro dishwasher boys knew those steps. They liked to bus tables when a band was playing on the mezzanine. They'd go behind the curtain and cut the rug a bit. They'd try to get her to join in. But the rollie chair got in the way, and her tail.

"Oh, yeah, like you know something about cool cats jamming, my ass." Quin scoffed at Jinks. He wasn't buying the cool cat act. He was right. Jinks wasn't anything like a cat, except for his funny little mouth and pointy teeth. He might be good for mousing, better than Mr. Whiskers, who was hiding again.

"Have you seen Mr. Whiskers recently?" she asked, done talking about dancing and tonight's big-wig party she might or might not be invited to and didn't give a hoot about anyway.

They both hemmed and hawed like they'd been caught.

"We've been too busy getting the Sand Bar gussied up pretty to notice Mr. Whiskers," said Jinks, winking. "But if I see him, I'll tell him you're looking for him."

"Next time I'm at the galley, I'll try to get you a can of sardines to set out," Quin added. He forgot to wink, but he probably thought one. The waiters left down the crew's narrow stairway, probably to get more tables and more swanky tablecloths and those little candles on mirrors. Those were pretty lit up at night. Romantic, like stars dripping sparkles over water.

Dang you, Jakub, where are you?

She'd forgotten to ask the waiters to bring her some food. She supposed sardines would do. The passengers loved to toss them to her. She liked to bite off the tails and spit them over the railing, being shocking just for fun.

She heard the two men mumbling:

"I wish someone would tell her about the damned cat. Why can't someone tell her?"

"Do you want to be the one?"

"No."

"Well, me either, so shut up."

She sighed a little whimper sound she hadn't meant to let out. She wiped her face, trying to make the sting in her eyes go away. What had happened? Mr. Whiskers was all she had on this stupid boat. Was nothing safe? No one safe? There was always talk about troublemakers going missing. But Mr. Whiskers was no trouble. He was useful.

She rubbed her eyes, hard, pressing the heel of her hand into her eyelids. She saw colors, reds and oranges like flames, bigger than candles flickers or lantern lights that gasped in the evening wind. She saw blue streaks and underwater currents and the faces of drowned sailors who had been tossed overboard eons ago. And there was a woman with long auburn hair flowing behind her. She was as naked as a jaybird except for long white gloves—on arms that reached out of the water.

"Come swim with me, Natalia."

CHAPTER 4

HALINA searched the cellar shelves for castor oil or milk of magnesia. One or the other might help calm wild man Janusz down a bit. She couldn't find either.

It was Theo's fault. Her husband had made her cut back on doctoring neighbors for free. He said it was enough to work at the hospital three nights a week. He didn't like her buying gallons of drugstore supplies or traipsing around the woods collecting roots and bark. But he didn't have to know everything, did he? What did it hurt? And Janusz, poor numbskull, needed something. Maybe a good swift kick in the pants if he didn't quit his hollering. She was down in the cellar and could still hear him up in the kitchen carrying on.

She stood in front of the near-empty shelves. A swaying light bulb cast roving shadows that went round and round like a carnival ride. The cellar, just off the coal room, had a dirt floor and cinder block walls, the chinking between blocks mostly crumbled away. It smelled like earth and springtime and roots and fungus. She kept what she could hidden on these shelves, in Mason jars and burlap sacks and pouches made from flour sacks tied with twine.

Theo always left early in the morning for the mill and came home late afternoon. That was plenty of time for her to mix up her brews. She usually kept some tonics and tinctures steeping and her other everyday ointments simmering on the back burner of the stove. But she seemed to be out of calming juice or sleepy-time tincture, what Janusz needed.

She pulled the blue jar down from the top shelf. It was her lucky jar, one she had kept her poker winnings in when she was just a kid. She used to bury it under Baba's peach tree, digging a hole with an old spoon and dropping in nickels and dimes she'd won from the weekly game with the menfolk on the street. Stach had taught her to play and saw that she won just enough to keep her adequately supplied with orange soda and black licorice. He also insisted she bought shoes that fit. He was a good man. Still was, even if he was moving slowly these days.

She wished he'd come help her with Janusz. She pictured a pigeon. It landed in the grass in the yard. Feathers were silky and silver with just a tint of pink, subtle like an April sunrise. She pinched her arm. A sticker burr pricked the bird's wing, a slight pain that nagged and needled. She sent the vision bird off.

Bring him back.

She and Stach had a connection for many years. They both knew Baba and exploited her heavenly connections for all they were worth. Stach's way was all about winning at poker, brewing moonshine, and avoiding the law, not that he had the gumption to get into too much trouble these days. Halina counted on the old woman to help her treat patients.

She came around plenty. Being dead didn't stop her. She lingered, nagging, whether she could be seen or not. The old woman was an idea that couldn't be forgotten, a light that couldn't be doused, no matter how much cold water and logic Halina threw on her spirit, trying to break free. She was stuck with the old woman who wasn't done teaching and healing.

Today the blue jar seemed awfully lightweight, only a few dimes and a couple quarters clinking around and a few dollars folded into squares. The paper might be worth more as kindling than anything else. Money just wasn't good for much these days.

Stomping noises carried through the walls and the floor above her head. Janusz. She had left him in the kitchen eating scrambled eggs, or that was what he was supposed to be doing. Didn't sound like he was cooperating.

For nearly ten years she'd been feeding this lost soul eggs from her chickens in the coop out back. He was like family, just as annoying and get-under-your-skin irritating as real family. At least he didn't whack her upside the head or trip her so she fell down the stairs like Pa used to do. Family. You can't pick 'em, that's for sure. Can't ignore 'em either.

"Hey, what's going on up here? Sounds like thunder," she said as she returned to the kitchen. "And what's all this mess?"

A plate was broken on the floor; scrambled eggs sprayed across the room. Janusz had a fistful of eggs in each hand. They oozed through his red, stubby fingers.

Janusz used to be a soldier in the Polish Blue Army, fighting with the British troops in France. He came home from the Great War a damaged man. His bald head had a scar that ran from his forehead to the back of his neck, a half-inch jagged seam where his skull had been cracked open. He'd been left for dead in a ditch. He had traveled a long path of wrong turns to end up in Hegewisch relying on the empathy of fellow Poles. Turns out that bond was enough, but barely.

He was dim-witted, with a knack for making trouble. For years, various neighbors looked after him, making sure he didn't do too much damage to himself or others. St. Florian took him for a few years, giving him a room in the basement until he nearly burned the place down. He lived in a boarding house off and on. But six months ago, he took a turn for the worse. His mixed-up head turned sour. Halina diagnosed a tumor, but she had no way of knowing for sure. The violent half of his brain was taking over, gradually pushing out the side that was naive and childlike. He was becoming difficult to manage, his pain pushing him into frenzies and emotional outbursts.

"Oh, Janusz, my man, what have you done? What the hell . . ."

Janusz flung his handful of eggs at her. He kicked over a chair. He climbed rungs of a ladder that wasn't there. She tried hushing and shushing him, but the man was beyond reason. And he was so big, a good foot taller than her, a hundred pounds heavier.

"Come on, now, big guy. It's okay. Calm down. Everything's okay." She whisper-cooed like she was hushing an infant. His face didn't react. It was like he didn't hear her. He was in some other place fighting for survival.

Halina got the kit from its hiding place under the mattress. The vial held enough for one more injection. Then it was gone.

"Looks like I'll have to go down to the dock to stock up," she said, holding the empty vial when she finally calmed the wild man down.

Janusz sat on the kitchen floor, slobbers dripping down his chin, his eyes glazed over, crying. He rocked back and forth, back and forth, a baby in a baby buggy. "Hurts. Hurts bad," he wailed, arms around his head like he was trying to wring the pain out of his skull.

"I know. I know, bubby. I'll get you more medicine. It'll be okay. Just let the sleep come and take you for a nice ride around town. Go with it. Be free of the pain, old friend."

"You're a good girl, Lina. I didn't mean to start the fire. I didn't mean to hurt Patcja. Or little boy, Jake-Jake, Jakub the good boy. I didn't mean to hurt Jakub or make him run away. Where is Jakub?"

"He got a job on some boat. That was a long time ago. We've all forgotten about it," she lied. She could never forget the damage this monster-man had done to her and her sister over the years. He used to peek in their windows and watch them dress when they were young girls. When her sister, Pat, owned the Corner Tavern, Janusz tried to burn the place down because Antonio had dared him to. Then Janusz caused a street brawl where Pat's son, Jakub, was severely hurt, his heart damaged. He stalked Jakub long after the boy healed, begging forgiveness when there was none to give.

But Janusz was of Polish blood. He'd fought for the homeland, and he needed help now. She couldn't ignore him.

"I'll take you upstairs. You'll sleep now. Come on."

The attic had been turned into a clinic-hospital years ago. She'd had a few serious cases up there over the years, when called for. Pa had his stroke. Major had the stomach cancer. Years later Matilda, his wife, had it in her bones, eating at her spine. The worst was Camel. Mustard gas in the Great War. Bandaged eyes. Hands that were melted into fingerless mitts. No voice . . .

She had loved the boy. They'd grown up together. That's why she did what she did. And why she still felt the guilt, still saw the feathers from the pillow flying in the half slant of the pre-dawn light coming in the single window. The boy had fought so little.

May God have mercy.

Janusz would be different. He'd fight.

To catch the man on the dock who sold the poppy juice, she would have to hurry. She worked tonight, so she would wear her uniform in case she needed to go straight to the hospital from the dock. She'd leave a note for Theo.

"Theo will be home at five thirty. He won't like seeing you, you know."

"I know how to stay out of sight and be good," Janusz said. "I am good."

"Right, bubby, you are good. Sometimes." Halina patted the man's cracked head.

She wondered how much opium she could buy with her grocery money from the blue jar. She might have to sit in on a poker game or two. She'd tested her luck at the boat's poker parlor a few times in the past. A daytrip to Mackinaw Strait and back should be good for a couple vials of medicine for Janusz.

She hurried to her bedroom to change. She slipped her extra queens into her satchel, just in case. She hated to lose.

Baba tsk-tsked along with the ticking of the clock.

Tsk. Tock. Tsk. Tssk. O'clock.

The old woman didn't approve of gambling, at least not with cards. Gambling with home-brewed medicines and guesses of dosages was perfectly fine.

Halina pretended she didn't hear. She had made up her mind to go, and no dead woman's tsking was going to stop her.

She heard the kitchen door open downstairs.

"Hey, Lina. It's me," Stach called. "I just thought I'd stop by, maybe get some of your ointment. You got some? I've got a splinter in my hand I can't seem to dig out. It's nagging at me like a bossy old woman."

I knew you would come.

CHAPTER 5

NATTIE knew she had to hurry. The rollie chair would be no help on the stairs, though. She'd have to make do with her lousy legs. She poked her bare feet through the slits in her costume and hobbled to the far end of mezzanine, her tail of gauzy fabrics following her, dragging like a weight.

The entrance to the rat-run was behind the curtains. She felt around for the button, pressed it, and the small door popped open. She took a deep breath and stepped in, her hands groping along the dank passageway. Single dangling lightbulbs here and there lit the way, barely. It was called the rat-run for a reason. She could hear them. Somewhere.

That was just more reason to hurry. Her destination, the clerk's office, was up a level on the bridge platform. She hitched up her tail as far as she could to better maneuver the metal ladder. Her arms did most of the work, pulling her body up rung by rung. She emerged and could breathe again, taking in the impressive view from the top observation deck. She could see most of the harbor, tall buildings surrounding it like royal guards.

The bridge was ahead of her, the clerk's office behind. She peeked in the office door's window. Empty. Seymore likely was still down on the pier checking off inventory as it was loaded. Squirely Seymore was a man who loved numbers. Weirdo.

She focused on why she came. Looking over the cluttered desk, she found a piece of paper and loaded it into the Underwood machine behind his desk. She had become a master at this marvelous machine, using it frequently to make new placards for the little silver frame mounted on a post near her station. It was her clever way of telling the gawkers the essentials. She typed:

SPECIES: Mermaid, freshwater variety

NAME: Natalia Izabela Wiśniewski

NATURAL HABITAT: Lake Michigan, USA

AGE: 16 (in Mermaid Years). That's a grown-up mermaid who can do what she wants

DIET: Maraschino cherries, orange slices, and martini olives. Requires mass volumes.

NOTE: Mermaids don't do tricks. So stop asking. And they don't sing either.

She found the red pencil on his desk and added some fancy scrolls and curlicues to the page, making it look old-timely, like the near-ancient library books she read all winter when the lake was frozen.

She had to update the sign to reflect her new status as all grown up, since she'd had a birthday. She also figured the bit about the diet might help get passengers to share the sugared-up garnishes from their Gin Fizzes or Polynesian Passions. Oh, how she loved those.

She tore the paper out of the machine, trying to be quiet so she wouldn't be caught. That was when she noticed pencil scribbles on the back side of the paper. Odd.

16-57-99.

Funny numbers. Sixteen like me. Heinz 57 and 99 bottles of beer on the wall.

She heard voices: Jack, the first mate, and Captain-Father. They were just outside the office door, heads so close together that their cap brims touched. She crouched down but was too curious to stay still. What were they whispering about? Looked like conniving if she'd ever seen it. She shuffled closer to the door, hoping to hear without the jingling of her shells giving her away, dang things. Shhhh.

"Captain, the two bankers are aboard. They're asking for a tour, the entire ship, bow to stern. They're insisting, I'm afraid," the first mate said. For a handsome man, he didn't wear a worried look well. He looked downright ugly with deep furrows between his eyebrows.

"Well, show our guests around, Jenkins. Introduce them to some of the girls, take them to the Sand Bar. Have 'Tender give them a tonic on the house. That'll fix whatever is ailing them."

"What about the mezzanine? What if they ask about the Mermaid Lagoon? The railing is still busted, remember? I could send a man down there to patch it up right fast. Might look safer that way, sir, if I can suggest."

"I've told you, I don't like men loitering around my daughter's station. I've issued warnings that were ignored, and that busted railing is one message that can't be ignored. That deckhand, the waiters, the damned musicians, that scrawny boy. Miss Margret keeps me informed. I know what happens on every corner of my ship. I want my daughter left alone."

"Yes, sir. Of course, sir."

***

Nattie shuffled back to her tank, pausing here and there to lean and rest. Alone. When she was back, she slipped the new sign with her proper age into the silver frame mounted near the tank. No one was there to read it.

Men laughed somewhere on the boat. She could picture them, with their dirty stories and nudges and eye squints that said they were talking about something she wouldn't understand. She understood a lot. She was sixteen now. *16-57-99*. She knew things. And she had a plan. The first chance she got, she was leaving this boat, with or without Jakub's help. Sometimes you gotta cut bait, fishermen say. If the odds are hopeless, why prolong a useless battle? She often heard them on the dock telling fish stories, trying to impress each other with their yard-long tales while they sliced open fish bellies, letting the guts fall all over their boots.

Hearing her father talk about the busted railing made her wonder if it wasn't an accident. Did he have something to do with the incident? He rigged it? Or had someone rig it? All because Buster and Quin and Jakub talked to her? Margret had snitched.

Now no one could talk to her? She'd be more alone than ever.

16-57-99 is weird.

It was time for her to cut bait and move on.

She had a knife. Pearl handled. Sharp.

She leaned back in her chair and rolled back and forth, going over the plan.

What would 16-57-99 stand for?

She had one regret, a nagging, noisy one that wouldn't shut up.

Maybe you could ask him. Maybe he would say yes.

It would have been nice to have one more beach day, just her and Captain-Father, like the old days. When she was little, he took her ashore once a month on sort of a promotional tour. Mimi got her all prettied up, did her hair in ribbons and curls. He wore his uniform, of course, even those pretend medals pinned on his jacket, ones he'd made out of old Christmas decorations, painted gold with ribbons. He put her in a wagon covered with shells and blue-and-green waves made of tissue paper. A poster on the back had a picture of the *Lake Maiden* and the price of a ticket. Two dollars for a day trip to the Mackinac Strait and back, including lunch. After he wheeled her up and down the pier and the sidewalks near the dock, they rested on the small beach on Lakeshore Drive. She got to play in the water, her long flowing tail cascading around her in billows of sparkles, aqua, violet, magenta, and jade green. She was special.

Until she didn't fit in the wagon anymore.

Captain-Father had taken her on a few other business errands in the city when he was negotiating deals. She was the magic that always clinched the deal, he used to say. Those trips weren't as fun. There was no sand or beach time. The Chicago River, where the *Lake Maiden* docked for passengers and supplies, jutted right up to the brick walls and sharp angles of Chicago's downtown warehouses, stores, and banks with columns and gargoyles leering down from rooftops. She hated edges and corners and the ugly bricks and iron fences and locks on gates and asphalt so rough it could tear your knees out if you fell. Being dragged around by your hair over gravel wasn't so fun either. It was hard on the costume, made Mimi pitch a fit.

Men on land were mean and hard edged, like they had a square turd up their butt they couldn't shake loose. Captain-Father got that way too. He was one of the sly talkers and grunters who spoke in single syllables, leaving their icy glares to convey their message, like it was code or Sunday preaching that only the preacher understood. She seldom followed the bargaining, which seemed more like squabbling, but it always ended in handshakes. Sometimes there were envelopes, sometimes not, sometimes gifts for her.

> *Captain-Father brushed her hair and tied the shawl with dangly shells around her shoulders. Then he lifted her way up high to ride on his shoulder, where princess mermaids always ride. She was supposed to be quiet, smile, say nothing at all. Important meetings were for captains and suppliers. She promised to be good. But the warehouse, when they arrived, was dark. She heard rustles and squeaks in the dark corners. Mice. She cried, coughed on cigar smoke and snot dribbles sliding down her throat. Captain-Father said hush. The men had raincoats and lumpy pockets and there was a cat, Mister Mouser.*

35

And another, Whiskers.

"I want a cat."

"You can't have a cat."

Captain-Father wouldn't let her down to pet Mister Mouser or Whiskers. He kept her on his shoulder, her lovely tail draping over his arm. Her sequins sparkled. Light from a dangling lightbulb danced over her scales, inky blue. The warehouse man was thirsty, licking his cracked lips, drooling like a dog.

"Please, can I have a cat?"

"No."

Captain-Father talked and talked, using his ugly voice, jabbing a finger in the air, poking at bugs that moved so fast she couldn't see them. The corner shadows were cold. Invisible mini-bats plucked hairs from her neck.

"I want down."

"Hush. Or I'll leave you here."

"We could keep her. Overnight. One night."

"She's got another performance tonight, the late show. She'd be missed."

They insisted that Captain-Father take a cat. "The mermaid wants a cat. She should have one."

"She should have whatever she wants."

"We'll be watching." One of the men winked.

She knew an outing with Captain-Father was unlikely. But she could dream. Just one beach day . . .

She remembered the Indiana Dunes: super high sand cliffs, mountains of sugary sand shifting endlessly. She had gone swimming there with Queenie and Queenie's special friend.

"Go swim," the black-haired man had said. But she didn't know how to swim. No one had taught her. It wasn't her fault. That was before her sequin tail and pen-drawn scales and before she realized that the waves chasing her didn't want to play. They wanted to swallow her in gulps, starting with her useless legs.

If only she could swim, she might break free of the pull. She tried. She tried harder. She tried to kick her stone-heavy legs.

Looking over the busted mezzanine railing to the deck below, Nattie saw some of the chorus girls had appeared, fresh makeup applied, all gussied-up, their respectable day-time outfits on. They were greeting passengers, offering to show them around. They called it the nickel tour, she knew. They would parade the passengers around, showing off the *Lake Maiden*'s attractions from the theater and stage to the gambling parlors, dining room, and cabanas. They eventually traipsed up to the mezzanine to show off the paddlewheel's mascot, the Great Lakes Mermaid, who also happened to be the captain's daughter. They always said that with a wink. She was so sick of the winks.

16-57-99-wink.

With or without the nickel tour, the gawkers eventually strolled up the grand staircase to see what all the mermaid hullabaloo was about. The signs pointing the way to Mermaid Lagoon were screwed into the walls, tamper-proof. She just needed a better screwdriver.

***

A woman's heels clicked on the metal floor. Nattie knew it was Margret-the-snitch before she turned the corner. Margret inspected the cast before each performance. Nattie tried to straighten out her hair tangles and her thoughts. That wasn't easy around Margret.

Margret was in charge of the dancers and entertainment, including the mermaid act. She also spent a lot of time playing chess with Captain-Father in his quarters. He was teaching her the moves of the masters. She was teaching him to rumba. They were both slow learners. They'd been at it for years, the old dancer dropping in for lessons at all hours.

That was why Nattie's cot had been moved out of the captain's quarters when she was just a tiny thing. They had made her a mermaid nest in the prop room behind the stage, the only spare place they could find, apparently. She didn't remember much effort going into the move, just some crying on her part. It was much quieter there, except for the mice. Fortunately, Mr. Whiskers kept their mischief in check. The good cat earned his keep.

Margret had her clipboard and pen, as usual. She was already dressed for the stage in her long silver gown, sparkly with silver shoes to match. The gown had a slit up to her thigh, revealing lumpy legs with ugly blue-and-green veins her fishnet stockings couldn't hide. They didn't hide her bruises, either. Margret was clumsy. She also had odd hands, misshaped, too small for her body, like they'd stopped growing when she was young.

Nattie had always thought Margret's deformity should make her more sympathetic to someone who was in the same boat. It didn't. Margret had it in for Nattie, always picking at her like she was fuzz on a sweater. Maybe she didn't want competition for the Poor Me award. Or she didn't like a constant reminder that people laughed at the peculiar and pitied the lame.

A ship was a risky place for the odd or weak and sickly. They could easily be culled and tossed away. Who would dare ask about them? Who would know? One angry decree or a dismissive wave of a hand could set their fate. Buster, Margret, Jakub—or Nattie—could easily be discarded, damaged goods put ashore on desolate rocky ledges or simply sent overboard, a careless, tragic slip or a railing giving way. *By decree number fifty-seven you're sentenced to ninety-nine years of beer in your bed.* They were in this precarious spot together, and Margret didn't even realize it, the nincompoop.

"Natalia, we will be departing slightly later than usual," Margret said, looking Nattie over. Nattie stretched her back, trying to be taller, trying to shape her bent spine into an elegant curve.

Margret frowned but made a checkmark on her list anyway. Seemed she didn't have a backup mermaid to plop in the tank. Or a trained seal. Or sixteen piano-playing chickens.

"Don't go anywhere. Stay at your station. Get on your throne, will you? And do something with that hair. Have you brushed it this week?"

Before Nattie could answer, Margret grabbed the clamshell suitcase and started rummaging through it. She had no business seeing Nattie's private treasures, including the postcard of her mother. And the knife.

Quick. Say something.

"Did you know my father used to scrape glitter off Valentine's Day candy boxes and glue it on my arms when we went on appointments?" Nattie blurted out.

"That's nice."

"No, really, he did." Nattie pointed. "There's the hairbrush. Right there." It was another stage prop, painted gold and sprinkled with sequins and glitter.

"Fine. Now, make yourself look presentable, please. Some big shots are going to board soon—two bankers who might be convinced to extend financing. There will be hell to pay if they aren't happy with what they see. Follow the right script during the performance, too. No crying for Neptune, for Christ's sake. We don't have a Neptune costume anymore. You know that, Daddy's little fishie."

"A mermaid is not a fish."

"Sure. Of course, right you are," she mumbled, eyes back to her clipboard. Then she took off, a silver scurry like a silverfish escaping the drain.

After a few strokes of the brush through her tangles, Nattie gave up on her hair. And on the strange number that kept bouncing in her head. 16-57-99.

Who cares what it means.

She watched the passengers streaming on board and strolling across the main deck. A cluster of dapper-dressed couples came to the ticket counter. They were all decked out, showing off—the men strutting, the women riding their wake.

A woman with a fur around her neck twirled a fancy umbrella over her shoulder, even though it wasn't raining. Her fella had a top hat and bow tie. Nattie knew their kind well. They were happy to lose money in the poker parlor and toss around silver-dollar tips because they could. Nattie studied the woman, hoping she'd turn around so she could see her throat. She put her hand to her own throat and her pearls. They were warm. She imagined the feel of diamonds against her skin. Ice cold. In her mind, she spun, twirling into the spiral of sun specks, lost in the glitter, in the promise of being pretty—for-real pretty, not made-up, not a fish-girl in a tank wearing sequins and dime-store jewels for the rest of her life.

The rest of my life.

The dressing room made of scarves closed in.
He pushed her against the wall, metal and ice cold. She shivered.
His hand groped in her hair, finding the ribbons, looking for something else.

She trembled. Her ankle buckled, and she stumbled to her knees.

The tin bucket in the corner tipped over, the noise jarring, piss spilling.

Diamonds could pay for her escape. She could buy herself an accomplice, one better than Jakub, and a ticket to somewhere. Some of the dock workers were the friendly sort. Jedidiah was a good man. Maybe he could be part of the plan. Jedidiah had a cart used to wheel off empty barrels at the end of parties on the mezzanine.

Maybe a mermaid could stow away in one of those barrels? Would anyone notice? Or care?

She would need shoes. Real clothes and a coat. She wouldn't take her costume. She'd leave it spread out on the floor where she slept in the prop room, on her nest made of old pirate sails from forgotten performances. Margret would find it, and then she'd be sorry. Nattie could picture it. She could hear Margret's pitiful sobs, just like she cried for Buster.

But Nattie wasn't sure what would happen after that. Where would she go? How does someone go about finding a place to live on land? That part of the plan was fuzzy, like old biscuits growing mold. Doubts had crept in when she wasn't looking. The floor under her feet was rotting. She might fall to the deck, just like Buster.

Nattie looked down to the deck and ticket counter. The magician was selling tickets, pulling them out of his top hat, the show-off. Still, Jakub was nowhere to be seen.

Would he be of any use on land? Did he know how to drive an automobile? Could he buy her shoes? A house to live in? Would he get a suit and fedora and a job and go to an office every morning? Or to one of the steel mills? Or the stockyard? Would he take care of her and her sickly legs?

Where was he? Maybe he'd been assigned to some other tasks below deck. He filled in wherever needed—including the boiler room. He really was too frail for that, though. He had a weak heart. He'd opened his flannel shirt to show her his awful scar once, a raised, ragged red crescent moon on his chest. Nattie couldn't hide her tears when she saw it. She had wanted to say profound and reassuring words, but she gagged on empty sounds, more fish-like than human. She tried covering with coughing noises, but not convincingly. He had flinched.

Her scars weren't as bad, but they were close. At least they went in straight lines. He wouldn't look, though.

> *"It's okay. You can see. Everyone asks. I don't mind if you look." She groped for the hidden snaps.*
> *"I don't want to see your scars, Nattie. I don't need to. I know you've got scars. And they're bad. We don't have to look at them all the time. We know. You and me, we know."*

Nattie knew her scars went deeper than skin. She was a tangle inside, twisted up, with girl parts and mermaid parts and Queenie parts that weren't decent. Nattie didn't belong on a stage, on land, on board the ship, or in water. She had to leave the *Lake Maiden* so she could find where she did belong.

Soon, she would do it.

She would do it. Soon.

Someday.

Until then, she might as well behave and be careful of railings that might snap. She could be the fanciest, best mermaid ever, she told herself. Maybe help woo some bankers, get some money to get her one friend— this old boat—fixed up. She nodded her head the way the boat bobbed up and down on the choppy waves.

"Boat, better settle down. We have a long way to go before we get to the strait. Be a good boat. Stop this bouncing up and down."

The *Lake Maiden*'s engine hummed, a droning melody. She settled, steady. The iron hull vibrated a song, the one her mother used to hum from the parlor late at night, when the land apartment was dark and the royal Queen of the Stage put on her crown and . . .

> *She danced. A gauzy nightie, ruffled wisps like candle smoke, white against night, clingy like mist and nothing. She shimmied and shivered; her legs perfect. And fine. She peeled long white gloves off her arms, tossed them to a voice who cheered from the parlor, "Bravo, bravo, my harlequin harlot. Encore. Encore. Honey. Queen Bee."*

Nattie parked her rollie chair within reach of her tank, the fetch-it rope tied to one handle so she could pull it close when she needed it. She pulled

41

herself up and into the tank, swishing through the shallow water to the throne, a wooden kitchen chair painted gold. When she was in place, she covered most of the throne and painted rocks with her tail. She liked to spread it out so the sparkle-jewels and ribbons and fishnet swatches flowed, like a wave had just washed her ashore, dropped in place, pretty enough for a postcard, if you had three cents for that kind of nonsense.

Her mermaid butt had worn away the paint on the seat in the shape of a heart. Jakub thought that was funny.

> *"You should carve your initials in the heart. You know, like people carve hearts in trees and put their initials inside?"*
> *"Why would I do that?"*
> *"Just because." He shrugged. "People do that. All the time. I've seen it."*
> *"Those people don't live on boats, I suppose."*
> *"Just any people. Like you and me. I could add my initials too."*
> *"Why would you do that?"*
> *"Just because." He shrugged again, hands in his pockets.*

They should have done it then. Now they never would. She had a feeling.

It wasn't a storm coming. It was something worse. There was an emptiness in her gut that was more than hunger. Olives or sardines couldn't fill this hole; neither could maraschino cherries or old biscuits or memories of her mother or planning picnics with a father who didn't want her.

She decided she'd go look for the boy, the dear, sweet boy. She wanted to love him. She needed him to save her.

The jerk. Clod. Dope.

Too bad for him she was mad. And she couldn't wait to tell him all about it.

And warn him that visiting her on the mezzanine wasn't safe. He should be careful. She didn't want him to splat on the deck like Buster.

CHAPTER 6

HALINA slid to the edge of the bus seat, antsy, her knee jumping around and twitching on its own. Her satchel on the floor jumped around too, vibrating with the motion of the bus, making the glass jars clink. She tried to steady it with her foot. She didn't need any broken tonic bottles, not today, of all days. She had a tight schedule.

She was ready to get out of this metal buggy. It had been creeping through the downtown streets like it had all the time in the world. She didn't have such luxury. She had a connection to make, and she worked tonight, the midnight shift at the hospital.

Chicago Harbor should be the next stop, not far from the mills. She watched for familiar landmarks and wrapped the satchel strap around her hand, ready to grab and go as soon as the wheels screeched to a stop.

There. He did it again.

The man across the aisle kept staring at her, not with a curious kind of look. This was more of a studying and thinking, like he was trying to decide if she matched the face in a dream or a sketch on a napkin, something hinky. She didn't like it one bit.

He'd been doing the sneaky side-staring for miles, ever since he got on in the warehouse district, the land of bootleggers and their suppliers. She knew this part of town. She had patched up enough of the reckless idiots: friends of Antonio and special friends of Patcja, her sister, the one who lived and breathed red sequins and booze.

And then there was me in my white uniform, fixing the busted up and bleeding.

She always got her fair share of curious glances, walking around in her uniform. Seemed some dumb snits didn't think a nurse could be out on the streets. Or they wondered where she was going. The big leather bag, rattling with glass jars, didn't help. And there were rumors that followed her and finger-pointing that went along with the talk.

She had inherited her duties from Baba, the last healer of Hegewisch. She was the one who got the stories started about ghosts of patients buried under the peach tree and the house with lights on at all hours of the night, making noises houses shouldn't make, wheezing and coughing sounds and a low growl if someone double-dog dared you into running up to the basement window to look in so you could see the shelves of powders and roots and leaves, feathers and dragonfly wings.

Baba had taught Halina everything she knew about healing with Old Country remedies—and about keeping neighbors at a safe distance. The mystery was part of the formula, the swirling of faith and fear and blind trust that miracles could be conjured out of roots and brews and words that sounded as ancient as misery and healing itself. Halina knew the science of her ingredients; she knew the part beyond logic, too.

It lived in her bones, a memory so true it was part of her and couldn't be erased, no matter how many fires were set, no matter how many rocks were thrown through her windows. She had to live with it, like it or not.

Halina reached into the satchel and pulled out a compact. She pretended to look in the mirror and dab her eye with a pretty hanky from Woolworth, the one that was just for show. The man's face was wobbly in the cheap mirror. She didn't recognize him, but he had that look: smarmy, crooked, conniving. He must be a bootlegger, in distribution or sales. She knew enough about how they worked to recognize the flashy suit, the expensive hat, the pale skin from sleeping all day and working all night. She saw the eyes and the yellow tint.

Liver troubles. Another sign of a bootlegger.

Maybe he was working up courage to ask her about some doctoring. That happened. People knew her along her usual route from the big old house in Hegewisch to St. Margaret Hospital, where she worked half days and some nights. They waited and followed her, eventually asking for healing, or as much as they could get for a dime.

She also put in time at her sister's tavern, the Corner. Bear ran it now, since Patcja took off after the shooting. It had been a hopping place back in the day, but Antonio had shut off the whiskey when he took off with Patcja. People still came 'round to the side door looking for the nurse. Sometimes she was there and would hand out tonics or do some lancing or stitching if they talked nice. She sent away the blasphemous and whiny.

Halina looked out the window, trying to judge how much longer to the dock. Seagulls flew among the pigeons. She could smell the water. She shivered. The baggy blue sweater she wore over her uniform was hardly enough for a damp April day like this, barely spring. Chicago always held on to winter as long as it could.

44

The uneasy feeling was still with her from this morning, like dread. Janusz needed help. He needed a vial of magic from the man on the dock.

Gray clouds hung low, nuzzling along the horizon and the tall buildings in the heart of downtown. The bus continued through the sprawling warehouse district: bridges and canals, metal girders, roads that lifted so boats could pass under. This part of town was always dark, long shadows across loading docks and giant overhead doors that were controlled by pulleys, contracts, and passwords. She hated the warehouses, hated the alleys, hated the piles of trash, empty barrels, crates, and sheet metal scraps used to make lean-tos that hid men with nothing to lose but plenty of anger and vengeance building up, like steam in a pot with a lid sealed shut. Sooner or later, it would all blow. Bricks would go a-helling.

She nudged her leather satchel closer and put one foot on each side. Her white stockings and white shoes looked shockingly bright against the dark, well-oiled leather. The contrast was comical in a sad sort of way. She never fit in.

She was the best nurse she could be, but that wasn't always enough. She had no saint-qualifying miracles in her bag, nothing to write the Vatican about. But she could dish up a good story and fizzy potions and vision-inducing tonics to go with any special-delivery messages straight from God. She didn't charge extra for the prophecies or preaching.

Maybe that was why the guy across the aisle was staring at her. Maybe she'd wronged his people. And vengeance was brooding. Wouldn't be the first time. She couldn't save everyone, no matter how much tonic and elixir and poultice paste and praying and smoke and amulet waving she did for a good show. Even stolen hospital medicine couldn't fix every ailment.

Wondering if she needed to be worried—really worried—she snuck another glance at him. Bootleggers loved their switchblades, all quiet and sneaky but deadly. There were no obvious bulges of weapons. He didn't have an overcoat, just his suit jacket over a white shirt that wasn't too white. She caught a flash of gold glitz at his wrists, cufflinks, engraved with XXX.

She almost laughed. How obvious and defiant of the law could a bootlegger be? He might as well have been wearing a sign: "I'm a bootlegger! Look at me!"

She knew all about bootleggers' three-step process to give their mash the wallop everyone wanted. They marked barrels with an X after each step. Three Xs and it was ready. Antonio's operation had turned the practical code into a stylish signature design to represent his business. Antonio had style, even if he was a louse.

Forget about him. Ignore him.

The man turned her way again. Their eyes caught. His were yellowed, watery and bloodshot, crusty around the edges. They drifted up and down, sizing her up.

So what? He's a bootlegger with a bad liver. I don't care.

Maybe he was wondering if he could swipe her satchel or if he could knock her over, rough her up a little, get what all men want from women. Maybe he just liked to look and he got his jollies off from daydreaming.

Pfft. Hardly. Don't flatter yourself.

He didn't look like much of a wolf. Even if he was, she was no lamb.

She had no delusions about her looks. She had an ordinary face, plain except for the scar over her right eye and a nose that had been busted once, from a punch and a tumble down the stairs. That was the end of the first baby.

Getting off the bus at the next stop might be the smart move, but she also had an appointment to keep, and she didn't dare miss it. The lousy boat had better still be at the pier, her contact still walking up and down the dock, busy with his real duties. He supervised the loading of supplies, crates, and barrels and bushels of produce for a passenger boat. It was a great paddlewheel, a big boat that had seen better days.

Her man was some kind of clerk. He did a lot of nodding and bossing men with muscles, grinning like he enjoyed telling them where to go. All the time, he watched for customers who might be interested in the small brown vials in the hidden pocket of his vest. She knew he had some regulars, like her, but he'd also do business with anyone who had the money and knew how to ask.

> *"Do you have some Johnson's Dyspepsia Tablets to spare? A liver lozenge for my mother-in-law's bowel winds?"*

The man thought it was funny. He made her say it, word for word, every time.

What an ass, making a joke out of digestive disturbances.

The odd man on the bus leaned over in her direction, as if he might ask for a match or offer her some gum. As he turned toward her, she saw the left side of his face was droopy, a clay sculpture left in the rain. He opened his mouth, but his lips froze around half-formed words that went nowhere. He wiped his face with a big, clumsy hand.

Something was wrong with this fella. Something serious.

The bus jerked to a stop.

Finally! The harbor. She could smell the lake, hear the gulls screeching, see the dock, hear choppy waves smacking at the pier. Halina grabbed the satchel and hurried off the bus.

"Wait. Don't go," the sick man said from the top of the bus steps behind her. He coughed and choked on the words.

She turned as some impatient ass gave the man a good shove. The sick man staggered. He tumbled and fell. His forehead hit the curb with a loud thud. A gash started bleeding.

He blinked several times, like he was trying to snap his vision back in shape.

She looked to the dock and sighed. He couldn't stay in the middle of the road. She turned around and went back, hearing minutes ticking, vials clinking in a pocket, and Janusz whimpering in the attic.

"Hey, mister. Can you stand? C'mon, I'll help you. Lean on me," she said.

Some passengers stepped around them; others stopped to gawk. Blood will do that, draw the looky-loos.

"Move along now. I'm a nurse. Give him some room," she said with as much stern authority as she could muster. Her nurse voice wasn't something to be ignored. She helped him up and led him to a bus stop bench, pigeons and seagulls sharing a perch.

"Here, sit here. Rest a minute."

"I knew you'd help me, Halina," he said with a peaceful little sigh.

She started to ask how he knew her name, but blood dripped down his forehead and over his eyebrow. He put one hand up, a reflex, trying to catch it in his palm like it was valuable.

"Don't do that. Look, you're going to get the sleeve of your fancy suit all bloody." She took the handkerchief from his breast pocket and pressed it against his gash. He winced. "Hold this," she said sharply.

His eyes were unfocused. One pupil was dilated. One a pinprick. She needed to get him some ice, somewhere to lay down. She'd stitch him up, good as new, then send him on his way.

Gurgling sounds came from his throat. His eyes rolled backward.

He sputtered, spraying a fine pink mist, mucus and blood and yellow fluid from somewhere, maybe his lungs. The scent of his sickness was sharp like ammonia and shit fumes. This was obviously more than a bump on his head. A serious illness had been festering for some time. Then the fall triggered a secondary event, a hemorrhage or a rupture, a blood clot dislodging . . . could be a dozen different conditions that had picked now for a dramatic climax. Not good.

She lowered his head and shoulders to the bench seat and pulled up his legs so he was flat. His head rolled to the side.

She kneeled in the sharp gravel so she was eye level with the man.

Another pair of stockings ruined.

"C'mon now. Hang on, fella. I can stitch you up and you'll be good to go . . . wherever you were going." She tried to dab his bleeding forehead with his handkerchief.

His eyes opened. He pushed her hand away. "Keep it. Save it. You'll need—"

"Your hanky? I've got plenty of hankies, mister," she said, trying to sound unconcerned.

"Not like this one."

She loosened his tie. She reached for her satchel—but what could she pull out? A bottle of holy water? Her rosary?

"Are you a believer, mister? If you've got any repenting to do, well, now might be the time."

He took a deep breath and spoke between wheezes. "Your sister sent me. She said you'd fix me up with a tonic to stop the cancer. And I'm supposed to take you to her."

It took a moment for Halina to register what he had said. "Pat? Sent for me?"

"She needs you."

A flood of questions overtook her, but he was in no condition to answer. His breath was shallow, weak. She tried to put on a reassuring face, all calm and under control like a nurse was supposed to be in a crisis. But her heart was pounding, her mind racing, trying to think of some last-ditch effort to bring this buffoon that knew her sister back from the edge his toes were already hanging over. But, really, he might as well go. Now or in an hour or in a day. What did it matter?

She had nothing else to offer. He had nothing else to say.

What could she do with him now? Wait for the end? Hold his hand? Talk to him of some heavenly promises?

She glanced at the dock, ships neatly lined up, bobbing on the choppy water. There—toward the end of the pier, her paddlewheel boat was still docked, the three smokestacks towering over the other smaller freighters.

Wind tore at her ears. She shivered, suddenly chilled. She pulled her babushka tighter.

"Mister . . .we can't stay here forever. You got some family I can call to come fetch you? Or some business associates, maybe? I saw the lighter. Do you know Nicky, the distributor?"

She poked his shoulder, shook him. His mouth dropped open. His limp arm fell, dangling from the bench, fingers already blue gray. He was gone.

She wasn't sure if she remembered the phone number for Nicky's warehouse. The brotherhood had several offices. Should she call the police? Maybe someone else would, someone who had more time and wasn't trying to catch a boat before it sailed off with the medicine she needed.

She stood. She heard Stach arguing with Janusz to get back in bed.

Think, think, think.

She put her satchel on her shoulder and wiped her hands on the man's handkerchief she still held. For the first time she noticed it was oddly heavy, oddly lumpy, oddly . . .

Holding something?

Black thread in ugly, rushed dashes had turned one corner into a flipped-up pocket, sewn shut. Something hard and flat, coin-like, was sewn into the blood-stained cotton, and there was a business card, she could feel, too.

It'll have to wait. I've got no time for games now.

She dropped it into her satchel for later, then untied the floral babushka from her head and draped it over the man's face. The silky fabric clung to his open mouth and the blood on his forehead. She made the sign of the cross.

"May God have mercy."

She left. Then paused. Went back. She reached into his pants pocket and found the lighter. Gold. He wouldn't need it now. She dropped it in her satchel.

She walked as fast as she could go, bits of gravel still stuck in her knees, her torn stockings drooping.

Cinders from the road blew across her legs, stinging. Another handful was tossed in her face, tiny sharp bits of gravel pelting her. She spun around.

"Who did that?"

There was only the dead man and an old woman. Baba sat hunched on the bench next to the man, her shoulders up near her ears, her chin down to her chest, like she was trying to lay an egg.

"Don't look at me like that," Halina said.

The woman didn't move, just glared.

"Well, be that way. I don't care. I have somewhere to be." Halina picked up her pace, wishing she hadn't left her babushka. Her ears were cold. The wind off the lake was brisk, damp, heavy with almost-rain and storm-brew.

It would have been a good day to stay home.

CHAPTER 7

CAPTAIN Wiśniewski paced in front of the long window of the bridge. From this vantage point, he had an excellent view—if his eyes were open. He preferred to pace with them shut, leaving the entire departure process to the crew. He trusted them, mostly, but remaining calm during the close maneuvers was much easier if he didn't see the infinite number of near disasters.

He just listened, and that was almost as telling.

Jack Jenkins, the first mate, was at the helm. He was a dependable lad, perhaps a bit too jovial for his own good but as capable as they come. He had been on board about a year, ever since the engine failed on his own fishing boat. As soon as he saved up, he said, he would get another. That would take one hell of a long time with the wages he got on the *Lake Maiden*.

Max Wiggins was also at his usual station, going about the routine in an orderly fashion, as it should be. Wiggins was a tall man who talked too much, always with a new joke to tell, mostly sarcastic quips only he thought were funny. He had weak, watery eyes and he blinked too much. He also had questionable oral hygiene. Those weaknesses could be forgiven, though, as long as he tended the maps and the radio and the weather forecasts and minded his own business.

Voyages on the Great Lakes were mostly routine. Until they weren't. Weather could be unpredictable, especially in spring when torrential downpours and gale winds could put an overworked vessel like the *Lake Maiden* in peril at the blink of an eye. She was not the agile beauty she used to be, capable of outrunning moon tides and dark currents and ghosts of drowned captains and their passengers.

One must stay alert but calm and confident. Never let them see you're worried.

Today would be a little choppy, that was all, he was sure. The morning fog said so. He had noted it in his log. He kept meticulous records of every voyage, all the legal parts.

The sound of water against the hull carried up to the bridge even though it was a yawning, undefinable distance. The wind could be heard, too, but he was reluctant to assign a number to its speed. Figures were far too one-dimensional and limiting for his official captain's log. He used a series of symbols to record the lake's temperament and the wind's demeaner, from hostile to consoling. Today he wrote {^V^} to indicate the wave patterns.

He heard a tug on their bow, an insolent upstart, a perky vessel. He hated tugs. Its engine chugged in a high pitch, one that sounded like a girl giggling at a joke she didn't understand. Girls were like that. Except for Queenie, who was born regal. She had been gone from their lives for a decade, but her presence still lingered, nagging, scolding him in his sleep. She stole things, like his fountain pens and jewelry that belonged to passengers too careless or inebriated to notice her ghostly hands. Sometimes the passengers had the audacity to complain about the thefts. He congratulated them on having a ghost story to tell their friends.

Captain opened his eyes to glare down at the tug. He stood rigid like a flagpole, his arms crossed over his chest. Tugs exhaled clouds of black smoke—poisonous, everyone knew. He had captained a tug when Queenie was alive, and it had poisoned her, made her sick and mean, spewing venom.

That's why he couldn't stand the things. One gave him The Cough, too.

The hacking started as it always did when he was angry, his chest constricting. The flask in his pocket was half-empty, but a couple of swallows were enough to get the fit under control. The whiskey and his strong resolve did it. He didn't want to cough, so he didn't. He was in control of everything on his bridge.

Wiggins was in communication with the tug captain. The men waved at each other like old friends. Captain ignored the gestures and Wiggins with his mildly treasonous act of conniving with a tug. He let it go.

It was big of him to be so tolerant, and the crew knew it.

Wiggins returned to studying the charts and the weather reports collected from the ports on today's route. "Looks like we might be in for some rough weather, Captain," he said, holding up his reports like he was Moses with stone tablets. "May I suggest we pick up speed, stay ahead of the front, divert toward the western lane—"

"And do your weather reports tell you April storms on Lake Michigan are seldom substantial, just showers, nothing to worry about, not like the gales of November, the real test of a crew's prowess?"

"No, sir, they don't," answered Wiggins. He swallowed and looked again at the charts, inhaling gumption. "Are you sure, Captain, sir? This report shows a front will be coming at us from—"

"Nothing more than some teasing, I'm certain, Mr. Wiggins. We can consider this forthcoming shower a training maneuver for more serious tests of our resilience to come. Nothing to worry about, lad." He clapped his hands together.

"Captain—did you at least look at this report? And the forecast, sir?" Wiggins's eyes were wide open, either panicked or angry. What had gotten into him? He must have thought today was his lucky day, a day to challenge the captain so he could brag about it, look smart in front of his pals.

Captain wouldn't put up with it.

"Mr. Wiggins, I don't appreciate your insolence. Would you like to spend the remainder of this voyage in the boiler room shoveling coal? I hear they're shorthanded below deck and could use an able body. You could take your charts and weather reports with you. How would that be?"

"Well, no, sir. Sorry, sir. I was just worried about . . . I mean, I know you want smooth sailing for our passengers, especially with Mr. Salvatore coming on board and all—"

Seymore, the clerk, entered the bridge without asking permission. "Captain, with all due respect, I must protest," he babbled, waving a bound book of green pages. "Your daughter has been in my office again. She's made a mess of the latest financial figures Mr. Salvatore asked for. Well, they were a mess to begin with. But now they're a sticky mess.

"A jar of maraschino cherries seems to have been spilled on the ledger. Just look at this. Pink goo. Everywhere. Sickening sweet smell. I won't tolerate this any longer. She uses my typewriter, uses my pencils and inks, and leaves a mess. How do you let her have the run of this boat?" Seymore took a breath, his hands in the air, the book's pages flapping.

Captain tried to picture his daughter in the clerk's office making a mess. He tried to picture his daughter as she ought to look. Perfect, like her mother. But he couldn't. His mind couldn't create the impossible, no matter how many times he cast that net into the abyss. She was an abomination. She never ran. Never would. Facts were facts.

"The *run* of the boat? Really? You think she *runs all over* this boat, do you?"

Seymore's color drained in an instant. "Of course I didn't mean literally running. It was a figure of speech, for Christ's sake, Captain."

"Get out of here. Off my bridge," the captain said, waving his arm.

"But Captain, we really should discuss these numbers before the meeting with Mr. Salvatore," Seymore said, tapping the book. "He's sent word that he wants to discuss obligations. Assets. Liquidity." Veins protruded from his forehead and his round glasses slid down his shiny, pointy nose.

The man is a weasel. Look at those beady eyes, that snout.

Captain knew Seymore and his talents. After all, he'd hired him. He knew his abilities with numbers. He also knew the clerk wasn't especially honest, loyal, or seaworthy. He would sink to the bottom in an instant, even without rocks stuffed in his pockets.

"I'm supposed to bring the adding machine," Seymore said as he turned to leave, ledger under his arm. "And the checkbook. He expects to settle up, I think."

"Leave the ledger with me. I'll handle it."

"Excuse me, Captain," Jenkins said from his place at the wheel. He pointed toward the bow, where the tug was pulling alongside the *Lake Maiden*. "Seems we have a late passenger who wants to come on board."

Highly inappropriate.

The tug captain waved urgently. Next to him, a woman waved just as frantically. She was dressed in a white uniform with a baggy blue sweater over it and a leather satchel hanging from her shoulder.

"It's the nurse," Captain said. "What does she want?"

"Seems she wants to board the *Lake Maiden*, sir."

"Well, I can see that, Jenkins."

He had heard of her and her medicines, her healing abilities. She'd been on the *Lake Maiden* before, selling her tonics and taking money from passengers over poker. She was something of a card player and mystic. Almost magical, some said, with her bottles of potions, ointments that fizzed and bubbled blue and pink. They looked pretty. Might just be the kind a mermaid would need.

> *"That nurse should be banned from the Lake Maiden. She has no business on board." Margret pranced around his quarters in that little violet robe that was missing its belt. "She preys on the sick and helpless. I tell you, she's bad news." She stomped*

> *her bare foot for emphasis.*
> *"Oh, Margret, dear, dear, dear." He patted his lap. "Come, have a seat. Calm down."*
> *"She's evil. Defiant of God's will, interfering and acting superior. It's not right. Unnatural. Unholy."*
> *"Since when did you get holy, Margret? And how the hell do you know so much about her, huh?"*
> *Margret dropped her robe. "This is how. Look what she did to me."*

Captain couldn't see the nurse's face from his vantage point, only the top of her head. She waved frantically, with a little jump and pleading motion. Women could be so desperate. And desperate women were always so accommodating, weren't they? They could be eager to please. Maybe she'd have something to offer. Something worthwhile.

And it was fun to get a rise out of Margret. Show her who's boss. He didn't listen to anyone, certainly not a woman from the stage. Performers were so dramatic.

"Let her board. Have them lower the ladder for her, Jenkins. Tell the deck hands."

Jenkins paused, looking at the wheel uncertainly, like his hands were glued to it.

A conscientious lad.

"I'll take the helm, Jenkins. Do as I say."

"Aye, sir."

"Just try to avoid Margret for now. Might be best. Don't take the nurse past the auditorium or the mezzanine. Tell her to stay in the Sand Bar. She can sit there. Out of sight. Safe."

"Safe from what, sir?"

"Trouble. Don't you feel it in the air, Jenkins? Electricity, static-charged. Something's coming our way."

"Um, sir, once again, I would like to suggest that is the pressure change from a storm front heading to us," interrupted Wiggins. "A thunderstorm with serious, sustained wind speeds has been reported—"

"Wiggins, shut up. I don't want to hear more about this phantom storm you've imagined."

"But—"

"Just shut up, Wiggins. Jack, go. I'll take the wheel."

Cappie stepped up to the helm and gripped the large wheel tightly, squeezing power from the metal. It felt good in his hands.

He focused his eyes on the lake. The water was a dark, muddy green, the muck along the lake floor stirred up, the runoff from the canals and city streets making the water dank, smelling like oil and chemicals, stockyard waste and untreated sewage. He tried to focus on the horizon, where the gray flannel sky reached down and anointed the water, a priest giving a dying child a blessing before it passed from this world to the next. The miracle spot of sky touching water was elusive, but he sailed toward it, certain he could reach it before darkness fell if he could only keep his thoughts pure and focused.

But Queenie had other intentions. She poked his ribs. She grinned. She twirled her long auburn hair around her hand, making loops and circles that were hypnotic. She might strangle him with the knotted ropes of hair or hang him from the hatchway. He could see her as clearly as if she were there. And he hated her as much as he did the day she died. Her perfume hung in the air, making a bubble of Queenie air and Queenie needle-nags around him and the ship's wheel.

She was sucking the air out of him.

"Wiggins, take the wheel."

Captain rushed to his quarters to collect himself. It was a small but handsome room with a bunk and desk, some shelves, and a cabinet of charts. There was a safe in the floor behind his desk. The key to it, which he kept in his pocket, had recently gone missing. Thank God he had a spare. After the door was opened with a key, there was another door, with a combination. No one knew it but him. He wasn't a trusting man.

Queenie followed, as nosey as ever.

She'd probably taken the key, and all the missing pens.

On top of all her sins, she was a thief, too.

She'd never get the combination. He'd take it to his grave.

CHAPTER 8

NATTIE parked her rollie-chair in the dressing room, out of the way. She would do her hobble-shuffle thing, slow going, and awkward, but less embarrassing than the chair.

She would start the hunt for Jakub on the main deck, at the ticket booth, where he was supposed to be, the oaf. Stupid boy. Two levels lower.

Going down the rat-run ladder was easier than going up. Her tail dangled down ahead of her. She was being sucked down a tube, feet first.

She emerged on the main deck near the paddlewheel. The wheel hanging off the side of the boat was huge, four times her height, but it had seen better days and could use a coat of paint. Now wasn't the time to ponder the ill repair of Captain-Father's boat, though. She had to find Jakub, and fast. She needed to be back at her station before departure.

Get going.

The wind was brisk out here, chilly for spring. They were sailing directly into a north wind, it seemed. Why didn't the helmsman divert slightly eastward? That would ease—

Oh, who cares. Surely, they know what they're doing.

But she wondered. Then worried.

She hobbled along, holding on to the handrail, taking small shuffle-steps. Of course, gawkers noticed and stared.

"Do you need help, miss?" A do-gooder eventually came up beside her and held out an arm. He seemed to be alone, no woman hanging on his other arm, no enforcer walking beside him with brass knuckles or pockets bulging with other tools of the trade.

She started to snap "No thank you," but realized—since she was in a hurry—a shoulder to lean on would help.

"Well, mister, if you don't mind, I'm needing to get to the ticket booth over there. See the stand and sign and the man with a cape—"

"Certainly. Happy to assist a member of the performing cast. Lean on me," he said. "Is this a recent sprain? Did you suffer a fall in a practice? A mermaid stunt gone wrong?"

He was a fatherly sort, curious and trying to make small talk—and not quite sure how to help. He reached out a hand but pulled it back and offered her his arm instead. Safer. Maybe he knew that talking to mermaids could be lethal. *Don't lean on a railing, mister*, she almost said.

She leaned on his arm instead.

"No, nothing recent. I'm like this always. A permanent gimp."

"I'm sorry," he said, looking down like he wanted to kick himself. Poor man. "I shouldn't have assumed—"

"No problem. I just do it for the attention of strangers. It lures them into my trap."

He didn't wink, but he chuckled a little, nervous-like. "Well, you certainly got me. Hook. Line. And Sinker. Bait swallowed."

She laughed. This guy was funny. Couldn't be a bootlegger or banker or . . . "So, this must be your first time on the *Lake Maiden*, huh?"

"Yes, I'm with the navy. Can't resist a sea vessel of any kind. Was curious about the paddlewheel and how it maneuvers on the lake and in the strait."

"It's my father's boat. He can make her do anything he wants. She listens to him. If he said tippy-toe through the strait, she would."

"That's one fine vessel."

"No, one fine captain. And, well, the boat's pretty good, too. She tries hard."

"I can see that."

The April wind tore at them as they started across the open deck for the ticket booth. He wore an overcoat, which he offered her. Such a gentleman, and handsome, too. Too bad he was twice her age. Of course, she was grown up now. So age didn't matter.

"No, no. I'm fine. Used to the wind."

"Of course, being a mermaid and all—"

"Yes, well, that would mean I was used to the water, not the wind. Mermaids live in water."

"How silly of me. I see your point."

"Easy mistake to make. Don't worry. I'm used to being misunderstood, too."

"I'm so glad you have a sense of humor about—well, about—"

"My large tail?"

"Yes, your lovely, large tail. It's very pretty. One of the prettiest tails I've seen."

He got flustered and hemmed a little like he was embarrassed.

"It does get in the way, though," she said, testing a coy flutter of her eyelashes, like she had seen Viola use so often. Maybe she didn't get it right.

He didn't have a smart response. But he did seem to be looking her over, looking for the back door, like long johns have, or a way to remove the tail. They always looked for that. Always. Even nice, funny navy men curious about paddlewheel maneuverability.

Fat chance that's why he's on board.

They reached the ticket stand.

"What gets in the way?" demanded Mario, the cranky magician, trying to hang on to his hat. "What do you need, Nattie? What are you doing down here?"

"We've reached your destination. Farewell, mermaid," the funny man said and slipped off.

Nattie transferred her weight to the ticket stand and waved so-long. She changed gears back to why she'd come down to the main deck. She had to catch her breath and think a minute. The nagging wind wasn't helping.

"I'm looking for Jakub. He was supposed to sell tickets today. Do you know what happened to him? Why isn't he here?"

"I wish I knew," Mario yelled. "I don't know jack shit about the boy or why he's not doing his job. You think I want to be here selling tickets? Margret sent me. Said they couldn't find the boy, and someone had to it. You're looking at someone."

"But—"

"Don't 'but' me. That's all I know. Now that you're here, help me pack up. I'm done selling tickets. The sad sacks on board are all we're going to get today, I'm afraid."

She tried to help, but her bare feet were cold and kept getting tangled in the gauzy fabric that whipped around her ankles. Then he wouldn't let go of the cash box, said he had to hand-deliver it to Seymore, no one else.

"So, we didn't fill up capacity?" she asked. Now she had something else to be worried about.

"Not even close. Maybe one-quarter. That's usual these days, in case you haven't noticed." He was obviously annoyed with her and her stupid questions.

"Yeah, but—"

"Just go somewhere else, fish-girl. I'm tired of you and this whole charade you play. Move, you're in my way."

"Can you help me below, so I can look for Jakub on the lower deck?"

"No, he's not there. They already looked for him, I told you. Margret looked. She sent someone to the boiler room. No one can find him. So forget it."

"But what if—"

"Stop with your butting and moaning. You can't go down there. You know it's hotter than Hades, don't you? What are you thinking?"

"I don't know—"

"You think Daddy can rescue you from that too? Rush to the boiler room to save you?" Think again, honeybunch. Those fellas down there aren't afraid of your father. And your father doesn't give squat about them. Or you. Or me. Or any one of us."

"But—"

"Just git. Now, I said."

Nattie started back toward the hatch to the crew stairs, the wind shoving her along.

Navy Man was standing just around the corner. Had he had been close enough to hear all that? She blushed. Knowing her face was red made her even more embarrassed. She wanted to crawl away. She tried to slip out of sight, but there were only some flimsy deck chairs bolted to the deck, hardly enough to hide behind. It would be nice if a giant wave came up and washed her overboard right about now.

Too late. Their eyes caught.

He rushed over.

"I'd be happy to escort you on the return route. It seems your mission is completed, and you're heading back. No?" He wasn't trying to be funny anymore. He must have heard. At least he had the decency not to ask nosey questions—she hoped.

"Yes, the mezzanine level, up one. That's my station. I'm supposed to be there."

"Let's go. Up the grand staircase."

"There's a crew staircase back this way."

"Ahh, but then the other passengers can't see your splendiferousness as we go up the stairs."

"Spediferishnose? Is that like seductress?"

"Much better."

"I just wish people would stop calling me names."

He took her back to the mezzanine. As soon as she was properly deposited at her station, he asked directions to the bridge. He wanted to meet the captain, he said. "Shake his hand. One nautical man to another."

She refused, locked her lips shut and threw the key over the railing. She made a lovely splash sound when it hit the water.

Introducing passengers to the captain wasn't a good idea. Never had been. Never would be. Passengers didn't mix well with the captain, especially the kinds of passengers that had questions, opinions, and ideas of their own. They irked him, and he didn't bother to hide it. He would start the finger-pointing and jabbing at the air.

Eventually the navy man gave up and said he could navigate to the bridge himself. He knew something about how vessels were laid out.

Another know-it-all. "You may know boats. But you don't know Captain-Father," she said.

"That's why I intend to meet him. Seems like a person I ought to know. You never know when the navy will need a paddlewheel captain. Or a paddlewheel boat."

Nattie laughed. "That's the silliest thing I've heard. You might as well strip her down to the bones and build a new shell over her. Isn't much else worth a dime."

"Hey now, the navy is many things, but silly isn't one of them. And good bones are valuable. That and boilers."

"Yeah, well, maybe the navy needs a mermaid, too?"

Now he laughed like he thought her idea deserved to be tossed in the Stupid can. "Well, I do suppose that could help with recruitment," he said skeptically, dreamy-weird, like he was picturing a world overrun by mermaids. He turned toward the bridge.

He didn't wave bye this time. He seemed to be thinking something, picturing that dream world of his. What an oddball he was, but smart-sounding and respectable. She didn't know many respectable fellas.

She guessed she'd said too much and probably made a real fool of herself. He probably thought she was a child.

I just hope he doesn't tell Captain-Father about our talk.

She flipped her tail smartly and saluted the back of the navy man as he walked away.

What a strange fella. A rowboat with one oar.

"Good luck, Mr. Navy Man."

CHAPTER 9

RICHARD took a notebook from his pocket and jotted down notes to help him remember details about the ship. It was a curious vessel with unusual qualities. He loved studying all forms of marine transportation. Fascinating. He often made notes about ships he encountered, wondering about possibilities and lessons that could be learned about maneuverability or buoyancy. His musings often went in unusual trajectories, speculating and building odd bridges of matchsticks and earwax.

He was an idea man. That's how he got the attention of his superiors and earned his rank. He could solve odd problems, which the navy had plenty of. He was supposed to focus on one: training aviation recruits. That meant teaching them to fly. Flying was the easy part, though, as any kid— hayseed from Kansas, rebel from South Carolina, Boston blue blood, California beachboy, or Chicago Kawalski—could be trained to pull back a throttle. The hard part was taking off and landing on a carrier tossing around on an ocean.

At all times, even in the latrine, he carried a standard-issue field notebook. When his mind ventured into speculatory territory, he took it out and noted the date, the time, the place, and the underlying problem that needed to be solved. He numbered his points and classified each for their reliability, potential, and merit for further consideration. One-star ideas had a slim chance of going anywhere. Five-star ideas deserved immediate attention.

He classified the *Sea Maiden* observations as a one-star. Unlikely to be relevant. Still, he completed his notes, speculating on the linear feet of the deck, the location of the bridge and the paddle wheel. The navy didn't have any paddlewheels in its fleet.

Fascinating.

CHAPTER 10

NATTIE was in place, ready for visitors. She had given up on Jakub for now. Maybe he'd show up for the late-night show.

She adjusted her shells, her hair, her tail. She smoothed the sequins and let the fine gauzy mesh of her tail spread out over the rock, the ends covered in the shallow water.

The water level was lower than usual. Every time she got out of the tank, she took water with her, leaving less and less. Cigarette butts floated, collecting in a corner. She'd have to type NO DROPPING TRASH IN THE MERMAID'S TANK on the next sign she made for the little silver frame on the post.

The sand in the bottom of her tank was littered with other tidbits that were far from trash. There were flat blue rocks, round and smooth, perfect for skipping. Then there were shells, mostly snail shells, mostly busted. At the very bottom was a gold bracelet with a charm, a mermaid, of course. It was a gift, the kind that could get a man killed. She couldn't stand to look at it, couldn't stand to throw it overboard either.

More jewels had found their way into her tank. There was an oval brooch with diamonds, a gold watch fob, red ruby earrings, a dangly necklace, a ring with every color in the world.

She had a lovely collection. She stirred the sand with a stick of driftwood, a prop that was quite useful for fishing in the sand and burying and unburying secrets. The bauble soup was a powerful remedy for lousy moods and for red-haired boys who didn't show up when they promised and a railing that got busted on purpose because a drunkard deckhand talked to her one time too many. The soup sparkled, sun specks skimming the water's surface.

Looking out over the onboarding passengers, she scanned for sparkles. She could always use more.

"Hello there, Nattie, honey," called Mimi in her honey-sweet voice as she popped out of the rat-run door near the curtains.

Mimi wasn't much older than the chorus line girls. She was like a big sister, looking out for them, scolding and nagging, doing her part to make the performances alluring. Mimi liked to say "alluring," and then she would do a mouth pucker and put one hand on her hip and the other in the air with her wrist cocked like she was holding up a bag of potatoes. Nattie only made the mistake of mocking her once.

Mimi had been a model when she was very young, or so she said. That was hard to imagine. She walked like a penguin on stubby short legs. And she wore glasses, big round frames that made her look like an owl. If Antonio was around, she took them off. Wasn't that an interesting fact to ponder?

Today, she was carrying a stack of costumes over her arm, all neatly repaired, booze stains laundered, ready to be delivered backstage. Nattie could see long white gloves with buttons and black lace and see-through fabrics with tassels and snaps for flinging off and dropping on the stage.

Ba-da-boom. Hey, baby.

Sometimes the girls ripped too hard. Or the men ripped too hard.

Ba-da-boom. Take it off, baby.

Snaps had to be reattached, tears stitched up or patched.

"What are you staring off to like that? Daydreaming?" Mimi asked, no glasses on today.

"Just waiting for the crowds, waiting to show off for them," Nattie answered with a halfhearted tail swish as she slumped back on her throne.

A photographer from the *Dziennik Związkowy*, Chicago's Polish newspaper, took her picture once. "Chicago's own *Syrenka*," the headline read. A mermaid was the symbol of Warsaw and had been on the town seal forever. She was called *Syrenka Warszawska*.

Captain-Father was born in the Old Country and had told her the story of the mermaid when she was little. She'd played mermaid in the bathtub before she knew that was what she would become.

"Well, you better fix that attitude, honey. Mr. Salvatore and his entourage are joining us on this route, I heard. He's got a bunch of bigwigs he's treating. Chicago top dogs, 'Tender says."

Nattie played shocked. "Me? Aren't I the very best mermaid possible? The best on the entire boat?"

Mimi's smile dimmed into a dark glare. She never appreciated Nattie's sarcasm. She had an ominous side, one that would prick you with her pins just to see how loud you yelped. "Just cooperate. For once. Be on your best behavior, please, Nattie. For all of us."

"For you, Mimi, I'll be magnificent!"

"Thank you, dear." She flipped the sweet switch back on.

"Can I have some gloves?" Nattie asked. "You know, those long white ones to go up to my elbow? They're pretty. And everyone likes them. We could sew some sequins on. I'll do the sewing if you don't have time."

"I don't think so, dear. You would have white gloves filthy in a day. You aren't a white glove kind of girl. But here, I almost forgot—"

Mimi reached into her smock pocket and pulled out an intricate, ornately jeweled crown, gold with diamond-like stones and red rubies, green sapphires, too, the colors of museums and olden-day paintings in fancy gold frames.

"A crown! For me?"

"For you! For the final number, when the pirates proclaim you're their queen."

The crown caught specks of light and scattered them around the mezzanine and the shallow water in her tank, star dust.

"Wow. That's actually pretty! Not the usual fake gaudy crap people bring me. Can I wear it now?"

"A crown for a princess," said Mimi, helping her put it on, securing it with hairpins she pulled out of her own messy bun.

"Your father had this made for you by a jeweler downtown. He picked it out," she said, huffing some breath steam on it and polishing it with her smock hem. "He said the cardboard one we were using was shameful. Imagine that. A man with taste."

"Oh, Mimi! I can't wait for Jakub to see me now." She hugged the seamstress. Mimi didn't hug back. Maybe she knew being kind to a mermaid was dangerous on this boat.

"I can't find him, though. He was supposed to come meet me before we left port today. And he didn't— I'm worried. What with Buster falling and—"

Mimi stepped back and shook her head. "Don't say that. Don't talk like that. Whatever you do, don't talk about the railing. Last I heard, Jakub took a shift in the boiler room. But there was some ruckus down there. I don't know. Boys will be boys. Always fighting; you know how they are. Well, maybe you don't know yet."

She smiled and patted Nattie's hand. "I need to run, hon. The afternoon performance is moved back to two o'clock." She pointed to the clock on the level below. "Be on time. Please. Don't make Margret angry. She takes it out on all of us, you know, when she can't find you." Mimi started toward the stage but stopped.

"And you hang on to that crown, hear me? You know how shiny things seem to disappear around here. Mr. Salvatore isn't happy about a possible thief on board. We don't need more things to go missing, do we? What if a passenger reported a theft?"

"Nope. We sure don't need that."

Mimi nodded and rushed off, leaving a trail of suspicion behind her.

Nattie's stomach clutched. Why did Mimi bring up things going missing? And why couldn't she talk about the railing?

Drat. Crud. Damn.

Did Mimi think she was to blame?

And Father bought her a crown? Right after he gave her a pearl necklace?

Something was off. It suddenly seemed absurd that her father would buy her an expensive gift, just because. It wasn't like him. There must be some catch or more to the story. There was always some hidden scheme, an ulterior motive that was far from noble. Her father was like that. Above water, he was full of self-righteous puffery. Below water, barnacles clung to the knobby knees that he kicked like mad to stay afloat.

She didn't trust him.

He had a dark side. He'd been at the shore the day Queenie died. No one thought Nattie could remember; she was only four. But she remembered plenty. Images flashed in her head like newsreel pictures at the movie theater downtown.

> *Captain-Father was hunched over Queenie in the sand,*
> *straddling her, slapping and shaking her, yelling and yelling.*
> *Her eyes were wide open, her lips red from her paint and red*
> *wine that dribbled down her chin.*
> *Ants crawled over her face—*

He had left her like that. What did he do to her? Did he squeeze her neck? Did he smother her face? Poison her whiskey? Leave her to bake in the heartless sun? Or did he just tell her she was a rotten mother and deserved to rot?

"Go swim," the black-haired man had said. But she didn't know how to swim. No one had taught her. It wasn't her fault. That was before she had a sequin tail and pen-drawn scales, before she understood she had to be quiet and mind her own business and go play, no matter how long the waves chased her back and forth, trying to eat her feet and swallow her in gulps.

Nattie remembered the sun and wind on her face, crisp, tingling with a mystery just out of reach. Trees along the top of the sand cliffs were barely greening. She remembered tiny leaves, lime-green sneeze-speckless scattered among the branches.

She remembered the wind picking up. It became relentless. Now, she felt it again, deeply in her girl parts, behind the snaps, hidden behind layers of fabrics clinging to places too secret for names.

She felt the motions and churning, lunging up and down. Mama and that man had danced in the sand, lying down. They had danced to a deeply buried rhythm that pulsed in roots in the sand. It was something instinctive and powerful, grand and shameful all at once. It was passed from mother to daughter, like traits, talents, and inherited diseases, like faulty muscles and bowed bones.

Maybe she caught it from Queenie. Maybe she would die in the sand like Queenie.

She took off the crown and buried it in the sand, at the very bottom so she couldn't see it. She didn't want it—at least not now.

She had to think. No, she had to unthink. She sat up straighter on her throne in her tank, her sequined tail spread out around her. She was almost pretty. She wiped away the almost-tears. She swallowed a big gulp of air in case she couldn't get another.

She braced for what was coming.

***

Heavy footsteps came from the crew-only stairway behind the curtain.

It was Jedediah.

He pushed his way through the scarves, rushing, eyes darting like he was being chased by a sheriff. He carried a bucket and mop, water splashing all over the mezzanine floor.

A young man followed close behind, tripping and staggering like he was drunk, or hurt. It must be Silas, Jed's nephew she'd heard about. He was the same brown color as Jedediah, had his expressions, too, and big calloused hands with pink palms like Jed's. But the young man was ten times skinnier, a sack of bones, like he forgot to eat or had a hole in his stomach.

Both men were out of breath, looking over their shoulders for invisible monsters on their heels.

"What's wrong, Jedediah?" she asked, getting his attention with a wave. "What are you two running from?"

Jedediah stopped and set the bucket down in front of her tank. The water in the bucket was pink. He dried his forehead with his sleeve, catching his breath. The younger man froze, wide-eyed, looking at Nattie like she was an apparition from the grave. Apparently, he had never seen a mermaid this up close before.

Actually, he didn't look so good. He wobbled, weak kneed, eyes drifting upward.

"Is he okay?"

Then she saw that a white towel had been rolled up and stuffed in his work shirt. The towel was soaking up blood, lots of it.

The boy swooned, a sack of potatoes falling. Jedediah caught him just as he started to keel over.

"Whoa there, Silas. No time for a nap, son," Jedediah said, making the boy lean on him. He slapped the boy's cheek, then tried to shake some sense into him. "C'mon, Silas, son. Clear your head. Stay with me, now. We need to get you off this boat before it leaves dock."

"Um, well, I think it's too late for that," Nattie said, pointing down to the pier. The *Lake Maiden* was pulling away, paddlewheel turning, black huffs and puffs coming from the smokestacks.

"Too late? Dang blasted. Now what? What now?" The preacher looked panicked. Nattie had never seen him like this. The good-natured Bible man was gone. The man left in his place was afraid. His fear was contagious.

"What happened? Was it in the boiler room? Did you see Jakub? Is Jakub okay?"

"It's a bad day on the *Lake Maiden*, Miss Nat," he said, wiping at his eyes, mumbling into his hands. "A fight. Tempers. Men-jokes gone too far. Women. Always over women. Fists. Then knives. He didn't do nothing wrong, not really," he sputtered. "And look at him, bleeding all over himself. Judgment Day is coming, I tell you. Judgment Day is coming."

A knife fight? Over women? On her father's boat? "What are you talking about, Jed? You know my father doesn't allow fighting among the crew. He'll toss troublemakers off at the next dock. You know that."

She couldn't help but look at the splintered railing and think of Buster.

The injured man was gaining his senses. He perked up, leaning on his uncle and gaping wide-eyed at Nattie. "Listen to that! The mermaid talks!"

"This is Silas, and he's an ignorant toadstool. Acts like a fool. All over the biscuit baker girl, too. Got in the middle of a boiler room tussle. Hotheads and young fools. Fighting don't solve nothing."

"Sorry, Uncle Jed, Sor . . ." Silas mumbled, sliding lower, going under.

The *Lake Maiden* picked up speed. Nattie felt the vibrations through her throne.

Her rollie chair escaped from the dressing room curtains, rolling out into the open for anyone to see. Dadblasteddamned thing.

"Miss Nat, here's your carriage," said Jed. "But you know better than to let it—"

He started to push it back, then stopped.

"I think maybe I'll just borrow this for a bit and let stupid Silas sit and rest," he said, then added, "That okay with you, Miss Nat?"

But he didn't wait for an answer. Jed dropped Silas into the chair. The young man slumped over, passed out. The towel at his waist looked like it needed a good wringing out.

Jed rolled Silas back into Nattie's dressing room. "I'm gonna park him here a minute. Find me some help. I'll be back."

"Don't forget to come back," Nattie said. She didn't like being left alone with a strange man in her dressing room, bleeding. What if he woke and started hollering?

"Don't you worry. I'll be back and fetch Silas as soon as I have a place to hide him and someone to bandage him up a bit."

"What do you know about bandaging up a bleeding man, Jed?"

"Not a thing. But I know someone who does know."

Before he left, he tossed the bucket of bloody mop water into her tank, as if it was a perfectly fine thing to do. Then he stowed the mop and bucket in the dressing room like it was his personal maintenance closet. He trotted away down the mezzanine. He didn't even look back or give a sorry wave or a don't-worry smile.

Lousy preacher man.

The *Lake Maiden* snorted and harumphed, ready to pick up speed. The vibrations pulsed up the metal hull from the boiler room to her mezzanine. The shiver began deep in the boat's bowel.

The *Lake Maiden* was in a go mood, wanting to leave Chicago far behind in her wake.

Nattie fumbled for the switch near her seat and flicked it on. The spotlight glared in her eyes like an interrogation lamp.

She refused to answer any questions. She wouldn't confess. Maybe she would be a statue today, unmoving and silent. Nothing could hurt her. She held her breath, completely motionless except for her heart, which she didn't know how to stop. She wondered how long she could stay like this.

She tried to avoid looking down.

Don't look. Don't look.

But the water in her tank was unsettled, still swirling, murky cyclones spinning. The pink tint matched the pink sequins across her belly. Sick. The blood-tainted water was gross. She didn't want it on her.

She could hear a trickle of voices, some giggles and booming gruff men. Passengers coming. She hoped Mr. Antonio and his important guests didn't make her sing. She hated it when they made her sing. What lame-brain got the stupid idea that mermaids could sing? They couldn't.

This one can't. Can't dance either.

She wasn't pretty like—

Oh no. She realized she wasn't wearing her charm bracelet gift from Mr. Antonio. He would expect to see that. Disappointing him was not a good option.

Nattie fished around in her tank with her stick of driftwood, looking for the bracelet among the sand and the tainted water. The thought of her jewels—and new crown— in this spoiled water made her squeamish.

She found something else. Metal. Silver. A handle.

An open switchblade.

A shiver ran down her spine. This wasn't one of her treasures. It must have been left by Jedediah. The knife had probably been in the bucket.

Of all the lousy no-good nerve!

She looked closer. She recognized it, the tarnished, dented handle and the button that was supposed to make the blade pop out. But it was bent, and he always had to yank at it. She turned it over in her hand, remembering Jakub suggesting they carve initials in her throne. Jakub's knife wasn't nearly as fancy as the one the First Mate used to carry.

She poked at the old thing with her stick. The blade was mostly clean, but some dark goo clung to the tiny screws in the handle. Gross.

She buried it deeper in the sand, halfway to China.

CHAPTER 11

MARGRET was mad enough to spit nails. She paced in front of a scattered, zig-zag line of half-dressed, lazy-ass dancing girls who thought they could test her patience and get away with it. They were wrong. She was tired of their lousy attitudes, and she would put an end to it. After today's performances.

She just needed them to cooperate for two more shows. Two more. Then she'd kick ass but good. From here to kingdom come. Fire them all! Hire some cute young things who didn't sass back and drink half the inventory, complaining the whole time, like these snotty, ungrateful things.

They were all on the stage, the curtain closed, only half the overhead lights flipped on to save generator power. She had called for a lineup so she could inspect their costumes for glaring issues to be repaired before the next show. Antonio would be in the audience today, she had heard. He was so critical and smart-mouthed cocky, spewing sharp snipes coated in sugar.

> *"Oh, Margret, you've managed to put on a lovely show for what you've been given to work with and considering your limitations and physical abnormalities. You still show your face every performance. How brave of you."*

She wanted this performance to be at least a little better than lousy.

But, as usual, the dancers were late and in various stages of undressed indifference, strutting around like their flabby asses didn't stink. They thought they were too good for her little troupe. Either that or they'd had enough.

The women certainly looked like secondhand merchandise. Effie slouched in the back, a putrid color, likely hungover from last night's commotion. Some high rollers had been going at it in the poker lounge long after the *Lake Maiden* had docked. Some of the women hung around, motivating consumption of inventory, as was expected. Must have been dawn before the party broke up.

Tula, the last to mosey on stage, moved in slow motion, holding her head and moaning for someone to make the boat stop rocking. Effie had one glove. Minuet didn't have her red headscarf. And in the front row was Viola, smirking. She bent over to fix the buckle on her shoes and show off her bare ass. She was missing her ruffle britches under her pirate skirt.

That was the last straw for Margret.

She threw her arms in the air. "What is wrong with you? Don't you care? Have any pride? Don't you want to be better than this? Any of you?"

"What? Why? We're all here," protested Minuet. Others joined in the back talk, always eager to argue.

Margret clapped her hands. The girls shut their traps and made an effort to line up in the appropriate order. Margret took another look, noting on her clipboard the essential repairs that would be needed, starting with finding the white ruffle-butts for Viola.

Ripped lace dangled. Threads of sequins hung in lopsided loops. Missing snaps left gaping holes, exposing pale skin.

Margret sighed. Mimi, even if she tried, couldn't possibly fix all the costume maladies on such short notice. Maybe she could touch up or hide the worst of the worst, though.

Maybe she should just let them all make fools of themselves. Go on stage like this. Let the money-bag investors see how bad things had become. Maybe they'd find more money to pay for some improvements, finally.

How can I be expected to put on a decent show when this is what I have to work with?

Margret took a deep breath.

She didn't want it all to go down the tubes. Antonio could pull the plug and let them all sink; the whole crew, cast, stagehands, and performers could all wash out, done. Then what? This little floating vaudeville act may not be much, but it was all she had. And she wasn't about to give up. She'd worked too hard to let some lazy chorus girls make her look stupid —or like a joke.

The audience had laughed last week. They weren't supposed to laugh. There was no comedic element to the scenes she wrote. But Big John from the boiler room had been a poor casting choice.

That horrible incident was still fresh. She could still hear the roar of the audience laughing in big, horrid, rolling waves.

As soon as Big John had stepped through the curtain onto the stage for his short appearance as King Neptune, she knew it was a mistake. His bare belly bounced around, more lumpy, blue-mottled, and grotesque than she had imagined it would be. His chest had flabby bulb-shaped breasts that looked big enough to milk. The stifled giggles from the audience turned into a roar of whiskey-fed commotion, men hollering insults and calling out ludicrous comments about whale watching and blubber tubs.

"Well, now," Margret said, collecting herself. "We have a show to put on, ladies. One way or another, the curtain will open for a performance. Despite some apparent garment issues—we must put on a performance today, and it needs to be our best, better than our usual slipshod stumble-crap. As you may have heard, there are special guests on board today."

That got their attention.

"Yes, Mr. Antonio Salvatore and his crew are on board and will attend a show, either the afternoon or the midnight show or both. We need to be prepared. Please."

The women stood up taller, adjusting loose garters and dangling strings of sequins.

"Let's do a run-though of the opener. Think of it as a dress rehearsal. Get in full costume, like I asked. Be back in five. This time, be ready."

The girls straggled back to the dressing rooms they shared.

She could hear them whispering to each other, wondering which of the henchmen would be tagging along with Antonio. Each of the girls had their favorites. Sometimes the hooligans brought gifts.

Margret didn't care for any of the distribution boys. Cappie managed to keep her desires satisfied without demanding too much in return. She didn't have much to give, being damaged.

As soon as she arrived in Chicago, Major had put her to work. There was a hardware store that didn't sell much hardware. But a fella could buy a screw real cheap. That was the joke. Rooms, little more than closets, were partitioned off, with filthy mattresses on the floor. She was popular. The girl with special hands had mastered the hand job, they used to say. They liked her small palms and tight grip—until she got sick. A pregnancy gone wrong. The pain had become too much. For days she'd begged God to take her and put an end to the misery. But even He didn't want her and her rancid womb, the infection eating at her.

The goodie-two-shoe sisters carried lanterns to the kitchen.
And mirrors, to reflect light, they said. Hogshit.
"I just want to die. Let go of me. No. Let me die. You can't cut
me open. You're no doctor. Student nurse, my ass. And your
satchel of potions."

Margret couldn't believe this place. She huffed. "And where is that mermaid?" she called in the direction of the dressing room. "Is she back there? Anyone see her?"

"She's not here," Viola called back.

"Not here," called Bubby, the stagehand.

"Not here, either," said Mario the magician, a strange man with a top hat, cape, and a chip on his shoulder the size of a cabbage. He waltzed onto the stage like he owned it.

"Hello, Madam Margret, I'd really like to talk to you about a new assistant for my act. Little Effie is too crying-out-loud stupid to follow my directions. She nearly ruins every illusion, I keep telling you."

"Mister Mario. I don't care. No one else is flexible enough to scrunch up in your stupid saw-box. Unless you want the mermaid. She'd be small enough. But you'd have to take the tail too. It comes with her."

"There's no way I want that smart ass little carnival sideshow attraction in my act. I have class. She has an attitude. And I don't like it."

"She can't help it, Mario. Give her a break. She's trying to grow up. She thinks she's in love, of all things. And now her damned cat got thrown overboard. It seems the first mate hates cats."

"She was on the deck looking for something. Maybe the cat. No, it was the putty boy, that Jakub—a runt of a boy."

"Well, Jakub's missing, too. No one knows where he went. I was going to have him come onstage in the final act and say a line . . ."

"Good luck, Madam Margret."

"Mario, how about you? I have a pirate hat that should fit you. You would make a lovely pirate."

He didn't move.

"You can have a black eye patch, too," she added, like she was offering a decadent dessert with chocolate sauce and cherries.

That hooked him, his sour disposition vanishing. He grinned. "Pirate Mario, at your disposal, madam."

CHAPTER 12

HALINA stood on the deck of the *Lake Maiden*, watching the tugboat chug-chug its cute boat butt back to the pier. She waved at the driver-man who had reluctantly given her a lift, but he didn't see her. He seemed intent on dodging bigger boats who were hogging the water and slow to move out of his way. He had been reluctant to give her a ride. It took some firm talking, Polish style, plus some sweetie-pie looks and hey-big-boy winking to convince him to deliver her to the *Lake Maiden*. Eventually he agreed, probably just to be done with her.

As long as it got her where she needed to be, she didn't care what he thought.

But the little bastard, as soon as she'd planted both feet on the *Lake Maiden*, turned around and left, not waiting for her like she had asked.

Another young fella, wearing a white uniform with a smart cap, had helped her climb up a ladder to the deck. He'd grabbed her satchel ("Be careful with that!") and held out a hand to help her make the last leg-up-and-over. She knew it wasn't very ladylike, but she didn't give a duck-quack about who got an eyeful of Halina ass. She had the good garters on, even if her stockings were a mess.

"Welcome aboard the *Lake Maiden*, ma'am," he'd said.

Now it seemed she was stuck on board and stuck with this navy boy who'd glued himself to her hip, asking nosey questions about why she wanted on board and who she wanted to see and more that was none of his business.

"It's eight and a half," she snapped at him.

"What is?"

"My shoe size. You've asked every other question about me. I figured you'd want to know my shoe size, too. It's eight and a half. And if you want to know the last time I had a good shit, it was yesterday. I'm due." She raised an eyebrow. Bringing up toilet needs was a tactic she used frequently. It shut down the questions fast. Zip. Every time.

"And all the up and down of this floating bucket is making me want to find a crapper, soon! You got one of those on board this canoe?" She moaned, dishing up a thick layer of malarky. She just wanted to ditch this fool.

His little-boy face blushed bright red. "Well, yes, ma'am, I can escort you to the ladies' room on the upper deck, behind the offices. If you follow me."

"Let's get to it. I don't have all day," she said.

Sailor walked in front of her, glancing back every few steps to make sure she was following. Of course, she was, but she was also looking for the man with vials to sell. She would make her purchase then enjoy an afternoon ride and be back to shore by dinner time. Simple.

She'd been on the *Lake Maiden* before, several times, as a passenger. She'd taken the short Sunday afternoon excursions that went out and back, just long enough for several hands of poker and two highballs. No more.

She tapped Navy Boy on the shoulder.

"Hey there, sailor, it just occurred to me to check. This is one of the afternoon trips, right? We'll be back to dock this evening, right?"

His eyebrows climbed up his forehead. "Oh, no, ma'am, this is the deluxe package trip. North through the Straits of Mackinac to Lake Huron, then south to Port Huron, then back, of course."

Halina nearly dropped her satchel.

"I can't be gone that long. I work a shift at the hospital tonight."

"Ma'am, unless you jump off and swim, that's not going to happen."

"Surely this boat can stop—just up a way, at the next corner, right? I don't mind walking a few blocks. I could get off, take the bus back to the South Side? Right?"

She tried some puppy-dog eyes and lip licking and hand wringing and toe drawing lines on the floor, one after another, her entire arsenal of sweet-plea asking.

Sailor just looked at her like she was a dog with two heads. "Ma'am, with all due respect, that's just crazy talk. Ships don't stop at corners like buses. We have courses we follow. We're going straight north, deep water, diverting slightly to minimize the impact of some weather we're due to encounter."

"Diverting! Ah, there we go, we'll just divert a bit more so I can get off. That's a plan, sailor. See, I knew you could help." She patted him on the shoulder like he was a good puppy. "Now, I need to find a fella with a clipboard. I have some business to conduct with him."

"Ma'am, you'll have to see our purser first. There's the matter of your ticket. You'll need to buy a ticket, I'm afraid. The purser handles ship finances, including tickets. This way . . ."

Halina's stomach dropped. She had no idea how much a ticket would cost. She had planned to buy medicine, and she had just enough paper money for one vial of poppy juice for poor Janusz.

I'm trying, Janusz. I am trying.

Of course, there was always the possibility of selling some of the tonic or good luck charms she had in her satchel They could be valuable in the poker parlor. She wouldn't be opposed to a couple hands, either. But this nurse's uniform didn't exactly lend itself to hiding cards, in case she needed to help her luck along. Maybe she could keep the blue sweater on. The long, floppy sleeves could host a whole deck of queens. Who would suspect a nurse of playing dirty?

That fish-girl.

The last time Halina was on board she met the odd girl in the poker lounge. The kid, in that sparkle crap, had been sitting on a fella's lap—an off-duty musician—and blowing on his cards for luck. It gave Halina the willies. The kid was involved in one wacky con and didn't even know it. It struck Halina that someone should let the girl in on the stakes, being she was the bait and patsy all in one. But then the smart-mouth fishy girl took an interest in the cards. She hobbled around the table, collecting cherries from empty highball glasses, peering over shoulders to get a glimpse of cards in sweaty hands. And, apparently, counting.

"How lucky for you! A deck with six queens!"

A sign for the Mermaid Lagoon pointed to the fancy staircase that curved like it was from a movie where men in tights would have sword fights up and down the marble steps. Halina followed. It would be interesting to see how the little stinker was faring.

She smelled the perfume before she saw the woman in the curtains spritzing it in the air from one of those atomizers French harlots used back in the day. She didn't get a good look at the woman, but she was small, walked like a penguin, and wore some kind of smock-robe. Then, just as suddenly as she had appeared, the woman slipped into the curtains, like there was a magic door. She vanished.

The perfume stink didn't disappear. It was fermented, like it had been in some floozie's boudoir nightstand for a decade. Strange, indeed.

Halina knew all about coochy-coo girls from postcards, the naughty kind. When she was a kid, she had found a whole stack of the postcards in Stach's shanty. She'd learned all kinds of things in that shanty about men and their proclivities. She was just sixteen. About the age of the mermaid girl. The poor thing probably knew a few things about men and their hobbies, too.

The mermaid tank was up ahead in the middle of the big mezzanine. It was a big open space that would hold lots of tables, she imagined, or could serve as a dance floor. Some portions were closed in with windows. Up front was mostly open, with rickety wood railings overlooking the deck below. The banister was busted right in the middle, like a bull had charged through it. Goose bumps ran up her arm as she shivered. She was glad she had her sweater. But this was one weird-ass boat.

The fish-girl sat on a gold chair in an oversized fish tank with water in the bottom. Halina wasn't sure if the girl looked absurd or pretty in her costume. Someone had spent lots of time sewing on those sequins and doodads. And she looked regal on that throne, if you squinted and put your pretend hat on. You could imagine her swishing that tail in the lake, splashing and doing flips in the air, mesmerizing sailors with flexy-bendy tricks. Teasing. Men liked that.

Halina snuck up from behind, catching the girl fiddling with a loose string on her shell top, turquoise sequins dangling in a sorry loop.

"You snag your sequins on something? Wasn't some caveman manhandling your delicacies, was it?"

The girl jumped. "Where did you come from?"

"Around. Just visiting. Came to say hello."

"Hey, I know you," the girl said, realization spreading over her face. "You're the nurse."

"What gave me away?" Halina asked, pointing to her uniform.

"Hmmm. The shoes. Had to be the ugly-as-sin white shoes," the girl said all serious-like. "Wouldn't nobody wear those God-awful shoes if they weren't required."

"Ahh, so I have a tell. My shoes. I'll have to remember to remove them if I ever want to fool someone about my vocation." Halina wiped a splash of mud off the toe of one shoe with the back of her hand.

"Are you a real nurse? I kinda figured you were a made-up one, just, well, you know, wearing a costummmme," Nattie said, stretching the word into something weird and evil.

80

"Now, why would I dress up as a nurse to come aboard your little boat?" Halina crossed her arms.

"I thought maybe Captain-Father hired you to heal me. You know some voodoo act. I was supposed to be cured. But then I caught you cheating at poker. You had extra queens. Remember?"

Halina nodded.

"But I didn't rat you out. I can keep a secret."

"Well, that's good to know. Smart," said Halina.

"I am smart. Very," answered Nattie. The girl cocked her head like a snooty librarian daring someone to test her. Halina had to admit the girl looked wise for her years. She wondered if this creature went to school, then snickered at her own joke. A fish-girl in *school*! A *school* of fish!

The girl cringed.

Crap. She thinks I was laughing at her.

Maybe she could make it up to her by some straight-talking. From the looks of this floating circus, this girl probably didn't get a whole bunch of truth told to her.

"Yes, I'm a real nurse and a poker player that invents her own luck. Well, mostly. I am a nurse's aide at the hospital." Halina smoothed the girl's tangled hair from her face. Nattie let her.

"But I have a clinic in my home, too, in Hegewisch. I tend to neighbors who don't have the money—or the trust—for doctors." Halina strolled around the tank, taking in the clever props and creative touches, even pink water to match the girl's scales. "I learned healing from a Gypsy woman, the Romani. Travelers. They crossed all of Poland before the Great War. Baba was a healer."

"You knew the witch lady with the peach tree?" Nattie asked. She leaned forward, her eyes suddenly the size of silver dollars. "When I was little—"

Words caught in the girl's throat. She choked and coughed, wheezing.

"You heard of her, huh? Well, rumors travel," Halina said, patting the girl on the back. "Baba had a way about her, a little strange. But she always meant well."

Nattie caught her breath. But she looked annoyed suddenly, squinting, like she was calculating sums in her head.

"Is that good enough?" Nattie snapped. "Good intentions don't mean much in my book." She tugged harder at strings and sequins again, yanking and snapping the thread, sequins flying.

Halina tried to catch them, but they flew too far, too fast.

"My father might mean well. Maybe Mimi and sometimes Margret too," said the girl, being an uppity, cranky cuss. "But that never seems enough to me. Doesn't change things at the end of the day, does it?"

"Like what? You're not treated right? Looks to me like you're getting the royal treatment."

"I'm just decoration. A moth that landed in the scenery paint before it was dry. I'm stuck now. Part of the stage set."

She flicked her tail around and stirred at the water with a stick. She looked to the curtains behind her tank, some kind of closet or dressing room or private shit can just for mermaids.

What could be back there?

"Maybe I can help." Halina meant it sincerely but realized how shallow her offer must sound. Lots of mother hen types probably tried to offer advice—or salvation—to the child who seemed to be missing out on manners and morality lessons. She was dealt a lousy hand, for sure.

"Well, if you're a real nurse, maybe you could stick around, maybe you could help some," Nattie said. "There's a lot of sickness on this boat you can tend to," the girl said, glancing down at her legs then over the railing to the deck below. Then the curtains . . .

Halina started to tell her she had no time to stick around, she had a brain-sick patient in her attic needing her. But the girl blurted out more.

"There's this boy I know. Jakub. He has a bad heart and scars on his chest, like a crescent moon. He got it from—"

"—a fight in front of the churchyard?"

"How do you . . .?"

Halina's stomach fell. She gulped air and choked on it, the lingering perfume catching in her throat like it was poison. She smelled blood and ruin and bandages and pain and horror and the basement of St. Florian, where she had treated the boy for four days before Sister Beatrice kicked them out for calling on spirits to help protect him from infection.

She didn't want to think about the horrible wound to Jakub's chest. She didn't want to chitchat with a dang fish-girl, the smart ass. She didn't want to explain to this girl that Jakub had almost died because she had been so proud and sure of herself, thought he didn't need to risk a trip to the hospital. She could save him, she had thought. Until the demons arrived.

She pushed him, slumped over in the wheelbarrow, over tree roots, rocks and cracks in the soil, busted headstones, clumps of sandy soil from recently dug graves. She struggled through the church grounds, gnarly fingers from bare oaks grabbing at the boy they wanted to claim. The ruptured stitches bled, soaking the strips of bandages torn from white sheets, creating puddles deeper than sanctimony and glacier made lakes.

She grabbed her satchel and took off, back down the stairs. She didn't say goodbye. She didn't look back. She needed time to think. Jakub was on this boat? He worked on board?

What a turn of events. Maybe she could find him. Maybe she could stay for the three-day trip. Maybe she could win a couple hands of poker and come away with enough money to pay for a ticket. Stach would take care of Janusz. Right? Theo would think she was working at the hospital. She'd send a message . . . something so he wouldn't worry. Something he would believe.

Emergency. Tragedy. Crash. Horror. All hands on deck. Nurses needed for double shifts.

She wrote the note on a cigarette. She smoked it, inhaling and exhaling words that would arrive on Avenue O with the afternoon newspaper, delivered by a newsboy with a splint on his arm, his bones tingling with messages and conviction and a compulsion that wouldn't end, like a song verse stuck in his head. The boy owed her a favor.

At the foot of the steps, she paused to get her bearings. The wind was picking up, the boat rocking. She remembered the basic layout of the deck, especially where the poker playing took place. It wasn't like the dang thing was some huge ocean liner. It was three levels of smoky rooms, fat men, floozy dancing girls, bored bartenders, and crew hands wearing silly white uniforms they bought at the dime store.

She took a turn around a post and nearly ran into the frosted glass doors of the Sand Bar.

Perfect! She could use a highball.

She opened the door, ducked in as nonchalantly as possible, and there he was: the poppy-selling man she needed.

"Yoo-hoo . . . Yoo-hoo," she called to him. He wasn't wearing the

83

usual coat and black vest with poppies he wore when he was strolling up and down the dock. He looked much stuffier now, like he belonged in a library, not dockside. Did he have the vials stashed in his pocket? Or had he left them in some safe hiding place? She hoped he had at least one left.

"Psst. Mister. Remember me?"

"What are you doing on board?" he snapped. "And in the Sand Bar? This is for our VIP guests and high rollers. I doubt you're either."

"Um, I need to make, um, a purchase," she whispered.

Behind her, the glass doors opened, and there was Navy Boy again. He rushed in, looking indignant. He obviously didn't appreciate being ditched. His sour face lit up with triumph when he saw her.

"There you are! I see you found our purser," he said, nodding toward her connection. "Did you pay him for your ticket?"

"Purser?" she asked. "You're the purser?"

"Pleased to meet you, ma'am. I'm Seymore Houseman, ship purser, chief accountant, and controller for Lake Maiden Maritime Industries."

She remembered the secret line she was supposed to use, as stupid as it was.

"Do you have a liver lozenge for my mother-in-law's bowel winds?" She added a coy wink at the end.

His charming smile turned to a sneer and he made a dismissive motion like he was brushing dandruff off his shoulder. He kept walking.

"Not now," he said as he passed her. "I'm on duty. I never mix ship duties with personal hobbies."

"Well, isn't that a fine how-do-you-do, mister?" she said to his back. "Did you hear me? A fine how-do-you-do." She was shouting now, not giving a crap who heard her.

The purser left her standing there, unsure what to do next.

She felt eyes on her, someone watching, and whipped around. Why couldn't people mind their own business? Several men who had been ordering drinks were turned toward her, curious looks on their faces.

"What? You've never seen a nurse before? Nurses drink whiskey, too, you know," she snapped.

"Not in here, they don't."

"Leave her alone, men. This is a famous healer. We might need her to save a life for us," said a familiar voice. "Her drinks are on me, bartender."

There, across the room, at the end of the bar, he sat on a stool. He was still the same lanky fella with a swoosh of black hair that fell over his eye, coerced into the perfect curve by a gallon of hair tonic. His eyes locked with hers for a good one-two count before he stood. He ambled over with a gait that said he had all the time in the world. No one could hurry him or make him do anything he didn't want to.

Halina knew all about him, his starched-shirt arrogance, and the thugs at his beck and call, wielding gasoline cans and matches.

> *The match landed on the gasoline-soaked floor. Flames went up with a loud whoosh. The two sisters stomped on the floor, a frantic dance, trying to put it out. Patcja's red shoes smoldered like her temper. "I'll kill him," she said. "I'll kill him."*
> *"Not if we die first," Halina said.*
> *"I wouldn't let him have the satisfaction." Patcja kicked at the radiator pipes until the valve finally gave, spraying water across her tavern's sad, scorched floor. "I'll show him."*

She knew about his one weakness, too. Her name was Patcja.

"Hello, Antonio. Long time, no see. How's my sister? You two still have that little love nest? Somewhere in Canada, isn't it?"

CHAPTER 13

NATTIE had no idea why that wacky nurse ran off like that. One minute they were talking about Jakub and the next she was flying off down the stairway like her tail was on fire. It was the strangest thing she'd ever seen. Not really. But it was up there.

She didn't have long to worry over it. Voices ricocheted on the stairway. More visitors, just what she needed. A young couple was on their way up, all chipper looking and optimistic, obviously excited by a voyage on the magical *Lake Maiden*. They were bouncy, more than was called for. Most couples didn't hop-skip up the stairs on their way to Mermaid Lagoon.

She groaned.

They're going to ask me a million stupid questions, I know it. I know it.

Nattie checked that her pearls were securely clasped, her tail properly positioned. She swirled the water in her tank with the driftwood stick, hoping the pink tinge wasn't too obvious.

I'll just pretend I don't hear them. Maybe they'll think mermaids don't have ears and they'll leave quickly.

She smoothed her hair down over her ears. She thought about hiding in the dressing room, but remembered that bleeding fella, Silas, was there. How could Jed do something so mean?

She looked over at the dangling curtains. Nothing moved. Not a sound either. What if Silas had dropped over dead, eyes open, creepy-ghoulie? What if Jed never came back? Her mind raced around the absurdity of it all.

Captain-Father would be so angry. He'd probably think it was her fault. *How'd a bleeding Negro man get in your dressing room, anyway?* he'd say. Then he'd read her the riot act. And forget about any picnic on the beach. He'd confine her to her quarters.

How'd I get myself in this lousy mess?

"Hey, you, how are you doing back there, fella? Silas? You hear me?

You okay back there?" she called, but not too loudly, not wanting the bouncy couple to hear.

Nothing.

The couple skittered in her direction like two chipmunks racing for scattered peanuts. The man had shaggy hair under a felt fedora that was horribly old-fashioned. His suit was even worse, baggy and droopy, shaped like a half-empty potato sack. She wondered if he was embarrassed. He should be.

She squinted. This man looked familiar, something about the blue eyes and the square chin that was too big for his face, like he got a second helping of chin when God was dishing out features. He was hurrying the woman along, almost shoving her in a playful sort of way, like they were racing and it was the lady's turn to win.

The woman, who didn't really look much older than Nattie, wore a dress that was outdated, too, and obviously borrowed from someone with a big appetite, a woman with dime-store taste. Maybe her mama. It seemed she didn't know the fashionable ladies were wearing hems at least a few inches shorter these days.

"We'll play dress-up. I'll be the mother. You're just the baby. Baby girl."

The man pointed to Nattie, waved like she was supposed to know him. The woman waved too. They both started jabbering, pointing, waving— excited, like they'd never seen a mermaid before. They practically ran down the mezzanine, knees pumping like kids chasing a ball . . . No, a cat . . . a little runaway cat, darting into the street . . .

"My kitty cat!"

"Stop, Kitty! No!"

She knew them. She remembered. Those days came rushing back.

Nattie laughed. It was a little-girl laugh, a sound that bubbled up from a place buried deep.

The apartment was in the basement of a building that was tall with a metal fire escape that climbed to the sky. Neighbors above and walked on the ceiling, stomping and shouting in Polish. All the neighbors were Polish, floor over floor climbing to the sky. They were all loud and angry. All of Chicago could hear their roar.

> *Her face was wet, hair plastered to her forehead. She cried, but that didn't make it better. She screamed, but that didn't help either.*

Papa carried her outside on his shoulder. "Hush now. You've caused enough chaos for the day."

The neighbor children cooed at her like she was a bird. Papa handed her over. "Just for a few hours, then the Missus will be home. Queenie has a performance today. A matinee."

They propped her up in a toy wagon. The girl with braids tucked a red blanket, doll sized, over Nattie's legs. "There, there, baby. Be a good baby today," the girl said. Her brother was a big boy with a big-boy coat and a big-boy bag of newspapers.

"Pa-per. Get your paper here. Read all about it."

"Szymon! Szymon, the best newsboy on the South Side. And dear sweet Anka, the good sister-friend to me. Oh my! You're all grown up. When I saw you last, you were . . . well, children!"

"Of course, you were little, too. A tiny thing. Frail," said Szymon, his voice trailing off.

"Look at me now!" she exclaimed, pointing to her pearls and her tail. "I'm the star attraction for the *Lake Maiden*."

Anka came closer. Close enough to see Nattie's sequins, the tattoos and ink on her arms, the fake shells glued in place, tied to Nattie's almost-flat chest with blue ribbons that had been tied and untied hundreds of times. And then the tail, shimmering like wet paint in the diluted light of the mezzanine.

Szymon read her framed sign on the post.

Nattie hugged herself, wishing she could dive into her tank and swim away. In the water she would move with grace, riding the lake shimmers northward, deeper, safer. She would swim to the end of the world.

Anka started to reach out to touch the hand-drawn scales on Nattie's arms, a baffled look on her face. At the last minute, she yanked her hand back.

"What did they do to you, Natalia? What happened?"

Before Nattie could answer, she saw Margret coming down the mezzanine, frowning, jaw clenched. Nattie waved her over.

"Miss Margret! Look who's here. Some old friends of mine. Come meet them."

"You're needed at rehearsal," Margret said, all serious, ready to launch into one of her lectures. "I came to wheel you over."

"Wheel?" asked Szymon.

"Hello," Margret said, turning all nicey-nice and syrupy. "Nice to meet some passengers and old friends of Nattie, and of the captain, too, I assume." But she looked the brother and sister over with her squinty eyes that could see invisible flaws. Of course, she would notice their raggedy clothes. "How did you meet Natalia?"

"We lived in an apartment above the Wiśniewski family," said Szymon, taking a step closer and squaring his shoulders. "Before all this silliness. When Natalia was a little girl. My sister and I took care of her when her father was out on his tug and her mama performed on stage. We took Natalia to sell papers with us."

"She rode in a red wagon. She brought us luck. We sold more papers when she was with us," added Anka.

"Well, that's nice," said Margret. "You knew Mrs. Wiśniewski?"

"Of course. Natalia's mother was famous, a performer, Queen of the Opera House. She wasn't home much."

Margret smirked. "And was she as evil as I've heard? Beautiful, but conniving?" Marget sounded eager to get the dirt on Nattie's mother, like she was a criminal who deserved to be strung up. Nattie tried covering her ears. It didn't help.

"She was caught with one of the brewery boys, caused a shakeup in the organization? Right? You were there? You heard about it firsthand?" Margret leaned in closer to Anka and whispered, "Did she really fall from grace? Dragged off stage? Drunk? Becoming bitter and blaming—?"

"We don't know anything about her except she liked to entertain, and she wasn't much of the mothering type. That's all. It wasn't Natalia's fault, though," Anka said emphatically. She touched Natalia's shoulder where the scalloped lines began and wiped at the ink, as if she could brush it away. "She limped a little, maybe. Maybe she was small for her age, and her legs were wobbly. She had braces that were supposed to help, but someone had to put them on. Szymon did it most days, didn't you, Szymon?"

"Until the braces disappeared," Szymon interjected. "Maybe we better go, Anka. I don't know if Natalia wants to be reminded of those days. It was ten years ago."

"Oh, don't go," said Nattie, pulling herself up from the shallows, pretending to be fine. Just fine. Really fine. Fine. A-okay. "I want you to see my performance. Everyone loves the show. They clap and whistle and hoot, cheering for the mermaid to be rescued. Come to the afternoon performance in the auditorium. Then, after that, I'll show you around the *Lake Maiden*. We have secret passageways just for the crew. They're fun to sneak through."

She winked and leaned over to them, pretending to share a ship secret. "And there are hidey-holes where we stash away *the whiskey*. It's so fun for spying on passengers. You see such naughty things!"

"But first, we have a rehearsal," said Margret sternly, heading to the curtained dressing room.

"No, don't—" Nattie yelled.

Margret would raise holy hell when she saw Jed's nephew bleeding all over the rollie chair. "Can you come back later, Margret? Just ten more minutes? Pleeease? I need to . . . well, you know."

Marget nodded her head like a co-conspirator who knew the plan. She would croak if she saw what was back there. Who was back there. Nattie felt like croaking herself.

Marget left, saying she would return shortly.

Szymon and Anka stepped back, eyes cast downward. Nattie didn't want them to see her shuffle awkwardly to the dressing room. She certainly didn't want them to see a bleeding man in her dressing room, a Black man and a preacher's nephew, no less.

"I suppose I need to get ready. The show must go on!"

"It sounds so exciting," said Anka.

"Well, come to the next performance. It's in the auditorium. Two levels down. Signs point the way. Please come. We have a magician. Music. Dance. Excitement. A chorus line of pirates, and a mermaid, of course."

"We wouldn't miss it for anything," said Anka.

"C'mon, Anka," said Szymon. "Let's let Natalia go." He steered his sister toward the stairway. Anka hesitated, looking back. She put her hand out like she wanted to grab hold of Nattie. Szymon took the outstretched hand instead.

"I'll see you two later!" Nattie called to her old friends.

As she watched them go, a sudden deep loneliness hit her. She had things to ask, things to say, so much she wanted to know about those old days in the neighborhood . . .

And now a void was left where they used to be, an empty room that would echo if she screamed. She kept her mouth shut, swallowing the uneasy feeling.

She smelled the perfume again. She saw Queenie's silhouette in the half-lit parlor as she danced for a man who wasn't Nattie's father. She heard Szymon selling newspapers and Anka hush-hushing her as the wagon wheels went *clippity-click, clippity-click* over the cracks in the sidewalk, block after block in the streets of Hegewisch, looking for the house with a peach tree behind it. That was where the old Baba lived, Szymon had told her. She was the Old Country healer of Hegewisch who could fix her legs if they asked pretty-please and promised never to tell. And they paid her five dimes. That was all they could take from the newspaper money.

Baba's hocus-pocus poultice did as much good as the doctor's braces, but it smelled worse. Szymon had said they never could tell anyone. They never did. They had a shared secret, and they had shame. They had been so young and naive and wanting so badly for the magic to work and make their little miseries all better.

It was funny that those two suddenly appeared here, on Captain-Father's boat, out of the blue after all these years—wasn't it? And on the same day that the nurse, the old witch lady's protégé, was on board too. Who arranged this strange little reunion? Couldn't be chance, could it?

I don't believe that for a second.

CHAPTER 14

JACK Jenkins walked back across the deck toward the *Lake Maiden*'s bridge, happy to be done escorting the mouthy nurse around. He had left her in the Sand Bar, jabbering with the clerk over her ticket, or lack of one. It appeared she knew him. There was plenty of glaring and eyeballing and stink-eye staring, the way old lady immigrants liked to do. This nurse wasn't too old, she just had a crotchety streak that she couldn't hide.

He had a great-aunt Anna-Maria who could condemn you to living hell with her evil eye. She gave cousins Alonzo and Leo boils after they laughed at her set of secondhand dentures bought from some undertaker.

As soon as Mr. Houseman started talking to the nurse, Jack had figured his mission was accomplished. He'd gotten her on board the *Lake Maiden*. Now he could get back to his job. He was supposed to be navigating, not babysitting.

He hoped Captain would see it the same way. The man was difficult to please, and he wasn't very clear in his directions. It was like he didn't know what he wanted. He always had his nose stuck up the ass of some rich passenger or some connected distributor or supplier, anyone that could keep the supply of whiskey coming and keep the port authorities from noticing. If he paid half as much attention to the *Lake Maiden*, they'd all be better off.

Jenkins huffed, irritated. He couldn't help being a purist. A boat captain should care only about two things: his boat and the safety of his passengers.

Rosie had been a fine fishing boat. He missed her more than anything. He'd never loved a woman that much, not even his mother. Not a one of these modern flapper women had the same grace as *Rosie*. They certainly weren't as obedient, either. Dames. Shouldn't be allowed on board. Every sailor knows a woman on a ship is bad luck.

He made his way through the scattered passengers on the main deck. Despite the damp, chilly weather, they had a rather good turnout, looked like. Of course, good weather wasn't needed to play poker and guzzle whiskey, but it helped. The rough water wasn't fun for passengers or for crew. Everyone knew wrecks could happen. Wasn't that long ago that one of the bulk freighters, the *Cowle*, went down, a collision with another ship in fog. Killed most of the crew.

Hell, anything could happen in a storm.

He heard an odd banging and followed the sound. At the railing, a young crew hand struggled to secure a set of four wooden lifeboats banging against the hull. Seemed like one of the ropes that had been holding them safely suspended over the side had snapped, the pulley dangling empty. The kid was hanging over the railing, trying to catch the mechanism that flung around in the wind.

Jack stopped to help. The kid obviously had no training in ropes or knots. Either that or he was a useless imbecile.

"Sailor, what's your trouble here? Can't you tie a proper knot? Secure a cable?"

"Well, sir, no. I suppose not. I don't know nothin' about no knots, except the slipknot on my pa's pouch of snuff. But that's it," he said sheepishly, like he was hoping the first mate would have mercy on him and help.

Jack wasn't feeling merciful. Poorly trained, lazy-ass, smart-mouth young fellas like this were dangerous on a ship. Their carelessness jeopardized the entire vessel, putting innocent passengers at risk.

He needed to be taught a lesson. His slow response to an emergency was unacceptable. Because of this man's blunderings, there would be four less lifeboats.

Jack searched his back pocket for his knife. Where was it? Damn thing must have fallen out. He saw the idiot had one on his belt. He took it and used it to sever the single remaining rope that held the lifeboats. They fell, still tethered together, and hit the water, lost in waves, the noise swallowed by the roar of the wind. Passengers on deck didn't even notice.

The boy's mouth dropped open in disbelief.

"Why'd you do that? They could've been saved. I know they could've been. A rope could've been used to . . . We could have . . . But, you cut the rope . . ."

"Because you failed, lad. It's your fault. Remember that," Jack said, and he walked on, leaving the moron to ponder his guilt. The boy was lucky Jack didn't send him over the side, too, to make sure he understood the lesson. Ignorance has consequences.

"I run a tight ship. See to it. Keep her decks clean and the crew equally scrubbed, gentlemanly to our guests and respectful to officers.
No questions. It breeds disorder."
"Right! There's no place for troublemakers on board a ship." Jack nodded to the captain. "They need to be plucked off, like plucking ticks off a dog's back."

Jack continued on, walking around the clusters of passengers, all snazzy in their finery. He wondered which ones would be quiet fretters or loud screamers in the heat of a storm. Which ones would be prayers and which would be pukers, seasick and clinging to the latrines, afraid of mussing their suede shoes with regurgitated dumplings and pea soup.

He thought again about the weather forecasts. The sky looked plain enough, just one continuous overcast grayness that hung low on the horizon. The problem with being socked in . . . you couldn't see what might be building in the distance, just beyond the blanket over your head.

He picked up his speed, trying to dart around a stately couple blocking the way. A porter followed them with four oversized pieces of luggage on a handcart. Why was it taking them so long to find their cabana? More incompetence.

The woman waved. "Oh, excuse me, Captain. Do you know when we'll reach the Straits of Mackinac? I hear it is a lovely view and I don't want to miss it." Her hair was dyed platinum blond and bobbed just below her ears, like the young women wore their hair these days. A sparkly headband held her chopped bangs against her forehead. A white feathery plume sprouted from the back, giving the impression of a plump crane with a single tail feather.

She also had a string of diamonds around her neck.

Those would be tempting for the ship's thief, whoever it was. He wondered if she'd be attending tonight's VIP dance on the mezzanine. He would have to be alert. Perhaps he could finally catch the scoundrel red-handed. That would certainly be a feather in his cap, gaining the favor of Antonio Salvatore, the money behind Lake Maiden Enterprises. It just might bring him one step closer to taking over as captain of the ship.

"Don't worry, ma'am, the captain will be making announcements over the speakers when there are attractions to see."

"You're not the captain? Well, with your snazzy uniform, I thought you had to be in charge," she said with a flirtatious smirk.

"No, ma'am. First Mate Jack Jenkins, at your service." He bowed and slid by. Being handsome was such a burden. He pretended he didn't see her appreciative survey of his trousers and went on his way.

Jenkins opened the door to the bridge and slipped in quietly. Cappie was at the helm, guiding the *Lake Maiden* to open water. His black eyebrows were pinched together. Jenkins glanced over to Wiggins to get a reading on the current mood. The poor man looked miserable, like he'd been recently beaten. Jack felt a ping of sympathy for the man, knowing how vicious the captain could be.

"I'm back, Captain. The nurse is safely on board. I can take the helm again, if you like."

"If I like? If I'd like you to do your job? Why wouldn't I want you to do your job? Is it my job to stand here at this helm? Or is it your job? Which one of us is the captain and which is the first mate?"

"It's my job, sir. I'll take her. Thank you, sir."

The captain stepped aside, letting Jenkins take his place. "I don't know why I put up with you, Jenkins. Or any of you."

"Sorry, sir," Jenkins mumbled.

"Sorry, sir," Wiggins added.

Each of the men focused on their jobs. The bridge settled. Only the sounds that belonged there pinged around the metal and glass bubble overlooking the *Lake Maiden* deck and the expanse of Lake Michigan opening in front of them.

As the *Lake Maiden* picked up speed, she sliced through the waves more easily, with less tossing back and forth. That was good. Maybe they could outrun the storm after all. Seeing the vast open waters ahead comforted Jenkins. The ship's bridge was like a step back in time. The instruments—the brass compass, paper charts, sextant—were nearly unchanged from the era of the great explorers. He could feel a connection somewhere deep in his blood, and he reveled in an exhilarating moment of clarity. He was on his way to his rightful destiny. He would be captain.

The captain wasn't acting like a captain at all, a disgrace to the title. He hacked and coughed, choked and sputtered like his lungs were sponges that had been sopping up swamp muck. He paced, stomped around the bridge, restless and red faced. He was either embarrassed or having a respiratory attack of some sort, or both.

"Captain, can I bring you a drink? Water? Something stronger?" Jenkins offered.

"Hmmm. No. Why on earth do I need water, Jenkins?" he asked. "Are you wanting to leave the bridge again?"

"Not at all, sir."

"Where'd the nurse go, anyway?" the captain added quickly. "Why isn't she here, like I wanted? Bring her here, I told you."

Jenkins shrugged. "Captain, sir, I left her in the Sand Bar. Mr. Houseman was talking to her over some business. She was attempting to make a purchase."

The captain made more disgusting noises. He coughed, spit something globby into a hanky, and studied it like it was fascinating. Jenkins watched him with quick little glances, worried. Cappie stopped behind him, close enough that Jenkins could smell the hair tonic and the throat lozenges he'd been chewing to mask the whiskey and illness.

"Buy something? What would a nurse buy from Houseman?" Captain demanded. "His Orient oil? Was he peddling his poison? Again?"

"I don't know about that, sir. I assumed she wanted to buy a ticket. The three-day package. She needs to pay. No one gets a free ride."

"Well, of course. That's absolutely right."

"Mr. Houseman will see to it, I'm sure," Jenkins added. "He had his ledger and adding machine. All business; you know how Mr. Houseman is about numbers and the *Lake Maiden's* business."

"What do you mean, Jenkins?"

"Well, he's serious about the *Lake Maiden's* business affairs, as if he knows more about how she should be run than you do. If I wasn't a trusting man, I would wonder what he was up to. It's almost like . . . well, that's crazy. Never mind."

The captain winced.

"But it's almost like he's plotting something," Jenkins added. "Hmm, funny, isn't it?"

The captain paced faster, building up steam.

"And after blaming your daughter for making his ledger sticky with something spilled on it. That Mr. Houseman is one comical fella, isn't he?"

"I see no humor in Seymore Houseman's unfortunate accusation about Natalia and the damned ledger," spat Captain. "He had no business leaving the books out!"

"Right you are, sir."

The captain stopped suddenly, hands on his hips. "Damn those books. Three days of bankers on board. They're supposed to enjoy the trip, be persuaded to see the potential profit, not sink the damned ship under my feet!" Captain fumed. He coughed and pursed his lips, sucking on his lozenge. "You have the bridge, Jenkins. Steady as she goes."

"Aye, Captain."

As soon as the captain was gone, Wiggins stood and clapped. His big hands made hollow sounds as they came together. "Quite a performance," he said.

"Knock it off, Wiggins."

"Yeah, what are you up to? What kind of bullshit was that?"

"Nothing to worry about. Forget it. Where'd you say that storm was going to hit?"

Wiggins looked at his charts again, turning his focus back on the immediate issue—weather. "Just off Mackinac. Right about here." He pointed to the partially unrolled chart on the counter. He had to tear at the stuck-together edges to open them further. Against the dotted gray lines and muted greens and blues of the map, a handprint stood out, bright pink, sticky, smelling like sickening sweet cherries.

"I see we've had a visitor on the bridge," grumbled Jenkins.

"Well, it sure as hell ain't been me up here sucking on pink cherry juice," said Wiggins. "Damn that fish-girl."

"Mermaids are NOT fish." It was Mimi in the doorway, mocking Natalia's high, squeaky voice, standing with an exaggerated twist in her back. She had costumes over her arm.

They all laughed little awkward laughs. Mimi blushed, looking slightly embarrassed for poking fun at the poor girl. Then Jack grunted, shutting them up. "Enough," he said. No one should laugh at the sick kid-fish.

"Here's the Pirate King costume, Jack. We'll use you in the first show. Mario's going to do the second show. Be backstage at least a half hour early. All you do is come on stage on cue. Wave a cardboard sword. The chorus takes care of the rest." She left before he could object.

Wiggins laughed and clapped again.

"Bravo for the Pirate King," he said.

CHAPTER 15

NATTIE stared at the empty seat of her rollie chair. Where did Silas go? Margret pulled the empty chair up to the tank and parked it within Nattie's reach. She made a motion for Nattie to pull herself over.

"Did you see anyone in the dressing room, Miss Margret? Was there someone back there? Maybe a fella who wasn't feeling so good? Someone looking woozy? Passed out, maybe?"

"Of course not. Who, for Christ's sake, do you think would be in your dressing room?"

***

Nattie waited backstage, as ordered.

She hid the handful of chewed-up orange rinds in the cushion of the red velvet settee where she sat, deposited by Margret, who had told her to wait there. On the way to the auditorium, they had detoured through the Sand Bar, and Nattie had swiped oranges from the bottoms of almost-empty glasses when Margret wasn't looking. Margret didn't notice her help herself to half a highball left on a tray, either. Nattie had figured a few sips would help chase away the uneasy feelings lingering in her bones. Then an abandoned Polynesian Passion went down while Margret had hobnobbed with 'Tender over some arrangements for cabanas.

So, now, she rested her head on the settee, which seemed to be spinning. Bubby, the light and sound man, dimmed the backstage lights, a signal to the cast and crew to get in place. Nattie didn't see how she could. She had to hang on to the settee to keep from falling off. She was droopy, slippery, slinky. She could seep into the floor.

Ten minutes to curtain. Lights were still up in the auditorium so passengers could find their seats. From her spot, Nattie could see through a gap in the curtains. The seats were filling up, couples filtering in, whispering to each other in secret codes. They were spies.

A gang of brewery boys came in, loudly claiming an entire row as their own, the hoggy-piggy brats. They all looked the same, dressed in their white shirts and buttoned vests. They probably worked for the same distributor who gave them tickets for the *Lake Maiden* as a reward for a job well done. Their mamas must be proud of them.

She didn't have a mama.

But she'd had too much whiskey, she was pretty darn-tootin' sure.

Five minutes to curtain.

The lights lowered. She slid under water, splash-less, into the dark murky calm that absorbed light and sound. She floated, tiny movements of her tail and hands keeping her from drifting off with the current.

She blinked underwater. Her eyes adjusted and she could make out the shapes of the other performers and the stagehands that moved in the half light. They all seemed to be in a hurry. Frenzy was above water. She was below, safe.

Above water, people went missing. Buster, Silas, Jakub, Mr. Whiskers. The boat was cursed.

Bubby stood in front of a tangle of frayed rope at the curtain edge. His knotted old hands were shoved in his overall pockets like he was saying it wasn't his fault, he didn't touch a thing and look what happened. He might cry. She might cry.

> *Just look.*
> *The poor innocent helpless rope broke.*
> *Doesn't anyone care?*

"Here. Eat some more orange slices," someone said, handing her a glass. "Have some cherries, too. Just stop whining, will you?"

She sucked at the orange as hard as she could, tasting the whiskey.

> *"I bet you could suck the silver off a trailer hitch, honey. Your pretty lips are so fine." The man with black hair pushed Queenie to lay her head on his lap like it was naptime.*
> *"Honey, go get her. Look, she's near the water again."*
> *"Let her go. She'll be fine. Don't stop now. We're going to town."*

"Why couldn't I go to town? Why didn't you want me?"

"You were too sickly to take anywhere." Queenie sat on the settee looking lovely, not very dead at all. Most of the ants were gone. Her eyebrows were still painted black, arched in dramatic curves.

"I didn't mean to be sickly. My hair was combed pretty, the headband in place. I said, 'Are you proud of me?' Do you remember? I said, 'Are you proud of me?' You said, 'For what?'"

> *I'm a big girl now. My bow is straight. I didn't pull it out and my hands are clean and I'm sitting up straight, not squirming even when it hurts to hold still, frozen like cement. I don't move. I don't cry once.*
> *Not once today. I didn't act selfish. I didn't ask for anything.*
> *"Are you proud of me?"*
> *"For what?"*

Nattie watched Bubby. He looked bewildered.

Someone should help him.

"He'll have to pull the curtain by hand," Queenie said. "The curtain is still on the track. He just needs to tug and walk it across, one side at a time. It's not so hard. We did it at the opera house all the time."

"Should I tell him?"

"No. He'll figure it out on his own, if he has half a brain."

"I have half a brain," said Nattie. "I'm smarter than you think. Why wouldn't you let me go to school?"

"I didn't want you to be disappointed when you realized you weren't up to it."

"I could have tried. I would have tried really hard. You wouldn't even let me try."

"Who are you talking to over here in the dark, Nattie?" asked Mimi, who had snuck up behind her with a hairbrush. The seamstress attacked her tangles with full engines, full speed, not waiting for an answer.

"I thought I heard Queenie."

"Oh, darling. Queenie isn't here."

"I smelled her perfume."

"No, honey, that—

100

"She dropped by. We had things to say to each other. Words needed saying."

Mimi got all flustered and sputtery, spit coming out her mouth like she was an old woman with loose dentures. Was she crying?

"The perfume was supposed to be a joke. Nattie, I'm sorry. I did it. Margret put me up to it. She found the perfume in your father's quarters. Margret was jealous you got those pearls, not her. She knew the perfume was your mother's. . ."

Nattie wiped the dribbles of lake water and tears from her face and sat up straighter, forcing the curve of her spine to stretch to pretend-straight, for her mother. She tried to ignore the muscle pains in her legs breaking through the whiskey fuzzy-wuzzies. She turned her head, trying to ignore Mimi. That was hard to do. The woman was leaking water, sorry-like.

> *She ought to be sorry. What a mean thing to do. Spreading*
> *perfume lies.*

"You know you need to be getting on your Rocky Shore platform soon. Bubby's going to push you out this performance," Mimi said, trying to sound like nothing was wrong.

"On thunderclap number two."

"Make sure he remembers to tie the rope around your waist. We don't need any more rope incidents this performance. Of all the shows, this is the one when a rat decides to chew through the curtain rope."

Nattie tried to focus, sit straight, and concentrate on the horizon to keep from spinning.

I'm trying to be good.

She looked down and realized her top was all askew, hardly covering the ittybittytitties.

"Oh no, just look at me."

She tried to untangle the strings of shells dangling around her neck, but they jingled too loudly and fought back. Mimi had to help. The woman's hands were cold and trembly. She looked dopey-sad. No, worse, she had pity on her face. She was biting her lip and wouldn't look straight at Nattie's face, like Nattie's dead mother would stare back.

Maybe they were one and the same, Nattie and Queenie. Maybe Mimi was afraid some of Queenie's vengeance would rub off on her. She would be contaminated forever, like Nattie. Poor Mimi.

"I'm sorry, Mimi, I'll try harder. I'll hushhh." Nattie sat up straighter. She had to try harder, for Mimi. She had to be the perfect mermaid, made of mystery and enchantment. She was a legend. "When I live underwater, will you come visit me?"

Mimi brushed harder, pulling on the tangles.

"I'm going to take my clamshell of treasures and Mr. Willie Whisker-Whispers with me." She broke out in giggles. "Mr. Whiskers has a tail, like I do!" She meowed. "Mr. Whiskers, where are you?"

"Shh, Nattie, no more now. Really."

"You haven't seen Mr. Whiskers, have you?"

"No, honey. I haven't."

"I know. He's swimming. I heard some waiters say he's swimming. Maybe he's swimming with dolphins in the lake."

"I don't think cats swim. And there are no dolphins in Lake Michigan," Mimi said, recovering from her bout of sadness. "You know that, silly girl." She stopped brushing and wiped her face with her sleeve, pulling her serious face back into place.

"There's no such thing as mermaids either. Yet here I am," Nattie said and winked.

"How do you come up with these things? And where is your crown? The new one? Did you lose it already?"

"I left it in my tank. It's buried in the pink sand."

"Oh, girl, are you trying to drive me batty? Is that your plan?"

"I have a plan. But that's not it. My plan requires empty barrels and shoooooes. Lots of shoes."

"Alright. Alright. I'll send someone to get it. You said it's at the bottom? In that slimy God-awful sand?"

"I don't think I want someone in my sand. It's. Very. Personal. And slightly pink." She realized her words sounded funny, slurred and slushy like almost-frozen puddles.

"Pink? You been eating whiskey fruit again? How many of those gin oranges you suck on this afternoon?"

"Margret gave me a hundredzillion so I'd be quiet. No, it was 16 kabillion and 57 million more and 99."

"Oh, she did?"

"Yep, but I'm not being quiet. I'm talkingtalkingtalking. Are you proud of me, Mimi?"

"Yes, honey, I'm very proud of you."

"I'm proud of me, too," Nattie said, her voice breaking like a brittle teacup.

"Hey, Bubby, over here," Mimi called to the stagehand, who was still inspecting the tangled, frayed rope.

"Can you come over here, please? You'll have to push Miss Natalia out on stage with her Rocky Shore platform so the pirate ship has somewhere to land after the storm."

Mimi made some gesture behind Nattie's back.

Bubby nodded and winked, all important and knowing and wise, like he'd been let in on a secret.

Maybe Mimi had told him the big secret: Captain-Father left Queenie dead on the beach for the ants to eat. Now Bubby knew the most horrid of all secrets and he would never be the same man, knowing what he knows. The burden might cripple the man and make him useless.

"She goes out on thunderclap number two."

"Sure thing, Miss Mimi," he said, all-knowing.

Bubby carried her to the Rocky Shore platform and set her on top of the mountain of chicken wire and plaster rocks painted brown.

"Okay, Miss Mermaid Fish-Girl, you sit here. Fix your tail all pretty like."

"Mermaids are not fish!"

She was so high on the rocks, higher than usual. There was no railing, busted or not busted.

She put a new sign in the holder. Mermaids like oranges. 16 like me, Heinz 57, 99 bottles of beer on the wall.

"Now you hang on tight. Here's the rope."

This perch wasn't quite right. There was no handle, like there was supposed to be there.

"Okay, get ready to go," he said.

Bubby didn't know what he was doing.

Jakub knew where she was supposed to sit and where the rope went. And that she'd rubbed a heart shape on her wooded throne just by sitting.

But Jakub had abandoned her, just like her mother had.

The perfume was a farce. Her mother was gone.

Nothing could be worse. No horrible sea monster nightmare and middle of the night screams could be worse than having no mother, alive or dead.

Having no mother meant a huge hole. No one was there to tell her she would be loved. No one could explain how to make a red-haired boy love her. No one heard her screams when she fell. No one came. No one woke her from the nightmares of ants marching off with human eyeballs on their backs. Sometimes the eyes blinked. Ninety-nine times.

She laughed at the eyeball parade, so bizarre that it was funny.

She was a little girl riding in a red wagon, laughing, selling newspapers with neighbor children because she had a lousy mother who couldn't be bothered to tend to her little girl.

Queenie was a star at the opera house, but she didn't sing opera. She danced. She had white gloves and took them off while she danced. Nattie saw her practice for man friends. Getting those gloves off was hard. She had to pull and tug-tug-tug with the rhythm of the music on the gramophone.

Queenie wasn't coming back. Ever.

Neither was Jakub, she knew. She felt it. His absence was becoming thick and cold and heavy, threatening to take her with him down the drain, like bathtub bubbles that washed away, out to sea. With Heinz 57 and 99 bottles of beer on the wall.

She had her own escape route to plan. She just had to do one more show. Maybe two.

She wondered if Szymon was in the audience, and Anka, too.

I'll wave to them.

"Me too," said Queenie. "Wave to me."

"No, I'm mad at you. I'm not talking to you anymore."

Queenie pulled the stage curtain open. The gramophone started. The chorus girls took the stage. The dance steps made the floor vibrate in time to the music and the waves hitting the shore, in and out, in, out-in, in-out-in-out.

Nattie's eyes closed as she slid under water, floating away, adrift in kind, warm currents to a place where someone loved her and stroked her back, proud of her, pat-patting her hand. She wore proper white gloves, each with three pearls.

A thunderclap woke her.

She jumped a mile high, into the gray storm sky where bald gulls hovered.

Thunderclap two.

Bubby pushed. Too sudden, too fast, too hard.

She fell overboard into the icy blue storm and was washed away.

Queenie caught her.

"Come with me," Queenie said. "We'll swim."

"But I don't know how to swim. No one taught me."

"I'll teach you everything you need to know."

"How to dance lying down in the sand, going to town?"

"This way," Queenie said. "Take my hand."

"Will you be proud of me?"

"Of course, my little *Syrenka*."

"Are you sorry?"

"Sorry for what, fish-girl?"

CHAPTER 16

JEDEDIAH huffed because he was angry and because he was out of breath and because was tired of trying to talk sense into Silas. The fool probably wouldn't hear him anyway. He was almost passed out, almost worthless, hanging on by his shoelaces. Jedediah doubted the man's ears were working. His feet weren't putting in much effort, that was for sure.

He pulled the droopy boy through the narrow crew passage that stretched along the length of the mezzanine.

"C'mon, now Silas. We've got a ways to go. You can do it, I know you can."

Jedediah had hauled Silas out of the dressing room while Natalia was daydreaming and stirring in her sand pile, half-dazed, that strange look on her face. No wonder most of the crew thought she was daft, a little light upstairs. Maybe she was. It wasn't his place to say. He had always liked the cripple girl and tried to help her out when he could, bringing her fresh water for her tank and emptying the piss bucket for her without her knowing so she wouldn't be embarrassed.

He had left the dressing room tidy when he hauled Silas out. There wasn't much wiping to do. The towel had caught most of the bleeding. There were a few dollops of red on the floor. He rush-wiped those as best as he could. Later he'd bring his mop. He left the wheelchair.

It wouldn't be no good in the rat-run anyway. Silas would have to walk a bit—if he could.

Christ carried his own cross to his crucifixion.

"Come on, Silas. Keep moving." Jed knew the boy's knife wound needed attention, and soon. How long could a man keep bleeding before he was out of blood and out of time? Jed was keenly aware of his lack of knowledge in this area. Being a man of God, he had spent most of his adult life shying away from violence. He had a pocketknife, but it was for cleaning his nails and whittling wood, nothing else.

"What got into you, Silas? A knife fight? What got you two fellas all riled up? Whiskey? A woman? What got into you?"

"Nuthin. . ."

"Nothing? Don't look like nothing to me. Looks like trouble. Deep trouble. You know troublemakers don't last on the *Lake Maiden*. Everyone knows it. Some curse. Maybe it's just plain stupidity run amuck. Stupid boiler room boys do stupid things, get themselves in a lard vat full of misery and trouble."

Jed paused to rest. His breaths came in gasps. Air was scarce in these rat-runs. Poor ventilation. Or he was riled up too? Maybe the dang boat's curse was after him too.

"A perty fish girl, was all," Silas mumbled, fat words sloshing out his mouth. "Fishy hoo-hoos and fish lips." He sounded drunk. Or stupid. Or on his way to half-crazy or plain dead, one foot in Purgatory, one in the long line for redemption.

Jed was so mad he thought he might help Silas to his demise. The idiot boy, causing trouble. Over a girl.

"You ought to know better than test a man's allegiance to his girl, even if she's part of the stage show. She still counts for something."

Jed wanted to slap the boy. Instead, he shoved and walked him forward, carrying most of his weight.

"That's it. Lean on me, Silas."

Jed's shoulders burned, muscles screaming. He had already been carrying around a heavy burden for days, the weight of a dead man. He was the one who had sent Buster to the mezzanine that night. It was an awful burden.

And the mermaid was tangled in that ill fate, too.

Buster was a fool, a bigger fool than Silas, for sure. All that drinking and talking. And pestering the girl. Wanted her to feel like she was worth something, Jed supposed.

Pestering. Pestering. Pestering.

Then he pushed the limit. And there was no going back to this side of right.

Righteous.

Jedediah stumbled. Nearly dropped Silas.

"You ain't the only one that got caught in the girl's trap, you know. She's an oddity, all right. Buster. He was a grown man. Ought to have known better."

Jed looked up at the markings on the wall. M8. Mezzanine 8. They had to go down a level to Galley level. Jed hoisted Silas up again. The boy moaned, miserable sounds like a cat in heat.

"Hush up, man. You're calling attention. Wailing. Like a ghost in the walls. We don't need none of that nonsense."

> "Nonsense, man. Hush up. You know you ain't got no business up here.
> M8 is for the rich and white. You ain't either," said Jed, stacking plates.
> "I am just strollin', getting air. I got a right," Buster shouted, his slurred words bouncing around the empty tables.
> "Yeah. Breathe all you want. Then, do me a favor. Stroll past the mermaid. See if she got any real food in her today. Here's a plate you can give her, if she's hungry."
> "Scraps? Like she's a dog? Ain't right," Buster mumbled.
> "Blessed are those who hunger and thirst for righteousness," Jed answered.
> "You can keep your holy horse shit, preacher. I see through it. You ain't no better than rest of them."

Jed's throat tightened up, dry as dust, thirsty as hell. He choked and coughed. He swallowed harder.

Holy horse shit.

"Come along now. That's it. Keep those feet moving, Silas. It's a good thing you're all bones, or I'd never be able to carry you through these walls. But nephew, you sure as hell gonna be sorry when I tell your mama, my dear loving sister, all the trouble you's causing me."

Silas drooled spit and blood down his chin.

"Come on, Silas. Keep on. Move those lazy feet."

***

Jed peeked around the corner to the galley, hoping to catch Mabella alone. He was near certain she would help, being a God-fearing woman. She attended his preaching meetings every Sunday in the auditorium. Mabella was a large woman, born in Alabama and partial to anything sweet, buttered, battered, or fried. She'd break your bones if she fell on you. There wasn't much chance of that, though. She was built low to the ground, just a few inches over four feet tall.

"Psssst, Eunice, over here. Come here, will you?"

"Preacher, what you want? You know Mabella don't tolerate no lollygagging." Eunice was a young woman, her brown face dusted with flour. Some was in her hairnet, too, some on her blue uniform dress. "I got work. We's got the main dinner meal cooking. I'm on biscuits. You know how many biscuits I gotta make for one dinner?"

"Eunice, I know. This is important. Go fetch Mabella for me. Tell her it's important. And give me that towel," he said, pointing at the dish towel over her shoulder.

"Preacher, what you need a kitchen towel for?"

Silas, who was propped up behind him in the doorway, slid against the wall and landed with a loud thump on the floor, leaving a red smear that couldn't be missed on the wall.

Eunice screamed, hands to her mouth, knees buckling.

"Shhh. Shhh. Stop that, girl," Jed said, slapping his hand over her mouth—but not fast enough.

Half the kitchen crew came running, including Mabella, who led the pack, pink slippers flapping on thundering feet.

"What's going on over here? I declare, girl, shut your mouth," she said, looking around to find the trouble. "Now what woe-is-me worries you bring in here, Preacher? You need to steal my slop pail for that fish tank again or what?"

She quickly saw that the situation was more urgent.

Jed was getting the boy upright again, or trying to. There was no chair in the galley, but Mabella brought over a three-legged wooden stool, fussing and griping the whole time about the interruption to her cooking and contamination of her clean kitchen. Germs were a blasphemy unto God, she declared.

Then she shooed everyone else back to work. Eunice held back, overly distraught. Silas might be something special to her. Jed had heard the rumors, like the rest of the boat had.

"What's wrong with him, Preacher? Is he going to be alright? Tell me," the girl pleaded, her eyes brimming with tears.

"Just you worry about those biscuits you're supposed to be baking, Eunice. Git to work now," Mabella said, shoving the young girl back to her job.

Jed explained the situation to Mabella as quickly as he could, keeping the story simple. Mabella didn't need the long version. She knew how to piece together the how-comes and the what-ifs and the what-next. She was a smart woman who knew how the *Lake Maiden* worked and why Silas could find himself swimming with the fishes if they didn't help and get him to shore.

"There's no place for troublemakers on board. They need to be plucked off, like plucking ticks off a dog's back."

Jenkins, the ass-kissing first mate, would be looking for Silas, that was for certain.

"How long you figure to the next port?" Mabella asked, thinking ahead, just like Jed.

"It'd be Mackinac Strait. Usually we'd get into port about midnight, but I hear weather's ahead of us."

"How bad?"

"How am I supposed to know, woman? The Heavenly Father doesn't tell me everything."

"You'd never know, listening to you preach," she snapped.

"Well, I saw some of the crew tying down crates, securing cargo, like they was expecting white caps."

"We're not going up to Superior, are we?"

"I'm not here to argue about the weather, May. I just need you to have one of the bus boys keep a towel pressed on the wound and keep him from smearing blood he can't afford to lose on the dang walls."

"And what are you gonna do?"

"I heard waiters talking about a lady who hitched a ride on a tug. Said she was wearing white. I think it might be that nurse who comes on board sometimes, plays poker likes she's one of the fellas. I'm gonna find her. See if she'll sew him up."

"That crazy woman?" Mabella asked, ducking her head like bats were coming for her. "You know she's got the Evil about her. And she's a seer, that's how come she wins at poker."

"Nah, she wins at poker because she cheats."

"Well, I don't want her in my galley. That's all I have to say about it."

Jed was losing his patience. He finally resorted to the one thing that always worked, that settled any argument: "It's His will. He told me so. Answered a prayer."

Mabella gave him the scrutiny, up and down, studying him for cracks in his devout layer. She usually had a good nose for sniffing out bullshit, but something threw her off her game. Maybe all the cooking commotion going on behind her was distracting. Pans rattling and dishes clinking, searing and sizzling sounds made a loud roar. She was supposed to be orchestrating that hullabaloo.

She probably wanted to get back to work, the good woman.

She nodded. "Alright, Preacher, but you be sure to put in a good word for me with the Lord Almighty for helping you, you hear me? You be sure to tell Him that Mabella answered the calling."

"Oh, He knows, Mabella, He knows all about you and your devotion, I'm sure."

Jed patted Silas on the shoulder and went to find the nurse.

"Where do you think she is?" he asked God.

God didn't answer. But Jed had a good guess: the poker lounge.

CHAPTER 17

HALINA stared at Antonio, her eyes locked with his. She wasn't about to blink first. She wanted to knock him off his high horse and have him feel her dark eyes boring into his—

He laughed, a dismissive scoff meant to brush her aside. Antonio wasn't the least bit intimidated by midnight-black eyes, it seemed. He was just as arrogant as ever, unsoftened by his years with Pat wherever the hell they'd been holed up. The poor fella.

"Well, how is she? How's my dear sister?"

"She's luscious," he said, drawing out the word and licking his lips like was talking about a lemon chiffon pie. "As voluptuous and audacious as ever."

"You eat a dictionary or something? Since when does my sister deserve such big words?"

"She's moved up in the organization, no longer tied down by that rat trap in Hegewisch and that man who didn't know a thing about how to keep a vixen like Pat happy."

"Yeah, well, she always did have *a fixin'* for living it up big. A big appetite. And lots of guts, too. Gotta give her that." Halina chuckled, her turn at being dismissive and rude.

"Vixen, I said. Not fixin'."

"I heard you the first time. I'm not deaf. Not dumb either, whiskey man," she said. "I'm just not sure I believe it."

She wasn't ready to believe all was well with her sister. How could it be? She was, apparently, afraid to cross the border, holed up in Ontario. Didn't even make it to Ma's funeral. And who knew how long it had been since she'd seen her son. God knows what Jakub was doing on this boat and what trouble he could be in, trying to make his own way in the world after what he'd been through.

The poor sweet boy, red hair and all those freckles. And a horrid scar left on his chest.

Jakub had been one of her most challenging cases. A chest wound. But he recovered. It took some hospital medicine, but he lived. Patcja never really appreciated the fact that Halina had saved her boy.

Halina thought of the man from the bus, spread-eagle on the street, gasping from some kind of hemorrhage, head bleeding, eyes yellowed, stinking of sickness.

"She needs you. She sent me to bring you back."

Her eyes darted to her satchel, at her feet, within reach. That's where she had dropped the bloody hanky. Maybe she should have examined it closer or hid it better. Maybe she should just grab the whole bag and run out of reach of this ass, Antonio.

Where could I go? Seems like I should have a plan first.

"You sure Pat's doing fine? Her asthma is under control? Those cigar burns on her feet got all healed up? The last time I saw her those burns weren't looking good. Your Uncle Salvatore's doing."

Antonio's face turned gray. But the cigar incident was years ago. The burns should have healed long ago. Then again, some wounds never do.

Antonio stood abruptly, knocking his bar stool into the next one, which fell onto the next one, which fell onto the next one . . .

The other passengers in the bar froze. The bartender jumped into gear, rushing to right the toppled stools.

"Anything you need, Mr. Salvatore? This lady causing trouble? I can have her escorted out, if you like." The bartender nodded to the black doorbell button screwed into the counter where he had been slicing oranges. On the cutting board, his paring knife glistened, orange juice shimmering on the blade. That blade looked sharp, sharper than was needed to cut orange slices.

Wonder where they get oranges this time of year.

"Nah, get her a drink, 'Tender. One of your Polynesian Passions. She just needs to relax a little, not worry about her sister and her ailments."

"Whatever you say, sir."

Antonio turned to the bystanders and spread his arm, like Jesus on the Mount. "Nothing to worry about, folks. Nothing to see. Go back to your business."

Halina realized she wasn't going to get a straight answer, not now, not from this ass-wipe. She pulled up a barstool and watched the bartender make her drink. Maybe she could remember how he made it and make them for herself at home. Why not? She still had a couple bottles of Pa's whiskey stashed away.

Theo didn't have to know.

The purser fella with his accounting books came back in, pointing his sharp nose toward Antonio.

"We're all set up in the mezzanine," he said from the doorway. "We can review assets, or lack thereof, from there. I had some waiters set up tables in the corner. That area's usually quiet in the afternoon. The mermaid has left for the afternoon show."

"You talk too much, Seymore."

"I know, sir."

"I'm going to watch the afternoon show," Antonio said. "Why don't you join me, Nurse Halina?"

"I'm going to drink my Polynesian Passion," she answered as 'Tender handed her the drink.

"So, why do they call you 'Tender?" she asked the bartender. "Can I have another one of those orange slices? Where do you get oranges this time of year?"

Antonio bristled and huffed off. Seemed he wasn't used to being told no. The Seymore character followed, carrying his all-important book.

"Looks like he's going to watch the afternoon show, too," Halina said with a shrug.

"Oh, I doubt that," 'Tender answered, warming up. "He's not much for theatrics. Unless it has to do with his books. Then he's got a different tune to sing."

"I was trying to do some business with the man," she whispered, "but he didn't seem to think this was the place or time."

"Well, I may be able to help you, ma'am. Seymore ain't the only entrepreneur on the boat. I can set you up, if you're so inclined for company." He leaned in, eyebrows raised. "I ain't one to judge. Our banjo player will do some private strumming. If you like 'em younger, one of the boys from the galley could be arranged. And if you prefer ladies, our Sally, from the chorus, is usually available for . . . a nap. I can set you up with a room any time you want."

Halina took a long swallow of her drink and let it warm her throat all the way down. She tingled in places that didn't usually tingle, not often anyway.

114

"'Tender, you're a matchmaker. But I'm married, and that isn't the kind of business I was wanting to do."

A panel in the wall behind the bar swung open. It wasn't big, just wide enough for a skinny man. That's what came out of the passageway—a skinny old man, dark skinned like those shantytown fellas on the other side of the tracks. He looked like he'd seen better days. His clothes were smeared, filthy. Was it blood? His face was frantic and tired and he was out of breath.

"Preacher, what you doing here? No one buzzed for an emergency cleanup."

The man ignored the bartender and the scolding. He pointed at Halina. "You!"

Well, at least somebody's happy to see me.

"You're the nurse. I am looking for you!"

***

Halina refused to follow Jedediah back through the rat-run and insisted on using the normal passenger route to the kitchen, no matter if it was longer. She wasn't about to get into no secret passageway with no idea where it was going and what was down there, all alone with some skinny old bum doused in dried-up blood, even if he did claim to a be a preacher man on Sundays.

But she did follow him to the kitchen, because he insisted. And he said a man was dying. She had a duty, she supposed.

A knife fight was the same no matter whether it happened in a boat's belly or at the end of a long alley. Chances of survival all depended on where the knife went in, not how deep or how large the wound. It was all about whether an organ was hit. Belly wounds were bad. If the bowels leaked bacteria into the stomach cavity, there wasn't much use in trying to stitch up the mess. Sepsis was bound to happen. And if the liver was punctured, there wasn't much hope at all. A man needs his liver, even if it is half-pickled with booze.

She tried to find reassuring words for the preacher as they walked. He looked frazzled with fear, an electrical wire overheating, about to short out.

It probably wasn't serious, she tried to tell him. It was hard to kill a

115

man with a knife, she said. She wasn't too worried. It did cross her mind that she had only one uniform, no change of clothes. Getting blood on the white uniform would be very inconvenient.

I'll ask for an apron. Surely a kitchen would have an apron to spare.

***

It was the biggest tiny kitchen she'd ever seen. Everything was on a small scale to fit in a cramped space, like a child's playhouse, but there was so much equipment and shiny metal counters that gleamed like they'd been polished. She counted five stoves and two huge metal closets that were likely iceboxes or Frigidaires. She marveled at a mixer as tall as a child and a silver bowl as big as an oil drum. She couldn't imagine how many cakes a mixer like that could make all at once.

"I have to say, this is one impressive cooking establishment you have here, Mabella," she said to the head cook when she was introduced. "Right nice equipment, and so clean, too. You run this whole kitchen? You? My ma was a cook, at my sister's tavern. She ran the kitchen. All the cooking. All herself. She had her skillet and a big wooden spoon. Nothing as fancy as this." She realized she was probably sounding silly, rambling about unimportant things when these two people were scared crazy thinking this boy might die.

But talking was a good remedy for the nerves. Theirs and hers. A calm voice did a world of good for the jitters. Baba used to make her patients sing. It's impossible to be frightened when singing "The Beer Barrel Polka."

"You know, Mabella, I bet you are one fine cook. You must be. For the boat captain and all these whiskey fellas to put you in charge of the kitchen, you being a woman and tiny sized. I bet you get your fill of short jokes. Being Polish brings on the ridiculing jokes, too. I understand your troubles, Mabella."

Mabella didn't look sure about this at all. Halina caught her side-glancing at the preacher man, like she was wondering what she got herself into.

"Just get this boy out of my kitchen. Fix him up and send him on his way," Mabella snapped.

Then Halina saw Silas, the wounded young man, propped up in a corner, perched on a three-legged stool. He could hardly be called a man.

He should be in school. He was barely old enough to shave and looked too skinny to amount to much. A good wind would blow him away.

A young woman with flour all over face came rushing up.

"Can you help him? Please help him," the girl said, oozing melodrama like she was in some kind of radio show, playing the part of the mortified girlfriend. She was sure milking it.

"Eunice, get back to making biscuits," Mabella said, hands on her hips.

"Let's see here what we have," Halina said. "Let's just stay calm and look-see what we're dealing with before we get too worried."

She bent down closer to her new patient. "How do you do, Silas. I'm Halina, a nurse, trained and educated. I'm going to help you, if that's okay with you. You can always say no thank you, but I don't recommend that."

"Help me. Please," Silas moaned, his voice raspy and weak. His chest sounded like it was rattling, ball bearings rolling around loose in his lungs. Sounded awfully close to the death rattle. She knew that sound.

"Alrighty, then. I'll do my best."

She started to remove his shirt, then she remembered.

"Mabella, can I have an apron, please?"

And from somewhere on the boat, down some corridors, across the metal passageways and through the rivets and galvanized steel, she heard music, ever so faint. A band tuning up. An accordion testing chords.

"The Beer Barrel Polka."

A whiskey bottle dropped on a kerosene lamp. Pa's drunk clumsiness.

Baba was at the stove, stirring more powders and roots and stems into the foul-smelling concoction. Patcja was huddled on the floor, her pitiful burned arm propped on the chair, charred bits of skin hanging.

"You're supposed to be singing, girl, I told you. Sing now!"
The old woman brought the kettle and a supply of torn sheets to the table.
"I can't."
"You can. Halina, you help her. Sing together. Big breaths for singing.

Air. You need air. Breathe. Sing." The woman slammed a hand on the table.

Halina started singing the only song she could think of.

"Roll out the barrel. Roll out the beer barrel of fun. Roll out the barrel of fun."

She used the back of her hand to wipe her sister's face of the soot and tears from the fire.

"C'mon Pat, you can do it."

Patcja opened her mouth and sucked in air. She gulped and swallowed it like it was medicine. She held her face up, locking eyes with her sister. She sang a word. Then another. She gulped more air. And sang

another word.

And another.

And her blue lips started to become pink again. As she sang words out, air came in and her chest started moving with the rhythm of the song.

She was breathing.

It was a quiet, slow whisper of half beats, but it was better than sobs.

Halina held her sister's good hand and she kept singing, kept her sister from looking to the table where her arm, gray and black from the soot, was propped on a white sheet, and the woman picked away the dead flesh.

The fumes from the concoction in the kettle made both girl drowsy.

Halina saw beer barrels rolling down the street and flying into the sky.

She wondered if she was drunk but didn't care.

Eventually Patcja drooped over, passed out. But her breathing wasn't so jagged as it had been. Color was coming back to her cheeks.

Or maybe it was the dawn that caused the pink flush.

Morning was coming. They had survived the night.
"You can stop singing now. That job is done." Baba gently
wrapped the burns in strips of sheets. "Hold her good hand.
Tap it. To the beat.
She'll breathe to the beat."
"How did you know singing would help her?"
"I know everything. Simple. Air. Breath. Beat. Pulse. And
focus. A distraction from the pain. Directions make her mind
work. Stops the panic. Brings her back to this world where
there are songs about beer."
The woman shrugged like it was simple fact, not genius.
Halina was awestruck. She cried. All of the God-touched
miracles that Baba had made happen and those that were yet
to come mingled into one powerful moment. She was part of
the circle. It was in her bones, and she knew it like she knew
her name.
"Will you teach me how to heal people?"
"You already know. It's in you. I'll help you remember. You'll
heal bones and hearts, fishes that breathe air and fliers
without feathers, sisters, sinners, and captains of chariots with
wooden wheels. You'll see."

CHAPTER 18

SZYMON pulled Anka along by her hand. She fell in line behind him and picked up her pace, thank God. She should know resistance was useless. Once he made up his mind on something, there was no stopping him.

Focus was important, and determination, of course. He had plenty of both, when it mattered. Like his plans for being a pilot. That was all he could think about these days. He planned to enlist. Most people didn't think of planes when it came to the navy. He did. In the last war, the pilots who took off and landed on aircraft carriers had a powerful impact, providing air cover for troops pushing back the ground forces.

He wanted to feel that kind of glory.

But he needed someone who would look after Anka while he was serving. He just didn't know who. She was going on sixteen, which ought to be old enough to look after herself, right? After all, their mother came from the Old Country at sixteen, all alone. But Anka wasn't nearly as independent or resourceful as their mother had been.

She was more fanciful, a bird with frilly feathers that couldn't fly. Couldn't cook, clean, sew, teach, or type, either, or any of the other things a woman might do to earn some money and look after herself. So he was stuck with her and her ding-batty flightiness until he could figure out a solution.

As they crossed the main deck, he wished they had worn warmer coats. Anka didn't have a hat. Her hair was flying all around in the wind, and she didn't have the smarts to tie it back.

It wasn't half as pretty as Natalia's hair. He didn't remember Nattie's hair being such a pretty wheat color when she was a little girl. She had sure grown up to be a lovely young woman.

Nattie was still just a girl, though, wasn't she? Was someone looking out for her? It didn't seem like it. He knew if he was in charge, he wouldn't let her walk around in that outfit. No mother would, either. Well, Nattie's mother, maybe.

Queen of the Opera House, my ass. That woman didn't know one lick of opera. Not a one. He wasn't even sure she could sing.

"Come on, Anka, you're dragging again. Pick it up."

"I'm trying. You walk too fast for me. You know that. But you keep doing it." She slowed down even more, just because.

"I should have left you at home."

"Well, you didn't."

"Do you want to miss the show? If not, move it."

The plan had been to find Natalia and tell her the news about Queenie's trunk being found at the opera house—that it contained mementos she would probably want, like Queenie's scrapbook and a diary. "The Joys of Motherhood" had been handwritten in a loopy script across the cover, blue ink all spattered and messy. Szymon thought Nattie might find comfort in the scribblings of her mother. He could arrange to have the trunk delivered to wherever Nattie and the captain lived now. Surely they had a house to live in, something besides this paddlewheel.

He had thought he and Anka could do a short little boat ride, talk to Nattie, then go home, back to where they belonged. He hadn't planned on a three-day trip.

Now he was regretting the whole idea. Did they really need to pass along the old crap from Queenie? It was a long time ago when he'd taken Anka and Natalia with him to sell newspapers, pulling the little kid around in that homemade wagon. Someone had to look after her, back then, didn't they?

And it had been his stupid idea to take her to the old lady witch, the healer. He had heard stories. Some of the fellas had dog-dared him to steal one of her potion jars. It turned out to be a joke. He got a jar and a poultice for Natalia and some singing. The old woman made them sing while she applied ointments to the child's stick legs. Nattie cried the whole time, scared to death.

But was he still obligated? He had tried his best. He'd put the braces on her legs and tightened the screws around her shoes. Then, one day, the braces were gone. Some rust-gilded guilt pulled at him. Should he have done more? Maybe the witch made her worse.

He slowed down to appease Anka, who was sulking. Plus, he wasn't sure he was heading in the right direction. He hated to have to ask, but this damned boat was bigger than he'd thought it would be. People in fancy clothes with their noses in the air were racing like they'd been invited to the Last Supper and there was a shortage of seats. No one wanted to sit next to Mary Magdeline. Or Judas.

He wasn't sure he wanted a seat at all. Some dinners were awfully high priced.

Finally, he saw a wooden signpost planted in a barrel that was bolted to the floor. Green moss dangled from the arrows, and he wondered if it was real or a prop. He was a city boy. The only thing he knew about the lake was that it was a good place to get rid of problems.

The sign pointed to main attractions:

MERMAID LAGOON

SAND BAR

POLYNESIAN POKER ROOM

SHARK BITES DINING ROOM

STRAIT SHOOTERS

GOLD COAST CABANAS

AUDITORIUM

"C'mon, this way," he said, tugging Anka, who was slowing down again. This time she was staring at a dolled-up tart coming their way. The peroxide hair piled on top of her head wobbled in the wind. Looked like some critter could be caught in there, trying to get out.

Szymon didn't dodge her fast enough.

"Hey there, big fella, you need help finding where you want to go? How about the nickel tour? I could show you all the best attractions on the *Lake Maiden*, starting with me." She didn't look much older than Anka, but she certainly had filled out more. She had a healthy frame.

She also had a red boa around her neck, and she waved it under his nose like she was trying to tickle him. It smelled like dirty sheets and old booze. He sneezed and pushed the ratty thing away. A little gray moth fluttered out. Anka tried to catch it and Szymon slapped her hand.

"Stop that," he snapped. He meant Anka, but the woman with the boa took offense, too.

"Well, don't come crying to me when you get lost on this floating rat maze, mister," she sneered.

She turned to Anka and fluffed her feathers at her, then followed them as they started to walk. He bet she got a nickel for every naive sucker she lured to some backroom for a shakedown.

Szymon knew how these operations worked. The *Tribune* saw its share of hustlers at the loading docks and the dispatch yards, where truckloads of morning editions could be torched because some rookie driver fell for a broad's wink or come-hither grin. Then the union boys would meet, gasoline cans in tow, deciding who got burned, whose dues got raised, and whose kneecaps would be busted to even the score. Payoffs kept Chicago running. And it looked to him like dames were always part of the machinery, one way or another.

"If you wanna ditch this sad sack and see how to really have a good time, just come backstage after one of our shows," Doll Face said to Anka with a grin that he guessed was supposed to be enticing. All he could see was her chipped front tooth and a sore on her mouth the size of a horsefly.

"Ask for Margret. Not Margaret. Or Margie. She's Margret. It's Polish. And Mimi, she's French, could get you something swanky to wear. The cat's pajamas. You can't have any fun dressed like that, baby."

"Really?" Anka said. She was caught in the net, snagged by imagination and desire, weaknesses that stood no chance against this temptation. She should be scouting for men of the marrying type. She certainly shouldn't be talking to floozies who wanted to lure her to some private lair of debauchery. He regretted bringing his sister on this mission. *Family.* The bonds could strangle the careless.

"We're not interested," Szymon said. "We're not here for fun. We're here for—"

And then he saw him crossing the deck, in a hurry, his eyes straight ahead, like he was avoiding eye contact with passengers or crew.

It was the captain in his white uniform. He wore a white cap, too, and white shoes like a nurse would wear. He had fancy gold rope things on his shoulders that looked like they came from curtains. And he had some metal doohickies hanging on his pocket, homemade medals, looked like painted Christmas ornaments with a pin stuck in them.

He looked ridiculous.

Anka saw him, too.

"He got old," she said. "He looks older than Old Stach, you know, that ancient vagabond who lives in the shanty. . ."

"It doesn't matter, Anka. Come on."

***

The auditorium was one level below deck and reminded Szymon of a church basement. The ceilings were low and sounds ping-ponged off the metal. He kept going, following signs and throngs of other passengers who seemed to know the route: frequent guests making themselves at home. They were mostly men, but some couples walked together, chitchatting and flirting. He figured they weren't married. The women were painted up, a lot like the floozy who had stopped them on the deck. They wore enough face paint to join a circus as clowns or one of those Wild West shows as the Injuns wearing war paint.

He found it disgusting, but he didn't have words to explain why. It just felt dirty, like cheating or lying, saying you're something you're not. Deluding yourself. Clowns trying to be funny, white men painted red, showgirls, sideshow acts, a mermaid . . .

Then he realized he wasn't much better. He was a pressman who wanted to be a pilot. What kind of delusion was that?

Anka was grinning ear to ear.

There were plenty of seats, rows and rows of wooden fold-up chairs with thread-thin cushions on the seats. How many hundreds of asses had to sit on these cushions to wear them so thin?

Szymon picked two seats for them near the front, where he hoped they'd be able to see Natalia.

Should he wave when she came out, so she would know where they were? Or would that distract her from her lines? Embarrass her? He didn't know what was polite. He hadn't been to many performances besides the holiday plays at the church.

It wasn't long before that Margret woman in her long silver dress came out on stage in front of the curtain and did some talking. Then someone started a phonograph, a needle scratching out music. It was in front of a microphone, must be, and was turned up as loud as it would go.

Anka was transfixed by the stage and the dancing girls who came on in two lines, high kicking and sashaying, waving their heinies in time to the music. They were dressed-up, sleazy caricatures of pirates, with red-and-white skimpy little tops and gold sequin belts. They wore little black skirts with slits up the side and white ruffles underneath.

They reminded him of a sundress Anka had as a child, with little ruffle-butt pants that went over her diaper. She'd crawl across the floor, her ruffled *dupah* wiggling so fast, a little bug scurrying across the room. She got all the attention. "Hey, how's my little ruffle-butt girlie-girl?" Pa would say when he came home from whatever odd jobs he'd found.

The pirate dance was supposed to be tantalizing, he guessed. But it was more on the funny side. Some of the girls had plenty of curves but no rhythm. They bumped into each other and stumbled—but they did it while grinning and gyrating. Then the music changed. Gray clouds made from gauzy material and stuffed like pillows were dropped down from ropes. They swayed on some unseen wind from some unseen storm, some unknown force, perhaps God. Or maybe a fan.

A pirate boat, a silhouette with a Jolly Roger flag hanging from sails, was pulled across the stage. Blue and green scarves on the stage floor waved up and down, tossing around like rough seas. The music became ominous. The pirates danced like they were fighting with the waves. Bit by bit, they tore off pieces of the costumes and tossed them to the stage floor. Occasionally they'd toss a glove into the audience for men to fight over. Then they started in with the glitter buckles, then sleeves, then the rest of the striped tops, leaving red sequined doilies with tassels glued in strategic places.

Anka gasped. Szymon looked away, ashamed. The rest of the crowd cheered and hooted.

The girls shimmied and the tassels twirled.

"How do they do that?" Anka asked him.

"Maybe they have strings. Or magnets. Or windup springs. I dunno."

Lightning and thunder came next. Someone backstage flashed lights on and off. The thunder sounded like sheet metal being hit with a mallet. Another thunderclap rattled across the stage, this one louder.

A platform on wheels was pushed onto the stage. It had plaster rocks on it, all jagged looking. There, perched on top, was a mermaid. A spotlight beam found her and cast a golden glow around her. She looked lovely. Sequins sparkled. Her tail was spread out around her. But Szymon focused on her sweet face.

Natalia!

"There she is, Szymon! Look!"

An old coot was pushing the platform. It got stuck for a moment, one of the wheels locked up. Old Coot gave it a good shove. The platform jumped, and Natalia—

She toppled off her perch, head-first to the stage, landing behind the rocks. The thud was loud and horrible. The crowd made a loud "OOOH" sound, one collective moan of shared dread.

They couldn't see her. The platform of pretend rocks was in the way.

The music continued. The dancing girls continued their steps, not seeing what had happened behind their backs.

Szymon stood up. Anka jumped up, too.

Old Coot ran off stage, waving for someone. The curtain closed. The squeak of metal pulleys and tortured rope made Szymon's teeth ache to the roots.

***

Szymon was prepared to push past the crowds that he pictured hovering around the girl, people springing to action. But when he and Anka got backstage, he saw . . . business as usual?

No Natalia. No old coot stagehand. Just some crew members sitting on an old couch. Others milled around, sipping on something. The chorus girls were reassembling their costumes, snapping sleeves back on, chatting in muffled tones.

"Where's Natalia? Where is she? Tell me," he demanded from the cluster of girls. "Is she okay?"

Some shrugged. Others shook their heads.

The floozy from the deck recognized him. "You're the man who didn't want a tour. Are you lost? What are you doing back here?" Then she saw Anka. "Ah, you decided to have some real fun!" She grabbed Anka's arm. "Good."

Szymon pulled Anka back. "No. We saw Natalia fall. Is she okay? Do you know where she is?"

"Oh, her. She's in the dressing room. Margret has her. Don't worry. She'll be fine. Mermaids dive off rocks all the time. Dive and splash, splash-splash, like little fishies."

"Mermaids are not fish," replied several dancing girls in unison. They snickered, pleased with their little private joke.

He stormed toward the dressing room where the girls had pointed. He realized Anka wasn't following him, but he didn't stop. He had to see if Natalia was okay.

He owed her that.

I'm coming, baby girl. Don't cry. Szymon will take you for a wagon

126

ride. C'mon, little one. Up you go. Here, we'll cover those braces with your blankie. You just sit pretty with the newspapers. People will think you're my sister, pretty as can be, all fine and pretty. A good girl. No one has to know the truth. Smile now. Little Syrenka. Syrenka Warszawska.

CHAPTER 19

HALINA took charge and got bossy, even more than usual. Once she'd agreed to treat this young man, she became the only authority in the room. That was her philosophy. Anyone who didn't like it could shove it where the sun didn't shine.

She met little resistance, none that she acknowledged.

She took off her sweater and Mabella brought her an apron, like she'd asked. Halina figured that might help with some of the spatters. But it didn't matter much. She wouldn't be home in time to make dinner. Theo would be getting home from the mill and wondering where the hell she was. And Janusz would be wallowing in pain in the attic clinic. She just hoped Stach would make sure Janusz got fed and got his next dose of tonic . . . without pissing off Theo. That could be interesting.

What a mess this was turning out to be.

Focus. Concentrate.

"I'll need a bed or a table to lay him on. I can't treat him on a stool in the corner. Where's the closest place to lay him down?"

Mabella and Jedediah both stared at her, dumbfounded, like they hadn't thought through the part about actual treatment and what that would entail. Apparently, they thought she would show up and wave some magic wand and he'd be fine.

"C'mon now. Think. Get your thumbs out of your asses. Where are we going with this boy? How about right here?" She waved to a counter that was dusted with flour. A round bump of dough was being rolled out by the young woman who had pleaded for Silas moments ago. Now she just looked scared. She kept chewing on her fingers, smearing flour on her face. The white smears looked like chalk on Sister Beatrice's black chalkboard in school.

"Go on, Eunice, clear off your counter," Mabella ordered. "Move your biscuits over to the back table."

While Mabella and Eunice cleared that counter, Halina and Jed got the boy ready for closer attention. Halina tried removing his shirt and the rolled-up towel that was wedged in place, held by a belt. "This all has to come off."

What a mess. Mess. Mess.

It took four of them to carry Silas to the counter once Eunice had removed the biscuits. A fine layer of flour remained, but Halina figured that was probably the best she would get, so she let it go.

How much could it hurt, really?

She didn't like what she saw. A man has only one of some organs, and some of those he can't live without. Basic. Didn't take a nursing school to teach her that.

The boy protested, moaning and wincing and trying to push her hands away, some kind of reflex.

Halina talked to him, scolded him for not cooperating. She used the tone usually reserved for training puppies. "No, no. No. That's enough of that. No more squirming. You need to be a good patient, Silas. Good, Silas."

"What happens now, Nurse?" Jed asked.

"Have you done much praying? Now would be a good time for the praying, Preacher. Lots of praying. Bring on the praying."

"Does that mean it looks bad?"

"It always looks bad. Sometimes it really is."

She knew she was giving a half-ass answer, but the preacher man could chew on it and take away whatever he needed, hope or caution, maybe a little of each.

She opened the satchel.

Prophesies, prayers, blooms and scents, psalms, and medicine in mist droplets of muse arose into a cloud that hovered over the satchel. Jars clinked in a cadence that was like windchimes in a storm. The bottle of holy water gurgled as she poured handfuls across the wound, washing it. There wasn't enough. A tidal wave wouldn't have been enough.

Mabella brought towels, as ordered, to sop up the runoff. The others stood back. They looked afraid. She made up jobs for them to keep them busy, sending off good juju but out of her way. She gave Jed candles to light, a small wooden Madonna to talk to, and bundles of sage and lavender for burning, good for calming the patient and the worriers hovering around.

She gave Mabella some roots to boil in a pot of water. "Add a spoonful of this and a handful of this when it boils," she said, handing her burlap bags that smelled like last year's garden and the one before that and the one before that.

Generations were represented.

"Put a towel up around your nose, like a holdup bandit. Don't breathe the steam or you'll be seeing beer barrels flying."

"Huh?"

The fumes from the concoction in the kettle made the girls drowsy. Halina saw beer barrels rolling down the street and flying into the sky. She wondered if she was drunk. Patcja drooped over, passed out.

"Just don't breathe it. It's powerful," Halina said. "Eunice, you stand over there. Hold his hand. And sing. A good hymn. Any song with heart to it. And lots of Godliness. Tap his hand to the beat."

"What? Sing? I can't sing. Why would I do that?"

Eunice wasn't much of a believer. She wasn't much of a girlfriend either, apparently. Halina wondered if she'd been wrong in guessing there was a connection between her and Silas. Maybe it wasn't a good connection. Maybe there was some bad blood there. Eunice wouldn't take her eyes off Silas, but she wouldn't move either. Something was off, like last year's calendar still on the wall, the neighbor's mail in your mailbox, phone calls but no one there when you answer.

Wouldn't be the first time a young man was stabbed over a cheating girl.

"Do it, Eunice, or leave. There can't be any 'what-for' here or 'why-me' doubting and asking questions. You either believe or you don't, and then you leave. I won't have you killing my patient with your doubt or some kind of guilt."

Eunice burst into tears and scrambled away.

"Well, that's just fine, and better to be rid of that now, before it causes a fester."

Mabella, standing and stirring at the nearest stove, started singing. "Amazing grace, how sweet the sound." She stirred, the motion of her hand matching the tempo of the song. "That saved a wretch like me. / I once was lost, but now am found, / was blind, but now I see."

She sang three verses beautifully.

She brought the kettle of pungent root juice to the counter where Halina was sewing. There was a perforation that wasn't good. The wound had jagged edges like the knife had been serrated, the kind used to slice bread. A bowel was seeping. Leaking and seeping and gushing with pulses. Her stitches weren't small enough or close enough to hold.

"What should I do with this?" Mabella asked.

"Dribble some in his mouth, under his tongue. Small dribbles. Don't make him choke."

Mabella followed directions carefully. She didn't flinch. "Is he asleep? Does he feel all this sewing and poking in his insides?" she asked. "Don't you need ether?"

"He's mercifully unconscious. Asleep. And those drops will help him stay that away. Besides, I don't have ether. Do you have ether?"

"No, of course not. This a kitchen, not a hospital."

"Is there any chance there's gauze on this boat? Bandages? I'm going to need something to wrap around his belly."

"Sheets? Will sheets work?" Jed asked from his safe distance. "The auditorium is close. They have sheets they use—"

"I don't care what they use them for as long as they're clean. Are they clean? Go get them."

She felt like she was losing the battle. Jagged edges didn't want to be stitched closed. It was like trying to darn a sock when the threads were frayed.

What would Baba do?

She thought of the old woman, her baggy old sweater, a babushka over her hairnet holding bobby pins and spit curls in place while she bumbled around her kitchen, making banging noises and ghastly scents, plumes of steam rising into spirit shapes that floated to the ceiling, whispered, and left as quicky as they came.

Halina saw her face, round and flushed pink with the heat of the stove and the steam. Her forehead was beaded with sweat, and she took off her babushka to wipe her face. Hair pins, small silver clips and bobby pins, and her fine filament hairnet, nearly invisible, tumbled into the boiling pot, leaving her hair standing out like a silver mane, curly and outrageous.

"What would you do?"

131

"I just told you."
"Will it work?"
"What else do you have? You could let him go."
"He has unsettled scores. He was wounded in a fight. There would be vengeance pulling at him, not peace."
"Then fix him just good enough so nature—or God—can do the rest. A bridge from here to there."

Halina saw a spider web made of angel hair, silk strings, milkweed seeds, and dandelion fluff stretched from grass blade to grass blade, swaying with the rocking of the boat.

The boat seemed to be rolling more than usual. Up and down. That wasn't helping her sewing problem.

She took a breath, trying to clear her head. She wished she could open a window.

"I think we've had enough of those drops," she said to Mabella, who was still putting dribbles in the boy's mouth. "I may have gotten a whiff."

Mabella sighed, a happy, contented sound. "I'll put a lid on it," she said, vigorously shaking her head. The cook might have gotten a whiff or two herself and was hearing great symphonies of "Amazing Grace" playing in her head.

Halina thought about the bridge from here to there. A web would help the stitches take hold. Then she could close the bowel that was oozing more than blood, stinking like rancid gut rot.

She used to sell a dandelion tonic for cases of gut rot. That was before she'd seen the opened insides of someone who had septic organs. A fifty-cent girl in the backroom of the hardware store—that sold pleasure, not hardware—had a pregnancy gone wrong, but the fetus didn't dispel. By the time Halina was called, the child-woman was near dead. She had to cut her open. That was the first time she stole ether from the hospital. It was the first time for lots of things. At least she lived. Margret lived.

Because I didn't give up.

"Mabella, put water on to boil. And let me see that hairnet. I just need about two inches, I think."

132

"What in tarnation—"

"We're going to make a bridge."

"Lord, help us," said Mabella.

"Please don't die, Silas. Please don't die," said Eunice from across the galley, tears smearing across her face, making a white flour paste, thick as misery.

CHAPTER 20

JINKS was not happy about being sent on an errand by Margret, the Queen of the Stage—and Delusion. He almost told her "I'm not your fetch-it boy," but why risk a shitstorm of nastiness? That woman could let loose a swarm of annoyances worse than hornets with a hard-on. He had better things to do than pick nasty words and insults out of his hide for the next week, so he went.

Mimi, the sewing lady, had said the mermaid girl left her new jeweled crown in her fish tank. Margret insisted they have it for their silly stage show. What a hoot. The audience only cared about seeing one thing in that show, and it wasn't a tin crown.

He grumbled the whole way to the mezzanine, in a lousy mood to match the lousy weather coming in. Waves were picking up and the boat was rocking hard. He didn't like it at all. Not one bit. This didn't happen in Iowa. Whenever the water got rough, he regretted leaving his nice-and-dry home state. He wasn't keen on the water, never a fisherman, never a swimmer, didn't even like puddles that were more than ankle deep. So it was odd he worked on a boat. But there was no work in Iowa. Pa's farm was barely scraping by. Plus, Jinks wanted to make something of himself. See some sights. Live a little. Then he'd go back to Iowa a rich man. That would show his father he had learned a thing or two about surviving in the city.

> *"You're just a lazy bum. Mooching and music are all you know. You think you can survive on that? It's sink or swim time, boy. Don't come back until you can pull your own weight."*

He could carry plenty of weight. In fact, he had about five pounds extra in his pockets right now, lovely items he had liberated from passengers. Later, working tonight's party on the mezzanine, he might have a chance to add to his coffers. He could accidentally brush up against a dame who'd had a couple Polynesian Passions too many, and one quick yank on the clasp would be enough. Gold or silver, didn't matter to him, as long as he could pawn it at the next port.

The waves were tossing. Making his way to the mermaid station wasn't easy. He had to stop several times and hang on to whatever was bolted to the floor. When he eventually made it and stood in front of the glass tank in all its shabby splendor, the bizarreness of the whole thing hit him in the face. The idea of sticking his hand in that slime-stink water to look for a crown in the sand made his stomach lurch.

Between cigarette butts floating and the oily scum making rainbow swirls, it looked rather gross. Was that an onion skin floating in the corner? And was there a pink tinge to the water? What the hell would make the water pink? There was also a chance he smelled piss. He wouldn't be surprised if one of the bus boys had decided to piss in it out of spite or on a dare.

He was tired of it all. Going back to Iowa was sounding better and better every day.

Jinks went around back to the hinged door with plaster rocks. He climbed onto the throne, a kitchen chair painted gold with some crap glued on it. He thought it might be easier to fish the crown out from that vantage point.

Just hope no one sees me up here.

He was sure he'd get a raft of shit from the other waiters if they saw him sitting in the seat of honor. Really, it was more like a seat of shame. The stupid fish-girl was good for a laugh, not much else.

The boat's engine sputtered and groaned, coughing like an old man in the morning.

"Shut up, boat," he growled out of the side of his mouth.

Jesus Christ, now I'm just as loony as the fish-girl. Screw this.

He started to climb down and realized he didn't have the dad-blasted crown he'd been sent to grab like he was a damned messenger boy.

He found a stick and dug around in the muck.

What the hell is this?

He pulled out a woman's brooch, a cluster of red stones in the center and diamonds all around. Then he found more. And more. And more.

A gold lighter. A hat pin, with diamonds. Necklaces. Pearls. Several more pieces of jewelry, all authentic looking, not hokey play stuff. And then he found a gold crown. The real thing. He was certain those were real gems. He hit payday.

Jinks was shocked. And at a loss of what to do. He looked around. The mezzanine was empty. The afternoon show had probably started by now. There were four empty tables in the corner, the ones he and Quin set up earlier when they talked to the girl. He remembered she'd been hungry. They'd promised sardines. Of course, they never had any intention of going to the galley for her.

Everyone lied to the fish-girl. Everyone lied, period. This whole boat was one big floating lie, drifting around in some cockamamie upside-down world.

"It's sink or swim time, son. What are you made of?"

He held the jewelry, wadding it up in a ball, trying to hold it all, while looking over the gems and appreciating the top-quality specimens. It was quite a haul the girl had collected. Not bad at all. How did she get it?

He considered putting it back. Maybe they were gifts passengers gave to her. Or the brewery boys. Some of them were sweet on the kid.

Or there was another thief on board. He had never even considered he might have competition. When rumors had started flying about a thief on board, it had never occurred to him that there might be two.

And she beat me to these.

Well, they were his now. He was keeping them. Why not? Screw the fish-girl. Screw the whole boat. He was going back to Iowa to rub his father's face in the loot.

He looked around for something to put the jewelry in. He tore down one of blue scarves hanging on the back wall dressing room and used it to wrap up the pieces, including the fancy crown he had been sent to retrieve.

I'll just say I couldn't find it.

It made a bundle the size of a hen. A golden hen. The beads were twisted around the brooch and tucked in the crown. There were hatpins and a diamond bracelet, necklaces and a watch fob, all gold.

So, how about that? Our mermaid is a thief.

Maybe she wasn't so daft and loony after all. Maybe she was smarter than all of them.

He heard gurgles in the boat's pipes, something under the metal floor. Vibrations shuddered and shook. Through the window, he saw waves splash over the deck.

His stomach wasn't liking this bobbing up and down and up and down and the funny sounds in the pipes. It was enough to make a man nervous.

The pink oily water in the mermaid tank was sloshing around, making little swirls like miniature hurricanes. They made sucking sounds that reminded him of the piglets he'd seen sucking on giant sow teats at a fair once. Disgusting.

The whole tank was disgusting, and he was ready to get out. He pushed on the hinged door, but the damned thing was stuck, wedged in place. He pounded on the latch. All the boat vibration had jarred it lopsided-wonky, and now it wouldn't budge.

A fine mess. Well, there's more than one way out of this tank.

He put his feet down in the water. His shoes squished in the sand at the bottom. It was slippery with muck, like a backwoods swamp. The water came up to his knees. It was only a couple strides to the front glass panel, but it seemed a mile-long trek. He heaved himself up and over the glass. Putting all his weight on the glass wall was a mistake. He heard a crack, felt it under his hand.

He swung his feet to the ground.

Half the tank's water came with him as his soaked trousers gushed water everywhere.

A hairline fissure spider-webbed across the pane of glass. It grew. And gave way in a sudden shattering of glass. Water gushed to the floor. The whole tank busted, falling in on itself. Water was everywhere.

Jesus Christ, Mother Mary, and Joseph, now what?

Run. Fast. Now. Before someone comes by.

Jinks slid through the dangling scarves and popped the hidden latch to the crew's rat-run. He paused to let his eyes adjust to the dim light and to catch his breath, then he went down a level on the ladder, deeper in the bowels of the boat. Galley level. He had to duck to avoid the string of lights dangling overhead. Damn, there was going to be hell to pay, he knew it. He might be sent packing back to Iowa sooner than he'd thought. He ran, checking the chalk mark codes on the wall to see where he was. He stopped at the next vault.

G8 \4/.

Remember it. Remember it. G8, vault four. Galley eight, vault four.

This vault was pantry sized, big enough for a small keg or two of whiskey. He stashed the bundle of loot in the far corner, deep in the back, and firmly shut the vault door. He swung his elbow up and broke the lightbulb dangling over the door, locking it in darkness.

I'll come back for it later. Galley eight, vault four.

He ran toward the auditorium, working on his story about not finding the crown. His wet shoes squished with each step. He left a trail, like a wounded animal dripping blood.

He had to change.

G8.

At least find some dry shoes.

Vault four.

CHAPTER 21

JENKINS was at the helm when all hell broke loose. The intercom that connected main stations had been buzzing all afternoon with reports of problems related to the rough waters. Most were minor issues that could be addressed with a mop and bucket. Stressed seams on a boat like the *Lake Maiden* tended to leak. Motion made cargo shift. Crates broke open. Valuable inventory spilled across the floor. Unsecured items were tossed around. Then there were the passenger complaints, the minor injuries, the interruptions to the regularly scheduled itinerary. He dealt with them all. He was rather proud of his efficiency and decisiveness.

He stayed calm, mostly. He reassigned BDs—below-deck crew—from their usual tasks to attend to the cleanup, and had the DHs—deck hands—see to securing supplies. Kitchen was on standby. Dinner might be postponed or CPO, cold provisions only. No one would be happy about that, but as long as the bars and the poker lounge stayed open and the entertainment stayed available, all would be good. Probably.

Of course, there would be the passengers who got a little green around the gills with the tossing, but there was nothing he could do about that except tell them to go to their cabins and try to sleep through it. For the VIPs, the waitstaff could bring tea with a little sleepy-time powder added along with the honey. It kept them happy, or at least quiet.

It was all under control.

Then it wasn't.

He got word there was a man bleeding in the galley, the mermaid tank was busted with water going all over the mezzanine so the combo couldn't set up, the mermaid was knocked out cold from some fall, and on top of that, a passenger's diamond necklace had been stolen. She was demanding a police investigation as soon as they docked.

First, he had to find the captain. Then the stage crew would have to deal with the stupid mermaid tank. As far as the bleeder in the galley, Ma Mabella could contend with that. Probably someone got sloppy with a butcher knife and whacked off a finger. Wouldn't be the first time, or the last.

He decided he should personally go looking for the captain to tell him his daughter was injured. The captain should know, right? He might care.

He would want to at least be informed, right?

"Wiggins, you take the helm. You know what to watch for in the weather. Stay alert and listen on the squawk box for anything else needing attention."

He guessed Captain would be in the Sand Bar, the usual place for entertaining dignitaries like bankers. He had to cross the main deck to get there. He refused to use the rat-runs. The thought of being closed in those dim corridors made him sweat buckets. He had no idea if there really were rats in there, and the chances of being locked in were remote. But he could see the scene vividly, hear himself shouting for help, pounding on doors no one would open. He knew what it would be like to die in there.

So, he took the long route.

Walking across the deck was harder than he'd thought it would be. Rain hadn't broken out yet, but the wind was out of the southwest and waves were hitting the *Lake Maiden* with a powerful force. Spray whipped across his face. He had to hang on to the railings and the ropes that had been put out as a precaution. He was glad he'd made that call. At least someone was thinking of safety.

Some passengers were ignoring the risks, out on the deck, marveling at the huge waves like they were on some amusement park ride. Others seemed outraged, blustery temperaments flaring. A couple stopped him, demanding answers. "When is this bobbing up and down going to stop? This isn't what I paid for, you know. How can we possibly enjoy a trip in this weather? Can't you steer around the storm? Take evasive action?"

"Don't worry. We'll be through the storm front soon. Nothing to worry about," he said over and over to passengers stopping him. He said it so many times it almost seemed plausible. Of course, it wasn't. This was just the beginning. They were in for worse, and there would be hours of this pitching ahead of them.

He found the captain at a table in the Sand Bar, schmoozing with the banker fellas and Mr. Antonio Salvatore. The bankers had stern faces and open ledger books, and fountain pens in hand like they were just itching to start scribbling away. Antonio was watching, shaking the ice cubes in his glass. Captain was refilling glasses from a bottle. Shoe Polish the label said.

Jenkins stood to the side a moment, waiting to be acknowledged by the captain. But the captain was in a mood, it seemed, not interested in being bothered about the ship's business. Jenkins thought about turning and leaving, but he was afraid repercussions from that move would be far worse.

He cleared his throat.

Nothing.

He cleared his throat again, louder.

One of the banker men pointed to him. "Captain, it seems this officer would like a word with you. Perhaps you should see what he needs."

"What is it, Jenkins?"

Jenkins could smell whiskey on the captain's breath. Jenkins tried to hide his disapproval, put on his fake smile, but this was hardly professional behavior from the captain. Jenkins felt the weight on his shoulders suddenly become heavier. Was he the only sane officer on board this ship? Again, he thought about returning to the bridge. Someone well-abled should be directing the ship's route and seeing to passenger safety. But he didn't go.

Jenkins stepped closer and leaned in so he could whisper. "Sir, we got a message on the bridge that your daughter has been hurt. She's backstage, unconscious. She fell during the afternoon performance. She may need medical attention."

The captain's face took a minute to register a reaction, like his brain was trying to decide which response to go with. Maybe it was a hard decision. Had Jenkins been unclear? Had the captain not heard?

Jenkins started to repeat the message, but the captain jerked into gear.

"Where is she?" he demanded.

"Is it serious?" asked Antonio.

This gangster buffoon is concerned, too?

"Well, I believe she's backstage," Jenkins answered. "I don't know if it's serious or not."

Captain took off with Antonio following. They left the two bankers with their matching derbies looking quite put out. Before Jenkins could think of what to say to the men, the clerk came bustling in, all in a tizzy, arms in the air like he was airing out his armpits.

"Ah, gentlemen, there is a change of plans. I checked on a place to sit and review the books, as you requested. I had some tables set in the mezzanine, but I have learned it is currently indisposed with a slight maintenance problem being addressed."

"Well, we just need a table or desk and some quiet. The discussion is very simple," said Derby One.

"Excessive words aren't needed. The *Lake Maiden* is seriously in debt. We need to discuss liquidation of assets," said Derby Two.

What?

Jenkins had known times were tough, but he had no idea it was this bad. It couldn't possibly be true. There had to be some bookkeeping mistake this weasel-nosed, nearsighted, number-freak clerk made. And the bootlegger boys would never let their baby go under. They would bail her out, surely. Mr. Antonio had plans. He knew it.

"Gentlemen, I know the balances and the amount of red in the books must seem to indicate a poor business plan and dismal cash flow," Clerk answered, rubbing his hands together like he was enjoying this little scene. "But the real problem is in operational management. Overhead indulgences just need to be curtailed so that the profit-loss returns to a manageable ratio—"

"The time for reform is long past. We've been patient for months," Derby One snapped back. Derby Two nodded as he stood.

The *Lake Maiden* pitched and rocked. Glasses on the counter behind the bar slid, several crashing to the floor and shattering before 'Tender could catch them.

"More assets wasted," said Derby Two.

"Please secure—"

She pitched up.

"—the remaining inventory."

She dropped. And rolled.

"We can't auction—"

Up.

"—broken glass," said Derby Two, trying to steady himself against the bar.

Down.

Derby One took a large gulp of the pink fizzy whiskey drink 'Tender had set in front of him. Then he ate the skewer of—

The Lake Maiden *pitched upward.*

—oranges and cherries.

Hung. And dropped.

"Feels like being in a pot—

She rolled.

"—of boiling water," said Derby One.

Tossed up.

"You get used to it after a while," said the clerk. "You just have to—"

Down.

"—roll with it."

Up.

"Don't fight it."

Jenkins decided this might be his best time to jump in. He stepped closer and offered an arm to the two men, who wobbled, trying to stand in place.

"Maybe you gentlemen would like to rest a bit before continuing business? I could show you to your cabanas, if you like. Perhaps lying down would be the best way to ride out this little patch of weather we've run into."

"Excellent idea," chimed in the clerk.

"I can have a waiter bring tea and honey to your room," Jenkins added, laying on the sugar coating nice and thick. Maybe he could get 'Tender to spike the tea with something to knock these fellas out for a few hours.

He wondered what it would take to persuade them to forget their ideas about liquidating assets. Would having a couple of the chorus line girls visit their rooms do it? Maybe a couple girls and someone with a camera documenting the party? He'd have to talk to Margret. See if that little Effie or sassy Viola were available. And where would he find a camera?

"Perhaps a rest would be good," Derby One said.

"Yes, just for an hour or two," Derby Two added, holding his belly like his innards were about to flop out.

The *Lake Maiden* had her own aches. She groaned hollow, miserable sounds. She sounded constipated, her guts cramping.

The poor ship was being tested. Jack was worried. Maybe he could improve conditions for passengers and outrun the storm by changing the heading slightly and getting more power from the boiler room. He was going to try, like any honorable captain would do—as soon as he took care of these bankers. Troublemakers.

PAM RECORDS

There's no place for troublemakers on board. They need to be plucked off, like plucking ticks off a dog's back.

"Come, gentlemen, I'll show you to a cabana near the auditorium."

CHAPTER 22

MARGRET waved a feathered fan over the girl's face. Strands of tangled hair fluttered with the back-and-forth breeze. Nothing else moved, not an eyelash, not a pinky finger. She was breathing, though. Margret leaned in closer over Nattie to make sure she could see her chest move. Yes, the lift and fall, in and out, seemed steady.

So why isn't she waking up?

"She must have really whacked her head good," Margret said. A few of the stage crew were gathered around. They had taken the unconscious girl to Viola's dressing room and laid her on the narrow fold-down cot attached to the wall. Bubby was there in the back, looking miserable and ready to bolt.

"Did anyone see what happened?" Margret's eyes drilled into Bubby's head. "How about you, Bubby? You were right there. What happened? Did you tie her to the rock, like I told you to? Did you give her the rope to hang on to? Or did the rats eat through that rope too?"

Bubby only shook his head, befuddled. He had a sudden case of Know Nothing. The more she grilled him, the more confused he became. His milky eyes were unfocused, just staring off into la-la land, where half this boat lived.

Of all days; of all shows. The damned kid picks this one to get conked on the head and pass out. The captain is going to—

"C'mon, Natalia, wake up now. Please," she said. "Enough snoozing. We have a show to put on, young lady."

Mimi came barging into the small dressing room, and right behind her was a large lad, all frantic and making noise.

"Where's Natalia? How is she? Is she alright?" he demanded, as if he had a right to be asking questions.

Margret remembered him. She had met him and his sister in front of Nattie's tank.

The big fella, the old neighborhood friend, pushed his way in.

"What happened? Natalia, wake up," he said, patting her cheeks. "Is she bleeding? Did she break anything? Maybe it's a concussion. That can be serious, you know."

"It's a bump on her head. No big deal," Margret said, not happy about his interference.

"Look at her. How can you say that?" he shouted, really cranking up the annoying level and being big-time pushy as all get-out.

"Mister, this isn't any of your business. You'd better return to your seat before I have someone help you there. How would you like that?"

He started feeling around in Nattie's hair, hands all over her. A groper.

"She's got a huge bump, back here. But no blood," he reported. He didn't seem too worried about being taken to his seat.

Margret heard more commotion outside the dressing room. Preacher was out there, arguing with a prop boy about sheets. Preacher needed bandages, it seemed.

Well, not from her prop closet! Or her linen closet. She had dressing rooms and private lounges to keep up. Clean sheets were expected at the hourly rate she charged.

"Whoa there, Preacher. Who needs bandages? Is someone else hurt?"

Preacher looked confused. He looked into Viola's dressing room and, when he saw the girl on the cot, his face did a contortion thing like he didn't know what to do, some big dilemma. He stopped cold in his tracks and put his hands together like he was praying.

Over a bumped head? What was Preacher's problem? Why the hell did he want sheets for bandages?

"I just want everybody out, now," she said.

No one listened.

Preacher and Big Fella did some arguing back and forth, trying to figure out which one had the bigger problem requiring medical attention. She couldn't hear the details, just enough to know they were irritating her.

"Let's just call a doctor to make a house call, why don't we?" Her sarcasm seemed to go over their heads. They both gaped at her, bewildered. Didn't they realize it was *her* show that was being loused up good? She was the one who had the right to be mad, not them.

"C'mon, Nattie, wake up now. Do you hear me?" she said to the girl, slapping her cheek.

Finally, a dishwasher boy from the galley arrived with a bowl of ice and a towel. Margret wrapped up a chunk of ice and held it behind the girl's head. She didn't have to search for the bump. It was right there, huge, bigger than a goose egg.

Maybe this is serious. What if she's bleeding in her brain?

"So, is there a doctor on board or not?" Big Fella asked Preacher. "Because if there is a doctor, this young lady needs his attention. Now."

Preacher started his praying nonsense and carrying on about God's will and what shall be. Between the God hooey and the mumbles, Margret didn't know what he was saying, and she didn't care, either.

She didn't hold much for doctoring of any kind. Quacks, all of them.

Preacher hemmed and hawed. The dishwasher boy who'd brought the ice tapped him on his shoulder.

"What about the nurse in the galley tending to your nephew? She's got a bag full of medicine. Maybe nurses can fix mermaids."

Well, that made the dressing room go quiet. Faces turned to Preacher. How could he keep quiet about a nurse, keep her in the galley for his nephew? How could he be so unconcerned about Nattie?

Preacher took off like his tail was on fire.

Big Fella, huffing mad, started to chase him, but had second thoughts. It seemed he didn't want to leave Nattie.

"Boy, you go and fetch this nurse or doctor or whoever. Bring 'em here," Margret said to the dishwasher. "Tell her the captain's daughter is hurt."

The hispanic boy backed up. "Oh no. No." He started speaking Spanish, and the only thing Margret understood was his fear. He was afraid of the nurse, her white uniform, and her big bag of medicines that were stinking up the galley.

"She makes smoke and magic, and she yells and the whole place stinks and everyone's singing," he added in English. "Loco," he said, shaking his head.

Margret instantly knew who the nurse was. Loco, indeed. That quack nurse had cut her open and scooped the infection and dead baby out, along with all her child-bearing organs. Just cut them out with a kitchen knife, then sewed her back up with the pieces not matching like they were supposed to. Since then, none of her plumbing worked right. She had to keep rags between her legs to sop up the piss she couldn't control.

"Well, I'll fetch her," Big Fella said. "How do I get to the galley from here?"

"I'll show you a shortcut," Margret said, eager to get rid of this guy. She led him past the dressing rooms to the skinny rat-run door in the corner.

"Remind me again, what's your name, mister?" She put on a sweet tone, like she was making up with the guy, sorry for mean-talking.

"Szymon," he said. "I'm just trying to see that Nattie gets help, ma'am. My sister, Anka, and I were close to her when she was little. I always felt she got a raw deal, her legs and mama and, well, all of it. So much more."

"Well, Szymon, you'd better be careful about sticking your nose where it doesn't belong. No one likes troublemakers on this boat. No one," she told him.

She felt along the skinny door panel and found the switch to pop it open. "This will take you to the galley. Follow the corridor."

She sent him on his way. She didn't feel the slightest twinge of guilt for not explaining the navigation system of the rat-run and how to find the next door or the exit to the galley.

At least she got his name. In case they never heard from him again, she could make a plaque memorializing the lost Big Fella, Szymon. Sure. He deserved to be brought down a notch, and the last person she wanted backstage was that no-good nurse. Halina.

She hurried back to the dressing room, hoping the girl had come to. It was time to get the performances back on schedule. She would just have to make sure the second show tonight was ultra-perfect to make up for this little snag.

Someone else was in the doorway. Jinks.

"I'm back. But I couldn't find the crown. It was gone!"

His trousers, soaked from the knees down, clung to his skinny legs. He dripped all over her floor, making a puddle big enough to drown in.

"But there was a small problem with the mermaid tank. It's gone, too. Glass broke."

Margret groaned. No mermaid display tank? Now where was she going to put the famous Great Lakes Mermaid? Some passengers believed the mermaid crap. Was there no end to the trouble this fish-girl caused? Oh, how she wished she could pack her up and send her off somewhere, to some boarding school or some cathouse that needed another girl.

Maybe Cappie would be more likely to get married again if the girl wasn't in the wings, barging into his quarters, seeing things she shouldn't see.

How nice it would be if she just drifted away.

Off to deep water.

Wouldn't it?

CHAPTER 23

HALINA was happy with the stitch work. So far, so good. She sighed and shook out her hand, which was starting to cramp from the tedious work. It felt like she'd been working for hours, but, of course, it had only been minutes. Still, the amount of blood loss was concerning. Only time would tell. He was young. He had that going for him. But the skin-and-bones thing wasn't good. Maybe he had a nutrition issue or something screwy with his gut or digestion. Or parasites, though she saw no signs of white wigglies in his gut. It was hard to say.

She wasn't sure about breathing, either. She hadn't realized until now how much she relied on skin color to judge oxygen levels. She just didn't work on enough brown-skinned patients to know how to judge a healthy color on the face, fingertips, and feet. There was no pink glow to Silas, but no blue-gray dullness either. She guessed that was a good sign, and hoped she was right, or close enough.

The preacher finally came back with sheets for bandages. He seemed flustered. How hard was it to go fetch sheets, man?

"Here's what I could get," he said, starting to unroll the linen.

She sniffed. It smelled musty. "Is it clean? Where'd you get it? Some fat-ass bootleggers haven't been rolling their hairy bare butts in it, have they?"

"It was in the back of the housekeeping supply closet. It was the best I could do," he said, a defensive shrillness in his voice. His forehead was scrunched up with worry furrows. A vein was raised and throbbing. He'd better not have a stroke and give her more problems to deal with.

She didn't much care why he was so riled up, except these sheets were lousy with stale stink. A moth fluttered by. Dust hung in the air, making her cough.

"Jesus, man, look at this," she yelled, waving her arm, scattering the dust in a frenzy, but trying to cover the patient.

Jed hugged the sheet. He tried to hug Silas, laying there on the counter. Halina shoved him away.

"Get your filthy shirt and filthy hands and germ-breathing snout away from my patient," she snarled.

Jed backed away. The man looked like he might cry. She had never seen a preacher cry.

Dear God, what am I supposed to do with this nincompoop?

Mabella came to the rescue with an arm around Jed's shoulder and some private whispers in his ear. Halina guessed there was some bad-mouthing of her and her temper. She didn't care.

Mabella took the sheet, wrinkling her nose. She sent Eunice off somewhere with it, God only knew where. But by the time Halina was done with her sewing, the sniveling woman was back with a fine piece of linen. It smelled clean; looked like it had been ironed, too. The only problem was the fringe around the hem, and the fact it was red.

"Fringe? Really?"

"A tablecloth. A VIP one. Ironed this morning by housekeeping," said Eunice. "I got it from Quin. He said he needs it back, but I figure he'll forget. I didn't tell him what it was for."

"Fine, fine, fine. Tear it in strips. About three inches wide. Wait, wash your hands first. Don't dangle it on the floor. And don't wipe your snotty nose on it, for Christ's sake."

"We're not idiots, Miss," said Eunice. "Just because we work in the galley doesn't mean we're simpletons. I would never wipe my nose on a tablecloth or a bandage." She huffed a brave noise.

"Well, thank God for that. So get your galley-cooking, tablecloth-fetching brown butt over here, stop your sniveling, and help me." Halina made a sideway glance at Mabella and raised her eyebrows so Mabella knew she meant good. Only good. *I'm plain talking, fire starting, gumption making*, Halina said to Mabella with her eyes.

Mabella nodded back. *I get it*, she said with her eyebrows. *Just don't bad-sass my staff*, she said with her chin clench.

Halina nodded.

"Go on, Eunice, you help the nurse," said Mabella. "And do that singing thing she likes, while you're at it. Go on. Silas would like that. He'll like hearing your voice, you know."

"Yes, ma'am," said Eunice, going to the sink to wash her hands.

Mabella led Jed to the stool in the corner and set him down, patting his arm and meowing nice talk to the poor man. He was explaining something.

From the look on his face, it was something bad. Something making the man crazy upset. Halina couldn't hear, or maybe she just didn't understand.

Her Polish ears didn't always understand the slang of other people. She knew expressions, though. And faces. And glances and eyebrows and mouths making shapes, not words. That was usually enough.

Still, she wasn't catching what was going on with the preacher, so she focused on bandaging the wound and talking to the patient. He should start waking up, so she could judge his response level, make sure he was doing okay in the breathing and heart-beating department. A lot could go wrong yet. A whole lot.

Eunice did a nice job of tearing the tablecloth, including removing the fringe.

"You should save that, Eunice, you could sew it on a plain dress and make one of those jazzy dresses the flapper girls wear. You could sew that on anything," Halina said.

"I don't have no place to wear a dress like that," Eunice answered.

"Don't you ever get a night off this boat? A day off?"

"Once a month, ma'am."

"I don't get much of a day off either," Halina said as she carefully wrapped bandages around the wounded man. Seems someone's always on the verge of croaking."

"Don't you want to help them?"

"Sometimes. Usually. Truth being that sometimes stupid gets what it deserves, and there's no point in saving a nitwit who's just going to find another way to cause his own demise."

"Silas ain't no nitwit."

"Right. How'd he get stabbed? Do you know?"

"Yeah, I know. And it wasn't his fault. One of the boiler room boys came and told me, because he knew I was sweet on Silas. That Big John was telling Silas mermaid jokes, like the boys all tell. And Jakub, the red-haired boy, didn't like it and told them to stop. Big John didn't like being told what to do. Neither did Silas. So they kept at it. Then the red-haired boy had a knife. And they tussled over it. Now the stupid boy is gone and run off."

"Is Jakub hurt?" asked Halina. This Jakub could very well be her nephew. He had red hair . . .

"Aren't you supposed to be singing, Eunice?" said Mabella.

CHAPTER 24

SZYMON tried to picture where he was. It didn't take long to realize that hussy woman in the silver dress had sent him down this maze as a stall, trying to louse him up. It seemed she didn't think Natalia needed the nurse. She had some grudge against Nattie—or the nurse. Well, he wasn't about to let some woman's pettiness get in the way of poor Natalia getting medical help, even if it was just a nurse.

This skinny corridor was barely lit. Lightbulbs dangled here and there. He had to keep looking up so he didn't hit his head. That was how he noticed the chalk markings. They seemed strange and random until he caught on to the pattern. The numbers went up as he walked. He was in section BS. He figured that was backstage. He knew the kitchen was on the same level. Finding his way wasn't that hard. If he could navigate the streets of East Chicago as a kid selling papers, he could navigate a stupid passenger boat. And here, bums and hoodlums weren't trying to steal his bag of dimes.

He only had to backtrack twice before he found the "G" series. He hoped that meant galley, not garbage. From the chaos of smells, it was hard to tell. Eventually he focused in on the smell of biscuits baking, which led him to the playhouse-sized door where scents came wafting through on a steady air current, steam venting from some stove or oven. It had a peculiar odor, sharply pungent, making his nostrils burn.

For a moment he worried he had stumbled onto something ghastly, but he could hear voices on the other side and started tapping, looking for the button to open the door.

Whoosh.

It magically opened and shafts of light flooded in with the smells and sounds of dozens of people rushing around in a frenzy of pots and pans big enough to boil an entire hog.

The chaos froze. Faces stared at him like he was an abomination, trespassing on sacred ground.

"Hi there, folks," he said, waving.

PAM RECORDS

It took some convincing, but the nurse eventually agreed to follow him back to the stage area. He didn't let her rest a minute like she wanted. He did go along with the washing and getting rid of the bloody apron she was wearing, mostly because he couldn't stand looking at it. The red dribbles and squirts were disgusting.

While the nurse wrapped up, Szymon did all the glaring at the preacher man that he could. At the same time, the head cook, a short little thing the color of chocolate, sneered at him for taking away the healer. It was quite the standoff of silent, almost deadly assaults.

It looked to him that the sewing and bandaging were done. This skinny young man, all bandaged up, just had to rest now and recover, right? But red bandages were a funny touch, he had to admit.

Apparently, she wasn't done. The nurse left all kinds of directions to the preacher and the cook and the sniveling biscuit girl, who kept sticking her nose into the matter like she had some part to play besides dribbling tears and snot everywhere. The girl's moans all seemed a bit of overacting to him. But what could he do besides tap his foot impatiently, trying to hurry the thanking and goodbyeing along? They all but put a medal around the nurse's neck, all for some sewing on some boiler room boy who probably deserved the knife in his gut.

Once he got the nurse moving, she refused to go back to the stage the way he'd come. He had to find another route, which took time. And there were crowds to push through, more people on the boat than he'd realized, all unsettled and shifting about, searching out a place to sit to worry out the rest of the afternoon and evening and complain about the storm. Many were on the railings, heads hanging over. The boat was rocking hard, waves splashing up and sending spray in their faces.

How stupid can these people be. One big wave and they could be gone. Just like that.

He managed to avoid the big washes and made sure the nurse followed. They held on to the ropes to cross one open stretch of slippery metal, textured with rivets and missing rivets and layers of chipped paint, rust showing through. The obvious flaws in maintenance were enough to make a fella nervous. Szymon also noticed the surprisingly small number of lifeboats. He didn't waste time counting. There weren't enough. That was plain.

They reached the signpost with arrows pointing to the auditorium, and Szymon pulled the nurse along. He offered to carry her satchel for her, and she reluctantly handed it over and held on to the rope with both hands.

"Maybe we should have used the skinny crew corridor after all?" he said to her.

"Not on your life," she snapped back.

When they reached the auditorium, a magician was on stage. He had one assistant, a woman so thin and malnourished looking, Szymon wondered if she ever ate. That must be how she fit in that box. The audience had dwindled, not nearly as enticed by magic as they had been by the dancing girls and the mermaid.

The old man who had tried to keep Szymon from going backstage was still in place. He didn't have such a good memory and hee-hawed around about letting them pass. Szymon was losing his patience and was about to show the idiot a fist when the nurse butted in with some sugar-sweet singsong, promising the coot a bottle of tonic for the bald spot on his head and balm for the mangey rash creeping-crawling up his neck. She had a name for it and condolences on how it must itch. She got his name, Bubby, and promised to come back.

Szymon huffed, not even trying to hide his irritation with all these delays. The simple job of fetching the nurse had taken far too long.

He yelled, "Come on! Let's go!"

A fella with a banjo hanging off his shoulder, came running out from backstage acting horrified, as if he had interrupted some great theatrical production, not an amateur hootenanny.

Again, the nurse spoke up, waving her hands for silence. "Don't worry. I'll keep Mr. Big Mouth quiet. Just show us where the mermaid is. I hear she's hurt."

Szymon remembered the way and led nurse to the dressing room. He pushed through.

"We're here, we're here. How is she?"

He shoved Margret aside.

Natalia was propped up on the cot, her eyes open but droopy.

She's awake! Oh, thank you, God.

He sighed. Relief washed over the anxiety. He didn't know he had been so terrified until the terror was gone, and a hole was left.

I should have done more.

The witch laughed over the boiling pots on the stove. "She
doesn't need medicine. She needs someone to care about her."

He listened to the patter of introductions and questions and orders and sharp directions and lectures and reassurances. There were weird, sharp glares between the nurse and the Margret woman that he didn't understand. He couldn't imagine how they knew each other. Very strange.

The nurse was a nosey thing. She asked question after question after question about Natalia's legs and spine, which agitated Szymon. She was supposed to make sure Nattie's head was alright, not harp about the sad state of the physical impairment she'd had from birth. That was all settled and accepted. Why stir it up?

"She needs someone to help her stretch the muscles, make
them move and bend. I can't do that with a poultice. Someone
needs to make her move, not give her a wagon to ride in. She
has to try," the old witch had told them.

Then suddenly the captain moseyed in, followed by a tall man with a swagger and a smug, cynical look in his eyes and the "I dare you" lean of his shoulders. He had one hand in his pocket. Maybe that hidden hand was busy, fiddling with himself. He had that kind of pinched smirk on his face.

"Our mermaid just has a little bump on her head, no blood, no broken bones," Margret said to the captain with forced optimism.

"Are you sure she's okay?" Captain asked, his voice seemed taut. Maybe he was genuinely concerned. He reached for Natalia's face, but the nurse slapped his hand. Then she shoved Captain and the tall lanky man out of her way.

"This is my patient. All of you get out," she shouted, louder than she really needed to. Then she told Margret she wanted to move Nattie, to somewhere with more room.

"We can take her to my quarters. I'll carry her," said Captain, trying to push Szymon out of the way.

"You don't remember me, do you?" Szymon said.

Captain paused. "Have you been a passenger before? Or a crew member?"

"We lived in the same apartment building. My father was the landlord."

Captain squinted at Szymon, eyebrows furrowed. He seemed to have no recollection of Szymon. How could that be?

"I was a lot smaller then," Szymon said, putting his hand out about chest high, the height he was when he learned all about women's anatomy from the opera star who didn't sing. But oh, she could scream and squeal.

Captain shook his head and looked away dismissively.

The brush-off was annoying as hell. The arrogant captain hadn't changed at all. He was just as uppity as ever, assuming Szymon was unimportant. He wanted to slap the man and tell him he was wrong.

I know things. I'm the one who told you. I told you what was happening.

Szymon knew plenty from the days in the apartment building. In his newsboy days, he had to be awake before dawn, picking up bundles of paper, getting ready to hit the streets. He crossed paths with men leaving the apartment building's garage. Captain used the stairwell as a meeting place, apparently thinking the concrete blocks made it safe. Really, all the cement just made the sound carry, vibrating over the coldness. Szymon had heard them talk. Jobs to do. Jobs done. The captain had stains on his hands he could never wash off.

Then there was the crack in the apartment doorway, wide enough to see through. When Cappie was out on his boat, Queenie had private parties. She liked to entertain male fans, young and old. Szymon had learned a lot from watching those parties. Those long gloves . . .

"Move, man," Captain said.

Captain tried picking Natalia up, but the cramped dressing room made the motion awkward. Nattie still wore that costume, which seemed to make lifting her more difficult, like she was slippery, a goldfish out of water. Then the captain made a heave-ho move, lifting her, and the dangling shells around her neck fell away. Szymon could see her chest, her small but beautiful breasts.

When did she grow up?

The captain didn't even try to cover her up. Maybe he didn't notice.

Szymon closed his eyes and looked away, embarrassed for the girl and ashamed for wanting to look. He was ashamed of so much—what he saw and did and didn't do when he was a kid. Why didn't he help her stretch her leg muscles like the old healer had said?

Because I liked having her in the wagon with us. I wanted her to need me. Need us.

Szymon looked around, suddenly realizing he didn't know where Anka was. He jumped up and started scouting backstage. The performance was still dragging on. Banjo music came from the stage.

"Anka?" he called toward the dressing rooms.

He was hushed by some stagehands who threatened to flatten him.

He walked around stealth-like on cat paws, ready to pounce on any sign of his sister. He whisper-called, "Ankaaaaa" as he walked.

He wandered into some kind of storeroom. A giant anchor made out of paper or plaster or nightmares leaned against a wall. One of those black flags with a white skull and crossbones hung in a corner, like something from a movie. He stubbed his toe on a toy treasure chest. A stuffed parrot perched on the open lid fell off. Dust and moths flew up, caught in the half-light streaming in from the doorway. Sheets were tangled and twisted on the floor, like a giant nest for one of those prehistoric birds that could screech and carry off a caveman in its huge beak.

He felt like he had walked into a hole in time: pirates, parrots, and pterodactyls all swarming around. In the middle of the sheets, he saw girl things, so horribly out of place in this nonsense. A nightgown was laid out, so simple, white cotton with pink roses, a child's size, far too small for Natalia. Next to it, two pairs of underpants, folded, white with a bit of trim, rather worn. Then a pair of white stockings, small, delicate anklets, like a little girl would wear with patent leather shoes for church. They were laid out neatly, arranged like someone was going to take a picture for posterity. But no shoes? No dress?

Someone had been sleeping here, and he knew who it was, of course. Natalia. He touched the folded sheets that had been made into a pillow, an indent where she had rested her head and tried to sleep. The fabric was cold to his touch, damp, and coarse.

His throat constricted like he was choking on pickle juice, and his eyes watered, burning. It was all too much. He rushed out.

This whole boat is crazy.

He had to find Anka. He walked by the bank of ropes dangling from rafters—and heard more voices.

There.

"Anka! I've been looking all over for you."

She was in a dressing room with one of the dancing girls. Something was wrong with her. He hardly recognized his own sister. She was dolled up like a floozy, with paint all over face: red on her lips and charcoal on her eyebrows so they went up way too high like she was surprised and pink splotches on her cheeks like someone had slapped her. Then there were the clothes—what there was of them. She wore half the costume. He covered his eyes, thinking she wasn't done dressing, but they laughed at him, and he realized this getup was it. All there was.

"What have you done?" he spat out.

"I got dressed up. Look! Do you like it? Vi says I could be a pirate on stage. Doesn't that sound like fun!"

Something in his head snapped. His vision squeezed smaller, like he was looking into a tunnel. He shook his head to clear it. He took off his suit coat and threw it around his sister's shoulders and tied the sleeves, like a cape. It didn't cover enough, but it was better. He grabbed her arm and yanked her up. She yelled and fought, but he felt like he had the strength of three men, and he was not about to stop because his sister was fussing. The stage crew couldn't stop him either, not with their swearing or the wooden bat someone pulled out or the punches and threats. Nothing could.

Szymon stormed out of the auditorium like a freight train dragging an uncooperative caboose. He tore up the track and didn't care. He found the signposts and followed the arrows to their cabana on deck four, the cheap ones.

By now Anka had shut up, except for the crying and sobbing and pleading for him to let go of her arm—he was twisting and breaking it, she yelled. He didn't listen, couldn't listen. He was being irrational, he knew, but the energy was unleashed and couldn't be recaptured. He had failed Nattie and wouldn't fail his sister. He had to fight for her. He couldn't fail again.

The tiny cabin had two beds that folded down from the wall, one above the other, and a small sink with a mirror over it. Szymon shoved Anka's face under the faucet and scrubbed at the floozy paint like it was poisonous. It had to come off. She sputtered, choking and sobbing and carrying on like a banshee. He saw her lips moving but didn't hear any of it through the ringing in his ears.

He unlatched and folded down one of the beds, which left barely enough room to stand. He didn't need much room. He tossed his wet, disheveled, half-dressed sister onto the cot and took back his suit coat.

"Dry yourself off. Get dressed. Make yourself presentable again," he told her, barely able to get the few words out. His heart pounded.

He locked the cabin door behind him when he left. He took his pocketknife and wedged the blade into the lock, jamming the tumblers. She wouldn't be able to unlock the door from the inside. That would keep her safe.

His ears still rang. He felt like he was looking through a tube. His legs were weak. His arms and shirt sleeves were wet up to the elbows from the tussle in the sink.

He made himself breathe slower, deeper.

He tried to return to the stage to check on Natalia, but the doors to the auditorium were locked. A handwritten sign was tacked to the door: *Next show at midnight.*

Then he remembered they were carrying her to Captain's quarters. He didn't think he could face the captain again tonight. He didn't think he could face any more turmoil.

He followed the arrows to the Sand Bar. He might as well wait there.

I'll just give Anka some time to cool off. Then I'll go retrieve her. She'll realize I just want what's best for her.

"What will you have, mister?"

"Whiskey, I suppose."

"This your first ride on the *Lake Maiden*?"

"Huh? Oh, yeah." He nodded, not exactly in the mood for chatter.

"So, you alone? Or need a friend to keep you company, a companion to liven things up?" The bartender did a little back-and-forth thrust with his hips to demonstrate what he meant.

Szymon laughed and threw back the whiskey.

It was hot going down his throat. He shivered.

Whew. What a boat, this Lake Maiden. *Some maiden.*

It was no place for his sister. Or Natalia.

He held out his empty glass.

"Make it a double," he said.

"You sound like a man with troubles," the bartender said, not knowing when to shut up and mind his own business. "Let me guess. Heart crushed by a woman?"

"No, it's not that." He threw back the drink in two gulps. "When she first moved away, I was crushed. But I was only 12 years old." Szymon tried to laugh, but the sound that came out was more of a whimper.

"Ah, they get their hooks in you early, that's for sure, those wild women, set on a handsome husband." The bartender filled Szymon's whiskey glass again.

"It wasn't like that. They just moved away suddenly, no reason, no goodbye, no forwarding address. They didn't even pack up their things. I would lay awake at night worrying, wondering where she went and why."

The next whiskey went down easy. Nice. The warmth radiated . . . to . . . his . . . toes.

He shook his head, clearing the ripples, and held out his empty glass.

"Maybe you should slow down, big guy. We have a three-day voyage, you know. Might as well spread it out—"

"I'll have another," he insisted.

"—and the waves are getting rough."

"I heard them leave, late at night, you know. The girl wailed. She just wanted her cat. The girl cried over the cat more than she cried over her dead mother."

"All women like to cry," said Bartender. "It comes natural to them. Flirt, prance, tease, cry, run to Mama. It's what they do."

"But she loved that cat. Ki-Ki, she called it. Couldn't say kitty. And the Queen hated it. Let it run in the road just as a truck was coming. Was her fault. She killed that cat."

"How old was this dame?" asked the bartender.

"Aren't you listening, mister?"

"I think you might need to slow down a bit."

"She wasn't exactly mmodel mmother mmaterial, you know." Words were suddenly hard to say. "She deserved what she got." Szymon held his empty glass up to his eye and looked through the magic tunnel to the land of faraway and waybackwhen.

"Who in Christ's name are you talking about?" Bartender asked.

"Queenie."

"I don't know what you're up to, man. Queenie's dead," said the bartender, backing up a step, hand on the doorbell buzzer on the counter.

"I have her trunk."

"She's been dead and buried ten years. Captain found her on the beach, dead. Everyone knows it."

"Oh yeah? But do they know who killed her? And why?"

The bartender shook his head.

"I know," Szymon said. "I know why she had to die."

CHAPTER 25

NATTIE opened her eyes and blinked two billion times. They refused to focus. Something was wrong. A train roared in her head, or maybe it was water rushing, waves. She was under a waterfall. Or at the bottom of a river that was flowing over her, washing her away. It hurt, whatever it was.

Her head hurt so bad she could barely think. *Why?*

She moaned. Winced. Her face scrunched up, her scalp throbbing, her hair screaming, the crown of her head about to explode in red and orange. Thinking made it worse.

A weight fell on her forehead, cold, hard, wet. She shivered.

Clenching her eyes closed, she concentrated on not moving. Her chest made slight shallow puffs up and down. Eyes seeped. Tongue checked her teeth; one was loose. Her jaw felt off track. Pulse quickened. She felt sick. Queasy. Seasick-nauseous like she had been cast adrift for eons with eyes glued shut.

No, she had the flu. She was sick with the flu and just needed to sleep.

Dizziness hit. She felt hot and cold at once. Her stomach lurched. Maybe an illness was coming on, one of her attacks . . .

> *"You have to stay still. Stop squirming. You're flopping around like a fish out of water. You have to rest to get well. The doctor knows best.*
> *Take this. One more spoonful. One more. Stop your whining."*

The bitter medicine was hot in her throat. Dread came next. Antiseptic smells and cotton balls and harsh lights and sharp needle stabs and metal braces on skinny little-girl legs.

> *"I won't be sick. I won't."* She took deep breaths, calming herself down.
> *"Go to sleep."*
> She couldn't.

She was being watched. She felt faces in a circle staring at her.

"I think she's stirring."

"Someone get more ice, in a clean towel this time, please. Clean. Have you people heard of soap?"

"It's about time you decided to rejoin us."

"Natalia, Natalia, dear . . ."

"Natalia, it's your father. Wake up now. Snap out of it, now."

"I don't think orders are effective in this case, Captain. Step out of the way. This is my patient. All of you people, get out of my way. You're stealing her air and squandering my space and getting on my nerves. Git, I say. All of you. Except you, costume lady. You stay. Help me get her out of this silly getup. You, go—fetch her nightgown, something more comfortable than this nonsense. Why are you standing there? Go, get me something to put her in. Clean. Cotton. Not a single sequin, either. Hear me?"

Nattie frowned at the voice. She blinked one hundred times and 99 more and the woman came into almost-focus. She wore white like a summer cloud. She didn't look like an angel, though. Or a lake spirit made of mist. She didn't look like she even belonged on the *Lake Maiden*.

She looked mean. And mad. And blurry . . . dipped in Not Real juice and hung up to dry.

"Who are you?"

"Ah, she speaks. There she is," said the woman. The voice seemed familiar, maybe a passenger? Nattie faintly remembered something to do with cards, a queen. Two queens. Six queens in the deck?

> *The case rattled when the woman set it down at her feet at the poker table. Glass bottles clinked.*
>
> *"What's in your bag? Is it glass? Is it going to break and spill and make a mess someone will have to clean up?"*
>
> *The woman sat at the poker table, chips in front of her.*
>
> *"It's medicine. Nothing for you. Never you mind none." She studied her cards like they were biblical scrolls.*
>
> *Nattie stole a look. Queens.*
>
> *"What kind of medicine?"*
>
> *"Tonics. Cures for curses." Then she turned to Nattie and got*

nose to-nose close and spooky-snarled. "Amulets for
protection. Antidotes for evil and potions for love. Charms for
luck. And something to make you shit if you're stopped up."
Her eyebrows raised.
"Do you need help in that department, Missy? Pipes
blocked?"

"Hello, Natalia. It's me, the nurse, Halina. We talked earlier today, by your tank, remember?"

"I remember your satchel and jars that jingle and you like queens."

"Good. And I remember you don't think good intentions are good enough. Right?"

"Did I say that?"

"Yes, most definitely. Was rather brilliant, too. A good observation, if you ask me."

Nattie's vision started to clear. She remembered telling the nurse about Jakub—

"But you've had a fall and a bump on your head. Your friends asked me to come check on you, see how you're doing." The nurse bent over so she was eye-to-eye close. Nattie could bite her nose if she wanted to, she was that close. The nurse smelled like cigarettes.

"How am I doing?"

"Well, I believe you have a concussion."

"No, I don't. I didn't take one."

The nurse laughed.

"A concussion is something that happens when you hit your head. You fell."

Nattie remembered. The morning came back to her in one flood.

"The performance! What happened?" Nattie tried to get up. "Did I miss my cue?"

She fought their arms. "Did Jakub come? Did he push the platform out? Thunderclap number two?"

"No, no. Now, Nattie, dear, don't you worry about that," Mimi said, trying to come in closer. "The performance went on. Bubby pushed you on stage. You fell. But the girls all carried on for the big finale. Don't you worry about that."

"You need to rest," the nurse said. "You have a bump on your head as big as a softball. Which is darn big for someone your size."

"Can I still be useful?"

"Well, of course. But not now. You can rest for a while," Nurse said.

"So, it's okay? I won't go over the railing?"

"Because of a headache? No, I don't think a dive overboard is called for. Except you are dripping a good deal of melted ice all over, making a nice fine puddle in your father's bed. I am a little concerned about what he'll say about that. He seems to be an opinionated, particular man, if you ask me."

"He's the captain. He makes the rules. All the rules."

"I have heard. I met him very briefly before I shooed him out. I've also met the first mate Jenkins, an overly enthusiastic Boy Scout, and Purser Houseman, a bit of a weasel man, and a bartender who is a romantic matchmaker, and then Mr. Antonio Salvatore, who looks so suave, like Rudolph Valentino giving dance lessons. Quite a wacky ding-dong ship."

"Don't say that. Don't make fun of Boat. She's home. The only one I have. It's not a joke, you know." All the talking made Nattie's head hurt more. She was tired.

"Hmm. I know. She's a nice boat."

"Yes! She is a very nice boat," she tried to say. But her head hurt too bad to make words come out.

"Shhh. Don't worry about the *Lake Maiden*," Mimi tried to reassure her.

Nattie was done listening. Listening and talking hurt. Laying there hurt. She tried to freeze. She tried to stop breathing because the in-out movement hurt so much. She felt liquid dripping on her forehead and wondered if it was blood or brains or ice water or tears or ninety-nine bottles of beer. Dripping. Dripping. Dripping.

> *The dressing room made of scarves closed in.*
> *He pushed her against the wall, metal and ice cold. She*
> *shivered. She trembled. Dribbles of pee ran down her bare leg,*
> *spread across the floor.*
> *He stepped in it.*
> *He looked at his shoes, piss under his hard soles. He stomped.*

It splashed her face. Dripped down her face.
Dripped.
He made a fist. His black hair fell over his eyes, swooping in a
curve, elegant like the swan's neck.

"Where's Jakub?"

"Hon, he didn't show up for the afternoon performance. I don't know where he is," said Mimi. "Don't you worry about him now. He'll be around. As soon as he hears you're ailing, he'll visit. But he's probably in the boiler room working."

"Jakub works in the boiler room? A boy that has a weak heart shouldn't exert himself in extreme heat," said Nurse. "I would imagine the boiler room is hot, far too hot. That kind of stress could kill a boy with a weak heart."

No—

Natalia dropped into the blue water, under the surface where it was cool and safe and dark and safe and swirly and safe and where she belonged. Waves rushed over her head, washing back and forth; they held her, rocking her with gentle movements back and forth, up and down, back and forth.

Mama rocked me once.

She was lulled to a lagoon made of blues and greens and singsong currents humming.

"We'll go sailing up the mezzanine," Jakub said. He jumped on the back of her chariot and away they sailed, flying off into the blue, like he'd said, like he'd promised. He held her baubles and jewels in his hand. She tried to catch them. They floated away with the current. So many.

Sixteen like me. Fifty-seven varieties of pickles, ninety-nine
bottles of beer.

She followed them. Safe in her lagoon. The *Lake Maiden* rocked her, glad she was home.

I'll never leave, she told the boat. I belong here.
Mermaids belong in water, the boat said.
I know, she said.
They have curved spines and withered legs and if they're not
careful they'll be left in the sand to be baked into a pie, the

gulls diving toward her said.

"No, that won't happen, now hush. Sleep," the nurse-lady said.

"I'll be good. I'll be a good girl."

"You were never a good girl," said Queenie. *"Unless you wanted something."*

"Where's the zipper on this getup? We need to get her out of this sequin mess. No wonder she can't walk, with her legs squeezed in like this. Either help me get her out of this contraption or I'll get the scissors and cut her out," Nurse said.

"Not the scissors! They'll ruin—"

The nurse got rough-handed, rolling Nattie around, this way then that, skinning her alive. Her lavender sequins and blue ribbons and fishnet trim and dangling shells were torn away. Nattie knew what they saw: raw skin, white-gray, wrinkled and withered and horribly ugly with red lines and scars from leg braces. She felt naked.

She screamed, "Noooo—"

"Nooo," cried the child on the floor, trying to kick. The braces wouldn't let her.

"Stop that, Nattie. We just need to get you comfortable. Hush."

"Stop that noisemaking right now."

"Someone go get her nightgown."

"I'm going to give you something to cry about."

"How could she not have one? What does she sleep in? Where is her bed?"

"Go to your room. Go to sleep."

"You mean she doesn't have a room, doesn't have a bed, doesn't have a nightgown?"

"Goddamn it, go to sleep."

"For the love of Christ. What kind of shit show is this?"

"For Christ's sake. You're driving me crazy-mad."

"Are you people nuts?"

"I said shut up."

"How could you people, all of you, be so God-help-me crazy?"

"I can't take any more. For God's sake, not another sound."

I've had it, I tell you."

"Yeah, I'm annoyed. You betcha. Damn right. Damn tootin'."

"About damn time. Alright, already. Fine."

"That'll do. Fine. Fine."

"Finally."

"Finally."

CHAPTER 26

HALINA sat on a wooden stool next to the captain's bed where the girl slept. The stool was a squat, ugly thing layered with hundreds of shoe-polish outlines of captain-sized shoes. It looked like the captain had been dancing some wild dance on top of the rickety thing, wearing shoes dripping with paint.

Of course, he'd done no such thing. He was too much of a fuddy-duddy with stupid notions about what was proper and what wasn't. He was big on decorum, like the white uniforms and his white shoes, and those little do-dads that were supposed to be medals but were just little cookie cutters painted gold. He didn't give a squat about raising his daughter.

At least he'd offered up his quarters and carried her here. How big of him. She'd wanted to slap him silly but had settled for yelling. Now she was out of words, her anger settling into a low simmer. The girl had been awake off and on, talking nonsense. Halina could smell alcohol on her. She guessed she'd been given some before her fall. So, in addition to her head bump, she was inebriated.

That would explain some of the gibberish she said. Halina hoped it was that and not damage to the brain. She would have no idea how to treat that. Nattie would need real medical care as soon as they reached a port.

I can only do so much. Maybe I have no business even trying to do that. But who else is there?

She thought of Janusz in her kitchen and his wild fit throwing eggs. Maybe she did him wrong by trying to treat his woes. She hoped he was tucked safely in a bed in the attic, sleeping, his pain dulled. She tried sending calming thoughts and a reassuring message for Janusz.

He must think I've abandoned them. Hell, he might even be worried. Maybe Theo, too. She should have tried harder to send word, in a more ordinary way. She wondered if the newspaper boy had delivered the message she had sent. Oh, how silly it seemed now. How stupid. But what else could she do?

I'll be home as soon as I can. Sorry, Theo. I meant well. I was trying to do something good. Stach, take care of Janusz. Tell Theo I'm trying.

Thinking of Theo made her feel like a homesick kid. Maybe Stach would make up some story. Or Baba would help with the message and let Theo know not to worry. But he never listened to the thumping and tapping and humming in the walls the old woman sent along with her hints and dribbles of memories good enough to eat. He wasn't that sort of man, never would be. Still, she was fond of him. And didn't want him to be aching with worry—or fuming with fury.

Oh, she had messed things up bad. It had been one hell of a day. And it wasn't over yet. She was so tired she felt loopy. She could use a smoke or a Polynesian Passion, maybe whiskey straight up.

"Nattie—wake up, honey. Natalia, do you hear me?"

After the fight to get her out of the costume, Nattie had fallen asleep again. Either she was exhausted or her head bump was worse than Halina had first thought. She just didn't know. Halina tried everything to wake her up: jokes, prayers, promises, threats. Nattie would open her eyes then drift again, like she had other places she wanted to be. At one point she started singing about bottles of beer on the wall, of all things.

Halina had a vague recollection that letting a patient with a head injury fall asleep was inviting a coma. She hadn't treated many concussions, though, and had to think back to the training at the hospital. She'd taken a six-month nurse's aide course when hospitals were desperate for help during the Great War. She had been desperate, too, barely fifteen, lying about her age, needing a way to earn some money besides her poker winnings so she could get away from Hegewisch.

She had wanted to get out of town so badly when she was young. She had hated the old-timers, including her parents, all Polish immigrants, hated their Old Country ways and their superstitions and the lopsided shacks decorated to the hilt with red shutters and symbols of scythes, roosters, baskets of loaves and bundles of wheat. So absurd. Wheat didn't grow in Hegewisch. Or in Chicago. Or anywhere near here. Did it? She really had not been far from downtown, at least not in person, just in those flying dreams she went on sometimes when Baba tried to teach her some lesson or show her a new medicine. The woman wouldn't let up.

Where are you now?

Halina twisted her hands, her knuckles swollen from sewing up the boy Silas, the stormy weather, and worry, which plugged up her juices and joints something wicked. She wanted to cry actual tears. She couldn't do that, not near a patient.

She looked up to the ornate tin ceiling. It looked like it belonged in the drug store, not a ship. Nothing seemed right. Nothing seemed to fit how it should.

"Can't you help me?" she implored the old woman healer. Or God. Whoever would listen. Whoever was up there, hovering, strings dangling down, like threads from a hem. Neither came running. But she heard a voice on the intercom box by the desk. A woman's voice.

"It's your turn. I tried once. I failed, sent her away with a boy and a wagon. Now you. You. You." The voice was gone in static.

Halina understood. It was up to her. No one was going to help. It was her mission.

> *"You'll heal bones and hearts, fishes that breathe air and fliers without feathers, sisters, sinners, and captains of chariots with wooden wheels. You'll see."*

She put her hand on Nattie's bare shoulder. The skimpy nightie, loaned by Viola, the sassy one, didn't cover much. *I hope she's not cold.*

"Natalia, wake up, little Polish mermaid. Talk to me. Where did you live before the boat, Nattie?" Halina shook the girl's shoulder. She looked so small in the captain's bed.

Halina closed her eyes. She looked again. Blinked. And looked again.

> *Nattie was a little girl, barely four. She was on a table in a kitchen, the walls red. Vapors came from the stove and swirled like spirits over the child. She held a small wooden Madonna in her tiny hand. Old woman hands kneaded the child's hips, like the atrophied muscles were bread dough needing to rise, yeast activated by the warmth of hands and the rhythmic motion. Pound. Pull. Turn. A little boy's voice sang.*

> *"Amazing grace, how sweet the sound."*

Halina blinked again.

The fish-girl, with those damned scales on her arms, was tucked snuggly in her father's bed. She didn't move. No one sang. She looked peaceful, like a corpse.

172

Camel had looked so peaceful when he finally surrendered.

Down feathers flew around the room in torrents, like the twisting legs, bicycling, an instinct he couldn't control. He didn't want to fight, she knew. She knew his heart. She knew with a fierceness, like her fierce grip on the pillowcase that tore at the seam and more feathers flew to the window like feathers on a duck returning to the lake. Where it belonged. Where he belonged. And he was well. And he was gone. Where he belonged.

"Did you know I'm Polish too?" she said to Nattie. "I live in Hegewisch. A house on Avenue O. When I was a girl, my sister and I slept in a coal room, sneaking in and out of the window. My sister liked to chase boys. There were two brothers. Camel. Bear. Those were nicknames. Camel had such skinny knees and a tan cap. Bear was round and had a brown cap. I played poker with the men who lived on the street and did odd jobs for nickels. Can you believe it?"

The girl's eyes fluttered. But they didn't open.

"Where's the rest of your family, Nattie? You must have lived on land some time. Where's your mother? Hon, tell me about it. Wake up and tell me," she begged, hands folded tightly.

Nattie's face changed, like a cloud passed over her. She frowned. She tossed her head, like she was trying to shake free from a bad dream.

The boat tossed, too. The lake fought back. It seemed mad as hell.

The weather seemed to be worsening. She bit her lip, patted Nattie's shoulder.

"Now, now hon. Don't worry."

The boat pitched up and down in uneven, ragged lunges. An alarm clock flew from the shelf to the floor. Books tumbled in a heap of dust and bookmarks, handwritten notes from a student's homework. Such a mess.

Halina leaned over Nattie, trying to protect her from more flying objects. The girl stirred. She tossed. She mumbled, "Pickles and bottles of beer. Ninety-nine."

"You're having some wild dream, honey. Come on, now, time to wake up."

Someone was stumbling around outside the cabin door. Mimi, the Frenchie, came in, carrying more hand-me-down clothes and a suitcase that looked like a giant shell. More hokey silliness.

Halina motioned for the woman to come in. "She's still out. I've been trying to wake her."

"I brought her collection of favorite things, and me and the other girls all pitched in some clothes, some underthings and such. They didn't have much that was appropriate for a girl, though." She held up a camisole that could have held two watermelons and some lacey pantalettes that would barely cover an ass crack and certainly wouldn't keep a fart in.

"Pfft. Don't talk to me about what's appropriate, lady," Halina sneered. "I'm not seeing much appropriateness, let me tell you."

"I know how it must look," Mimi said. "We all did our best." She shrugged and averted her eyes.

Mimi was young herself, but it was hard to pinpoint her age. Maybe mid-twenties? Oddly, she seemed to be trying to cover up her age. The messy bun, the old lady shoes, the glasses, the accent that came and went. They were all part of her own costume. What was this gal's game?

Halina was fairly certain Mimi had been the woman spraying perfume from that atomizer earlier this morning. What the hell was that about? Trying to drive Nattie out of that damn tank with perfume stink? Off the mezzanine? Why? She thought about grilling her. But, then again, maybe keeping that bit of knowledge to herself might be more useful. Some secrets were good to keep close.

"Here, sit down. Before you fall down," Halina said, hanging on to the bed frame as the boat lunged.

Another book fell from the shelf. This one looked like it was world explorers, old turds with fancy hats. On top of that, another fell. Of all things, it was a book of Polish fairy tales. The *Syrenka Warszawska* story. Quaint. Silly. Nattie looked nothing like her.

Mimi fell into the desk chair and hunched protectively over Nattie's shell suitcase, eyeing the flying objects.

"Must be some valuables stowed away in there, eh?" Halina asked.

"Oh, I don't know. Mostly girl things, I think. You know the tidbits a girl saves, romantic notions. She doesn't know yet what's important to her, so she saves it all."

Curious, Halina took the case and popped it open. Rocks, twine, a brush, an oversized brass key, old and fancy. There was a jar of dragonfly wings. Dandelion fluff, seeds, a matchbox of bent fishhooks. Nattie had fountain pens, the fancy kind. And jewelry, the sparkly kind, nearly pretty enough to be real. And a cardboard crown that was so childlike it was sweet. Precious.

"Girl things or grown-up things? Seems to me Nattie isn't quite ready to let go of one for the other, hanging on to some trace of innocence for dear life. Then again, maybe she's ready to face reality head on. Look at this."

From the bottom of the case, she pulled out—she could hardly believe it—a switchblade with a pearl handle. It was old looking, some kind of antique; maybe it didn't even work . . .

"Why would she have that—" Mimi asked, shaking her head.

"Maybe she's ready to fight for something worth fighting for," Halina said and snapped the case closed, done intruding on the girl's private world.

"Maybe," Mimi said. "Maybe it's time for her to leave the nest. Maybe she needs a shove. Or two. A kick?"

"Like perfume in the wind?" Halina blurted out, raising an eyebrow.

"Exactly." Mimi fumbled in her skirt pocket and pulled out a small silver flask. "Who can do it alone? Sometimes you need a shove out the door. A friend to say enough pretending. Enough fairy tale. Face the truth, as crass as it may be."

"Oh really?"

"Like me," Mimi added, her French accent suddenly gone. "I'll fess up. I'm as French as a powdered poodle at a dog pound." She took a short swig and handed the flask over.

Halina slapped her on the back and laughed. "A poodle!"

"And you, Nurse—well, I would bet the bees in my bonnet you've had about as much medical training as . . . as . . . as . . ."

Halina took a swig, then another. It was the good stuff. She raised an eyebrow, waiting to see what the seamstress might come up with to describe her questionable qualifications. But the woman seemed at a loss.

"I'll have you know I had an entire six months of training," Halina offered with her own touch of stage-acting indignation. She held up three fingers on each hand, wiggling them around. "Just enough training to be a night shift aide. In charge of bedpans and ass-wiping."

"Ha. I knew it!" said Mimi. "No one with a real medicine diploma would risk drinking this homemade moonshine that could turn you blind as a bat, or worse." She pushed the flask to Halina's mouth, laughing.

Halina took a swig. She felt warm from the booze, a calm dullness coming on. Her eyelids felt like they weighed a ton. Her neck was a limp noodle. It was sure hitting her quickly. Too quickly. Too hard.

"Do you need to take a nap? I can sit with the girl awhile if you want to take forty winks. Put your head down . . ." Mimi suggested. Too eagerly.

Without the silly accent, the woman seemed so much friendlier, almost trustworthy.

Up went the boat.

Maybe . . .

Down.

. . . for a minute?

"Lord, I wish the boat would stop this rocking," Halina said. "Does this happen a lot? Should we be worried?"

"Nah, nothing to worry about. Nothing at all," Mimi said, pushing the flask back in Halina's hands.

"So, Mademoiselle Mimi, if you're not from France, where are you from?"

"Quebec. Canada."

"My sister's in Canada. Hiding out from the law."

"I know. That's where I met her."

Halina understood in a flash of clarity. She'd been tricked. She was swallowed alive by a flying turtle. She tried to fight it, but the damned thing was big. And the whiskey in the flask was jacked up. Maybe the clerk's poppy tonic. The turtle was a mighty thing wearing armor and a party hat. It wasn't a turtle at all, and the whiskey wasn't whiskey at all, and the seamstress wasn't a seamstress at all. Or a French poodle. She seemed rather sober, though. Oddly turtle-free.

"You know my sister, do you?"

"Yes, I do. Indeed, I do."

"How is Pat?"

"Distraught."

"Why's that?"

"Antonio has a new sweetie. And dear Antonio kicked her boy to the curb, tired of him hanging around, sickly and weak. He was a reminder of that Polack bar in Heg-witz-something."

"Hegewisch."

"Yeah."

"She told you all this?"

"No, Antonio did."

Well, isn't that funny, Halina thought as the flying turtle soared to the ceiling then sputtered out of fuel and crashed, plummeting down to the bed where the mermaid in a provocative nightie slept. Halina parachuted down and landed in the bed beside her. She put her head on the pillow next to Nattie, who smelled like the lakeshore late at night when the smelt came out to feast on moonlight and star droppings.

She couldn't move. Couldn't talk.

She could breathe. She could see through a fringe of eyelashes, eyes half open, half closed, half of this world, half underwater, where mermaids go and where nurses afraid of dying hide.

She had just enough sense left in her head to fight the temptation to go under completely. She kicked her legs, trying to surface. She tried sucking in air, billowfuls, pillowfuls. She tried to think. If she were a patient, what would be the treatment?

Baba rode up on a bus with advice. Restore blood pressure. Steady rhythm of pulse. Heartbeat. *Padum, dum.* Music. Sing. Clickety-clack, the wheelies on the buster went over the crack-track. *Padum, dum.* Clickety-cack, the welts on the bus went over the track. *Padum, dum.* Clickety-clack, the wheels on the bus went over the track. And faster. *Padum, dum.* Get the blood pumping. Faster. Burn off the tonic fumes. The clicketyclackthebus went. Over. The track. Clickety-cl—

Antonio in the doorway.

Deep breath.

"Are they both out?"

"Both. Burnt out lightbulmbs."

"Bulmbs?"

"I may have had a little sop . . . sip . . . too," Mimi said.

Antonio slapped her face. "That wasn't in the plan," he snapped.

"Ah, Tony, baby, what's the big deal?"

"Did you find the safe?"

"Yeah, here in the floor. But it needs a key."

"I thought you knew locks."

"I know dials. Not keys. Not like this one. It's strange, old and fancy and brass." Mimi stood behind the desk, one foot on each side of a little door in the floor. She was looking down at it like she wanted to piss on it.

"Then forget it. We'll get it later. C'mon."

CHAPTER 27

THE captain slipped off the bridge as quietly as he could, moving in slow motion like his thoughts. Time had lost its rhythm and was muddled. The erratic lurching of the lake caused it. The beat was off. Unpredictable. Choppy. Chaotic. As random as the lightning flashes lighting up the bridge, blinding, making the leftover blackness more consuming . . . until . . . the next . . . flash.

The clerk's desk was cluttered: papers, bills, receipts, inventory logs of shoe polish, bleach and seltzer. There was a notebook of deliveries. Full barrels came on board. Empty barrels were wheeled off. Captain ran his finger over the report, but he saw no discrepancies. He didn't know if he could spot an error in the books even if one was there. He wasn't much for numbers. He would need something clearer, proof Seymore had ulterior motives.

Captain sat on the corner of the desk scanning the entire room, from the typewriter and colored pencils that his daughter liked to borrow to the classic globe and the books of charts, the ones spotted with red cherry juice. A bit of an overreaction, wasn't it, the way Seymore carried on about Nattie spilling the juice on the maps? A conniption fit over nothing.

Then he saw it.

Half a Nattie handprint. Her palm was there, but the fingers were cut off, like some other panel had been there and was gone now. He felt around. The boat had doorbell buttons here and there that opened the sliding panels to the rat-runs. He didn't know of one in the clerk's office.

He found the button. A panel on the shelf slid open and bundles of cash tumbled out. More were behind that. Then more. So many that he couldn't guess at how much had been stashed away. Houseman had been skimming off the top, stealing cash from ticket sales and the bars. More than skimming, it looked like. No wonder the *Lake Maiden* was floundering. The bastard. Captain seethed, clenching his fists, gritting his teeth to hold back an explosion of fury. It looked like this was a long-time endeavor, not some one-time breach.

The boat pitched up and dropped down, and more bundles fell to the floor. Then more. If he hadn't been so furious he would have found the waterfall of cash to be comical, something from a Keystone Cops movie. He wasn't laughing.

Captain picked up what he could and shoved bundles into his pockets. He would have to come back for the rest. He had to think. He needed some peace. He also needed to empty his pockets. He couldn't walk around with huge bulges in his pants. He didn't want to tip his hand until he knew how he wanted to handle Houseman—and whoever else might be in on the scheme. He needed to be careful, to watch his back. And there was Nattie to think of, too.

He pushed open the door to his cabin. She was still in his bed, the nurse still sitting with her. When he walked in, he was overwhelmed with the disarray. The room smelled of chaos. The quarters were dimly lit; a lamp was broken, the shattered glass bulb on the floor. His papers were disturbed, and his books were a mess.

But Natalia was asleep, looking peaceful, perfectly arranged in the bed, no odd angles of legs sticking out askew. The nurse was next to her on the bed, her head on the pillow too. Her eyes were half open in an odd sleep-stare he recognized. She was doped up, high as a kite. Probably opium.

Natalia's costume was on the floor. It looked like it had been shredded. He had come to hate that convoluted getup, more added on to it every year, another layer of sparkle-crap, another dangle of plaster shells and toy pearls until it had become a monstrosity, weighing her down and choking her with some horseshit Polish myth. *Syrenka.*

It wasn't cute anymore, he knew. But if his daughter outgrew the game, she also outgrew him. If she stopped being the ship mascot, what would she be? She would leave him, go far away, live on land, meet some man who would take her away and convince her she had lived an odd life, on the fringes of appropriate—so much whiskey, poker, Margret and her girls. Her mother's daughter.

He crept closer to the bed, careful not to wake her. He didn't know much about head-wallops, but there wasn't any blood, so it had to be minor. Just a bump. Right? She had to be fine. The nurse would have told him if it was more serious, right?

Natalia was a resilient kid. Brave. Smart. Sometimes too smart for her own good. Resourceful. She had half the crew wrapped around her little finger, bringing her things. He knew Antonio gave her gifts every time he came aboard. That had to be how she had such a collection of jewels.

Antonio was trying to win over his daughter, bias her, pollute her thinking.

That was why Captain gave her the pearls for her birthday. And the crown. He couldn't be outdone.

He touched her face. She was lovely, even if she did look too much like her mother. Sometimes he couldn't bear to look at her, couldn't bear the reminder of the woman who'd ridiculed the child and flaunted lovers in front of him. Those were difficult days he would rather not remember. The doctor had no answers for Nattie's legs, none they could afford—just some stupid braces she was supposed to wear. He couldn't stand to see her in the things. Hideous contraptions.

He had tried burning them one night. He was drunk and couldn't look at them any longer.

> *The fire in the trash drum climbed into the black night sky,*
> *chewed at the leather straps on the metal braces, sucked on*
> *the metal bones and the bolts that screwed to her shoes.*
> *The braces wouldn't melt. They wouldn't turn to ash. They*
> *mocked him, gleaming white hot.*
> Now who will save your daughter? *they shrieked.* Can you do
> it, stupid man?
> *"What have I done? No. No. Stop."*
> *The metal was too hot to pull them out. He burned his hand*
> *trying. He had to let go.*

He would have to let go of her, too, he knew.

He heard commotion on the bridge. Shouting carried over the roar of wind and beating rain. He thought he heard metal tearing and crunching. But it couldn't be. He was wrong, had to be.

Hurry.

He rummaged among the books on the floor to find the Encyclopedia of Explorers. The spare key to the floor safe was tucked inside the back cover; a good thing, since the key that he usually kept in his pocket had gone missing. Queenie and her ghostly thieving. She liked to take his fountain pens too.

He opened the door with the key, then turned the combination dials to open the vault and started dropping in the bundles of money from his pockets. Five or so bundles were already in there, a tidy sum he had managed to put away, out of reach of the whiskey men and the nosey clerk. He had to plan for his future and the girl's. Maybe he would buy a new tug when this was all said and done. Maybe he'd get the girl a house, a real nurse, some clothes, shoes and stockings. A doll? Was she too old for dolls?

He started to leave but turned and came back. He took the cheap homemade medals off his shirt and dropped them in the vault too. If they were boarded by the authorities in port, he didn't want the coast guard laughing.

Men in uniform could be so full of themselves, couldn't they?

"Good night, Nattie," he whispered as he slipped out, making sure the vault locked, the door closed, the key in his pocket.

CHAPTER 28

HALINA woke up face-to-face with a girl. It took her a second to remember who the girl was.

Natalia. She studied the girl's face, trying to remember the rest of why she was here, nose-to-nose with this blond imp. She was little more than a child, her whole life ahead of her. If not for some scalloped scale lines drawn on with a blue ink pen, she'd be beautiful.

Well, not that wild hair. She needed a haircut.

She thought of her nephew, Jakub. He'd be about the same age, probably, maybe a little older, almost eighteen.

She wondered if Jakub cared for Nattie. The girl obviously was sweet on him, the way she had talked about him. She wondered where he was now. Was he safe? This boat was full of trouble. Maybe it was cursed and needed a good cleansing of spirits.

She thought of the whole scene with Mimi. And then Antonio in the doorway. So, ol' slimy Antonio and fake Mimi were an item. Ooh-la-la. She wondered if Pat knew, the poor thing.

Concentrate.

She sat up. She rubbed her head. She took some deep breaths.

The conversation between Antonio and Mimi came flooding back: the brass vault door in the floor.

Halina poked the girl, shook her arm.

"Nattie, wake up. Please."

It felt very late. The boat was still pitching up and down. Bottles in Halina's satchel clinked. She heard voices on the bridge, men shouting at each other.

"Did you try the radio?"

"Did you call—"

"Did you try—"

"Did you—"

"Nattie, wake up. You can show me around this boat. Show me your

182

favorite places on the boat. And your clam suitcase. Wake up and tell me about all the things in it. Lovely things. Like a key."

She was curious about the key and the safe. She was worried about the weather and the boat. She was frightened for Nattie. Worried about Jakub and wondering how Silas was getting along. She hoped the cook was watching his bandages like she had instructed. They probably needed a change about now. She was angry about Mimi and Antonio. And she wasn't too happy with her sister, either.

She also felt like a fool for letting Mimi drug her.

She kicked the satchel on the floor, the bottles tinkling, bottles of mystery and promises and herbs, roots, and extracts from petals and seeds. Yeah, some had medical properties. But some were for nothing but colorful fizzes and smoke, the fancy razzle-dazzle to convince patients she was connected to the mystic world beyond reason. Some of it was nonsense, sure.

Mimi had guessed she had little medical training. One liar could spot another a mile away. They saw through each other's scams.

She had been so much like Nattie. Living in her own world. People had talked about her, laughing behind her back, eye-rolling and making cuckoo faces. There had been rumors, the stories of the haunted peach tree that said she buried her dead patients there. That wasn't true, of course, but she had loved all the talk. She fed and nurtured the mystique. Just like Nattie fueled the mermaid bullshit, Halina had fueled her own far-fetched story. The mythic mermaid. The mystic healer. Yeah. Too much, too far? Maybe. Look what happened to the girl.

What do I do now?

She felt like stomping around or slapping something. She at least needed a smoke.

"Nattie, wake up. I know you've been dealt a lousy hand, but I can help you get better. We'll get you real doctors. Good medicine. You just have to wake up. Then we can show these conniving, back-stabbing people that you deserve better than this, and a better doctor than me."

She wished she had some miracle tonic to pull out of her bag to fix it. She was certain there was no bottle in the satchel labeled "Make a girl face reality rather than hide in a delusionary mermaid world" or anything close. She wished there was.

"Nattie. C'mon, hon. Hey. Mimi brought you some clothes. Let's get dressed. Let me help you. Then we could get you some shoes. Shoes are— shoes are, well, useful."

The girl stirred, eyelids fluttering like a butterfly set free.

"Useful?" she whispered.

Yes!

That's it, Nattie, let's get you dressed and in some shoes. Halina rummaged in the satchel. Maybe she could find something to help snap Nattie out of it. She tried again to find her smokes and the matches. Tonic bottles, candles, no . . .

"Well, how about this?"

She pulled out the heavy, lumpy handkerchief from the odd man on the bus this morning. It seemed like a long time ago. She ran her finger over the quick-stitched flap.

"Should we see what we have, Nattie? I suppose we might as well, eh?"

She pulled on the thread with her teeth. The hanky unfolded.

The boat pitched up.

A gold coin fell out of the flap and into her hand. A business card came with it.

Madam Salvatore's Rare Coins and Treasures
739 Portside Street, Ontario

Halina flipped it over. A note, in handwriting she recognized:

Halina—
Please, help me. I'm worried about Jakub. Antonio sent him away. My
asthma is worse. I'm sick. Find my boy for me. Coin is yours, in
payment. Please.
—Pat

Halina read the card and the note several times, rubbing the coin between her fingers, feeling the raised letters and the profile of some big-nosed man with curly hair and a fancy wreath on his head like a crown. King Somebody. She couldn't read any of the words on the coin, not even the country or the value. But it was gold and old and not worth beans to her. The Woolworth didn't accept gold coins. Neither did the Food Mart. Or Stout Brothers Shoes. What could she do with an old coin? Wipe her butt?

The card and note were even bigger mysteries. A rare coin store? Madam Salvatore? Pat had married Antonio? But she was still married to Bear—the poor idiot, left tending the bar in Hegewisch. The bar with no booze, thanks to Antonio.

Halina huffed. She was mad enough to spit.

She heard more commotion on the other side of the door, men rushing around the bridge just yards away. The captain's voice; the sailor boy, Jenkins, shouting about the straits of something and Huron and docking for something. Damages this and that something. And calling for something. And Antonio's voice.

And she was sick of Antonio.

I have a sick kid I'm worrying about here. Right now. Here. Now.

"Hey, will you people be quiet out there?" she shouted. "What's your trouble? Have you no sense? There's a sick kid in here. So keep your weather troubles and docking troubles and stupid boat nonsense to yourself." Her hands bunched in fists. She kicked the desk. Her shoe caught on the safe door in the floor.

A safe! Brass. Ornate.

She scrambled for the clamshell case and took out the brass key.

With some fiddling, the little door opened. Then there was another one. This one had a combination dial. How could she ever guess the combination?

"Nattie, do you know the combination? Three numbers. Combinations are usually a series of three numbers. Nattie. Think. Please. It's important."

"What? Why?" The girl moaned, groggily, waking up, trying to focus.

"Quick. The first three numbers to come into your head. Just shout them. Don't think. Just say them. Go—"

"SixteenlikemeHeinzfiftysevenandninetyninebottlesofbeer."

Halina was shocked that Nattie had managed to say three numbers. 16-57-99. She was even more shocked when the dial turned and the safe door opened. It opened!

Several stacks of cash wrapped in paper bands were jammed in the small space. She grabbed them. Nattie deserved this. Nattie would need help, the kind that took green money, not gold. She tossed the coin and bundles of money in Nattie's clamshell.

Scraps of words filtered through the door. Canada. Ontario. Rat-runs. Inventory. Vaults.

The mixed-up bits of phrases made no sense to her at all; all context was stripped. It was like two or three jigsaw puzzles mixed up together, and even if she could sort them, none of the pictures were pretty.

"Nattie, honey—are you listening to me, honey? Please wake up. We might have to hightail it off this boat. I don't think I could carry you, honey. You're going to need to walk if you can, maybe leaning on me . . . can you do little baby steps?"

She tried to think of options. Her mind was spinning, spinning like wheels.

That was it. She needed the wheelchair. But where was it? She tried to imagine. She called out to it. She closed her eyes. She saw Silas, eyes wide open. Jed pushing the chair. Sure, that made sense. Jed would use the chair to move Silas off that kitchen counter. She would start there.

She patted Nattie's shoulder, reassuring.

"I'll be back soon. I'm going to find your wheelchair. And check on Silas. I have to know how he's doing. And maybe I can find Jakub too."

She took the clamshell with her, just for safekeeping. There was a thief on board this ship, she had heard.

The stairs to the mezzanine level were safely under cover from the lashing wind and rain. Halina was surprised at the noise and the frenzy of passengers and crew. The crew members seemed to have one thing on their minds: moving the inventory into those secret catacombs they called rat-runs. Passengers were occupied moving inventory in their own way—gulping it down.

"Whiskey? Shots on the house," a waiter said, carrying a tray of shot glasses filled to the brim.

"You're giving it away?" she asked. She was tempted but knew she needed to keep her head sharp, and she still felt a little foggy, thanks to Mimi's potion.

"The best remedy for bad weather. Want a shot, ma'am? Complimentary, of course," said the roving bartender.

She wouldn't be surprised if there was something extra in the whiskey, too. People were snoozing here and there, on benches and at tables, their heads down and their fat faces snoring. It was funny in an odd sort of way. But if they did have to evacuate this boat, how were these drunk, drugged fools going to get off?

And how was she going to move Nattie? Or Silas? In the dark and the storm, getting to shore could be dangerous for a well person.

She glimpsed Jedediah at a distance, but he was wielding a mop and bucket, his mouth puckered up tight, jaws clenched. She waved to the preacher, but he didn't see her—or didn't want to take time to respond. He seemed busy cleaning. The boat tossing for hours had made messes. Food, drinks, and broken dishes were rolling on the floor every which way.

And water. There were a concerning number of puddles. The *Lake Maiden* was taking on water. This was becoming more alarming every minute. But Halina didn't have time to stop and worry.

The lower levels were the same: more messes, more water.

She retraced her steps from earlier and found the galley, where the absence of cooking smells was like a big hole. The crew were all cutting and slicing and stacking sandwiches, making trays of cold foods. No one talked. No one looked up. It was like she was invisible. Maybe she was. She looked at her hands. She saw them as clearly as could be.

Eunice slathered butter on biscuits, maybe the same biscuits she had been making earlier. She stood at the same counter where Halina had stitched up Silas only hours ago. It felt like days had passed, a small eternity.

"Hi there, Eunice. Looks like cold sandwiches—" Halina hung on to a counter so she didn't topple over with the next lurch. "How's Silas doing? Where is he?"

Eunice looked up. Her tear-streaked face was swollen and blotchy, her lips bleeding from being chewed raw. There was a second delay, then the young woman screamed like a wild hyena. She grabbed for a paring knife and lunged across the counter at Halina. "You—You—"

Halina stepped back as far as she could in the cramped space.

Mabella rushed in and grabbed Eunice. She took the knife away. Eunice didn't put up much fight. She was all despair and moans. Mabella held her, patting her back, hushing her with motherly sounds. The young woman fell in a heap of sniveling sobs and anguish, arms clamped around her belly like it ached.

"You best leave, Nurse. This is no place for you now."

She started to leave but froze.

"Is the girl's wheelchair here? I'm sorry to ask. Do you know?"

"Yeah, we know," Mabella said. She nodded toward the big icebox freezer. "Juan, show her." A Hispanic boy opened the door for Halina. Cold mist rolled out, like spirits running to greet her, enticing her to their ethereal world.

Halina stepped in, surprised at how cold the air was. She had never walked into an icebox before. She almost laughed at how silly it seemed. Until she saw.

Silas was propped up in the chair, white frost on his brown skin, ice crystals on eyelashes, his eyes wide open, seeing nothing. His mouth hung open. Spit dripples were frozen into icicles hanging from his chin.

Halina gasped, her hands to her face to hide from the horrible image. She ran from the galley, leaving the chair; leaving Silas; leaving Eunice, still sobbing on the floor.

PART TWO
CHICAGO, 1941

CHAPTER 29

NATTIE sat hunched over the scarred bar top, sipping an iceless gin fizz from a lobster-red coffee mug, her eyes focused on the black and white tile floor, waiting for it to transform into a cavernous mouth and swallow her whole, ending the boredom with one gulp. It could happen. Any moment now. She had been hoping, even threw up a prayer pulled from the Why Not pocket. What a silly waste of air that was. She was certain God didn't give a rat's ass about random SOS signals from Anchors Away, a dive bar on Rush Street that harbored wayward souls, tainted, stained and ignoble. . . including one lost mermaid who appeared nightly.

Besides the low-life bottom-dwellers, Anchors Away was popular with the navy boys. It ought to be. It held enough nautical crap to make Jules Verne pant and Robert Louis Stevenson drool. Herman Melville might get a woody. The enlisted sailors, stationed at the nearby Great Lakes Naval Training Station, ate up the hokey props, confusing lakeshore and ocean lore with patriotism. White stars on blue, starfish and sand dollars, conch shells, turtles, lighthouses—and battleships.

Yeah, they go together.

"Hey, I know you! You're the fish girllll," said a customer who wobbled and lunged toward to the bar, holding his bottle of beer over his head. Was he toasting her or saving his drink from waves crashing at his waist, threatening to pull him out to sea? He plopped down on the bar stool next to her and tipped his hat, a gray fedora that looked like some hooligan moths had their way with the poor thing.

Nothing's safe these days.

"I don't know what you are talking about, sir. I clearly am not a fish. Look at me. Breathing air. See?" And she inhaled and exhaled as noisily as possible.

> *"Can't you just be a little bit nice to the customers? Maybe flirt a little? Help business? You need this place to be success-ful as much as I need it. Where else could a fish girl go? It's not like you have someone else to mooch from, do you?"*

Then she winked at the fella. He was just a smidge shy of cute, in a naïve farm boy sort of way, maybe one of the Indiana boys in the big city for a lark. He probably had a couple buddies close by. Those farm boys travel in packs. Quaint, like piglets.

She managed a small smirk, trying to look playful. It was lost on the dunce. He was more intrigued by her feet, it seemed.

"Where did your get-up go? The whole tail business? You turn back into a dame when the tide goes out—or something?" The confused man, obviously semi-snookered, looked her over, frowning, confounded. The poor clod looked like he had been trying to lay an egg and got shit farts in his pants instead.

Poor boy.

"Oh, some secrets have to stay secrets, sir. I couldn't reveal more," she said, wrapping her arms around her chest and turning away like she was hiding a treasure.

"Well, don't get caught! Watch out for baited hooks, fishyfishgirl," the man slurred as he slid off the stool, apparently done with this game.

She laughed at the absurdity, a little disappointed that he had cut bait so quickly. He could have at least tried to question her about mermaid ways or asked to see her scales. Or offer to buy her a drink. Or something to eat. Hell, even on the *Lake Maiden*, the gawkers brought her biscuits and sardines!

She laughed and shrugged, not really surprised, not really wanting biscuits, sardines, or the attention of a hayseed with granddad's fedora.

It was funny he had recognized her without the costume trappings. She looked almost normal before the first show. She wore black dance leotards with a short skirt that wrapped around her waist and tied. She also wore a matching tank top and the shell necklace from the act. It weighed five pounds at least and could choke an ox. Oversized fake pearls, marble-size gems, garish glitter-shellacked shells, and silver charms dangled off fishing line.

Rest of the costume was backstage. She seldom wore it out front, among patrons on nights when the place was crowded. She'd freeze to death for one thing. Plus, splintered chairs and sharp table corners played havoc with the gauzy fabric of the tail, the sequins and shells sewn on in intricate scallop and swirl patterns with yards of flowing see-through pastel colors that followed her, wherever she went. The top was a too-small brassiere, shell-shaped with sequins and strings to tie it. The necklace covered more than the flimsy fabric did.

Then there were the tattoos. The days of fountainpen ink on her arms were long gone. Pastel-colored fish scales climbed her arms, spiraling toward her neck, dipping over her subtle curves, circling her breasts in artsy flourishes, seldom seen. It was all too intimate for casual encounters with customers—unless they paid extra. Everything at the Anchors Away had a price.

> *"Captain Wiśniewski, I am afraid your blatant disregard for the 18th amendment and your careless disregard for passenger safety have consequences. There is a price to pay for such outlandish transgressions, sir. A steep price."*

Nattie looked at the clock behind the bar. Maybe it was time to get ready for the first show. Or maybe she could sweet talk Davis into another gin before she went backstage. There was a limit to how many freebies the girls could get every night, but Davis was bad at math.

Davis mixed a highball and a whiskey sour, heavy on the ice, and set the drinks on the far end of the counter for Flossie to pick up when she eventually flounced by.

"Flossie, dear, there are thirsty sailors waiting for these drinks." Davis shouted in her general direction. Flossie didn't seem to hear. She was at table sixteen, squeezing biceps of sailors and giggling.

Nattie hoped that meant a good tip. They were short on rent money. Again.

She hovered over her mug, inhaling make-me-invisible fumes. She wasn't much help on the rent issue. No one thought to leave tips for her. What would they leave? Shrimp? Goldfish flakes? Maybe some juicy night crawlers from the bait shop?

She let her uncombed hair fall around her face, her shaggy bangs drooping over her eyes. She looked like a stray sheepdog in desperate need of a grooming. Boss Lady Pat told her that every night. On the rare occasion when Pat was too busy, Syd, the bouncer, dished out the critiques. If that wasn't sufficient to get her in a humble state of mind, there was good ol' Margret, who was always happy to eliminate any telltale wisps of self-esteem lingering in Nattie's sequined crevices. Like fog on the mezzanine.

Some things never change.

Her messy hair wouldn't matter soon enough.

She checked the clock behind the bar. Twenty minutes until show time, the first show of the night. After the first show, she stayed backstage. Walking around in the full costume. . . Well, it wasn't practical. She would drip.

> *Don't think about it, fish-girl. It's a job. What else could you do? Dig ditches? Shovel coal?*

Her lack of schooling certainly didn't help in the employment department. She had spent plenty of time in libraries and reading Captain's naval history books when the *Lake Maiden* was moored over the winter. *Moby Dick* and *Treasure Island, Twenty Thousand Leagues under the Sea.* Little good that did her. She knew two things: boats and men. And pirates.

> *"You know what I want, honey. You know the price of pearls. Nothing's free."*

And bootleggers. All those gifts had price tags. Pretending she didn't understand didn't make them free.

She wiped her eyes and tried to focus on the bar top.

Ah, Silverfish Fred was still creepy-crawling over the bar. He was a scrawny little thing. Too bad he didn't bring a friend. She could have staged a race—like Millie and Billie, the snails in her little tank on the *Lake Maiden*, until they dried up into little snail boogers she had to flick overboard. A long way down, like the dive Buster made when the railing gave way. That old coot always made her laugh, telling little jokes and saying he was wooing her, wanted her to be his girlfriend. And he brought her cherry lemon taffy from the boardwalk shops. And even that had a price.

> *"Come sit on Buster's lap. See if you can find which pocket I hid the taffy in. C'mon, search harder. Where's the taffy hidden? Keep looking.*
> *Give a yank on the knob. Maybe you'll find it there. Right there."*

Then Buster paid. That railing didn't just happen to snap. She had eventually figured that out. It seemed obvious once she was older. But who tampered with the railing was still a mystery. She'd probably never would know. Maybe someone took a hacksaw to a joint or whittled a bit with a jack knife…at that curve where Buster always leaned, chatting her up. He might as well have been groping.

Maybe someone had been looking out for her after all. Maybe.

Nattie drew a line with her finger in front of Silverfish Fred. It turned into a swoop and swirl as she leaned down to look Fred in the eye.

"What do you think, Fred the fancy slivership? No. Silvership. No silver. Fish. Silverfish.

Say that three times fast, fish-girl.

Fancy. Shelfishsilverish.

Maybe she had enough gin.

Fred must have ventured up from the cellar through the drainpipes. The cellar was where cases of booze were stored, she knew. The girls sometimes took guests own there to see the stockpiles and do some buckle-jingling and knee-knobbing. Or so they said. Maybe it was all talk. Maybe someone should bust the railing that was along the stairs to the cellar.

Where are all the sanctimonious henchmen when you need them?

Silverfish Fred should have stayed in the cellar. She corralled him into a circle fence made of ice dribble and a loose sequin thread she found dangling from her necklace.

"Are you playing with that thing? How disgusting," said Davis, pausing to watch her fortify the entrapment with another mildewed thread.

"Just humoring myself, passing time doling out prison terms and destinies for the lowly creatures of Anchors Away," she said with an exaggerated orator's tone. "Yes, here we have bottom dwellers in the tank of life. What tragic fate awaits this creature? He calls himself a fish, but is he really? Pretenses abound here at the bottom. Let's see, shall we?"

She poured the last swallow of her watery gin into the circle. The silverfish floated past the thread barrier. Free! . . . until Davis squished him with the heel of a whiskey bottle. Then Davis wiped the shiny smear away with his white rag. Not even a leg was left to brush to the floor.

"Well, so much for Fred. I didn't get to say goodbye." She fake-sulked.

"Goodbyes are for wussies," Davis said.

"And for chicken-hearted boiler room boys . . ." she mumbled.

Nattie sat up.

"Maybe I should wander a bit," she said, knowing Pat would be out of her office soon. Boss Lady was due for her strut-n-sweep, the usual walk around—

"Natalia!" shouted a man.

She turned.

Oh no. The Aquarium and coffee man. The sweetest—

"What are you doing here?" he asked, his eyes blinking quicky like they weren't working right. He couldn't believe them. "Of all the places to run into you—"

"Frank! I could say the same about you," she hugged herself, covering her bare shoulders as best she could, pulling her hair around her neck. "What are you doing here? I doubt they serve coffee. Or sell books. Or have exhibits on freshwater habitats. Do they?"

He chuckled, that good natured little laugh of his that she liked so much.

"Probably not. My buddy here, Gus, is getting himself hitched. So, a bunch of us from the Water Quality team and Tank Maintenance decided to show him a night on the town. Right, Gus?"

Frank pulled Gus out from behind him. Gus had a head as round as a pumpkin—and just as bald. He was also sweating buckets, like he was being accused and interrogated under a bright light.

"Umm, hello, ma'am," Gus said, his voice cracking like he was fourteen years old. Gus' attention was fully transfixed on her chest.

Nattie adjusted her necklace, patting the shells, making sure they were all in place.

"Darn necklace," she said. "Isn't it silly?"

"Well, that is one fancy necklace," said Gus, still staring. "Where'd you get something like that?" Gus tried to whistle, but Frank elbowed him.

"Natalia's studying marine biology, aren't you? That's how we met. I was on my lunch break and strolling among the new lake flora and fauna exhibit at the Aquarium. Freshwater crustaceans. You know, crayfish or other invertebrates belonging to the group called the Arthropoda. Really fascinating. Natalia knows all about such things. And then we had coffee . . . Now every other Thursday, we meet in the cafeteria . . . if she doesn't have a class, that is."

"Yes, I do love crustaceans," she said. "Just love them to pieces," she said, pointing to her necklace, shrugging her shoulders, feeling utterly stupid, flustered. She had liked this young man, in an innocent, lovely sort of way. He was so courteous and, well, different from most of the men she met. He didn't try to grab at her. No stupid jokes, either. Just the history of the aquarium and exhibits. And now, the gig would be up. Damn.

She tried backing up, putting some distance between her and Frank, hoping he might not notice the scales on her arms or how oddly she was dressed. The few times they met for coffee, she always wore a scarf, carefully spread over her tattoos.

She knew he wouldn't understand. Nice men never did.

Frank and Gus both looked perplexed, like someone was trying to play a joke on them. Frank squinted and blinked, his eyes darting around, looking for the exit or someone who could explain this goofy scene to him.

"I was just heading to the ladies' room, back this way, I think it is. I'm here with a girlfriend, too. She insisted we come. Twisted my arm," Nattie said.

"Oh?"

"Bye, Frank. Nice to see you. Congratulations, Gus. Good luck." She continued backing up toward the hall that led to the facilities. She could hear the flushing water and smell the dribbled pee.

And Pat's perfume.

Nattie stepped on Pat's sequined shoes, bumping into the Boss Lady as she came out of her office. Black sequins screamed. So did Nattie. So did Pat. So did crustaceans and silverfish and Davis who rushed to save spilled drinks and shattered glass as Nattie and Pat fell into each other.

It was a mess. And Frank saw it all. Gus too.

Nattie pulled herself up from the floor in time to see Frank suck in air, mouth open, eyes wide. Then the hurt rolled out. He looked like he had been socked in the gut.

"Nattie? What?" he mumbled.

"Will you watch where you are going, please!" Pat scolded. "And get back to work, dear," she said while trying to keep a smile on her face. Pat always smiled in front of paying patrons. But her gritted teeth and clenched jaw gave away her true feelings. Pat was furious.

Nattie apologized, fretted and promised to be more careful. When she collected herself, straightened her necklace, pushed her hair out of eyes, she realized both Frank and Gus were long gone.

Another one lost. He worked in the maintenance department at the aquarium seeing to water quality, temperature, filtration systems, circulation. It had been fun to listen to him rattle on and on about his job. She had told a small fib about what she did. She had always meant to get around to the truth. Someday. Maybe.

She plopped down on the stool. Davis wiped at the bar top in front of her. His rag brushed too close and made the shells on her necklace jingle, fragile edges clicking. He poked her, teasing, wiping at splashed whiskey that dripped into the tank top.

"You missed a spot," he said.

"Yeah, I guess I messed that up good."

She stiffened, pushing his hand away. She didn't need his help. She could louse up things all by herself.

"We had a bartender on the *Lake Maiden* everyone called 'Tender. It was years later when I realized that was short for bartender," she said to Davis, resting her chin on her hand. "I was stupid back then. Not anymore," she said.

"No one would mistake you for stupid, dear."

"He used to make me give him a kiss to get some of those maraschino cherries I loved so much. He called them pucker-ups."

She pursed her lips, her Devilish Red lip paint all moist and glistening. She smacked the air. Then slammed the bar top with her open hand. Invisible silverfishes ran. 'Tender wished he could swim. Ghost boiler room boys vanished. Buster flip flopped in his watery grave. Queenie bowed in deference to the new star attraction, and Captain-Father wished he had listened to the weather forecast.

She couldn't hold back the tears. Davis took the mug away. He had some decency after all.

"You know what happened to 'Tender? He's dead. Drowned. No one bothered to help him ashore when the water rushed in. No one—"

"Oh, geez Louise, cut it out. No one wants to hear about the big storm. Again. Suck it up, Fish."

"Mermaids aren't fish."

"Yeah. And sailors aren't dicks. Tell me some other made-up story. Go find a nice cute paying customer to talk to before it's stage time. Someone who won't mind that you are part fish and have scales and work for a living. There are real men out there who aren't afraid of some ink and a costume. Go find one. Go be your usual sarcastic saintly star of the lakeshore and stage that we all love—like we love bill collectors and board of health inspectors."

"I love you too, Davis, like I love foot fungus," she said, wiping her eyes.

"Glad we see eye to eye, both equally enthralled with each other and overflowing with mutual respect. Now go mingle, before I flick you with my towel." He waved his menacing white rag at her like it was a deadly weapon—laced with silverfish slime. She hated towel snaps on her ass, and Davis knew it, the jerk.

"You know I might have to settle for you," she warned, recovering her senses.

"The hell you will," said Flossie, coming up behind her. "You're a prude and you know it, Mermaid Maiden." She play-whacked Nattie's backside with the empty serving tray. "Under those shells, you're a Goody-Two-Shoes stuck in the good old days on Papa's fancy boat, waiting to be swept off your *tail!*"

Flossie broke out in a high-pitched giggle. Davis joined in, laughing at the stupid tail joke and shaking his head at the girl-squabble, the usual banter he had to endure night after night.

"What's so funny over here?" chimed in Anka, her large feather fans in hand, ready for the show. "I want to hear the joke. You two always leave me out of the fun." Her bottom lip quivered on cue.

Does she practice that in the mirror?

Viola appeared. Suddenly, this corner was crowded. "Now, girls, stop your squabbling," she said, always the big sister. She pulled everyone in for a hug-huddle, turning serious. "Ten minutes to show time. Has anyone made rent money yet?" she whispered into the circle. "Landlord promised to start selling peeps through the peephole, you know."

"Oh, Vi, who says he doesn't already? I get chills," said Flossie.

"It's early," said Anka. "Too early for extra dances. Maybe after the second show."

"I have to get into my costume," said Nattie. "Will one of you zip me up?"

"Maybe some of the sailor boys would like to help?" suggested Viola, raising an eyebrow in a question. "A table in the corner has been asking when the mermaid comes out. They're practically drooling. Those boys might pay to see the girl transform into a mermaid and all the breathtaking wiggles it takes."

"You don't have to, Nattie," Anka said. "I can sit on some laps after this next show."

"It's okay," Nattie said. "Bring them backstage. One memorable transformation, girl to fish, coming up."

"I'll tell them two bucks each."

They broke the huddle, Viola heading to the lucky table.

"But tell them no touching," Nattie called over her shoulder as she walked toward backstage, barely limping, swishing her butt back and forth, like a silverfish swimming up a drainpipe.

Silverfish Fred would be proud. Buster, too. And Mama, Burlesque Queen who died in the arms of her lover.

"Mermaid! Mermaid! Mermaid!" the audience chanted, thumping their tables in rhythm.

***

Four sailors stumbled through the dressing room curtain all at once. They filled the tiny room, stepping on her toes, bumping into each other, pinning her against the wall. She held the costume up high, protecting it. They smelled of beer, old socks, and hair oil lavishly applied. Viola was herding them, like a junkyard dog rounding up vermin.

"Welllll, hellllo, there, honey. We're here to help you get ready for the show," said one sailor, hat in hand, his huge yellow teeth showing in his horse-faced grin.

"I was expecting you darling boys. I've been waiting for you."

They hooted, cheered, and jeered like goblin children after candy.

"Okay, calm down. Behold the majestic artistry of . . ." Vi began, building up the drama.

Nattie tuned her out. Movement by the water tank caught her eye.

What the hell?

A woman hovered there, nudging at the tank's base, poking at the generator with her foot, inspecting the air hoses inch by inch. She wore a black lacey burlesque costume, the old-fashioned kind from the twenties, when flappers wore long sequined fringe and corsets with garters to hold up black fishnet stockings. She looked just like Nattie remembered her. She even had the long white gloves.

And there was that smell of Woolworth perfume, sweet like bubble bath and funeral flowers the day after.

"Queenie!"

"This contraption doesn't look safe. I don't trust it," the woman said, pulling back the curtain.

There was the tank. Nattie's tank. It made the tanks in Frank's aquarium look tiny.

The spotlight made it glimmer, water bubbles reflecting stage lights. Magical. Ten feet tall. Ten feet wide. Gallons and gallons of water. Huge. Sand and rocks at the bottom. Air was piped in through tiny tubes, fastened to green and gold plants along the back wall. *Pip-Pop. Pip-Pop.* A lulling fizz, like Seven-Up pouring from waterfalls.

Then, the bubbles stopped.

Silence.

Nattie held her breath.

The woman kicked the air compressor. Then kicked it again. Then once more, harder. It sputtered. It groaned. It smoked. Plumes of exhaust and spirit steam flew skyward in swirls as elegant as the flowing waves in Nattie's long hair, tangle free, and the billows of turquoise and magenta sparkles trailing behind her, cascading in ripples.

The girl swam, part fish. She was underwater, soaring, arching her back, stretching her arms toward the moonlight that kissed the water's surface, a pucker-up that was grander than grand. She didn't have to pretend she was something other than herself.

I am real. I breathe air. I breathe water. I am nothing. I am whole. I am me. I can be loved. I deserve to be loved.

The woman in black lace and white gloves was gone.

Queenie would be back. She always came back. Always annoying and nagging and never letting go of her grip on Nattie's lungs that breathed bubbles for a living.

Nattie was in her dressing room. Dry. Feet on the cement floor. Viola slapped at the men's groping hands. The noisy, panting sailor boys didn't stop. They closed in. Sucking up the air, their salty sweat dripping on Nattie's illustrated arms.

"Give us a little pucker up, baby."

'Tender!

CHAPTER 30

MARGRET leaned on the hostess stand, her bunions killing her almost as much as the wires holding her jaw in place. She couldn't keep her tongue from running over the wires and poking the gap where two molars used to be. She also had a mouthful of blood slobbers she hated to swallow, but spitting into a cup was so unladylike. Standing at the door, she had to put on a good act, make the tavern seem somewhat respectable —no matter how farfetched that might be. They couldn't afford to be put on the navy's Do Not Associate list.

She just hoped the caked-on makeup kept the sick purple green under her right eye hidden at least long enough for Mailman to come and go. He delivered messages from the downtown boys and picked up envelopes, and he was due in tonight for the monthly grease money, the arrogant ass. She hated to give him the satisfaction of seeing her like this. He was the one who'd arranged for her broken jaw, she suspected, payment for mouthing off to him on his last visit. Apparently telling Mailman to stick his delivery fee up his ass wasn't such a smart idea. Well, the reply message was received, loud and clear.

She figured the blue neon glow from the sign in the window helped cover up her colorful condition. "Anchors Away" flashed on and off in electric blue, casting the whole entrance in an odd, pulsing, underwater feel. They wanted the navy boys to feel at home. Really, the aim was to entice them in and make them spend their month's pay. Whether they felt at home hardly mattered, at least not to Margret. She'd been running this dive bar for the boss lady since Prohibition was repealed back in '33. She was far beyond caring what some sailor boys thought, as long as they paid their tabs and didn't break anything.

Margret tried rubbing her aching jaw, but that only made it worse. She motioned for Flossie to bring her another highball with a straw. That was about all that helped now that her magic pills had run out.

Flossie delivered, carrying her tall drink on a tray. She'd even put a cherry on top of the ice and a stir stick and napkin under it—very swanky, but a waste of inventory. Margret hoped Pat didn't see.

"Still bothering you, eh? Maybe you need to go back to Butcher for more pills. Or maybe it's time to get rid of the wires," Flossie said, leaning on the opposite side of the hostess stand and giving Margret an eyeful of cleavage. A wad of dollar bills was stuffed between the twin peaks. Margret hoped those were all tips, not cash that ought to be in the till drawer.

Skimming was rampant in seedy dive bars like this. One enterprising waitress could bust the place. Margret should know. She had been that kind of waitress at the old tavern in Hegewisch back in the day. She'd been so young. Hell, even Boss Lady, Pat, was young back then; voluptuous, too, with her signature red dresses. Now black sequin getups were more fitting of her mood—and the whole operation. There was a darkness to the business these days, not like the good old days when the G-men were the ones to fear. Now, the men running the booze racket unlocked a whole new world of treachery.

Margret started to grill Flossie on the wad of cash, but decided she didn't have the strength. Talking through wired teeth wasn't easy.

"How long are you supposed to be wired up like this? Seems like some bizarre torture treatment, if you ask me." Flossie shuddered.

"He said to come back in four weeks, not before. He's being watched. Heat's on him," Margret said. "He must have stitched up one gangster too many."

"Well, I don't know how you can wait another month. That's a long time to suck soup and highballs through a straw."

"That Polish healer, the one who comes 'round sometimes to check on Nattie, I might ask her for a twenty-five-cent miracle, if I see her." Margret licked her dried, cracked lips. "I could use a miracle."

"Well, pay your dollar for the mermaid's magic wish and maybe your healer will walk through the door. Wouldn't that be something?" Flossie laughed.

"That would be something, alright."

Halina didn't come around much these days. Halina and Pat were still feuding, it seemed. They didn't see eye-to-eye about the mermaid. It had all started that night of the wreck and just kept festering. The storm—

She shivered, suddenly ice cold, like the frigid water of the strait.

Margret saw her reflection in the window. Her agony was showing. Who was she fooling? All this talking was too much. She bent over and, for just a moment, she put her face down on the hostess stand. The cool surface, oak polished to a waxy shine, brought a fraction of relief. It wasn't nearly enough.

"Maybe we should track down that Polish healer for you, get you some of her magic medicine. Do you know how to find her?" Flossie asked, looking concerned.

"I could find her easily enough. I know where she lives. Avenue O. But I think hell would have to freeze over first for her to come around here." Margret sipped on her highball, washing down the iron-tasting blood in her mouth. "She's made enemies with the Salvatore organization."

"Well, that means half of Chicago," Flossie said, looking out the window like she was surveying the city and the Salvatore turf. She shook her head. "The woman must be crazier than I thought."

Margret nodded. That was enough. She didn't have the energy to explain to Flossie. It was complicated. And sad and it still made her mad to think of the lives lost. And blame being tossed around. Hell, storms happen all the time. Dying happens, too. People stop being useful and their time is up. Death sort of sneaks up and snatches them. Inevitable.

On the other hand, neglect could kill, too. Denial. Locked hatches. Not enough lifeboats. And greed. There was wrongdoing on that boat, no doubt. And the score still wasn't settled.

Vengeance is like a cesspool, growing fouler the more it steeps and stews.

Margret sniffed the humid air. The street smelled of trash, and runoff from the last rain was still backing up from the storm sewers. Rank.

She hugged herself. The stink was familiar. It reminded her of the hardware store, a filthy mattress caked with her own waste. She shouldn't have survived that backroom surgery when she was so young, and cheating death had a steep price. She would eventually have to pay.

Margret caught Flossie staring at her, looking doe-eyed and dopey. Curious?

Oh, how I could shock dear, sweet Flossie with the stories I could tell.

"Better get back to work before Pat comes out of the office and sees you loitering. Go on. I'll be fine." Margret shooed the waitress back into the Saturday night commotion. "Looks like table nine wants another round."

Flossie snapped up. "I'm coming, big boys!" she called to the group of ensigns who were waving their cute sailor-boy white hats around, trying to get some service. It was probably their first leave since being stationed here for training. They had the same doe-eyed and dopey look as Flossie.

Maybe it's youth.

It was time for the second show. Margret always knew when it was showtime, no matter how much booze—or pain pills she'd swallowed. The clock was inconspicuous among the jumble on the wall. Didn't need sailors to know how late it was—or how early. The rest of the wall was a mishmash of colors and words. Framed pictures of sailboats and lighthouses hid water damage from the leaking roof. A flyer for Sunny's Hearts and Arts Tattoo Salon was tacked near the cash register, so boys who were so inclined could jaunt over for some ink. Maybe an anchor. Or a mermaid.

Near the stage curtain, signs promoted the main attraction.

$1 HAVE A WISH GRANTED.

$2 BE MERMAID MESMERIZED

$3 MEET THE MERMAID IN PERSON

DON'T TAP ON THE GLASS.

Idiots always paid their dollars for the extras. And there was always someone tapping on the glass. Maybe they couldn't read. Or didn't care. Or the mermaid allure was too strong. Every show. Some fools just couldn't resist trying to get the mermaid's attention, like she was something special.

Margret was sick of it.

She put her head down on the hostess stand, wishing she could slip off into nothing.

CHAPTER 31

JINKS cringed when he saw the neon-blue sign for Anchors Away. He wanted nothing to do with a boat ever again. He had a strong aversion to the lake, too. He didn't even like to take baths, much to the frustration of every woman he met—or bought. He'd had a few try to return the Lincoln once they got a good whiff.

He was fine taking care of that business himself. Dames were almost as bad as boats. Both left a bad taste in his mouth.

This one wasn't a regular dame, though. He stood on the sidewalk, his legs wobbling with indecision as he argued with himself. Should he go in or not? The night was muggy, humidity hanging in the air. The wind off the lake seemed heavy with moisture. It pushed him toward the door.

APPEARING NIGHTLY: THE GREAT LAKES MERMAID.

SHE SWIMS. SHE DANCES. SHE GRANTS WISHES.

FROM HER UNDERSEA ENCHANTMENT BEHIND GLASS.

He had seen the showbill on the sidewalk, tossed like trash. A couple of size thirteen boot prints had mucked up the artsy drawing of a mermaid on a rock. But he could make out the address, which was all he really needed.

She'd be all grown up by now. Had she turned into the beauty he'd thought she would be? Or had her life gone down the crapper, too?

He wanted to know, but at the same time, he didn't. He couldn't have it both ways. It had taken him a couple weeks after he saw the flyer to work up the gumption to find the place. Now what?

"Hey J. Hey man, Stinky-Jinky, that you? What you doing up here? This aint your haunt."

Jinks froze and turned, covering his head with is arm, like he could hide. But Winslow was all over him, punching at his sleeve, arm around his shoulder, mouth up too close to his ear. Winslow was a stage man for one of the combos that played on the opposite end of the street—where the jazz still had soul.

"Yeah, it's me. Get off me, Winslow. I am walking here. I can walk here."

"The boys in the combo been looking for you, man."

"Let them look. My pockets are empty, man. Inventory drained."

"Not even some of those fancy ones? Sax-Moe likes those, man, you know. He can hit those high notes with those babies."

"No, I said. I can't help him. Or the boys. I have my own problems," said Jinks. He wiped his nose on his sleeve. And skittered to the edge of the sidewalk, out of the way of the crowds streaming past. Shoulders bumped his shoulders.

"You always got a problem, Jinky. Well, don't you come round the back door no more if you ain't bringing the merchandise. I ain't going let you listen for free if you ain't supplying."

"Alright, Winslow. I know. I know. I will see what I can do. Now git out of my way."

Winslow moved along, lost in the stream of bodies.

Jinks was between jobs so he was low on funding for his backdoor enterprise.

He could use some help, too.

Here he was, hunting a mermaid. All hyped up. His skin itched, needing a special scratch. He chewed on his thumbnail and his knuckles, sucking remnants of this and that out of the cracks in the callouses. That was good for something. It might get him through.

He paced outside the doorway of the navy bar, working up nerve. He felt out of place. The over abundance of youthful optimism exuding from the establishment was foreign and disgusting. He didn't belong.

He tried acting like he was waiting for his buddies. He would tag along with the next big group of pals who came in together, sort of blend in, scrunch down behind them, play it low key. No need to scream, *Hey, look at me, the one who stole the mermaid's buried jewels, lost them, and broke her tank, all in one night! Glad to see me?*

He thought he'd aim for a more subtle, incognito approach. Yeah, he was still clever that way. He had some brains left.

He wasn't counting on the sailors all wearing white. He stood out like a sore thumb. His brown shirt was crumpled and ringed with sweat stains.

It looked like he had slept in it, because he had. The flop house he was living in had vermin. It wasn't a good idea to sleep with no shirt. The beasties could nibble.

What the hell. He followed a group of jovial buddies in anyway. He needed a drink. And curiosity was eating at him.

Could it be her?

The boys were a noisy lot. They didn't seem to notice the extra head bobbing along behind them as they found a table. They were busy complaining about a course instructor that had it in for them. Training. It sounded like hell. And they didn't have the slightest idea how lucky they were.

The place wasn't crowded. Maybe because it was still early, or maybe Anchors Away wasn't the big hot spot for these fellas. Maybe the navy boys weren't as drawn to undersea enchantments as you'd think. Maybe mermaid was an acquired taste.

Jinks licked his lips. His stomach lurched, disgusted with his own thoughts. He wanted to spit out the sourness but was afraid someone would notice and not approve. He swallowed the bile rising in his throat.

There was an empty chair just behind the boys he'd followed in. It was against a wall, near the toilets. His undershirt's reek blended with the distinct piss scent coming from that direction. Seemed navy boys couldn't aim.

That's pretty funny. Funny as hell.

A blonde wearing a cute little sailor skirt with a square collar and a blue handkerchief around her neck came by. Her eyes matched the denim blue of her handkerchief, and with her bright red lipstick and matching red shoes, she looked very patriotic. He was tempted to salute or sing the national anthem. Or slap her silly. She looked too absurd to be allowed to exist. He was tempted to tell her, but once again, he resisted the urge. How noble of him. He deserved a medal, or at least a life better than this.

The waitress reminded him of those dancing girls on the *Lake Maiden* with their ridiculous pirate getups and long legs and fishnet stockings and their puckered-up lips painted red. Even as that horrible storm had snuck up on them and the damned ship was tossed around like it was a toy boat in a bathtub, those girls strutted around, showing off, brazen. Hussies. Not enough sense in their heads to be afraid of dying.

That was some night. He'd been sure they were all going to die. Dead sure. As sure as he was sure of his name.

"What will you have, mister?"

He ordered a beer, hoping he had enough cash in his pocket to pay for it. "Hey, I hear you have a mermaid act? When does she come out? Does she just come out on stage, walk around singing or something?" he asked.

She looked at him like he was crazy. Maybe she could see his thoughts. Maybe they were on his forehead.

"Mermaids don't just walk around. They swim," she answered with a hip cock and eye roll. She might have gotten an accidental whiff, too, which would account for her perplexed look.

"Well, when's the act?"

"Every hour. Next one is at eleven. Then midnight. Last one at two."

When she brought the beer a few minutes later, Jinks was leaning against the wall, trying to blend in with the blue and green waves painted on the plaster. The paint job looked like some third grader's art project.

Water. Waves. Blue. Green. Blue silky scarves hanging from wires,
making a wall that could strangle a person.

The beer was only so-so cold, but it still went down. He wished he had skipped the can of beans for dinner. They were gassing up, making him feel like a bloated beached whale. And this whale wasn't enjoying all the waves, blue and green, painted or not, up and down. Water.

Waves crashed at the hull. Sheets of rain beat at the deck with a fierce,
driving force. The sounds were deafening. The metal hull vibrated, the
waves hitting again and again and again. Unending. Relentless.

He didn't want to die. He crouched down low against the hull. The roar of waves filled his head, beating him down. Down. Up. Down.

"Did you lose something down there, mister? Drop something? Need help?"

Jinks looked up, startled. A waitress was talking to him? He was surprised to realize he was under a round table, the red tablecloth tented around him.

He jumped up and scrambled into a wooden chair, clearing his throat. "Oh, no. Found it. Dropped . . . something. Found it. My wallet. Got it. Thanks."

"Well, good. I was afraid you were trying to ditch me without paying or something," the blond waitress said, one hand on her hip, the other waving an empty tray around, like it could be a paddle. "You wouldn't do that, fella, would you? Cause Margret—see her over there?—she would take it out on me, you know."

"No, I wouldn't do that."

"Then let's go ahead and settle up now, okay? You pay your tab and call it a night? I think you've had enough."

"But I want to see the mermaid. Another beer. I'll have another."

"Hey," she said, locking eyes with him, her voice dropping an octave and finding some gravel to go with it. "Mister, don't make me call Syd. Don't make trouble for me. Or you. There's no storm here. No diving under tables and hollering about drowning."

"I didn't mean to. I have a problem. Water."

She smiled, like his predicament had a funny side to it.

"Well, Mr. Ding-dong, you came to the wrong bar. We got water. A tank full of it."

"Yeah, golly." He straightened himself up, fixing his collar, smoothing wrinkles. "I'm fine now. Really."

She brushed a smudge off his shoulder and patted it, suddenly friendly-like and mothering.

"Okay," she said, batting her eyelashes. "But stay off the floor, will you, huh? I'll bring you a beer. If you behave."

"Thank you . . . what's your name?"

"Flossie."

"Thank you, Flossie."

"Yeah, sure, honey," she said and bounced away, her flared skirt swinging back and forth.

Back and forth. Bobbing, up and down. Like tossing waves. Back . . . and . . . forth. Like a storm that was coming for him, to take him out to open water and toss him away, a soul to be lost in the endless surges falling to the bottom of the lake, miles deep. It would be ice cold at the bottom and black.

He couldn't do it. He smelled foul water. He heard the roar of wind. He had to escape. He fumbled in his pocket for some dollars. He found enough—he guessed—and left them on the table for Flossie to find.

He rushed toward the door, head down, concentrating on his feet.

Moving. Them. One. By one. To. The. Door.

He didn't want to drown.

He knew the woman at the door, Margret, from the doomed boat. She looked used up, a washrag that needed to be wrung out. He lurched toward her.

"Margret, we have to go. Now. We're all going down—"

"What the hell?" Margret pulled back and stared at him. "Jinks? No one is going down anywhere tonight." She was talking funny, like her teeth were glued shut.

"But I—"

She gestured to a big old boy with arms as thick as ham hocks. "Syd, help my old friend here to the sidewalk."

"Yes, ma'am."

"Go easy, though. He's had it rough."

"Just like all the others. These old losers are all the same." The beefy guy took Jinks by the arm and walked him to the shore, where there was no more storm and no more waves, thank God.

"Go home, buddy," Syd said. "Get your head right."

"Aye, aye," Jinks said. He saluted the big guy's backside. "Tell the mermaid that Jinks was here. And he has her crown! I have her crown! And her jewels. I took them. Tell her."

CHAPTER 32

NATTIE had an hour before the next show. Another show. Then another. They seemed to never end. She needed a break. Fighting off those sailors in her dressing room had rattled her resolve and put her on edge. Syd had to intervene, hauling their asses out when she and Viola started to scream. But what if Syd hadn't been there or hadn't heard them? She was so tired of skittering on the edge of chaos, teetering, about to fall.

She wanted out. She needed money to make a major change. She needed to get more serious about finding what was rightfully hers.

Nattie had been following clues for years, most ending in nothing but frustration. She knew it was a silly quest. But she had to find her stash of treasure and the crown from her father. They had vanished the night of the storm. The diamond jewelry she had pilfered from passengers was simply gone. Maybe the trinkets had been mopped up with the sand from her tank and the storm water. Maybe someone had pocketed them or they'd been washed overboard or they were buried in the muck that had settled on the poor boat's rusted decks. They could be in some corner, under tattered tablecloths and broken deck chairs abandoned on the boat. Or scattered among broken dishes, cracked glasses, and empty whiskey bottles.

On nights when she couldn't sleep, she stared at the ceiling, trying to imagine where they might be. Were they still worth something? Surely diamonds would still be valuable. Gold would endure. There was a chance. She needed them. She would buy a house on a beach and a boat for her father. No more spotlights for either of them, no more ridicule and pointing fingers. No more shame—or illustrious fame. They could both be anonymous, plain people, no different from the average father and daughter. How wonderful that would be. Peace.

The *Lake Maiden* was dry-docked now at the Calumet Shipyard and Dry Dock on the South Side, off the Chicago River. Ownership was tied up in legal issues and bank maneuverings that were dragging out, long past reason. At least the *Lake Maiden* hadn't been salvaged for scrap, a fate that would be unbearable for everyone who had loved that dang boat. Just thinking of that made her gut clench.

TANGLED IN WATER

Nattie had managed to get into the shipyard once, shortly after the trial. The bank's lawyers had felt sorry for her and arranged it. She fumbled that chance, though. She didn't have a firm plan. So stupid. She was still in her rollie chair back then. She'd managed to ditch the lawyer, saying she needed some time alone. But then she had looked up.

"Is that my boat? Are you sure? It can't be."
Out of water, with her hull exposed, the Lake Maiden looked bigger than she ever had docked in the lake.
The underside was unnatural, perverse, like seeing a priest in his underwear.
She stared. Poor boat. Poor thing. I'm so sorry.
She rolled her chair closer. Closer. She pushed herself up. Shuffle-step.
She could smell the rust, the old water, the chemical stink of paint eroding.
She's dying.
But how to get aboard? A ramp? It was blocked. Wood scaffolding was built around the boat.
Nattie tried. She climbed. Stumbled, her weak legs giving out. She crawled and climbed, clinging. She slid through narrow gaps, through the maze of wood beams and scaffolds, chains and pulleys, mechanisms that had hauled the boat here and kept her captive, a prisoner.
Nattie pulled herself higher with her arms, dragging wobbly legs that held her back like anchors. She found the hatchway. Don't look down. Don't look. You fool. Don't look down.
The deck was barren like a ghost town, nothing but silhouettes and shadows and half creatures that used to be functional: the stairs to the bridge, the smokestacks, the massive wheel that had once been the heart of the ship, rolling through the water, chomping waves, tossing them back over its shoulder.
"You! Girl! What are you doing? How did you get up there?"
A worker in dungarees and a red flannel shirt rolled up above

his elbows waved a giant flashlight like it was a club. He
stormed up the scaffolding.
Grabbed. Yanked at her like she was a ragdoll.
She scratched and fought, clawing at his muscled arms. They
were covered in tats: an anchor, a lighthouse, a mermaid.
He slapped her face.
She saw stars and blackness, night over the lake.

***

Sunny from the tattoo salon knew a man who claimed he could get Nattie into the shipyard, for a price. She was supposed to meet him tonight.

Sunny, a good friend, was always listening, alert for shipyard connections. She was watching for the man with an anchor, lighthouse and mermaid on a muscled bicep, too. Sunny got so many navy men and sailor types in her place that there was a chance the beefy guard might come in for a touch-up or a new addition. Sailors loved their ink.

Nattie had had a good share of near misses over the years. Something always went wrong. Tonight she was going to lock in details with this fella, make sure he could get her in. For real this time.

She rushed. At the top rim of the tank, she flipped her tail up to the wooden deck, a platform just big enough to sit on. She fumbled for the zipper and peeled the bottom portion of the costume off, leaving the shimmering fabrics draped over the rim, dripping into the tank. She toweled off her black tights and stepped into a skirt and flats from her locker. She wrapped her dripping hair in a scarf and pulled a sweater around her skimpy top, shells jingling.

She was at the back door when she heard Syd's heavy footsteps.

"Hey, Nattie, where you going? You got another show, you know," Syd said.

"I know, Syd. Don't worry, I'll be right back."

"Funny thing. I just tossed out a customer who said to give you a message. He said, 'Jinks has your crown.' How crazy is that?"

Nattie grabbed Syd's arm, her knees wobbling. "Crown? Where did he go?"

"Down Rush, toward the blues end of the street."

She ran, cutting through the bar, past customers, past Margret, and out the front door to the sidewalk.

> *"She's outgrown cute, that's all. She's not quite the seductress. She's got some developing to do."*

"Jinks!" she called. She darted among men on the sidewalk, searching for a face she remembered.

> *"I hear this combo is pretty good. They were playing at Dukes Downstairs on Rush Street—you know, where the cool cats jam."*
> *Jinks. I should have guessed.*

She didn't see him anywhere. She walked as far as she dared. Then turned back. She couldn't miss the next show.

But she would find him. One way or another, she was going to get what was rightfully hers.

She had it coming to her.

CHAPTER 33

MARGRET looked at the clock behind the bar and breathed a sigh of relief. It was only a few minutes before the midnight show. She was eager to get this night over with so she could collapse in bed and sleep.

The droopy velvet curtain, dark blue and moth mottled, was rustling, telling her the girls were taking their spots on the stage, getting ready. Riggs would be pulling the thick canvas cover from the tank about now. Sure enough, she caught a whiff of lake water, rocks, sand, grasses. They had made the tank look as natural as they could, hauling sand, water grasses, and wheelbarrows of rocks from the lake. She had to hand it to Pat for that. The boss lady didn't scrimp when she set up the place. But then something had changed. She'd run short of money, for one thing. The whiskey business, now that it was legal, just wasn't as lucrative as it used to be. A real shame.

Margret could use more ice for her jaw, but Flossie looked busy.

She'd try to tough it out a little longer, but the pain was radiating down her neck now, making it hard to hold her head steady. She searched for a position that didn't hurt. There wasn't one.

"This is it, Benny, I tell you. This is the place they was talking about," said an enthusiastic sailor in the doorway.

"Yeah, this is it. The place with the mermaid."

"No such thing as a mermaid, fellas. I'm from Maine. The coast of Maine. I would know."

"You're just a wet dishrag spoiling the fun, Stevens."

"C'mon, fellas. Look, the curtain's about to open."

The blue curtains were inching back, ropes squeaking on the pulleys. Music came from blue-painted box speakers at either side of the stage. Two musicians sat in chairs to the side, one playing an accordion, the other a clarinet. Their sounds were masked by the hoots and whistles of the men in front.

Two dancers strutted gracefully across the stage like long-legged herons picking their way along a shore, sure footed, perfectly balanced, moving in time to the flow of sounds around them. They waved large fans that looked like seagull wings crossed with clamshells, white and sparkly and ethereal. The women wore long white gloves and black stockings held up by lacy garters.

Behind them was the ten-foot-tall tank of water.

With a loud splash, the mermaid made her entrance. She swam into view, long blond hair billowing behind her. Her sequined costume glittered, catching bits of light as she arched her back in a graceful curve. Flowing around her were ribbons and strings and patches of fish netting that moved elegantly with her slow-motion swirls. Her tail swooshed gracefully, propelling her through the water, a magical sea creature.

The phonograph played a heavenly classical waltz with violins and a harp, while the two musicians added jazzy harmonies. The result was an odd battle of two styles, two worlds. The mermaid was caught in between.

She did circle-swishes in the center of the tank, her flowing tail cascading behind her like a mile-long train on a royal bridal gown, delicate yet enduring and timeless. The tail ended in two points, each perfectly pinprick sharp.

Hidden among the fabric green grasses and sea plants growing in the tank, among the rocks and sand, air tubes bubbled, cleverly disguised. She took a gulp of air from a small face mask without missing a beat to her routine. It happened so quickly, men in the audience wouldn't even notice.

She smiled and waved. She blew kisses.

She froze. In an odd, awkward pose, she hovered. Unmoving.

What the—

There wasn't supposed to be a pause in the choreography. No skipped beat for dramatic effect.

What's her problem now?

Margret started to get up. The girl was pointing an accusing finger at someone in the crowd. She missed the beat. And another beat. Five, six, seven, nothing.

C'mon.

The whole routine was off track.

Damn that woman.

Natalia hadn't changed a bit. She was still a royal pain, all the way from her tangled hair to her scaly tail. At least she wasn't as puny and misshaped as she had been when she was a kid. The nurse had done her

217

some good, Margret had to admit; Nattie had transformed from a mermaid to a Mermaid.

Too bad for her the change wasn't more substantial.

Margret had no time or inclination to feel sorry for the girl. There were worse jobs in this world, and the fact was, the girl was lucky to have any work. She owed Pat a lot for giving her a chance.

She had better get her act together.

Margret started toward the tank, waving at the mermaid. The dancing girls and the musicians seemed to have no idea the act was off sync. The lame-brain mermaid floated, frozen, staring at the audience like she saw a ghost.

Margret waved her arm like she was going to clobber Nattie with a club—or crack open the tank. Nattie jumped, startled. She made a big splash . . . and, got, back, on, track, six, seven, eight. Again, three, four, good, six . . .

Margret wasn't sure the audience had even noticed that something was off. They were the usual noisy bunch, full of crude, rude comments.

"Now, that's some good-looking tail I'd like to haul in. I could eat that all night."

"Open wide . . . Blow some bubbles my way, honey. One big blow right here."

"How can she spread her legs when she ain't got no legs, huh?"

Margret stopped at the bar, alternating between watching the tank and watching the crowd, looking for a face that may have spooked the mermaid. No one seemed particularly threatening or sinister.

But there was a redhead man with freckles and a slight built that looked vaguely familiar, something about the way he walked, like he was on a lilting ship and had been for a decade. But he looked disgusted, lips curled on the edge of a gag reflex, like he'd found a cockroach in his beer. Maybe he had. He rushed out the door.

"Davis, I'll have a whiskey," she said as loudly as she could through clenched teeth.

Davis made a note on a piece of paper for the books as if she'd be paying for this little job perk.

Fat chance of that, Bucko.

Syd strolled by, making his rounds and looking intimidating, his bald head reflecting neon colors from the window and classic whiskey tones of amber and gold from the bar

"Syd, did you see anyone in the audience who didn't look right? Someone or something spooked the mermaid, it seems."

"No, ma'am. Just the usual badass boys with their rooster strutting and stiffies. Squawking one minute, dirty heckling the next. The usual crowing." He did a little strut, wing flap, crotch thrust like he was a rooster showing off. He crowed. Apparently, he thought he was funny. He was wrong.

"Syd, keep your cock-a-doo-hoo to yourself. Just watch the crowd. Someone spooked her. We don't need another incident of her seeing ghosts, do we?"

"What's that, ma'am? Couldn't understand you," said Syd, rooster strutting some more, yucking it up with Davis, who thought this was hilarious. Maybe they were sampling the inventory, too.

Childish. Truly moronic.

"I'm so tired of this shitshow," she grumbled.

She didn't bother to tell the boss she was leaving. Pat could figure it out herself.

She went to the back room to get her bag and coat. She searched her bag hoping she might find a stray pain pill that was left. She searched corners, pockets, under her wallet, behind the snotty hanky and the business cards from men who were more than interesting. No pain pills.

Oh, God. Now what? I can't—

Then she remembered another line of treatment she could try. Sure, she could stoop that low. She'd crawl. She'd kiss his slimy ass. Or anything else.

She tried to give the cab driver the address, but he couldn't hear her through her clenched teeth. She pulled out a card and gave it to him, pointing to the address, a warehouse on the canal.

Eastern Sun Imports. Seymore Houseman, Proprietor.

CHAPTER 34

PAT sat in her office, the ledger opened on her desk, the page of numbers one big blur. Her eyes weren't focusing. Neither was her mind.

She fiddled with stray black sequins that had fallen on her desk pad. She lined them up like a sparkly caterpillar, winding across the green page, but they had nowhere to go, no purpose to serve in a caterpillar world—or on Rush Street. She thought about getting out a needle and thread and sewing them back on her dress hem. But what was the point? Another thread would just break and dribble more sequins. The dress was winning the battle. Who knew a dress could be so vengeful, conspiring, and vindictive? Plotting moves when she wasn't looking?

She rubbed the burn scars on her left arm, reminders of the whiskey bottle and kerosene lamp that had fallen at her feet when she was a kid, thanks to a drunkard father. The pink skin, mottled and stretched to translucence, itched when she was nervous. It itched often.

She returned to the numbers in the ledger, which were still taking a defiant stand, taunting. She wasn't stupid. She could figure out this mess. How could it be so hard to make a profit as a business on the up-and-up, no funny stuff on the side? She'd tried raising prices, but the stingy sailor boys just drank less. She'd tried watering the booze, but they bought one drink and moved on to the place down the street. She hired pretty girls, but they were a dime a dozen. Every bar had them, and in some places, they showed even more skin. G-strings and pasties were enough to keep the law out.

She was the only one with a mermaid gimmick, though. She'd thought it would be a bigger moneymaker. It ought to be, right?

When she invested in the tank and the equipment, she had big plans and big money she needed to spend from Antonio's coin shop. She'd been certain men would line up around the block to get a glimpse of the mermaid. Maybe her mermaid wasn't seductive enough. She wasn't very curvy. And she had that attitude. Whoever heard of a stuck-up mermaid?

Pat decided she would think about it tomorrow. She just needed to hold on for another hour, then she'd slip out the back door and up the fire escape to the small apartment upstairs. The place wasn't much, but it was comfortable enough, piles of floral pillows strategically scattered so she could prop up her legs and cushion her back.

Her legs ached terribly, especially her knees. Her ample proportions taxed her joints.

Her sister, the famed healer of Hegewisch, had told her many times that her exuberant size was hindering her walking—and her breathing. Yes, her asthma was getting worse, it seemed.

She was used to breathing through wet cement. When they were girls, her sister had taught her techniques to get her ragged breath under control, to find a rhythm. It was almost magical. It had saved her life several times. Sometimes she could still hear her sister's voice, so young but confident, as she tapped beats on Pat's heaving chest and waved foul-smelling tonics under her nose, making the world seem brighter as air returned in rhythmic dribbles.

> *Settle in God's magnificent lap. Feel his hand. His pulse. Your pulse.*
> *Your heartbeats are steady as rain. Hear the whisper. Air fills your lungs. One, two. Fills your heart. Air and goodness. Three, four.*

Her sister had a way about her, no doubt. But she also had a huge head, so big that it was amazing she could hold it up. It was all because Baba took a liking to her when she was a kid. Now the old Romani woman opened the window and yelled out directions from the afterlife, while Halina took the credit.

Pat put her head down on her desk, just to rest. She didn't like thinking about her sister. She didn't like admitting she needed help from the Great Healer of Hegewisch.

Years ago, she had sent for her sister from Ontario when she was in a desperate state. It was a stupid, last-ditch move, one she'd regretted ever since. She had been so worried about Jakub, the dear boy. And what did her sister do to help?

Nothing

Pat picked up a small frame from her desk. The boy in the picture. . .

"Stop squirming and let me fix your hair."

"Aw, Ma, stop it. The fellas are going to laugh."

"You want me to go give them a fist full of what for?"

"No. Just hurry up. Ooo. Did you spit on my hair?"

"Just where it sticks up. Here. It's our turn for the picture booth."

They had been at a street fair. There was a newfangled picture-taking booth where a man put your photo in a tin frame in just a few minutes. She talked Jakub into sitting with her on the small fold-down stool behind the little half curtain.

The picture was the last she had of him. He'd be in his twenties now. All grown up.

Flossie came in. Uninvited.

What happened to privacy? At least she came bearing gifts.

Flossie handed her a fresh cocktail. "Davis said to bring this to you. Said you were due." Pat set the frame down and took a sip of the highball. *Strong.* She shuddered as the drink warmed her throat.

Flossie picked up the frame, touched the boy's face. Her hand moved sensually, like he was a lover.

"Is this your boy?" Flossie asked. "He's might handsome."

Pat grabbed the frame and set it back down firmly.

"He was a good boy. Is a good boy. A young man, now."

"Where is he? Does he come visit his momma?"

"I haven't seen him in years. I'm not sure where he is," Pat said. Her voice sounded strange, like she had swallowed a mouthful of crackers. She threw back a couple gulps of the highball to wash down the crumb dust and guilt globs collecting around her tonsils.

Another gulp.

"Wasn't long after this picture was taken that he was sent away. Mr. Salvatore relocated him, as they like to say."

"Gee willikers," Flossie said, shaking her head, blond tangles bobbing. "Why'd he do that?"

"I don't know, Flossie. I suppose he didn't like Jakub being sickly. He had a bit of a heart problem is all. But Antonio couldn't tolerate any weakness, no matter how small."

"But he's your son."

"Yeah, well, that didn't matter, did it? Mr. Salvatore, the hotshot bootlegger, was more concerned about what the other cousins would think. And the rivals. It was all about reputation for bootleggers back then."

"Big bullies, if you ask me."

"No one asked you, Flossie. Just go back to work, will you please?"

"Yes, ma'am. But I'm still sorry about your boy. And I hope you find him."

Pat stood up. She didn't want more talking. "Me too," she said. "Me too."

When she had sent the message to her sister with the coin, she had been desperate, hoping Halina could help find Jakub. She had even sent that silly coin from the shop. The laundry operation. Antonio had been using it to convert whiskey money into legit money. It was the only thing of value she could get her hands on. Antonio watched the cash too closely.

Did Halina come? No. She got on the damned boat Antonio wanted to buy. The one with Miss Mimi with her French accent and French ass and sloppy French tongue kisses, and her French goose-down pillows doused with French perfume Antonio came home wearing, like a French whore hiding her French lover's French crotch stink behind gallons of dime-store French toilette water.

> "Polish women don't do that kind of knob sucking and back door slamming and slut strutting."
> "They lovely ones do. And smart ones. The ones who know what's expected of them."
> "If you want that that French trollop, then go. But don't bring that French flower stink back to my bed."
> "If I go now, I won't be back. Ever."
>
> "Go. We don't need you."
>
> "You can't stand on your own two feet. Neither can that pansy boy of yours."
> "He has a bad heart. What do you expect of him?"
>
> "I expect him to work. Earn his way."
>
> "Like you, a thieving crook? Heartless swindler?"
>
> "My dear, that's better than stupid or crazy. Like your family. All of them. Stupid Polacks."

"How dare you," she said and slapped his face.
He slapped her back.

She sighed. Thinking of Antonio made her tired. Thinking of Jakub made her heart hurt.

She looked at the clock. She just needed to babysit this sinking operation another hour, at least through the midnight show.

"Davis!" she yelled over her shoulder.

She waited, fiddling with sequins, watching the clock.

"Davis, where the hell are you?"

"He's busy right now. On the floor, picking up some teeth he lost, I think," said a strange voice. A large man filled the doorway, wiping traces of blood off his knuckles with a handkerchief.

"Who the hell are you?" She leaned back in her chair, stretching her arms, her "you bore me" act. She practiced it often. Had a nice flair-finish when she cracked her knuckles. Man-like.

The man didn't seem to care. He barged in, snazzy suit moving just right to show off a trim waist, arm muscles, thick thighs, and a bulge at his hip that was likely a weapon. Pistol? Revolver?

"I'm waiting. What do you want? Should I call Syd. He won't fall to the floor so easily."

"Pat, we're getting off on the wrong foot, I'm afraid." But he didn't look afraid at all. He looked uppity and cocksure of himself. He probably had a woman who called him handsome. She was right. But he was infringing on her territory.

"Times a ticking," she said, glancing at the clock. "I'm a busy woman."

"The Ontario boys asked me to pay you a visit. Just a courtesy call, as they say."

"The Ontario boys can take their courtesy call and shove it where the sun don't shine."

"You should take this visit more seriously. You should listen."

"Listen to what? You got something to say, say it."

"Don't make a mistake, Pat."

"Oh yeah? I don't think I need to listen to a damned thing the Ontario operation has to say. Ever again. Antonio is done. His Prohibition racket is done. We're done. I run a legitimate business now, and I don't need his

Ontario maple leaf sweet whiskey. There are some lovely gents in Kentucky who distill a nice barrel. So, get back on your high horse and skadoodle off."

"Not so fast, honey bunch," stranger said, slinking his way into her office, taking air that was rightfully hers and hers alone. She didn't want to share. There wasn't enough. She wheezed.

"Antonio's retiring. Settling debts. Cashing out. He wants the coin back. He's short on the total he needs to pay off accounts, and he figures the coin would put him right with his debtors." The stranger shrugged, as if he knew the story was somewhat silly.

Downright lame.

"And what puts him right with me? He owes me," she said, standing, pounding her chest. Sequins rattled.

"He might see it differently. This last transaction between you two would settle the score, he figures. He wants the Caesar coin from Madam Salvatore's Rare Coins, his little business venture you help float—and sink."

"I wasn't the one who thought of buying gold with whiskey money. And I certainly wasn't the one who pulled the plug on the laundry operation. I don't know what you're talking about."

"Of course you do."

"No, no, not really. I only remember Antonio cheating with that Quebec-Frenchie Mimi woman. Maybe she has the coin you're talking about."

"He knows you took it and had it delivered to your sister. Cousin Alfonzo was the messenger, before he croaked right on the street. Antonio knows. Now, he wants it."

"Well, good luck with that! Tell him I said so. Good luck. Good riddance. Good gravy and Good Lord Almighty. Now git. Time's up."

"I'll be back. You've got thirty days. Find it. Get it back. It can't have gone far. What would a crazy Polack nurse do with a coin worth a small fortune?"

"Wipe her ass with it? That's what my sister would say. She'd have absolutely no use for a gold coin. None."

"Good, then you can get it back."

She laughed, trying to cover the gurgle sounds in her throat and chest.

"Syd! Show this fool out," she managed to spit-scream. "He's not welcome here."

"So long, Pat. By the way, nice mermaid you have. How is the air compressor working? Everything in good working order? Would be a shame if there was an issue with her air supply one night when you were least expecting it. Wouldn't it?"

"Syd! Get your fat ass in here. Get this buffoon out of —"

Syd stormed in, a wooden billy club in one fist. Iron knuckles on the other. "Do you want him in the street, the lake, the hospital or morgue?"

"As far as you can throw him."

She swiveled in her chair, yawning a big, fake yawn. Nonchalant. Really, her heart was pumping and she could feel her chest constricting. She wheezed and rattled. She turned her face so no one could see the red creeping up her neck. She could feel the sweat beading on her forehead.

Don't pass out. Don't make a fool of yourself.

Davis rushed in, blood specks down the front of his white shirt, hand to his jaw, arriving late to a party. He made a big show of holding the door open so Syd could lead the cocky stranger out. He went without much protest. Syd would make sure he was gone, she knew.

Pat swallowed the last dibbles of her highball and handed Davis the empty glass.

"I'll have another," she said.

Then she looked in the desk drawer, rummaging among old papers, scraps, receipts, notes, plans for a better life. She might have a phone number for her sister scribbled somewhere. Maybe she could try calling that big, old, spirit-filled house where she lived with her wall of roots and seeds and dried herbs and pretentions of being a healer.

She didn't find a number.

Maybe a visit would be better than a call. It would be fun to tell Halina to her face how much she appreciated her sister's nothing-help. Worthless, help. Non-existing help in finding Jakub. And she could tell her to go to hell—after she returned the coin.

Her dumb ass sister better have it.

CHAPTER 35

NATTIE hung to the side of the pool, doing her kicking exercises as she'd been instructed. She was supposed to be counting, but she lost track somewhere in the thirties and just kept going. She figured she would know when she'd had enough. Usually, one hundred kicks each leg was her max, which was pretty good, considering that when she started the work with Halina years ago, she was lucky to manage ten kicks before the cramps started in.

Halina was sitting on a lounge chair at the side of the park pool, smoking to Nattie's rhythm. One puff for every ten kicks. One exhale for three kicks. Pause for ten kicks. Nattie wondered if she was doing it deliberately. Probably not. Halina wasn't the kind to count. Precision just happened, if it was meant to be.

All winter they went to the German Athenaeum Club's indoor pool. Halina's husband, Theo, was a member. They pretended to be German like him. But when they tried talking with a German accent, they could barely keep from laughing. Nearly got them thrown out a few times. Theo had to come and smooth things out. He was a good man. Didn't put up a fuss at all when she moved in. Thank God.

Today the park was crowded. Noisy children splashed, enjoying the reprieve from the heat. Nattie enjoyed it too, the break from Anchors Away was always refreshing—even if Halina worked her to death.

Halina never got in the water. She didn't want anyone to see her feet, she said, and smelling chlorine gave her a sore throat. But still, she met Nattie at the pool once a week.

When they first started the swimming regimen, it had been three days a week, mixed in with other treatments of tonics and stretches. Nattie had no idea which of the treatments worked, so she kept up with them all, even the sleeping with oven-warmed bricks, a saucer of ammonia under her bed and her legs propped up on a sack of potatoes—supposedly for improving circulation.

"What number are you up to? Are you counting or just showing off?" Nurse barked from the sidelines, shouting to be heard over the noise of the rambunctious children in the pool. "Are you trying to break a record or waste time so you don't have to do the squats? Which is it?"

Her voice sounded hoarse. She had been shouting for hours, along with smoking and drinking from a large jar of dandelion-cucumber-dill-something that looked green and disgusting. Nattie had refused to try a sip. It smelled like pickles.

"You caught me. I was hoping we'd run out of time and I wouldn't have to do the evil squats—or lunges." Nattie looked up to the clock, wondering why time was creeping so slowly today. Maybe the woman was moving back the minute hand. Nattie wouldn't be surprised.

"I said ten more leg kicks. You can do that. Come on, lazy girl. Kick like a mule."

"I'm not a mule." She wiped sweat from her forehead. Halina's attic was hot.

"You're stubborn like one. Stop stalling. Kick."

"The stupid can is too heavy. I can't kick with it tied on so tight."

"Well, kick it off. Go ahead. Kick until the can comes off."

Nattie tried again. Her muscles burned. "I can't, I tell you."

"I dare you."

Nattie's head burst into colors. Fire pulsed in her limbs.

"You dare me, crazy woman? Really? How dare you! I am sick of these made-up exercises you invent to torture me."

Nurse got up from her stool and kneeled on the floor, nose-to nose with Nattie on the floor.

"Yes. I. Dare. You. I double-dog dare you," Halina snarled, her voice was barely more than a whisper. Her black eyes sizzled loudly. Nattie heard flames cackle like an old woman's laugh.

The open window slammed shut.

"Or what?" Nattie's voice was steady like a ship through calm waters.

"Or else," a voice in the attic rafters said.

"C'mon you can do it," a young soldier standing in the corner said.

His hands were bandaged. He had no eyes.

Nattie heard the windowpane crack.

A chill ran down her back, her curved spine stretched, she reached, muscles flowing like water and gathering strength like a rushing current.

She lifted her leg, the can tied around her ankle was light as a feather.

Nurse had been known to enlist the help of spirits now and then. Nattie didn't usually mind the conspiracies between astral planes, but today she had a stop to make before she went to work. She couldn't spend all day at the pool.

"Fine, fine. If you don't want to walk anymore and want to go back to being Gimp Girl, that's fine with me. You decide," Halina said, turning her back to the pool. "I'll go home and cook for my husband, who appreciates my efforts."

"Don't say that. I want the full-blown Nurse Halina treatment. I really do. But I'm ready for the rubdown. Let's do that next, okay?"

Nurse got up from the lounge chair and put down some towels so Nattie could spread out, facedown, water dripping, her tangled hair hanging down her back. Nurse helped towel off her legs and started rubbing the tingly white liniment oil into the muscles of her calves and ankles. The women in the next lounge chairs got up and moved, making horrid faces and pinching their noses.

"Sorry . . ." Nattie made a feeble finger-wave goodbye, childlike. "I know it stinks, but it helps. Really, I swear it does," she called after them. The women just glared. Their uppity attitudes reminded Nattie of the hoity-toity Gold Coast women on the *Lake Maiden*.

"Oh, don't talk to them. They're just jealous," Halina said. "Ignore them."

Nattie pulled her striped beach cover-up tighter around her shoulders. "It's a good thing they didn't see my newest fancy scales, huh? Then they'd really be jealous." Her newest tattoos climbed up the left side of her neck, fading off behind her ear. Mysterious.

"Jealous of that garbage on your neck?" Halina shook her head.

"It's not garbage. It's art."

"I don't call that art. I don't understand why you want to deface yourself like that. Don't you have enough ink on you? Why do more? What Mimi did when you were a child was bad enough. Now you add more lines?"

"Just get in your chair. I'll push."

"Where are we going, Mimi?"

"To visit my friend Sunny."

SUNNY'S HEARTS AND ARTS TATTOO SALON

She squirmed in the seat, trying to push away the tiny woman's hands.

Mimi pinned back Nattie's arms and held her still.

The pain kept coming, line after line. Curves connected with curves and connected again, linked like chains, never-ending.

Nattie shrugged. "It helps sell the illusion. If I'm going to be a mermaid, I need to do it right. I deserve to be the best freak I can be. All in."

Halina reached for more liniment and spread it in long strokes over smooth skin and legs that were almost normal, almost straight. "This isn't who you are. It's what you do. Have you not learned anything? Don't you think more of yourself?" She squeezed Nattie's calves harder, kneading the muscles like bread dough. She dug her knuckles in—

"Ouch!"

"What? You can't take authentic leg massaging? I thought you wanted to do it right. All in."

"That was angry massaging, not authentic. What's wrong?"

"You! You tire me. You cheapen what you do, trying to further the lie. And that cheapens what I do. I don't like that. I thought you knew better. I thought you were smarter. I went along with you playing mermaid when you were grown up because it was a job. I didn't know you would take it too far. More tattoos—defacing your body that I worked so hard to heal. I don't like it."

Nattie rolled over so she could look Halina in the face. The woman was taking her protective nature too far. Who was she to judge? All because she had some ink work done on her neck, now Halina disapproved?

"I haven't done anything wrong. I can do what I want," Nattie snapped. "It's my decision. I didn't invent this game. I'm just playing the hand dealt to me, and playing it my way."

"I know exactly what you're doing, and that's why I'm mad. You gave up on the real Nattie. You're betting on the fish-girl with scales up her neck. The neck God gave you was perfect. Now it's ruined. Dirty. You did this to yourself, that's what disgusts me. You should be ashamed."

Nattie shivered from the chill of Halina's words. Disgust? Her eyes welled up with tears, but she refused to cry. "I haven't been perfect for a very long time," she whisper-snarled between her gritted teeth. "I am used, secondhand merchandise, tainted by all those men, their eyes and their hands. And God doesn't give a shit about my neck. So why should you?"

"Just go. Go now. Enough today. Get dressed and go. I'm done working on your legs." Halina gathered her bottles of liniments and oils and returned them to her well-worn satchel. She looked old. When did she get those wrinkles around her eyes? Were her hands shaking? Was she sniffing?

Nattie had never seen Halina cry. She hadn't thought it was possible.

She sighed. She was no longer a child. She had the right to make this decision about her appearance, what she wore or didn't wear, or what lavender and teal and magenta inks she had etched into her skin in perfect rows of scallops.

She sat up, grabbed her towels, and ran to the changing room, limping slightly. She didn't say goodbye. She didn't wave over her shoulder like usual. She didn't try to explain, because she couldn't.

***

Sunny's Hearts and Arts Tattoo Salon was a hole-in-the-wall at one end of Rush Street. It would be easy to miss if not for the throng of sailors gathered around the door all night. They waited outside for their turn, sharing a single dangling lightbulb and a pie-shaped swatch of light with a handful of moths. A small nondescript sign hung in the window, black letters on white, not a single flourish or curlicue, not even a heart or sun to pay homage to the name. Sunny didn't believe in unnecessary frills of any kind, and she was too humble to promote her work. The funny part: her modesty wasn't an act. Her broken Chinese accent was.

She was petite, the size, shape, and demeaner that her customers expected of a Chinese woman, with black, bluntly chopped hair and bangs. She dressed the part, too, all the way down to little white cotton socks and black cloth shoes with a strap and button. For the sailors, she spoke broken English.

To her friend Nattie, she spoke like a salty deck hand, all bluster and bravado, plenty of profanities thrown in for good measure. Her English was perfect, taught by Polish nuns who considered improperly conjugated verbs and misplaced prepositions to be blasphemy.

The salon was open, but business was slow in the afternoon. Men needed the refuge of darkness to bolster their tattoo ambitions. Most were too chicken for daylight commitments that couldn't be undone. The place was small, the entrance dimly lit and cluttered with scrapbooks of designs, sketches, and photographs of patrons showing off their finished tats. They always looked like happy customers despite firmly set jaws and pursed, never-smiling lips.

A couple of men in sailor uniforms paced in the entryway, walking the walls, looking and waiting, pretending to be picking out their designs from the hundreds of curled, discolored samples tacked to the walls.

A doorway with long strings of beads sectioned off the main salon where the work happened. Nattie pulled back the beads and peeked in. Sunny had a sailor in the chair. Ironically, he was getting a mermaid on his arm. His mermaid sat on a rock, bare chested, well-endowed, and curvaceous. She looked nothing like Nattie. Well, she had the same hairstyle: long and flowing.

The second chair was full, too. Rodney was finishing a classic blue anchor on a big man's shoulder. Sunny's much younger brother and protégé, Rodney, was dressed like a banker, in a plaid suit with a vest and a pocket watch, its gold chain hanging in a graceful loop.

Nattie wasn't up for waiting. She went through the beads, like passing into a different world.

> *She pushed through the silk scarves dangling down, sectioning off the dressing room. She held them to her face. Everything was blue and green, including the pearls the man held out and draped over her shoulders. His fingers groped in her hair, his hand lingering on that intimate place behind her ear where her hair became her neck.*

"No one will see us here. You can show me how this outfit works."

Sunny looked up from her work. Their eyes connected. Sunny nodded and smiled for a fraction of a second before she seemed to remember she was mad.

Nattie expected the cold shoulder. She deserved it. She waved anyway, trying to look innocent, a far reach. "Hi, Sunny. It's your favorite repeat customer here. I thought maybe I could get another row of scales added."

"Really? You show up today, out of the blue? You're just a few hours late."

"I know I missed the meeting. Something important came up. I couldn't get here because—"

"I can always find time for you, dear. But are you so considerate? No."

"Seriously, Sunny, everyone knows mermaids are timeless, enchanted creatures not bound by earthly hours," Nattie teased, trying to get her friend to laugh.

"You're full of bullshit; that's all, nothing more."

"Alas, I am found out, my ruse uncovered," said Nattie, her hand to her forehead in feigned melodrama fitting of the stage. Maybe she was just like her mother, after all.

The man in the chair laughed.

Sunny shoved Nattie into the wall and whispered to her, so the other customers couldn't hear. "Why didn't you show? He was here, and you weren't. He wasn't happy. I arranged a meeting, and you skipped it? You made me look bad."

Nattie whispered back, "Someone came in the Anchors Away. I ended up chasing him down Rush, trying to catch up to him. He got away, though."

Sunny grunted and returned to the customer in her chair, her back to Nattie.

The sound of ink being punched into skin was deafening. No one spoke. Nattie leaned against the wall, watching, rubbing her arms, imagining the ink mixing with her blood.

An eon later, Sunny finished the mermaid masterpiece on the sailor's beefy arm. Nattie admired the highly detailed image as the sailor got up. It had turned out truly lovely.

He returned the appreciative stare. "I've seen your show," he said, acting like a smitten admirer, unsure what to say. He asked her to autograph his arm. Sunny wouldn't allow it, saying it would mess up her hard work.

"Come by and see me tonight. I have all new choreography," Nattie told him. "I could offer a mermaid wish just for you, big fella." She gave her best coy smirk and eyelid flutters. Maybe this one would take the bait.

He left, promising to drop in with his pals.

"Can you make me look like that?" she asked Sunny, nodding in the direction of the sailor's mermaid.

"Like a sailor with a hard-on?"

"No, like the mermaid on his arm, silly."

"No, of course not. You're far too skinny. Who ever heard of a skinny-as-a-stick mermaid?" Sunny motioned for Nattie to take the chair.

Nattie's leg buckled and she stumbled, falling into Rodney, jostling him.

"Hey, be careful," Rodney said. "I'm doing delicate work here."

"Sorry," Nattie said as she recovered her footing. Trying to be more graceful, she sat down and leaned back in the chair, hands in her pockets.

Rodney didn't suspect a thing.

She figured the watch and fob might be good for a twenty. She'd buy some groceries. She was tired of eating peanuts from the bar between shows.

CHAPTER 36

HALINA woke up with a headache. She had tossed and turned all night, plagued by dreams she couldn't remember but she knew were bad. Her jaw muscles hurt from clenching and grinding her teeth, and her legs were tired like she'd been kicking and running. The bed linen was wadded up in a ball. Theo was gone already, left for the mill. She hoped she hadn't kept him awake. He was grouchy if he didn't sleep well. One grouch in the family was enough.

Halina knew she'd been overly cross at Natalia yesterday, and she wasn't sure why. She just hated those tattoos. The girl shouldn't be defacing herself like that. It was bad enough how that Frenchie woman forced her to be permanently marred when she young, but for her to take it up again now was absurd. It made Halina mad. She realized she was probably a little bit hurt, too.

She sat in her kitchen trying not to think of Nattie. She stared at the red walls. The color vibrated. The walls were very Polish. Poles loved their red. She had hated these walls for a long time but knew she couldn't paint them herself. What did she know about painting? Not a thing. The fumes would be too much for her. She didn't dare ask Theo. He was still perturbed from the last project she gave him to do—the henhouse fiasco.

It wasn't her fault that the stupid chickens had skittered into the road while he was replacing the chicken wire fence. The fact was, if he had first shut them inside the coop, like she'd suggested, there wouldn't have been a problem. He could have put up the nice new pickets, painted them, *then* removed the chicken wire.

He said he didn't need a boss lady.

Boss lady.

Ma had been like that. Always the boss, in charge, sassing everyone around and slinging orders left and right while she reigned over the grill at The Corner, the tavern in old downtown Hegewisch. Prohibition couldn't interrupt that neighborhood cornerstone, nor could it interfere with Ma's rule over the kitchen business. She had been one headstrong, fierce woman until the weight on her shoulders became too much. There's only so much guilt and regret a human heart can bear.

Maybe I could hire someone to paint the walls?

Then again, money was awfully tight right now. Theo would put up a fuss over the money. His German temper could get riled up over her spending. He was so afraid of being broke. That was a big black brooding cloud that always hung over his head, reminding him of what could happen. Everything could be lost. That was how he'd come to Chicago as a young man. His family's Nebraska farm had turned to dust and locusts. He never could get that bitter taste of dust out of his mouth, it seemed.

So, hiring someone to paint was out. She wasn't ready to give up the idea, though. Something would come to her. Had to, because all this red on the walls was closing in, making her nuts.

"Argh!" She let out a little half scream, but there was no one to hear, no one to come running to see what her problem was, offer condolences, or try to help. She was alone in this fight.

She reached for her cigarettes and one of the stick matches usually reserved for lighting the stove. They were in a Ball jar on the shelf, the red tips matching the red walls. The rest of the shelf was empty. The absence of her roots and powders and seeds and crushed petals and bark was an ache she still wasn't over. The empty shelves were a tribute and a heartache, deep and dark.

She only made liniments for Nattie now. And maybe it was time to stop that, too. Nattie was grown up and ungrateful and had ideas of her own.

Halina went outside, letting the screen door bang shut behind her. The August heat was oppressive; the thick, humid air was hard to breathe. It wasn't quite ten o'clock and already the sun was intense, determined to bake the garden and fry the petunias she had planted. Even the peach tree, usually defiant of all weather conditions, looked droopy and tired of battling the heatwave.

She and the tree had been through a lot together.

"Hello, tree," she said. "How you doing?"

Tree didn't answer. A tin pail next to the trunk held her clippers and a small trowel and the sprayer nozzle for the hose. She flipped the pail over and sat down on it to finish her cigarette in the shade. Butts were scattered among the tree roots. She smoked here a lot. The tree seldom complained, usually happy for the company, even if she did leave her butts scattered at its feet like a lazy ass. She picked them up and dropped them in the rusted two-pound Hills Bros coffee can, her ashtray. A few had red lipstick on the filter. Those were old ones. She didn't wear that stuff much these days.

She didn't dress up or go out, except to Jerezana's for groceries and to meet Nattie for her weekly swimming, stretches, and rubdowns. Didn't even do church much, only when the need to complain and rant got the best of her. She figured God would listen. He didn't seem to mind her raving about her side of things and the injustice of all the accusations and the blame she was carrying around. He might even believe her.

She wondered what He thought of Nattie's tattoos. He couldn't be a fan.

She felt a tap on her shoulder and turned quickly. No one was there. She stood up, knocking the tin pail over. As she bent over to put her shovel and other gardening supplies back in it, she felt another double tap on her backside.

She turned. Nothing.

She walked around the tree. Nothing.

Finally, she thought to look up, half expecting God to hand down a tablet with his position on tattoos.

It wasn't Him.

"Well, good morning, Mr. Michael. What are you doing in my tree? And what are you doing poking at me with that stick?"

"I wanted you to notice me," he said. The boy, seven or eight years old, was perched on a low-hanging limb, tweed hat down across his eyebrows. His chubby little-boy cheeks were red and sweaty from the heat. He was missing a couple more teeth since last week. The gaps in his mouth made him look silly—and adorable. It was hard to resist scooping the kid up and hugging him until he hollered.

"You could have just said something. You didn't need to poke me."

"I didn't want to scare you. I didn't want you to put a hex on me."

"Well, good thinking. Stick poking. That's always safer than talking, I suppose."

"It is if it's a good stick."

"Oh, I see. So, this is a good stick? You think?"

"Yep, I've been breaking it in and teaching it for near a week now. Ain't let me down yet."

"Does your mother know you're in a neighbor's yard and neighbor's tree, poking at them with a stick—even if it is a good stick?"

"Not exactly. But she don't care none. She's baking. She told me to stay out of her way."

"I see. Well, get down from there before you fall and hurt yourself and I get blamed for that too."

"I don't want to get down. You've got ghosts down there under your tree. I'm gonna stay up here where they can't get me."

"First off, my ghosts sleep during the day. They only come out at night. And second, if they wanted to get you, they could get you in a tree. But why would they want to get you? You're not exactly big enough to eat."

They argued about whether he was big enough to be eaten or not until Halina ran out of patience and humor. Then she simply reached up, grabbed a dangling leg, and pulled him down.

He was heavier than she anticipated, and they both landed on the ground. She cushioned the fall for the boy, thank God, but she landed in a pile of rotten peaches.

"Now, look at what you made me do," she said to the boy.

"It wasn't me. It was the tree."

"I think you're awfully quick to blame someone else when you ought to take responsibility."

A lecture on that topic wasn't much use. The boy was off to the chicken coop. And she had a soiled dress to contend with.

"Hey, Jakub, be careful. Don't poke at the chickens with that stick. They'll peck you back," she said.

"Who's Jakub?" he asked. "I'm not Jakub."

She shook her head. Jakub had been such a mischievous boy, like this one. "Sorry, kiddo. The wrong name slipped out. I know you're not Jakub. Jakub was my nephew. He got hurt when he was about your age, maybe a little older."

"How'd he get hurt? Did he fall out of your tree?" His curiosity diverted his attention from the chickens. He looked eager to hear about a gruesome fight.

"Nope, he was in a fight with some bullies much older than him, right in front of the churchyard. He was running, took a running leap at the bully. The problem was, that other fella, Janusz, was in front of a fence. One of those old-time iron fences with pointy barbs sticking up. Janusz moved. Jakub landed on the fence. It punctured his chest. Put a nice big hole in his chest next to his heart."

Michael leaned on his stick and squinted at Halina. "That stinks," he said.

"Yep, it did, for sure. Stank to high heaven and then some."

"So what happened?"

"I saved his life, that's what happened," she said. "I sewed him. Treated him. For days. Sat by his bed and saw to him. I didn't give up. Even when the fever came . . ."

She found herself crying, tears streaming down her face as she thought of the horror of those days, not knowing if Jakub would live or die as she treated him. He had needed so much stitching. The puncture was so deep.

> *"He needs to go to the hospital. He needs a doctor."*
> *"He won't last that long. He'll bleed out before we get him there."*
> *"Do something."*
> *"Fetch my satchel. Carry him inside. Boil water. Clean sheets. I'll need more white cotton thread . . ."*

She had been so afraid to move him, even after she got him stabilized. She thought they were out of the woods, though, past the worst of it. Until Sister Beatrice got on her high horse about her tactics.

> *Candles, one in each of the four directions: western sea, northern wind, eastern light, southern warmth. Call the ancestors before us, those strong with healing and powers to guide . . .*

The nun called it blasphemy. Of course, it wasn't. It was just Gypsy talk. She had learned her craft from Baba, who had learned it traveling with the Romani in their brightly painted wagons as they crisscrossed southern Poland, long before the partitions and the Great War.

It was just their way, and there wasn't anything wrong with it that she could see. Tradition. She kept God and the Holy Mother in the picture too. A little wooden Madonna in the center of the circle, priest-blessed holy water, anointed oils. She prayed. Oh, how she had prayed for the boy and for guidance on how to treat him.

"Hey, what's wrong? What did I do wrong? You mad at me?" asked Michael, backing away, like he was suddenly worried he had crossed her.

"Hmm?" Halina answered, startled by the boy's concern.

"I was just gonna see your chickens. But I won't if that makes you mad. Or sad. Or if it makes the ghosts come out."

"Nope. My ghosts are all busy right now. They're on a boat milling over other mistakes I made. Hang on, I'll get the chicken feed and you can feed the chickens for me. But you can't let them out of the coop. Promise me you'll be careful."

***

It was long past noon, and she was still chasing hens, trying to get them back in the damned coop. She was about to give up on the last two little banties. They were fast little buggers, and smart, considering they had pea-sized brains. Once they had a taste of freedom, they wanted nothing to do with being fenced in.

> *"I can do what I want now. It's my decision. I didn't invent this game.*
> *I'm just playing the hand dealt to me and playing it my way."*

"Well, just go off into the road, get run over if you want. See if I care," she yelled to them. Then she thumbed her nose at them for added insult.

She had sent Michael home after she realized he was no help with wrangling loose hens. His arm-flapping and mouth-yacking did more scaring than rounding up. Besides, he asked too many questions. Every other question was about ghosts.

She'd had enough. She was hot and sweaty, and now she was behind on the housework.

Worse than that, though, she was mad. She had already been mad about Nattie's show of disrespect yesterday. But now, thinking about Jakub and his injury—and the unfair, misplaced blame—had made things worse. She belched, bitter bile rising in her throat. The turmoil of memories was making her digestive tract squeeze and clench, spasm and misbehave in a rude display of gas bubbles that had to find a way out, north or south. It was a good thing she had sent the boy home. He'd be laughing at her, then telling the whole neighborhood about the crazy healer with a bad case of the winds.

TANGLED IN WATER

"Do you have some peptide for my mother-in-law's bowel winds?"

She wondered what had happened to the little weasel man on the boat with his stupid password phrase to buy his vials of poppy juice. What was his name? Seymore? She wondered what had happened to all of them. She'd kept track of the captain and his sailor-lieutenant, Jenkins, through Natalia. But she knew very little about any of the others from that last excursion on the lake. The storm had come on so suddenly, and it got worse as they came up to Mackinaw Strait.

> *The boat pitched. Lunged. Up and down. Jagged and jarring lurches.*
> *With each plunge down, her stomach flipped. Outside the captain's quarters, voices rose, a chaos of sounds. The girl, in her father's bed, moaned, tossing, trying to surface from her unconscious state.*
> *Halina went to the cabin door. A few yards away, the bridge was crowded with men in white uniforms shouting orders. She could see them through the windows, hear voices carry over the roar of waves and wind. Damage to the hull. Taking on water. Mayday. Harbor.*
> *Coast guard. Evacuate.*
> *Inventory. Stow inventory. Toss inventory. Just get rid of it.*
> *She heard bits and pieces of words, but they were garbled and disjointed. They made no sense. She knew she had to get this unconscious girl off the boat. She would need help. "You, sailor, who can help me with the captain's daughter?"*
> *"Stay in the captain's bunk. It's safe. It's the lower levels at risk. I'll be back for you."*

That sailor had never come back to help, but she'd managed to get the girl off the boat. Not everyone was so lucky. Men in the boiler room, a bartender, and those two bankers . . .

She thought of Jedediah and his nephew, Silas. The hole in his gut had just been too much, bowels leaking blood and acids and poisons.

That desperate effort to use a bit of hairnet to help hold him together could have worked, she was sure. When she left him, he was showing signs of coming through. She'd thought he had a chance. But something went wrong, apparently.

She could still see him: White frost on his brown skin, his open mouth, his open eyes, eyelashes crusted in ice crystals. He was dead to this world, in the *Lake Maiden*'s freezer, slabs of meat hanging from hooks around him.

She shivered.

The sun was high in the sky, a hot August day, yet she felt a cold chill. She saw her own breath in front of her face, like it was the middle of January. Her hands went numb from the cold. Her teeth chattered. Breathing hurt as icy air pierced her lungs like needles.

She looked around.

"Where are you? What do you want?"

The chickens clucked and flapped their wings, making a ruckus like a fox was in the henhouse. It wasn't a fox, though, she was certain.

She knew what it was. Who it was. And she wasn't about to be intimidated by any old lady, especially one that had been dead twenty years.

"Baba, leave those hens alone. You'll scare all the eggs out of them. What do you want?"

The peach tree rattled its droopy arms and knotty fingers, leaves rustling. It sighed. It moaned. It whispered warnings that only Halina could hear, if she chose to.

She didn't. She went into the house. She had dusting to do. And sheets to change. And dishes to wash. And she was still wearing the dress with peach slime caked on the backside where she'd fallen with Michael. She supposed she should change.

Change.

What a stupid annoying funny word.

She didn't like it one iota. It was pulling her under.

Drowning would be a terrible way to die.

Like suffocating under a pillow of feathers.

CHAPTER 37

JACK took *Lulu*, his tug, out into the harbor. He had one hand on the wheel and one on the giant mug of coffee, still too hot to drink. The squawk box was flipped on, receiving. But he only heard static. The harbormaster didn't start dispensing orders until dawn. He had a half hour to himself, at least. Cappie was on deck, of course, stowing the ropes. But he didn't say much. Didn't do much either, other than routine. He was good with routine. Unless he had been drinking.

Jack liked the time right before dawn. Fog was thick this morning, like most mornings, the lake hanging on to the moist night air as long as it could. The horizon was blocked by tall buildings, but a pink hint was starting, the sun making its appearance, the temperature warming.

Soon the faint pink streaks would become yellow then part-blue, part-green, part-nothing. Next, seagulls would appear, taking their first trips past the shore, looking for breakfast. They always woke the last of the sleepers with their cries, shrill and melancholy, sometimes mysterious, a warning of something amiss in their world. But Jack didn't speak the language, so he could only wonder.

The harbor was stirring, waking up, getting to work, like generations of fishermen, shippers, cargo carriers, sailors, and tugboat captains had done before. He was part of an endless timeline made of grand, elegant loops through centuries where water intersected with commerce. He was proud of his place on this ribbon of time and water.

It was time for Jack and his crewman, old Cappie, to get to work.

Jack had a small wood stove on the bridge. It was good for heating the place in the winter and keeping coffee warm in the summer. Cappie was supposed to keep the wood box next to the stove full. He had forgotten, again. Cappie's memory was as faulty his lungs. The days—and years—after the Mackinac incident had taken a toll on the man. The tall, confident captain in his striking white uniform that used to command the *Lake Maiden* was gone. A stooped, bitter man with emphysema was left. Still, he made a good first mate, if he could keep the sarcasm in check.

Jack didn't mind too much. He just returned the man's sass. Or he ignored it. Sometimes he wanted to slap the man, tell him he got what he deserved for trying to make deals with Antonio and his lot, the scum of the earth. But there was no point rubbing salt in the wound. Cappie knew.

When it had become obvious that the *Lake Maiden* was going to be boarded by the US Coast Guard, they'd had no choice but to dump barrels. The crew hid what they could in the rat- runs and the vaults, but that was a small fraction of the inventory. The bureau had a field day. Cappie was lucky he didn't spend more time in jail than he did.

That wasn't what broke the man, though. It was losing the boat. The debt had become too much to find his way through, no matter what creative scheme he tried to imagine. Then the emptiness, after the *Lake Maiden* was sold, was more than the poor fella's mind could take. He tuned out, silent for days at a time, his mind gone to who knows where. When he came back, he was bitter.

Jack hated what had happened to the man because it could happen to anyone. Despair was never far, especially for men who worked on water. The tides ebb in their bloodstream, pulling at them, threatening to take them under. The deepwater darkness is always there, as inevitable as Judgment Day and the day after. A man had to be ready. Jack was.

"Cappie, hey. Looks like we need more wood. Can you grab some from the tinder box?"

"Why? It's August. It's going to be too hot for the stove."

"Dammit, just do it, huh? For the coffee. And I'll heat some canned hash for lunch later."

"Yeah, yeah. Yeah." Cappie mumbled the whole time, but he brought in wood and re-stoked the stove.

"Thanks, man," said Jack. "You're moving kinda slow this morning. How late did the poker game go last night?"

Cappie's bunk was below deck. He slept on board *Lulu*, and sometimes he and the other dock rats played cards into the night. Cappie held his own, surprisingly. Some of the other fellas helped look after him, making sure he didn't lose too big, or win too big either. Extremes weren't good for Cappie.

"Yeah, we broke up about two, I suppose. Hawkins was winning big, and everyone kept saying they needed a chance to get even. I sat out the last couple hands, saving my cigarette money."

"Smart move. A man can't risk the cigarette money," Jack said.

As if on cue, Cappie broke into a coughing fit, gasping and choking, heaving and wheezing. Jack slapped the man on his back.

"You alright, old man?"

Cappie finally caught his breath and got the coughing under control, but he was pale and visibly shaken.

"Maybe you should have lost the cigarette money, after all. At least cut back? You're killing yourself, you know."

"Yeah, yeah. I'm just fine. Just fine as always. Fine as I can be. Worthless. Robbed of my life's work. Duped. Betrayed by people I thought were partners. My paddlewheel stolen out from under me. Blamed for grounding her in the strait and taking on water. My daughter hates me. And now I'm stuck on this damned tug with you, Jenkins."

"Well, so happy you're grateful to have a job, Cappie," said Jack, who had heard the rant many, many times. "Suck it up, man. You're living. That's better than the alternative. Just cut down on the smokes, will you?"

"Why should I?"

"I don't want you dying on my watch. I got a job to do. I don't want you kicking the bucket when I'm busy. You think I could take my hands off the wheel long enough to toss your sorry dead bones overboard? Nah. So stick around. Besides, your daughter would blame me. She's almost as hotheaded as you."

"Yeah, wouldn't want to impose."

"And who would fill the wood stove? You don't expect me to do that, do you?"

"Bastard."

"That's the spirit, Cappie."

"Asshole."

"Thank you. Want more coffee? Or want to go below and take a nap?"

"You think I'm a child that needs a nap?"

"Nope. I think you're a highly skilled and ruthless card shark who was taking his buddies all night—possibly cheating—and you deserve to sleep in a little."

"Damned right."

"I knew it. I'll holler when it's lunch."

"Don't bother. I'll be able to smell the crap burning, I'm sure."

The radio barked directions for Jack. He steered *Lulu* toward the nearby ship carrying cargo crates. His job was to help nudge it into its spot at the dock. The Chicago River was rather calm today. Without much wind, it would be another hot one. He hoped it wouldn't be one of those scorchers that made you want to do nothing but plop in a tub of ice. He had plans. Big ones.

He tapped his pants pocket. The box was still there, where it had been twenty minutes ago and twenty minutes before that . . . and twenty minutes before that.

He was tempted to pull it out and look at it for the hundredth time today, but he was too worried about dropping it and it somehow rolling overboard. He had picked it up last night when he finally made the last payment. Took nearly a year to scrape together enough money.

The diamonds were a carat each, the real thing. Ace had sworn on his mother's grave that the ring was worth double the price he was selling it for. Just because it had been pawned didn't mean it wasn't worth plenty. Gold is gold, new or not.

"Where'd you get a ring like this, Ace? I thought you went straight. I don't want anything on a hot sheet that's going to get me in any trouble with the law. I've had enough of that, after the incident, you know."

"That wasn't your fault, Jenkins. Everyone knew, including Cappie."

"Yeah, well, it wasn't easy to convince some people. Someone had to be at fault. Those bankers died, too doped up to find their way off the damned boat. Those two deaths were what caused the ruckus at the trial. No one cared about the boiler room boys or the bartender.

Everything would have blown over. Except for the bankers."

Jack was getting anxious just talking about it. Sweat started beading on his forehead.

"What a shame. Two less bankers in the world. So what?"

"It means we're all mortal, Ace. All vulnerable." He paused, wiping his damp forehead. "Especially if you're locked in a room below deck on a boat that's taking on water."

"You think buying her a ring is going to make her forget that

she nearly drowned?"

"No, but it'll help."

He wanted everything to be just right. He would pick her up after the last show at two. She usually needed some time to unwind from the noise and chaos of the evening. They'd walk toward Lake Shore. He hoped she wouldn't be too tired. Maybe they'd just sit on a bus bench. He could rub her feet. She had beautiful feet, even if they were calloused from dancing in shoes that were too small. A hazard of the trade, she said once, embarrassed by the blisters and corns on her toes.

He didn't mind. She was perfect as she was, as imperfect as she was.

He had to admit he was feeling nervous. Would she be surprised by the proposal?

Will she say yes?

Would she be willing to walk away from the spotlight? The damned stage? Give up all those navy boys cheering for her every night?

She seemed to enjoy it—in an odd, delusional sort of way that he didn't understand. He would have thought a proper young lady would find dancing in skimpy outfits to be demeaning. But she saw glamour, like she was a movie star. She liked the attention. Anyway, it wasn't like she completely stripped down to nothing. It was just a tease.

That's what he told himself, again.

But he hated to think of men leering at her, show after show. Their risqué comments, lude and rude, were like assaults, each one creating another ping in her virtuous veneer. That protective layer was thin, barely skin deep, he feared.

The whole charade was obscene. The big feather fans, the phonograph music, two has-been musicians, and a mermaid in a big ol' fishbowl with piped-in air bubbles.

How could it be safe? The men got riled up, he knew. He had seen how primitive they acted, no manners at all, no respect for what was proper and orderly. Troublemakers.

Troublemakers need to be plucked off, like plucking ticks from a dog's back.

There was a bouncer, of course. Syd was a burly fellow with huge shoulders—made him look like that buffalo on the nickel. And someone was always stationed at the door. Margret. Ah, Miss Margret, who thought she was a Broadway choreographer. She was little more than a burlesque reject, another wash-up that had landed on the shores of Anchors Away.

He knew about Margret's little side business, back in the day, how she set those dancing girls on the *Lake Maiden* up on "dates" with passengers. She and 'Tender split the money. Some of those girls did more entertaining on their backs than on stage.

Back then, he didn't think much about it and did nothing to discourage it. But now he was in love with a dancer, and his perspective had changed. He wanted her to be safe, to be respected and admired, not drooled over and shouted at, men wanting to pummel her beautiful face with their moronic, crude comments.

Thank God he met Anka that night on the *Lake Maiden*. Thank God he had heard her banging on the cabin door.

> *"Help! Help! Someone, please, help me."*
> *Water rushed in the dark passageway, roaring.*
> *"I'm here," he shouted. He rattled the doorknob, but it was jammed.*
> *"I'll have to get an axe."*
> *"Don't leave me. Please. I don't want to drown. I don't want to die alone."*
> *He tried again. Hanging from an overhead cross beam, he swung his whole body and kicked the door with both legs. Then again. And again. The door frame splintered; plaster gave way. It was enough to pry a gap. He saw her hands and arms, reaching.*
> *He pulled her free.*

Now he had to pull her free from Anchors Away.

The sooner the better.

CHAPTER 38

RICHARD indulged himself in another cup of coffee while he sat at his desk and read the *Tribune*. He came in early to the training center just so he could read the paper over a second cup without being nagged about cutting back. She meant well and had his health in mind, but the wife's glares of disapproval started his day off wrong. Coffee wasn't good for his blood pressure, he knew. But it did help him think. As his pulse and heart cranked up, so did the ideas.

That's what he needed right now. Ideas.

As aviation aide to the head of the navy's Great Lakes Training Center, the challenge looming in front of him was big. He needed to figure out how to train pilots, and a lot of them, quickly.

No one knew when the US would be pulled into the war in Europe, or how. But most seasoned officers and strategists seemed to think it would happen eventually, to some extent. Either an ally would demand support or US interests would be threatened. The latter seemed farfetched, but it was possible. Richard's job was to examine such scenarios, analyze risk, and present possible courses of action.

As he leaned back in his chair and read of the latest incidents in Europe, he was certain he needed to escalate his proposals.

It had been two years since Germany invaded Poland, starting the spread of bloody chaos as nations fell like dominoes, one after another. Denmark and Norway followed Poland. Western Europe, France and Belgium, the Netherlands, and Luxembourg. Then Italy entered the war, invading southern France. Then British-controlled Egypt.

The immense scourge of war across multiple worldwide fronts was staggering. The loss of life was a deep, dark stain of anguish on all of humanity. Every officer in this navy felt the burden and instinctively knew what was ahead, just as every mother of a young man knew he would likely be called to face this scourge.

There was one encouraging element from last year. The air war—the Battle of Britain—had managed to hold back Germany's blitzkrieg. The Royal Airforce made an exceptional showing. The important role of aviation in modern warfare was becoming quite clear.

He felt a bit of pride in that fact. But it also meant great responsibility.

Richard had followed the RAF's show of resilience carefully, especially the immense training program that had been set in action to turn out the pilots needed to keep up the vigilance. The Brits had done a commendable job, exceptionally executed.

He had a far more complicated challenge. He needed to train pilots to take off and land on carriers. That was assuming the fighting would stay centered in Europe.

He heard stirring in the outer office. Colleagues were arriving.

He turned the page of the *Tribune* to the business section.

An advertisement caught his eye. He read it and read it again. He stood up and read it again. The box was no more than three inches tall. The headline was three words. It would hardly seem monumental to most people. Few would imagine it had the potential to change the future.

But he saw it. As clearly as he knew that the sun would rise tomorrow, he knew this was the idea he needed.

He was so excited he nearly spilled his coffee on the open newspaper. That wouldn't have stopped him. He picked up his phone and called Manley. He would understand. He had the engineering brain. They had toyed with ideas like this before. But they always got stuck on the width of the New York . . .

He answered. Thank God.

"John. It's Whitehead. Did you see this morning's *Tribune*?" . . . "No, forget the Cubs. Forget the White Sox." . . .

He wished he could grab the man through the phone.

"John. Shut up. Turn to page twenty-seven in the Business section."

"Well, don't sit there with your cornflakes dripping. Go get the paper from the sidewalk."

He paused, tapping his fingers on the desk, losing patience.

"Then put on pants. Or don't put on pants. Dangle your tidbits and go. I'll wait."

What is taking the man so long?

"Yes, page twenty-seven. Business section. Auction." Richard sucked in air, biting his lip. "See it? I know. But look at the length. See, the deck size. It's almost right."

He nearly shouted, "I said 'almost' right, didn't I? It's close. Admit that. It's close to carrier length. Maybe close enough."

He scribbled some calculations on his tablet while he half-listened to the irritating voice on the phone.

"I was on this ship. I walked the deck. Years ago. I remember it. I paced off yards then. I made notes about the wheel and the smokestacks. They could be moved to the side, if I remember right. The deck could be widened, the wheelhouse could come off."

He tore off the sheet of paper and tucked it in his breast pocket.

"How many knots would she have to go to generate enough windspeed for takeoff?"

He listened, swallowing more coffee.

"Well, if she's light enough, she could do that. Three stacks. Three boilers. Stripped down to bare necessities. She might do twenty-five, don't you think? Hell, they don't call Chicago the Windy City for nothing. Have you been down there? Felt that wind whip off the lake?"

He didn't know why Manley wasn't getting on board right away. He was usually so bright. So enthusiastic, happy to apply that educated, engineering brain of his.

"It would be close to ocean conditions, though. Close. Better than taking an active-duty carrier out of the Atlantic. We might have five carriers. They're still bogged down in budget."

He whistled then made exploding sounds.

"No, the Pacific is out of it. No one is looking to a Pacific theater."

"Right. We won't know until we scope her out." He was getting antsy. "True, but it's not like we can take her for a spin around the block. She's dry-docked."

Richard pounded a fist.

"I remember. Right. The Mackinac Straits. Yeah, that's the one. So what?" He shook his head as if Manley could see. "I don't care. Hulls can be fixed. You're a shipbuilder, aren't you? Meet me at the shipyard in forty minutes. Alright, well, fifty minutes."

Richard groaned, then interrupted, "Then kiss her goodbye or bring her. I don't care which. Be there. Or I call the next engineering genius on my list and ask him to make maritime history. Okay. Thanks, John. You'll see."

He hung up and left. He was halfway down the hallway when he turned around and went back to the kitchenette outside his office. He poured himself another cup of brain fuel for the road.

He had more thinking to do.

He was going to turn a paddlewheel into an aircraft carrier.

CHAPTER 39

NATTIE yawned, wishing she could take a nap before the next show. But climbing out of the costume was such a hassle. She slumped on the tank ledge, letting her sore back curve and her tail dangle down into the water. Her hair, still wet from the previous show, dripped down her back, tickling.

"Hey, mermaid, you're making a puddle. I'm not gonna mop that up," scolded Davis as he walked past carrying a crate of whiskey from the back room. "Drip in the tank, will you?" He winked as he looked over his shoulder.

She laughed. The wink. She still couldn't escape the wink. How she had hated that when she was young.

"You know you love mopping up after me, Davis," she called after him.

"You betcha, babe."

She squeezed more water out of her hair, letting it stream to the floor. "Here you go. A little more, just for you. Mermaid water. Almost enough water to swim in."

"Gee, thanks, honey."

"No problem. If you want more, I have to pee. I could dribble in your direction if you want."

The dressing room made of scarves closed in.
He pushed her against the wall, metal and ice cold. She shivered.
His hand groped in her hair, finding the ribbons. She trembled.
Her ankle buckled, and she stumbled to her knees. The tin bucket in the corner tipped over, the noise jarring.
Dribbles of pee spread across the floor. It smelled like ammonia.

She was so ashamed.

He look at his shoes, piss under his hard soles. He stomped.

He slapped her face.

He stormed out, throwing the charm bracelet in the yellow puddle.

Blue gauzy fabric, bunched around her ankles, sopped up the urine.

She picked up the charm bracelet, looking for something to dry it.

She used her hair. She wiped the tiny, gold mermaid clean.

Dry. Safe.

"Davis! Aren't you supposed to be at the bar? Get back to work!" yelled Boss Lady. "What do you two think this is?"

"Ah, Boss, we was just funning. Don't you worry none, don't you get your pretty black sparkles all in a tizzy," answered Davis as he went back through the swinging doors.

"Sorry, Pat," said Nattie, trying to look contrite and put the memory of the dressing room incident out of her mind. "I think your sequins are pretty. They make a lovely trail, like a dotted line following you." She winked.

Pat glared and huffed and sputtered as she looked for words.

Nattie instantly regretted teasing her about the sequins she was continually shedding. But she did think it was funny that she finally met someone who had more sequin troubles than she did. How odd that she and the boss would have that in common. Sequins. Of course, they both also knew Halina. Another oddity to share.

"The clock says two. Where's Anka? Why isn't she starting the record?" asked Pat, clapping hands to get the crew into action.

From the tank rim, Nattie had a bird's eye view of the backstage. After the last show, she'd watched where the other entertainers had scattered. The musicians were in the alley playing craps with their crooked dice. It seemed there were one or two gambling boys in Chicago they hadn't tried to fleece yet. Anka was in the ladies' room, regretting that last shot of tequila some sailor had bought her. Viola was on the lap of a navy lieutenant, sharing some Juicy Fruit and gin.

"We have one more show to do! Everyone get in their places. Now!" Pat clapped her hands and stomped around, and somehow the vibrations of her thundering steps found the performers. The musicians came in through the alley entrance as Viola pulled herself loose from the navy man. Anka emerged from the toilet and found her oversized fans and her spot on the stage behind the closed curtain. She forgot to start the phonograph.

"Allow me, ladies. My privilege," said Syd, who happened to be standing next to the phonograph player.

Nattie didn't care who dropped the needle on the record, as long as someone did. The sooner they started this show, the sooner they could go home.

Riggs pulled the curtain open. The music swelled and the audience cheered. The spotlight shone through the water, lighting up the plants and props in the tank. Nattie had to be careful not to look directly toward the lights, or the glare would temporarily blind her, making it hard to start the routine on the right beat. Once she got her bearings in the tank, though, she had no problems.

She often swam with her eyes closed. The space—her stage—was a cube ten feet in every direction, every dimension. She knew the routine so well, she let it take over: the vibration of music through the water, the ripples, the pumped-in bubbles, the flow of braided ribbons and strings of pearls cascading around see-through gossamer shapes, vaguely fish-like.

Sometimes when she opened her eyes, she was surprised to see faces staring at her. And she wondered how long they had been watching.

Last week she had opened her eyes and saw a red-haired young man that looked so familiar. She had been sure it was Jakub. She had frozen, floating, trying to see through the bubbles and glare on the glass. Their eyes had locked. But she had needed air and swam to the hose. Then he was gone. She tried to convince herself she had been imagining it. It couldn't be him. Why would he come back?

***

They reached the end of the show, only the wish granting to go. Schmucks paid a dollar for a chance to come on stage and get an up-close dance from the fan girls and the mermaid. Their wishes were usually disgusting and dirty and their buddies sucked it up big. Nattie hoped tonight's wish was something less horrid than usual. She was tired.

Anka made a big production of reaching into the wish jar and grabbing just one wish while the boys hooted and whistled. She prolonged the suspense, slowly unfolding the piece of paper, drawing out the tension with big eyes and a sultry smirk. She opened the wish and froze. Her face went pale. The musicians repeated their fanfare. She still didn't move. She stared at the crowd, looking for someone, saying nothing. The crowd shifted in their seats, some standing, some shouting. Men in the front pounded on their table, making their mugs rattle.

"C'mon baby, who gets their wish granted?"

Viola huffed, strutted across the stage, and impatiently grabbed the paper from Anka's hands. After a dramatic pause and some pouty-face expressions and exaggerated shock, she read the wish. "I wish my sister would come home with me where she belongs. And leave her *shameful* life." She hammed up the word "shameful," making a horrified face, her mouth puckered up. "This wish is from a lad named *Szymon*." Of course, she knew who Szymon was, but she hammed it up anyway, waving her arms in a grand flourish, like the magician used to do on the *Lake Maiden*. She just needed a top hat. All for the show. The farce.

"Where is Szymon? Are you here? Come up on stage, Szymon!"

Szymon, big shoulders drooping, climbed the two steps to the stage. He wasn't laughing. Anka recoiled, looking shocked her brother had dared to go along with this farce. She stepped backward and tried to cover herself with her fans.

Viola carried on. "Here's our lucky man, Szymon!" She started her little lucky man dance around him, wobbling her assets in his face, shimmying and shaking and plucking his nose and his belt and spanking his butt—moves that usually got the wish boy riled up and the crowd cheering. But Szymon acted like he didn't see Viola at all. He crossed his arms. He stared at Anka.

Nattie set aside her shock and snapped back into performance mode. She did her wish-granting dance, waving her wand and her chest, then she sprinkled a handful of marbles and glass beads in the water in a colorful explosion, timed perfectly with a robust fanfare of music and shimmies. She did one last ass-wiggle-tail-flourish near the tank wall, and the show was over. The lights dimmed and the curtain closed. Anka ran off stage, clutching her fans to her almost-bare chest.

Nattie swam to the top of her tank. As she pulled herself up, she called to Anka. "Wait! Where are you going? I can tell Szymon to go away. I can tell him—" Sitting on the edge of her tank, she struggled to undo her zipper so she could climb out of her costume.

The alley door opened, and Jack came in. Of all the times for him to show up backstage.

"Hey, big Jack, the heroic first mate," called Syd. "The show just ended. Your girl is in the dressing room."

"Thanks, I'll just wait for her," Jack said. "Hey, mermaid," he called up to Nattie, waving.

"Help me with this stupid zipper, will you?" she answered. "What a night. Anka had a surprise visitor in the audience tonight. Her brother was in the crowd."

"You're kidding, right?" he sounded skeptical and annoyed at once. He climbed the ladder reluctantly, like he wasn't sure he wanted to get too close to the fish-girl in case her sequins were contagious. "The brother that locked her in the cabin of a damaged ship so she nearly drowned? That one?" he asked, his face becoming redder.

"Yeah, she only has one brother. Szymon."

"Of all the nerve to show up here." Jack held his hands out. He obviously had no idea where to grab the zipper, or he was afraid to try.

Nattie pointed to the zipper pull.

"There, pull that. Tug harder," she ordered.

"Like this?"

"Yeah. Well, he made a wish. Yank it harder. One of those stupid one-dollar wishes, and Viola picked it. Read it on stage. It said he wanted his sister to come home."

"Where is this asshole? I'd like to give him a piece of my mind. Anka isn't going with him anywhere. She's going with me. She's my girl, and—and—"

The zipper moved then snagged again.

"That asshole is right here," said a deep, low voice. Szymon had found his way backstage. "I'm Szymon, Anka's brother."

"Well, this is for you, from Anka's future husband." Jack swung his fist into Szymon's jaw. Szymon blinked and punched Jack back, hard in the gut. Jack doubled over. Szymon used his knee to knock back Jack's chin, then followed with a fist to his nose.

"Szymon, stop!" screamed Nattie.

But Szymon swung again. Jack crumbled to the ground, unconscious, blood dripping from his bashed nose.

Szymon stood there, motionless, blank. He looked like a balloon deflating, all the anger dribbling out on the floor. Nattie hiked up her dangling tail to protect it.

Pat stormed out and took charge. "Syd, get this clown out of my bar," she said, motioning to Szymon. "We've got enough big hairy idiots loafing around, dirtying up the place. We don't need another."

"Jack! Jack, are you alright?" cried Anka as she ran out of the dressing room. Her skimpy costume had been replaced by a respectable dress. She cried over him and slapped his face. Her hand came away bloody. "Talk to me, Jack, talk to me."

Nattie had to get down from the tank. Maybe she could help. Her legs were still trapped. "Will someone just help me out of this blasted costume?" she begged. "The zipper—"

"Alright, hold your horses," said Pat. She started to climb the ladder to the tank rim, but she wasn't very steady on the rickety ladder. Her ample size made the homemade wooden steps bow, creaking; they weren't meant to hold more than—

"Never mind, Pat. Don't come up. It won't hold . . ." Nattie realized her mistake and wished could take the words back.

Pat glared at her, eyes ice cold.

Crap.

Pat stepped down off the ladder, brushed her hands, smoothed her dress, adjusted her neckline so it better covered her cleavage. She said nothing, at least not with words. Nattie got the message clearly.

It had been a mistake to call out Pat's size in front of the entire crew. Not smart. But Nattie was more concerned about Anka right now.

She tore the zipper and pulled her legs out of the heavy, flowing fabric, then pushed past Pat and rushed to kneel beside Anka, bent over Jack on the floor. Jack was still out. Anka squeezed his hand, shook his shoulder, begged him to wake up.

Nattie hated to see her friend like this. Her face looked twisted up, distraught, probably thinking the worst. What if Jack didn't wake up?

He was probably just winded, a little bump on the head. He would be okay in a bit. Of course he would. But seeing Anka's panic made Nattie realize Anka honestly cared for him. This wasn't a game to irk Szymon. It was something more.

Syd escorted Szymon toward the alley door. Szymon dutifully looked remorseful. He was going without a fight. But at the last minute, he paused and turned to his sister.

"Anka, I'm sorry. I just want you to forget this life and come home. Aren't you ashamed?" he sounded pathetic, pleading like a kid. "Aren't you embarrassed to show yourself to men like this? I hear how they howl for you, and I'm sick with grief."

"Were you sick with grief when you locked me in that cabin? When you left me? When the water started rushing in under the door?" Anka waved her hands in the air and made wild motions like waves hitting and hitting and hitting the door. "Where were you then? Were you sick with grief then? Were you, Szymon?"

"As soon as I realized the boat was in trouble and you were in danger, I came. I came back for you," he said, his voice rising an octave. "I did. I swear."

"Someone else beat you. Jack saved me. He heard me—"

"But Anka, what was he doing in the bowels of the ship when it was taking on water?" Szymon said. "Have you thought about that? I have. I've thought about it for years. Was he hiding from someone? Or hiding something? Why would the first mate be visiting the boiler room? When he should have been saving the ship?"

"There was a fight in the boiler room earlier," Nattie interrupted. She had to speak up. She had her worries about that, too, had thought about it often. "Silas, the preacher's nephew, and Jakub, my friend, got into a knife fight. Maybe Jack was settling things. You know how he talked."

"There was trouble in the boiler room alright. It was Jack," said Szymon over his shoulder.

"What difference does it make? I got out. That's all that matters."

"You're right. That's all that matters," Szymon said, as Syd pushed him into the alley and shut the door.

"But there are still scores to settle, aren't there?"

Nattie wondered if she heard that or thought it or said it aloud. She just wasn't sure anymore. She wasn't sure about anything.

CHAPTER 40

NATTIE walked straight from the bar to the beach on Lake Shore Drive after the bar closed. She wanted to be on the shore at dawn. She went alone. That was really the only way to visit the beach. Confronting a lake like Lake Michigan had to be done alone. It was every man for himself. Every woman. Every lowly sea creature, sequins or not.

***

Cappie was awake before dawn, as usual, waiting for Jenkins to show up to take the tug out. The air was crisp, the wind sharp. Pale pink light crept higher, the sun barely clearing the horizon. To the east, a sliver of gold shone through warehouses that loomed higher than logic.

But no Jack yet.

This had never happened before. Never. Jack was the most dependable, reliable tug captain on the Great Lakes. Just like he had been the reliable first mate on the *Lake Maiden*. Jack was a good man. Usually. Except for his temper.

Something must be wrong. Something big.

"What do you think happened, Mr. Whiskers? Our boy get into some trouble? Wonder if his deal with Ace ran amuck. Maybe our old jeweler friend didn't deliver on the ring?"

The old tabby cat rubbed against Cappie's leg, meowing, only concerned with the can of tuna in Cappie's hand.

Cappie knew Jack had been seeing Ace, making payments on a ring. Jack thought he was keeping it a secret, but Cappie knew. He knew Ace, too, a bit too well. Ace had his fingers in all sorts of businesses, most with questionable ethics. He'd helped Cappie sell a few trinkets after the storm, just enough to get by. Legal troubles were expensive.

***

260

Nattie sat on a bench, eyes closed, turned to the east. She would feel the sun on her face when it started to climb the sky. She was patient. She had been waiting ten years to get the mess sorted in her head. War was coming. Cappie was diminishing. It was time to be done with old hurts and shame. She needed to move on.

***

Cappie craned his neck to see if Jack was coming up the pier. No sign of him. Maybe he went out drinking with some fellas and tied one on. Buying a ring could drive any man to drinking.

Jack had his eye and heart set on that girl from the neighborhood. Cappie didn't approve. His snide jabs about Anka's dancing profession didn't deter Jack, though. The love-sick man was blind to the shame that would cling to that girl and rub off on him. And forget kids. There could be no kids. Shame flows from one generation to the next, as sure as a river runs downstream. No child deserved such a burden.

Like having a mother who . . .

"Well, I don't think we should be too alarmed yet. It's early. He'll show up soon. I know it," he said to the cat, dumping some canned tuna on a plate. "Now, you stay out of everyone's way, Mr. Whiskers. We've got work to do."

***

Nattie heard gulls in the distance. They were loud creatures, always complaining, protecting their territory, like they were the only ones with rights to the lake. *Dream on, birds.* She came here often. A pilgrimage of sorts. She wasn't exactly sure why she did it, just that it was something that needed to be done, an obligation. No, more like a toll. The problem was, she wasn't going anywhere. She was stuck.

. . . like a moth in almost-dry paint.

***

When orders started coming in on *Lulu's* radio, Cappie weighed his options. He could pick up the receiver and admit *Lulu's* captain was

261

AWOL, or he could ignore the call, pretend he didn't hear it and loaf around until Jack showed. Or he could take the tug out himself.

It took no more than three heartbeats to make up his mind.

"Hang on, Mr. Whiskers, we're going! We've got a job to do."

He picked up the radio receiver and confirmed the orders. Then he set about gearing up *Lulu*. The engine needed tending, the stove, too, to take some of the chill out of the air, then the ropes. He was just about to put her in high gear when he saw a woman on the beach. She waved. She looked familiar in a vague sort of way, the way an old dream comes back at you while you're shaving and then hops off again before you can trap it.

She wore all black.

***

Nattie opened her eyes. Dawn's chill was damp and sharp around the edges, like it always was in early fall on the lake. She walked closer to the edge of the water. She thought of Buster, who fell over the edge of the mezzanine. She thought of Jakub, who said they would go flying down the mezzanine in her rollie chair. She thought of Silas, who died in the galley. She thought of Bubby the stagehand, who pushed the Rocky Shore too hard, making her tumble to the stage floor, busting her head.

I'm here, Jakub. She waved to him. She waved and waved. See me, Jakub? Let's go somewhere far away.

***

His eyes weren't quite what they had been when he was a young man, but the skinny woman on the shore looked familiar. Nattie?

He couldn't imagine why she would be on the beach at dawn. No, he knew. She'd come to yell. It seemed like she did nothing but yell at him anymore. Every time he saw her—which wasn't often—she had another ancient grievance to lament, something else to blame him for.

Of course, the incidents were almost always true. She had her right to be annoyed. But there was only so much apologizing that he could do, and he couldn't be responsible for every God-dang time someone had winked at her. What the hell was her problem about being winked at and butt-patted and head-rubbed and cheek-pinched once in a while, if it made the passengers happy and the investors happy? It wasn't like he fed her to wolves.

Maybe some had crossed the line. Antonio had brought his daughter gifts too extravagant for a child. And there was that drunkard crewman who spent too much time leaning against the railing, bringing her candy. The busted railing took care of that. He should have thought of that himself. Someone beat him to it.

***

Nattie gave up. He wasn't coming. She choked back tears. She missed Jakub—or the ideal of Jakub. He was innocence. Hope. He cared about her for who she was, not what she was.

***

Captain choked. He coughed and wheezed. He bent over, hung his head over the side of the tug, but nothing came up, probably because he couldn't remember when he last had something to eat. He didn't have long to live. He was pretty sure of it. Breathing was getting harder. Keeping things straight in his head was getting harder. Following Jack's directions for the boat was getting harder. *Lulu.* No, the *Lake Maiden.* No, *Lulu.*

He wiped his mouth with his hanky, then wiped his forehead. Sand from his pocket smeared around, along with some tuna slime left on his sleeve from feeding Mr. Whiskers.

***

Nattie turned around to leave. She felt a tug on her sleeve.

Tap. Tap. Tap. Tap. Five, six, seven, eight. You're out of step.

"No, I'm not. You're out of place."

"Out of line," screamed a gull.

"Out of your mind," screamed another.

"Stop it," Nattie wailed into the wind.

"Out of time," said Queenie, pointing to the clock behind the bar.

"No!"

"There are scores to settle, you know," said Queenie.

"No. You don't belong here."

"Then why did you call me?"

"I didn't. I hate you."

"Someday you'll understand."

"You left me."

"You can't get rid of me."

***

He opened the throttle to full speed, eager to leave Chicago behind.

> *The little girl was on the water's edge, too close. Her skinny legs were in metal braces. She was covered in sand and something red and sweet smelling. It was on her hands and face. There was sand in her mouth.*
>
> *She sucked her fingers. She batted at the empty jar, scratching the label with her tiny fingers and fingernails stained pink. Maraschino cherries.*
>
> *"More. I want more. I'm hungry."*
>
> *A wave knocked her over, sending her face first into the water. She flapped and splashed, just out of his reach. She rolled, being washed out. He ran, in slow motion, the sugar-sand slowing him down.*
>
> *Finally, he reached her. He grabbed her collar with one hand and pulled her out of the water. She screamed, spit out water, kicked at him like it was his fault.*
>
> *"Hush, hush Natalia." He patted her back, brushed off the sand, tried to find her face under the snotty, sticky slobber and sand. She was a mess.*
>
> *Queenie and her friend had apparently indulged in the whiskey all afternoon, passed out in the brutal sun, and left the child to finish off the jar of cherries then fend for herself at the water's edge.*

Yeah, that was smart. Very responsible of Her Royal Highness. He tried using a beach towel he'd found to wipe away the\ mess on Natalia's face and the red cherry goo down her neck. But he only smeared it more and made the girl cry louder. People noticed. A lady pointed. A couple of do-gooders started walking his way.

He turned his back on the woman who was facedown in the sand next to her lover. The idiot man was bald and red from too much sun. He was waking up; the child's crying was disturbing his beauty sleep.

He had an empty bottle in one hand.

His hairless chest was beet red from the sun, and so were the knobby knees sticking out of his swimming trunks. He thought he was some Casanova.

Queenie stirred, opened one eye, tried to focus. But she was too drunk.

She was plastered—and more. He had added some of Seymore's poppy juice to the whiskey. Just a few drops to make sure she would be out.

Dead to the world. Her eyes rolled upward and her tongue fell out, stained burgundy red, like her lips.

He put *Lulu* in gear and steered her toward the open water, away from the harbor.

It felt good to have *Lulu* responding to his motions. She was well trained and quick in her response to his movements on the controls. She deserved better.

Mr. Whiskers went below deck. He strutted in long confident strides, mocking him for being old and useless. Even the cat judged him.

Cappie shut down *Lulu*'s engine and let her drift. She could go where she wanted. She was free, for at least a couple hours.

He followed Mr. Whiskers below deck. He could use a swallow. He had a bottle stashed away for just such an occasion. A free day on the lake would be grand. He could drift off into that bottle, floating leisurely, the lake making lapping sounds as the waves hit the hull of the boat, pushing her along on her course to somewhere better than here. He felt lighter already, more buoyant, an inflatable dinghy.

If storms were brewing, they were miles away. There wasn't a bootlegger in sight, either. Nor a coast guard ship. Nor a Canadian border patrol. Nor the Ontario boys trying to reclaim their inventory. Nor the bank or the shipyard men who wanted their share of the *Lake Maiden*, nor the men with derbies who got extra doses of sleepy-time powder so they would stay out of his way.

"Maybe we can outrun them all," he said, grinning as he patted the *Lake Maiden*'s hull. "Shall we try, old girl? Should we try to outrun the storm?"

She didn't answer.

But he heard the sticky sand-baby cry and then the sick mermaid moaning, lying on his bed in his quarters, her head wrapped in towels with ice.

He heard Margret accusing him of failing in his duties as captain.

> *"You think you're going to yell and intimidate this goddamned sinking boat to a safe port?"* She laughed, first a tee-hee then a full-blown guffaw fueled by panic. *"Don't fool yourself, man, you're no Magellan or Columbus, no Bligh either, although you might be just as pompous and crazy."*
> *"You've been reading my* Encyclopedia of Famous Explorers, *I see.*
> *Don't test me, Margret."*
> *The spare key to his floor safe had been in that book.*
> *"The storm tested you, baby. You flunked. Let Jenkins take over if you have any compassion and hope of us surviving this storm. Stop yelling useless orders. Shut up. Listen to him."*
> *"Why should I do that?"*
> *"I want to live, Cappie. And so do you. That's why."*

As he floated all morning and all afternoon, he thought of Margret. And Queenie. The two women were in cahoots. They conspired, whispering behind storm clouds and hiding in the shadows of seagulls that swooped down on him from above, trying to steal the tuna from Mr. Whiskers.

He thought of the storm. He shouted warnings and gave the commands that he should have that night but didn't because he was afraid of the whiskey being found. He'd thought it would be better to go down than be boarded.

Then he plotted what he would do next to set it all right. He needed to course correct.

He didn't have much time, he knew. His lungs were filling with sickness and dread of dying. He doubted he would be welcomed anywhere near heaven. He had diverted too far off course, long ago. There was no forgiving his sins.

His daughter . . .

"With surgery and a regimen of exercises, there's a chance—"
"How much money? How much time?"

He sat upright on his captain's throne, an old wooden chair stripped of paint and varnish from exposure to the harsh elements above deck, bolted to the wood planks so it wouldn't wash away.

The sun was gone. The sky was black, speckled with a few stars that poked through the building storm clouds. He realized he didn't have a clue where he had drifted to.

How far did I go?

The bottle was empty.

How did that happen?

Maybe it had a hole in the bottom.

He was too wobbly to stand or to steer *Lulu* back to the dock.

Surely she knows the way.

"Let's go home, *Lulu*. Back to the dock. Jack will be looking for us. And the mermaid will be hunting us, trying to capture us with her mermaid nets and mermaid strands of pearls and mermaid bullshit, all pink and turquoise. What kind of bullshit color is turquoise? Or lavender. La-ven-der," he said as he stretched out on the bunk below deck, where he would be safe from the dive-bombing gulls and assassin whales, the haunting queen and the revenging mermaid.

"The mermaid will be on the pier calling for us in the dark. She's like that, you know. Half a brain." He tried to wink, but he couldn't quite coordinate such a complex feat. So he went to sleep instead, Mr. Whiskers curling by his feet.

CHAPTER 41

HALINA was in a mood. A bad one. She sat at the kitchen table in her slip, waiting for the coffee to finish brewing. She tried not to look at the walls that were the color of beets. It was in the Polish flag. It seeped through white bandages. It was the color of horror, festered wounds, seeping gashes.

Coffee. Think Coffee. Coffee's not red.

She needed coffee, strong and hot, to steady her nerves. She was still frazzled from being outside for hours with Michael trying to recapture the chickens. She should have known better than to let the boy near the chicken coop.

Her dress was soaking in the sink. She hoped the rotten peach gook she had fallen into wouldn't stain it. That was one of her favorite dresses, one she had made herself on the old Singer from Ma's house.

Ma's kitchen tile was red.

Halina's tile was a dingy white. Sun streaks cast shadow shapes on it that bobbled across the floor, flying. Minnow fishies and birdies. So childish. Where are they going?

Can I come?

The smell of rotting peaches added to the oddity of Halina's small kitchen. It combined with the smell of brewing coffee, becoming more intense. Her throat burned. Mold spores were probably attacking her airways.

She wondered if Pat's asthma was under control. There were new medicines for it now, she knew, although it had been years since she'd worked at the hospital. They weren't as desperate for nurse's aides as they used to be. And all that hullabaloo after the strait sort of ended her healing days. Thank goodness she had Natalia to focus on for a while. That took her mind off the fiasco and the finger-pointing. The charges were eventually dropped. She didn't drug those bankers or the bartender.

Those days when Nattie came to live with her and Theo were grand days. How she had come to love the girl. She gave her a purpose.

269

When the coffee was done, she sat with her mug at the table. Between sips she hunched over the cup and let the steam waft up to her face, hoping it would help open her congested sinuses.

She didn't want to get sick. She had no time for such indulgences. Wasting all morning with that boy had been a mistake. She should have been dusting or running the Hoover.

Why are these walls red?

Theo liked a neat house, and she tried to keep the place tidy for him, because without him, she would be lost. She had a knack for getting herself into trouble, messy situations, and he had a way of smoothing out the kinks and sopping up the spills. He made her feel safe, even though safe was boring—and never lasted long.

She could use some excitement. Something to break her out of this lousy, mopey mood. She needed a plan! A project to wake up her tired bones. She was a smidge past thirty, and still there was no baby. Apparently, her skills as a healer didn't apply to prenatal care. Being tossed down the stairs didn't help, either.

She had been thinking about painting the red walls, ridding the house of the last remnants of Baba. Now that seemed silly. Just covering the paint wouldn't remove the stains and the telltale traces of loss. That would still be there, hidden underneath. And there were plenty of other bits and pieces that had belonged to the old woman, conjuring up the spirit footsteps and thumping and cold drafts that whispered in her ear. A Mason jar of dried dragonfly wings was still on the kitchen windowsill next to a jar of dandelion seeds, a bottle of rain, and the small wooden Madonna, the one she used to carry in her satchel as she made her rounds.

Those days were over. And she didn't miss them one bit.

Except for sometimes. Well, many times. Most days, really. Maybe all the time.

She went upstairs to the bedroom to find something clean to wear. The closet didn't hold much. The white nurse's uniform was still in the back, hanging limp on the hanger, a layer of dust on the shoulders. She'd been wearing it when the coast guard took her and Natalia to shore. The uniform had saved her. She'd been mistaken as part of the crew and wasn't questioned about what she was doing with the captain's daughter, who was in and out of consciousness, mumbling incoherent gibberish about sailing and flying off into the blue.

No one had noticed that the clamshell-shaped suitcase held a stack of cash from the captain's floor safe. No one had stopped her as she walked off with a small fortune in tainted money, bootlegger slime all over it. How did they not smell the gutter stink that clung to the bills? Maybe all that French woman's cheap perfume threw them off the scent.

There was so much confusion that night. The roar of waves, the fury of wind and chaos of shouting. It had all been overwhelming.

She was lucky. Nattie was lucky.

Maybe it's true that mermaids are good luck.

She heard knocking on the door that grew louder, becoming continuous bangs. She found a dress to slip on and went downstairs, fumbling with the side zipper.

***

Halina and Pat sat at the kitchen table, both drinking old, bitter coffee that had sat on the stove for hours. It gave them something to do with their hands. They could grip the mugs with all ten fingers and take a sip when they needed to swallow ugly words rather than let them slip out. They could hide behind the barriers while they collected their excuses and blinked the salt out of their eyes. The clock ticked and they both clutched their ceramic mugs like they might float away any minute, simply vanish, like God on Monday morning.

Neither had talked for nearly thirty minutes, unsure which injustice and insult to tackle next. There were so many to pick from. Pat should have made a list. That would have made this little exercise more fruitful. As it was, neither woman seemed to feel vindicated, just feather-ruffled and irritated.

"If coffee cups had legs, these cups would run away," Halina muttered.

"What did you say?" Pat asked. "Are you completely nuts? Have you really fallen off your rocker?"

"Just seeing if you were awake or snoozing over there. Saying nothing, just staring kinda creepy-like. Or maybe you snuck off, went home, left me to sit with an empty sack of bones."

"Creepy? Did you call me creepy? I swear you have some nerve," said Pat, gearing up for another round. "What makes you so superior? Huh?"

"Well, it's not my taste in fashion. You obviously have me outdone there. All my sequin gowns are at the cleaners. I'm afraid it's plain cotton for me. It's what all the housewives are wearing for dusting these days."

Pat looked down at her dress and the bodice encrusted with black sequins. They sparkled in the slanting afternoon light that trickled in the window. "Do you like it?" She stood up and twirled, laughing.

"Lovely, dear. Lovely."

"I only wear black now, you know."

"I know. Is that for you or for Jakub? Who are you mourning?"

Pat clutched the mug, took a sip, and held it in front of her face. If she was trying to hide her trembling lip, it wasn't working. Halina realized she had pushed too far.

Jakub had been at the center of this sisterly clash from the start, but neither had mentioned his name. Neither wanted to take that risk.

Halina finally decided what the hell.

"You know, you don't have to sentence yourself to a lifetime of dreary colors. It's not necessary," she said. "It won't change anything."

"There is nothing dreary about the way I dress!"

"Just the color."

Pat rolled her eyes.

"But you're right, the sparkle is definitely not dreary," Halina said. "Is that why you're *really* here, Pat, to show off your wardrobe? Bum coffee off me? Or what?"

Pat stood and paced. After six laps back and forth, stove to shelves, she seemed to finally find the words she needed.

"I need the coin back, the one Alfonzo delivered to you. I need it back. I borrowed it from someone, and the ass wants it back."

"What? After all these years, you think I still have it?"

"Of course you do. Because you're not smart enough to know what else to do with it. You have no idea how valuable it is."

"Oh, I have some idea."

"You know I sent that message to you, desperate for help. And what did you do? Nothing. You ignored me."

"I didn't ignore you, dumb butt. I tried to buy some medicine from the stupid clerk on the *Lake Maiden* and found myself stuck on the boat. I would have come looking for you. But a funny thing got in the way. The damn boat crashed on rocks. There was a storm. That wasn't my fault."

"What about after?"

"After? I couldn't do anything after. I couldn't crap without someone asking me what color it was. And you know why. Someone drugged those bankers. It wasn't me, but I was in the Sand Bar about the time they were. So Margret pointed the finger at me. She was protecting that bartender, I figure. I didn't put my tonic in their drinks. But how was I supposed to prove that?"

"You could have helped me find Jakub."

"How did you want me to do that? Dive to the bottom of the lake? We both know he was tossed off that damned boat. He couldn't survive the boiler room. Not the hard work or the bullying men. They were ruthless."

"I don't know it. I don't. He could have been alive then. There was a chance."

"No, there wasn't, Pat. I'm sorry, dear, but he was gone before I stepped on that boat. I know it."

"How do you know? How? Why didn't you tell me?"

"I sewed up the man who killed him. Silas. Silas had a knife wound. His gut was a mangled mess. Liver and intestines. Stomach contents. Acid. Bile. More blood that you could stand to see."

"Why are you telling me this now?"

"I don't know."

"Why? Just to be cruel? Do you hate me that much?"

"I don't hate you, Pat. But you have to stop looking for Jakub. You have to know he stabbed Silas. Silas stabbed him. It was in the boiler room, over the biscuit girl and mermaid jokes. They fought over women and honor, ridiculous things men have fought over for centuries. The men and Silas were telling stupid mermaid jokes. Jakub didn't like that. He tried to stop them, then they laughed at him, and he couldn't take being laughed at. The fight got out of hand. Jakub had a knife."

"How do you know? How could you possibly know that?" screamed Pat, her voice shrill and scratchy. She started coughing, gasping, fighting for air.

"Because Silas told me. He came to as I was finishing the bandaging. He said he needed to confess his part. And I was the closest thing to God on the whole boat."

"You? Closest thing to God? Have you even been in a church in the last decade?"

"Maybe Silas was seeing angels. Maybe he knew his time was up and he thought he needed to fess up and repent for starting the fight. I had the galley women singing "Amazing Grace" for him. Maybe that did it. He was thinking about his soul, not whether I'd been to church recently."

"You tried to save the man who stabbed my boy?" she wheezed and gasped to get the words out.

"I tried to stitch up a young man who was bleeding to death because he was in the wrong place at the wrong time, telling stupid jokes with some big burly fellas. He was just a skinny man, probably just trying to fit into their clan of boiler room hulks—all hotheads."

"I can't breathe," Pat gasped, her hand to her throat where the air was trapped.

"I know, Pat. I know," Halina said, getting up to help. "Hang on—"

Halina looked to the empty shelf. None of the remedies she needed were there, where they should be. She had nothing . . .

. . . except a jar of dragonfly wings, dandelion fluff, a bottle of rain, homemade candles, and a wooden Madonna with her gown painted blue, the finish worn from so many hands, in pain, wringing the poor statue, squeezing it for hope.

That was all she had so that was what she used, and words she had used before when her faith was strong and she believed she could heal someone with the craft stored in her bones, passed on from one generation to the next, uninterrupted, because life is never-ending, just changing . . .

> . . . *like heartbeats and breaths of air, gentle and warm, life*
> *restoring, God touched. God sent. Flowing in and flowing out.*
> *In-hale, three, four, ex-hale, seven, eight. Inhale.*

Halina handed her sister the jar of dragonfly wings and told her to study them like windowpanes, filament outlines, speck-wide, stained-glass windows on morning glory churches where God sits waiting for visitors to come on sparrow songs and sun slants. She used her hypnotic tone and powers of suggestion. Pat was easy to put under because she wanted to go.

"Trace the lines with your eyes, follow the cells to the center of God's birthday wish as he blows soothing wax candle fumes to calm the airways." Her candles made of wax and herbs sparked a slow, simmering flame releasing analgesics and relaxers. She tapped beats and talked the air back into Pat's lungs until the frightened woman was no longer afraid and she could breathe again on her own, the airways relaxed, muscles calmed, fury's toxins turned to oatmeal mush.

"You need to rest. No exertion for a few days. Let your lungs have a break. No sitting in rooms full of cigarette smoke, either."

Pat didn't answer. She stared at some invisible spot, maybe the porthole to oblivion she had almost fallen through. Or just a mouse turd on the floor. Who knew? But she didn't seem in a hurry to leave.

Theo was due to be walking in from his shift at the mill. He didn't need to see Pat and start another ruckus of words and insults. Pat and Theo didn't see eye to eye on much, especially the topics of booze, bars, and stripping women.

Halina's ears were tired; so was her heart. She didn't need to hear more yelling. She'd had enough for one day, enough for a lifetime. She just wanted peace. Her momentary desire for excitement earlier in the day seemed absurd now. She'd gotten what she'd asked for.

Stupid me.

"Go home, Pat. Go rest."

"You should have helped me years ago when I asked for your help," Pat said, always needing to get the last word in.

"You're right. I should have."

"And I need the coin," Pat said from the doorstep.

"I'll look for it." Of course, she knew exactly where it had gone. She had cashed it in with some sleazeball named Ace. The cash went to a very good cause, where it was used wisely, she was sure. There was no getting it back. This good deed had sprouted roots and taken hold, multiplying tenfold.

Her throat felt scratchy from all the talking. She coughed and shut the kitchen door after Pat left, trying to keep the words inside. She didn't need them flinging all over the street, stirring up the hens and the peach tree and the ghosts again. Some stories were too private to let them sneak out into the yard to cause rumors and trouble. Some secrets, some lies, needed to be kept close, locked up in the dark so they didn't get ideas about flapping on the wind spreading doubts and mischief, gaining strength from the midnight stars. Pat didn't need to know everything about Jakub and what had happened and why. Neither did Theo.

Theo might not understand this one. Pat certainly wouldn't.

"And you, old woman, better not tell either one. Hear me? Jakub deserves some peace. He doesn't need his mama chasing him."

But she misses him, said the tick of the clock.

She should know he's alive," said the whistle of wind through the window.

She has a right to know, said the creak of linoleum under her feet.

"She does know. That's why she won't leave it alone," said Halina. "And why she might ruin everything."

No, no. We can't allow that. Be careful, said the rustle of leaves as the peach tree wagged a gnarled finger, warning her to guard the secret with her life.

She intended to do just that. Jakub deserved another chance—on his own two feet, without Pat sniffing after him, leading Antonio straight to him.

CHAPTER 42

JACK was furious. *How could Cappie do such a thing?* He and Nattie were at the US Coast Guard station trying to explain the problem to two desk officers who weren't very sympathetic.

Lost tugs taken out for a joyride by the first mate hardly seemed like a crisis to them.

They didn't understand Cappie's precarious perch on reality or his intermittent sense of what was right. The man was competent enough to be dangerous, insane enough to be a threat.

Nattie started to explain that her father wasn't well and may not be in the right state of mind to find his way back. The men became a little more sympathetic. Jack figured it was Nattie's emotional appeal—and her appearance—that persuaded them.

Nattie leaned on her cane. She wore a dress and a light jacket, but the tattoos of scallops, like fish scales in blues and greens, climbed up her neck to her ear. She still had small braids in her hair, woven with pearls and shells and bent fishhooks dangling down, along with bits of torn fishnet. She looked like something hauled in from a fishnet herself, a real catch. The men looked . . . *enthralled.*

Nattie was used to it, it seemed. Jack wasn't. He didn't like the way the two kept eyeing her and nudging each other and pointing with their chins and side glances. They might as well have asked her what was up with the fish scales, but they had a professional duty, and they seemed to be making an effort to stick to the standard operating procedures, thank God.

"Anything you care to add about his mental state?" the duty officer asked, sounding accusatory, like being a little daffy was a crime and Jack was an accomplice.

Jack already felt guilty. He had a sudden worry that they could smell it on him, like he had a sliver of Shame wrapped in newspaper and jammed in his pocket. He looked down for telltale drips. None yet.

"It's nothing overly problematic, usually. He just has spells sometimes where he's not one hundred percent grounded in this world. Usually, I can keep my eye on him, but I had a bit of a problem myself . . ."

Obviously, they could see from Jack's bruises that he had been in a fight and hadn't come out the winner. He was busted up, all right. Szymon was a good six inches taller and probably fifty pounds heavier, all muscle. He had a powerful punch, the bastard.

Jack had a temper, too, but it had petered out when his nose was broken.

His nose was swollen. Bruises under his eyes were bluish with a yellow-green tint. Whenever Nattie glanced at him, she winced, as if she could feel the throbbing pain.

"Yeah, you look a bit on the poorly side, mister. But why'd you leave the tug so this sick fella could power her up? Seems pretty careless on your part. I might even say negligent. Suppose we don't find him in one piece—or at all. Suppose he does damage to another vessel, causes some cargo ship to capsize; you would need to be the one held accountable, wouldn't you say?"

"No, No! It wasn't Jack's fault. It was purely my father. Jack was good enough to give Captain-Father a job, trying to keep him busy and let him stay on the lake. He loves the lake. He loves—"

"Alright, lady. We get it. But sick old men can't be allowed to go powering around Lake Michigan just because they were a boat captain in their glory days. It's not safe. Do you know how many people drown in Lake Michigan in a year?"

That opened the spigots. Nattie started crying, wringing her hands, making fists, trying to hit at anything in reach, including Jack's arm.

Ouch, Nattie.

Jack couldn't tell if she was actually mad at him or mad at her father or just plain mad. Maybe she was just afraid. So he let her pound on his arm. What were a few more bruises?

He wished he had brought Anka to the coast guard station, too. He didn't feel right putting his arm around Nattie, but he couldn't let her wail and do nothing. He also felt responsible. As the man at the desk had said, he was the one who let Cappie have access to *Lulu*.

"Now, now, Nattie. Don't cry. Stop, please," he said, patting her shoulder. "These men are going to help us. Cappie will be back at the dock in no time, and he'll be surprised we're worried about him. You'll see."

"He'd better be back soon. He'd better be just fine, or I'll . . . I'll . . . I don't know what I'll do. But he'll be sorry, I know that. He'll be good and sorry."

"Now, ma'am, there's no need for that kind of talk. It's not becoming of a lovely young woman like yourself," said the officer. He tried to pat Nattie's hand.

Jack didn't like that. "Alright, officer. We'll go back to the dock and watch for him there."

They exchanged contact information. Nattie gave the number for Anchors Away. That, of course, led to the two men rambling about times they'd been to the bar. They were amazed to be talking with the star attraction.

"Sorry, I didn't recognize you right away. But I knew when I saw your —your doodads in your hair and the fancy tattoos that you weren't some ordinary girl . . ."

That's an understatement, Jack thought. *She's a troublemaker, always has been.*

***

Jack woke before dawn. He had a small place near the dock: two rooms, a hotplate, a table with two chairs. Not much, but enough. There was space for two to live comfortably. Anka would fix it up nice, he knew. It could use a woman's touch, like curtains, embroidered pillows, and some of those crocheted doilies that women like.

He walked down to the dock, hoping to see *Lulu* back where she belonged and Cappie looking sheepish for having borrowed the tug and scaring them. But that wasn't the case.

They were both still missing.

He walked up the stairs to the harbormaster's office. They knew nothing.

"What were you thinking, Jack?" Marlin, the dispatcher, lectured. "Now we're a tug short. We've got ships to move through here, Jack. Commerce. This is no old folks' home for retired captains to play at being skipper. We need tugs working. We need reliable tugs." He was not happy.

Neither was Jack.

He felt incredibly stupid, having jeopardized everything he had worked so hard for. All he'd ever really wanted was his own boat—and to have a good life with Anka. She deserved better than dancing at a bar on Rush Street, navy boys ogling her night after night. The ring box was still in his pocket, simmering with pent-up elation, dying to get out. But the timing wasn't right to ask Anka, not while this cloud hung over his head.

He could lose everything, and it was all because of the captain. Jack had thought keeping the old man close would be smart. He could keep an eye on him, make sure he didn't get chummy with anyone asking questions about what really happened at the strait in the storm. He didn't know what Cappie might say, now that Judgment Day was coming closer for the old man. Would he keep his mouth shut?

Jack picked a spot on the pier to sit. He'd watch for Cappie, he decided. He leaned back against a post. He thought about Cappie and what he might say. He wished he had tossed that skinny troublemaker, the preacher's nephew, overboard right after the fight. But he hadn't.

It had all happened so fast. Jack had fetched Jedediah and told him to take his nephew home. "Get him off the boat. Now."

But the preacher was too slow. Then the damned nurse got involved, and Jed's nephew ended up in the galley freezer.

Then the storm. Just thinking of it made him feel a surge through his blood. Power. The storm had been the most exhilarating experience of his life. The force of the wind, the rain, the waves, the lake convulsing in giant cliffs of water that rose and fell. The intensity had fed on itself and seemed never-ending. It was a powerful force. But he was stronger.

Survival had depended on him alone. The entire ship, its crew, and its passengers looked to him for answers, because the captain was an idiot.

He remembered thinking that, finally, everyone would know that he was really running the ship, while the captain palled around with his bootlegger friends, sucking down inventory like it was water. He would get the credit for saving the ship, he had been so sure. He would be captain!

But there had been one loose end. The grounded, damaged ship would be boarded by the coast guard, of course. They'd be looking for contraband or booze. They'd find a dead man in a freezer. He couldn't have that.

Only auxiliary power was on, and only in main areas. He took the rat run, despite his misgivings. He brought a lantern. When he got to the galley, the women were in a panic, in near darkness. Five of them, cooks and dishwashers, were huddled together, crying and praying, arguing about which way to go or if they should wait for help, water rushing in from who knows where, ice cold, knee deep, rising quickly.

He led the women to the ladder to the second level, where they would be safe.

"Stay here. A rescue boat is coming. It'll be here soon."

He went back down.

This time the water in the galley was up to his waist, rushing fast, pushing at him, threatening to pull him down. He hung on to anything he could grab: a counter, an open cabinet, the freezer door that was ajar.

The dead man was still there. Floating facedown in the icy water, white frost on his short-cropped black hair. The oil lamp's gold light reflected in the frost crystals. Jack could see his own breath in the cold air. For a moment, he wondered if it was his soul leaving him.

There was no time . . .

He heaved the dead man over his shoulder. But where to take him?

Another light bobbed down the corridor toward the galley, coming his way.

"Jenkins! What are you doing?" Captain held a lantern high.

"Cleaning up."

"Is he dead? Where are you taking him?"

"The boiler room. Help me."

Captain said nothing, but helped guide the way to the boiler room, carrying both lanterns.

It took both of them to fight the current of rushing water and carry the body.

The individual boilers were each on a platform. Boiler number three was above water, for now, but the wheel locking the door wouldn't budge. Jack's hands slid. Captain leaned in and helped turn the latch.

It took every ounce of strength they had to pull the door open against the force of rising water. They only managed a few inches. They tried again and made more progress. But water was rising.

Jack was careless with the lantern, water sloshing over it. It went out.

He threw it against the hull.

Water could put out the entire boiler if they didn't hurry.

One more heave and they pulled the door open enough. Barely enough. Each man took a shoulder and arm of the dead boy and fed the corpse into the dwindling flames.

Ice popped and sizzled as it met flame. Fabric and flesh seared. The fire chewed at the dead man. Soon he'd be soot and ash.

Maybe they'd get away with it.

The captain made the sign of the cross, moving his dripping hand from his forehead to his chest like it weighed a ton. He looked oddly remorseful. Jack had never seen that look on the captain's face before.

Jack didn't understand the big deal. What was done was done. The skinny kid had no business on the Lake Maiden *in the first place. He was a troublemaker. Jack hated troublemakers.*

They pushed the thick metal door shut before the boiler was completely flooded. It took two of them.

They were both guilty.

Jack snapped out of the old memory.

He ran through the usual excuses for his behavior, justifications so he could live with himself. He had plenty; they seemed to multiply every year. Really, he and Cappie had only cleaned up a bit. It wasn't like they'd killed the kid. Someone else did that.

And it had been his job to see that there was order on the *Lake Maiden* and that everything was running smoothly, as it should be. A ship must have order.

Then, after Captain was paroled, keeping him supplied with plenty of free whiskey was the best way to keep him from talking—or being taken seriously, if he did talk.

Would anyone believe Captain if he suddenly became remorseful? Nattie might.

Maybe it wouldn't be such a bad thing if Captain didn't come back.

There, on the horizon, was a tug. He recognized her. *Lulu*. A coast guard ship was towing her into the harbor.

"Thank God," he sighed. "Lulu's safe."

CHAPTER 43

Anka helped Nattie out of the costume, unzipping the tail for her so she could slip out of the layers of gauze-thin shimmers and fish-scale pastels. Up close, the getup wasn't as luxurious as it looked from a distance. Sequins were missing here and there, and small tears had been patched with crude black stitches. But it was still lovely, and much better than the moth-eaten fans she and Viola had to wave around.

"Are you sure you can cover for me?" Nattie asked, her voice uncertain. "Just stall for a bit. If you can give me another thirty minutes, that ought to be enough time. I'll be back as soon as I can."

"Sure, I can stall. But how? Lie? Say you'll be back soon?"

"No. Don't say I'm gone. Just find a reason not to start the music right at the hour."

"Maybe I can break the phonograph machine. Or drop the record." Anka was warming to the idea. It was nice to be invited into a scheme. For once, she was an accomplice, not the one begging to be included in the hanky-panky. This was fun. She liked being ornery.

"No. Something less . . . less harmful. I don't want to make Pat mad. Just off schedule."

"Alright. I'll think of something," Anka grumbled. She stuck her lip out to let Nattie know she didn't appreciate her ideas being dismissed.

Nattie sighed. "Maybe I should just ask Viola."

"No! I'll think of something."

Nattie rushed around backstage, wrapping her wet hair in a scarf and pulling a skirt on over the black tights. She didn't bother removing the shell top, just pulled a too-big sweater over it.

Anka watched. Even in this wet and messy, dripping and disheveled state, Nattie looked at ease with her single-focused vision. She was a mermaid and wasn't hiding it or apologizing. There was no shame in those blue eyes, no fear either. It was a funny thing: being able to walk seemed to make her better at playing mermaid. After all those sessions with the nurse, Nattie had gone from being a smart-mouthed, cynical kid to being . . . well, whole. Almost healed up.

284

Anka knew she would never be as elegant as Nattie, would never be a star like her. She was just too plain, another Polish blonde wishing she could be an inch closer to glamorous or at least stand out from the crowd of immigrant faces with the same disappointed expressions, the same dopey eyes and sagging cheeks turning to jowls. They just wore slightly different shades of Misplaced.

There were no sequins on Anka's costume. But she had a fan with white chicken feathers glued on.

She was the second-string fan dancer. Nattie and Viola liked to sit by themselves, gossiping and snickering about patrons. Nattie never included her when dirty talk and off-color nasty jokes were flying around. She sent her on made-up errands so her innocent ears wouldn't be tainted by the smut.

It was like Nattie forgot which one of them was older, who had the right to be the bossy mother hen. Nattie had no right.

> *"Anka, pick another table to flirt with. Leave those fellas alone."*
>
> *"Stop telling me what to do. I used to wipe your snotty nose in that wagon when you were a baby. I tucked a blanket around your legs. I looked after you."*
>
> *"Now it's my turn to look after you. Stay away from those men at the back table, the ones talking about leather, chains, and whips. They're not talking about a circus, like you think. Trust me."*
>
> *"But he said—"*
>
> *"I heard what he said, Anka. And he's talking about whipping women for sport, not taming a tiger. And you were goofy grinning, like you were ready to play his games . . ."*

Nattie was right. Anka knew she didn't always understand the innuendos and the dirty jokes with a million ways to rhyme with Nantucket, like she knew where the hell Nantucket was. So what?

Anka played with a strand of hair, wrapping it around her finger, thinking. "So, where you been sneaking off to all these nights?" she asked.

Nattie hesitated as she zipped her skirt and stepped into her flat shoes.

"I don't have time to explain the whole story, Anka, not all of it. I'm just looking for someone from the *Lake Maiden*. He was here and left a message. I need to find him."

Anka wasn't sure she believed that answer. It didn't make sense. Who could Nattie be hunting down? She remembered Nattie had been sweet on a red-haired boy who sold tickets. He was one of the people who disappeared the night of the storm. Maybe he just walked off the boat and never looked back, tired of life on the water.

Imagine that. Nattie, the expert entertainer, optimal tease, able to entice any man and put him under a spell, needed help with a rendezvous with an old flame—and a ruse for a cover-up. So maybe Nattie couldn't do everything, after all. Maybe she wasn't perfect.

"Is it that boiler room boy, Jakub? Is that who—?"

"Anka, not now. I need to go. Later."

Nattie darted out the back door. She popped her head back in. "Remember, don't let Boss Lady know."

Anka waved to Nattie as she shut the door. Then she waved to Pat, who stood in her office doorway, hands on her hips.

"And what was that about?" Pat asked.

"Uh, nothing. Nothing at all," Anka said.

***

Anka sat on a stool at the bar so she could watch the clock behind Davis. Ten minutes to showtime, the clock said. The place was still packed, plenty of sailor boys eager to serve their country after one last wild ride on the town. It was a boisterous crowd, all worked up, itching for trouble of one kind or another. She'd been fending off gropers all night, some of them testy. Tension in the place seemed to be cranking up. Maybe it was just her, nervous about her assignment.

She finally had a plan.

She would need to make her move soon, or Pat would come out of her office stomping her foot and demanding to know where the all-important mermaid was. The world revolved around Nattie, of course.

Here goes nothing.

The three-legged barstool she sat on was wobbly. She jostled it, leaning to the left so she almost tumbled into the lap of a stout, serious young man who was studying his beer suds.

"Oh, excuse me!" she squealed.

Then she wobbled to the right, so she almost spilled the beer of a man chomping peanuts with an open mouth.

"Oh, I'm so clumsy! Look at me!" she cried as she made a dramatic show of trying to steady the rocking stool.

"I think one of you boys is trying to push me off my barstool, you naughty boys."

They both were eager to help her, grabbing at her anywhere they could.

She rocked further to the left, then rocked further to the right.

The boat heaved up and down, rocked side to side, tossed in the storm.

She rode the barstool like it was a bucking pony.

Water rushed under the door, faster and faster. She was trapped.

Suddenly she couldn't breathe; the barstool wouldn't stop, even when she tried.

She was going to drown in this tiny room, filling with water, tossing back and forth.

She had to get out. She made her big move, flinging herself down on the ground, legs in the air, kicking at the barstool, pulling both sailors down with her.

"Whooopsie-daisy!"

They all went down in a tangle of uniformed legs and arms and man-hands groping for swatches of plump flesh, taking their chance to get a handful of Anka ass. One pinched. The other fondled. She slid out of the knot, leaving them in a puddle of beer. She didn't go quietly.

"Help! You brute! Help!" she shouted, loud enough for the whole place to hear.

Plenty of sailors came to her rescue, fists swinging. A full-fledged ruckus bloomed.

"Oh, you bad boys, stop that!"

Syd eventually came and did his thing, the bully.

She glanced at the clock. Twenty-two minutes past the hour. A pretty good stall. Mission complete.

Not bad for someone who's innocent and naïve.

Davis was laughing behind the bar, shaking his head at her, marveling at her little staged performance. Star quality, indeed.

At least I impressed someone.

CHAPTER 44

NATTIE pushed her way through the crowds on the sidewalk. The night air was chilly. She was cold, her wet hair dripping down her back despite the scarf. She had one more place she wanted to hit before the last show tonight, at the far end of Rush. It was a long walk. But she was determined to find Jinks. She wanted her jewelry and the crown. They were hers, and she deserved to get them back. She'd hang them in her window or over her bed and pretend they were the stars on dark nights out on the lake.

Hell no. She'd sell them. No question. A porkchop or steak dinner once in a while would be so human-like. Something to chew would be good for the molars. She was sick of soup that was mostly water.

She couldn't imagine how Jinks had found the diamonds. He must have been nosing around her tank where they'd been buried in the sand. Maybe he saw her stirring her baubles or dropping some new trinket into her stew. He and that other waiter had always lurked around, watching her. Creeps.

She remembered them talking her up as if they were halfway decent fellas, promising to bring sardines for Mr. Whiskers. At the time, she had enjoyed the attention. Of course, they were both full of shit.

> *"I hear this combo is pretty good. They were playing at Dukes Downstairs on Rush Street—you know, where the cool cats jam."*

Jinks had liked the jazz and blues dives at the end of the street where decent women didn't go. Maybe an inked mermaid with shells on her tits would fit in. She walked faster, keeping her heart pushing blood to her legs.

The crowd thinned. Faces were dark, blending with the night. They stared, studying her a pulse-beat too long, like they were interrogating her with silence, demanding to know what she was up to.

You don't belong here, a radio's electronic voice from nowhere said.

"Go home," said a man passing on the sidewalk.

"Weirdo white girl, you lost?"
"Lilly white, cracker face, stands out."
"Asking for trouble, girl?"
Don't mind me. I'm just walking. Just a mermaid walking.

There were fewer streetlights at this end of the block, leaving longer, deeper shadows, thick enough to hide monsters with fangs and maniacs with switchblades. Taverns here didn't have neon. Hand-painted signs, simple block letters on wood, hung over doorbells wired into brick walls.

She scanned both sides of the street as she walked, looking for stairways. She saw none going down, plenty going up: metal fire escapes and rickety wooden stairs on the sides of buildings, seeming to go nowhere.

After a night of swimming, she was tired, her legs achy, her back tensing up like spasms were coming on. The limp was worse, her right side tensing up, making her walk lopsided. She thought about turning back.

There.

Cement stairs went down to a basement door that was propped open. There was no sign, but music came from the open doorway, thick with patrons. It was a bluesy tune on a piano; sounded like a saxophone, too, maybe a clarinet. She started down the stairs. A couple on their way out bumped into her. Nattie's shells jingled. The scarf hiding her blond hair fell.

"I don't think you in the right place," the woman said, laughing at the shells. "There's no beach here, baby."

"Is this Dukes?"

"Yeah, but it's all filled up. You better go back to your end of town." The young woman squinted at Nattie, her face curious. Maybe she noticed the tattoos of fish scales up Nattie's neck. Even in a dark stairwell, something like that stands out, screaming, *Freak!*

Nattie didn't blend in. She was plainly dressed compared to the snappy patrons of Dukes who came and went, pushing past her on the stairs. Some paused to stare. The women wore flashy dresses with fringe and hats with feathers. The men wore boxy suits and shiny two-tone shoes and fedoras pulled down on their foreheads. There were no sailors here, no mermaids, no other white girls looking for a drunk man who'd made off with her treasure.

She realized her tattoos were exposed. The sweater had fallen off her shoulders, revealing shells dangling and fish-scale tattoos climbing her shoulder, a disease taking over, a horrid disfiguring fish disease. One woman gasped. A man shook his head, confused. She pulled her sweater closer, wishing she could disappear.

She was used to being different. Tonight, she felt worse, lower than low. Guilt was mixed in with the shame. She was to blame, no one else, for the freakish way she looked. She'd asked for the lines to be etched into her skin, staining her. She was an adult who had other choices. She had chosen to be fish girl. Somehow that made it worse, didn't it? That was what Halina had said. Maybe she was right.

Another young couple came out of the door, dressed in fancy duds, starched and ironed, dipped in shellack to keep them stiff. When they saw Nattie, they frowned and blocked her from continuing down the stairs. They glared at her. Both had fierce eyes full of resentment. Anger over some infringement simmering. Why?

Nattie wanted to defend herself. She didn't deserve their hostility. She didn't badmouth their people or look down . . .

She didn't do much to help them, either. She'd given Silas her roll-chair, but what else? She'd said thank you to Jedediah when he brought buckets of water, but she still had expected him to bring more, do it again, and again. She thought of the dishwasher boys who'd tried to teach her to dance. She didn't dance with them. She said she couldn't.

Fact was, she was afraid to. What would people say?

Flashes of the *Lake Maiden* brought out the tears. She wiped at her face with the corner of her scarf, wishing she had never come this far down Rush, where there were few lights, but she suddenly saw plenty of past sins clearly. Nattie stood up straighter. She couldn't give up now.

"I'm looking for someone. He comes here sometimes. I have to find him," Nattie said to the couple in the doorway.

The young woman studied her. She looked younger than Nattie, too young to be out so late at night. What would the girl's mama say? Her fella was lanky, his head and shoulders still music-bobbing to a rhythm vibrating on the steps.

Where the cool cats jam.

"Hang on a minute, Walter. This idiot white girl with fish skin is going to get herself into some trouble, like a fool," she said. "She doesn't know her kind ain't welcomed here."

"A fish-girl ain't welcomed anywhere, honey," he snapped back.

"Oh, hush your mouth, Walter."

"I perform as a mermaid down at Anchors Away," Nattie said. "I have a costume. A tail. It's an act."

"Well, see, that's something fancy, not freakish, I suppose!" the woman said, her tone changed. "So, what's this man's name you're looking for? You tell me, and I'll go in and ask around. If he's there, I'll send him out." Nattie couldn't see the woman's face very well. But her voice sounded sincere.

"His name is Jinks. He's a skinny man. Used to be a waiter. Now, well, he's fallen on some rough times, I hear. He's afraid of water."

Walter piped up. "I know that scrawny dude, sells pills to the band boys. Tends bar some, too. Goes crazy if he sees a puddle." He shook his head. The woman nudged him for more, and he went on. "He still shoots up every chance he gets. He sleeps in the garage around the corner."

"Damn, Walter, don't tell this girl about the garage. She can't go down there where those devils go to spawn. You want her blood on your hands? Fool."

Nattie shivered. This was getting worse by the minute. She wasn't willing to risk facing any devil-spawning street thugs in a garage. She wasn't that desperate or stupid.

"Well, never mind. Thanks," she said. She would have to call it quits for tonight.

Cut bait and run.

"If you see him, tell him that you saw Nattie. Tell him I want my diamonds back. My crown, too. Tell him that," she said over her shoulder.

As soon as the words were out of her mouth, she realized the mistake.

Now she wouldn't be the only one interested in finding poor Jinks.

CHAPTER 45

MARGRET stood at the hostess stand, concentrating on staying vertical. She picked a line in the doorframe and focused on making her legs line up with it, then her shoulders, then her neck. A line. Like the doorframe. It was a magic door. She was a magic hostess.

She had powers. She was so strong she'd been able to tear the wires out of her mouth all by herself because she couldn't stand them anymore. That was days ago. Seymore had fixed her up with some of his imported extracts of the amazing variety. They got her through the worst of the pain.

She was trying to cut back, at least enough so she could work. Pat wouldn't keep her on forever if she wasn't useful. She had to be useful.

"Margret! Are you sleeping or high? What's going on with you?" asked Pat, who appeared from nowhere.

"Hello, Boss. I'm just getting my bearings. I'm fine. A little tired, maybe. But fine."

"You better be fine. I need you to be alert. I need you to be watching for trouble. No more brawls. No odd men, alone, looking like they're up to no good. You holler for Syd if you see anything." Pat was standing too close. Her sequins glared, each one a vibrating ball of light. Some sang high notes.

"What exactly does 'up to no good' look like? What am I on the lookout for? Will this scoundrel have a sign that says No Good and an arrow pointing up?"

Pat didn't find that funny, apparently. She scowled like a mean beastie.

Margret thought her joke was hilarious and broke out in giggles.

Pat slapped her face.

The slap tore through Margret's face to her bones, shearing her face in two. She saw colors and sparks and boiling black fury. She felt her eyes rolling up to her brain.

Pat was mumbling, holding her up. Hands were everywhere. A rag was on her face. Someone held ice to her cheek. She tasted salt, warm, the opposite of the ice.

Pat talked but no sound came from her lips. She looked worried. She looked sorry.

She patted Margret's hand and held it. Margret realized she was shivering and shaking. Her magic had run out. She might be crying; she wasn't sure. She heard a ringing in her ears.

Then coffee came. She smelled it but couldn't taste it. She sat at the bar on a stool. Davis was staring at her, handing her another cup. This one went down easier.

The throbbing was letting up and sounds were returning.

"You doing better? Landing on two feet? You were pretty out of it for a while," Davis said while filling mugs with beer for waiting customers.

"Yeah. Coming in low for a landing. Damn, that hurt," Margret said, shaking her head, trying to shake off the cotton clouds.

"Yeah, Boss Lady forgot about your broken jaw. She was real sorry about hitting you there, when you were already broke. She felt bad."

"Not nearly as bad as me."

"Yeah, that's probably true. But you know, things have been tense around here. While you were out chasing pink bunnies, we had some excitement."

"I wasn't chasing pink bunnies. I was recuperating from a serious injury. One caused by Mailman. Has he been around?

"No. But one of the Italian Stallion's men paid a visit. Me and Syd had to take him out."

"You mean Syd took him out and you held the door open. I know you. You didn't want to get your hands dirty."

"I played a crucial part. I led the way and cleared a path."

Margret started to laugh but winced. Laughing wasn't good for the jaw. Neither was talking. "Forget this coffee, I need more ice."

Davis used the ice pick to break off a big chunk and wrapped it in a towel for her. Then he filled her in on the other gossip and news: Anka's brother showing up and making a ruckus, then Nattie's father taking off with Jack's tug. Then a brawl started by Anka playing a silly game with the wobbly barstool.

"You've missed all kinds of fun. And now we're watching for trouble, waiting for it to show."

Margret remembered Pat's instructions. That was what had started her trip down Pain Lane.

"Right. I made the mistake of asking Pat what 'up to no good' looks like."

"No wonder she slapped you."

Margret decided she had better get back to the front door. The adrenaline rush of the slap to her broken jaw had burned off the last of the juice in her bloodstream, it seemed. She was no longer magic. The throbbing lingered.

I can live with it. I've dealt with worse.

It was a Friday. Payday for these nice wholesome navy boys who were so eager to impress their mothers, make their fathers proud, and serve Uncle Sam. They all looked too young for such gallantry. Didn't they listen to the radio? While she'd been crashing with Seymore, he'd insisted on keeping the radio on. He was obsessed with news from Europe and the East, where his magic in a bottle was from.

She didn't want to think about these sailors being called to war. She didn't want to think at all. She took her place at the hostess stand, alert for trouble.

It didn't take long.

She was fairly certain that a dopey-looking guy carrying a gas can would classify as someone "up to no good," but that was just her speculation.

She left her station to tell Syd. She found him behind the closed curtain, near the mermaid tank. He was fiddling with the air hoses and the oxygen tank, like he was some diving expert. His baffled expression was comical, like a school dunce at the blackboard. She laughed at the absurdity—until she remembered that laughing hurt.

"Syd, some guy just got dropped off out front. He got out of a truck, like a delivery truck, and he was carrying a gasoline can. One of those red and yellow cans with a spout on it. You know the kind . . ."

"Yeah, so what? Maybe his car ran out of gas. What do you want me to do about it? Where'd he go? Did he come in with it?"

"No, I don't know where he went, around the corner, I think to the alley behind the bar. Maybe you should look for him. I think he's up to—"

"No good?"

"Yeah."

"Honey, everyone on Rush Street is up to no good. And ever since Boss Lady told the cast and crew to watch for trouble, that's all they see.

Trouble. There's only one Syd. And right now, trouble has hit these tanks. Someone tied a knot in the hose."

Pat came out of her office. She looked pale and was rubbing the scars on her arm.

"What did you say, Margret? Did I hear you say gasoline?"

"Yeah, a man with a long overcoat, like he was hiding something. He had a can, red and yellow; he was carrying it out far from his legs, like he didn't want to get it on him, like it was dripping."

"Come with me," Pat said, and she led the way to the back door. She opened the door to the alley, slightly, just for a peek.

"There, there he is," shouted Margret, pointing.

The man with the gas can was a few yards down the alley. He stood there, holding up the can for her to see. A line of gasoline on the ground reflected moonlight from him to the back door.

The man held a match.

"Hello, Pat. Me again. Did you find that item we talked about? Antonio is hoping you found it."

"Get away from my place with that. You can tell Antonio I have nothing else to give him. There's nothing left from those days. Nothing but the misery he caused. And that still hangs over my head. Tell him that. Tell him to come himself, instead of sending his messenger. Tell him I want to tell him to his face to go . . . go . . ."

"Go jump in the lake!" shouted Margret, finishing Pat's warning for her.

The man lit the match and dropped it. He ran.

The fire caught and traveled down the line of gasoline snaking through the alley to the back door, where it stopped with an exhausted pfft.

Pat and Margret stomped out the last bit of wimpy, smoldering flames.

Syd came out. "You ladies need help out here?"

"No. We took care of it ourselves," said Pat, wheezing. She caught her breath and turned to Margret. "Jump in the lake? Really? Is that the meanest thing you could think of? The very fiercest, awfullest threat you could manage?"

"Well, the water would be cold."

Pat laughed. And Margret laughed too, holding her jaw.

"I need more ice," Margret said, and she turned to go inside.

"I need to see my sister again," said Pat.

CHAPTER 46

Richard Whitehead

Aviation, Great Lakes Training Center, US Navy

Chicago, IL

HE found the envelope addressed to him on his desk when he came back from lunch and knew instantly what it was: the official "No!" from Washington. He had already heard their answer to his proposal over the phone, but the navy liked to put its most asinine proclamations on paper, so they could be saved for posterity and laughed at for generations.

This was one of those decisions.

Military analysts—always so smart *after* the battle—would be pointing to this pivotal point long after Whitehead was court-martialed for gross negligence. They would identify this as the moment when the navy should have run the ball, and they punted.

And his name would be right there. The man who didn't supply trained pilots.

He had to try again. Maybe this time in person.

He went home to pack.

CHAPTER 47

CAPPIE was a fish out of water. He sat on the edge of the foldaway cot in the apartment on Rush Street, a two-room hole-in-the-wall shared by his daughter and three other young women, equally low on funds and equally lacking in proper employment and appropriate wardrobe. They all worked the bars on Rush. None of them could scrounge up a dress to adequately cover their asses if their lives depended on it.

On top of that, they slept all day and worked all night. It was no wonder they hadn't found suitable husbands yet. They didn't sleep enough. They didn't eat right. They painted their faces with goop that made them look like hussies.

Nattie looked just like Queenie, only skinnier. The likeness was disturbing. His wife had liked to paint her lips red and draw on high-arched eyebrows with a black pencil. She had added a fake beauty mark high on her cheek. "For a touch of drama and air of distinction," she'd said when he scoffed at it.

Cappie took his blue bandanna out of his pocket and wiped his face with it. The cotton still smelled like the lake air, the night wind, and freedom. He had almost escaped with the tug, *Lulu*, the good gal. Loyal. Trustworthy. Jack didn't deserve her. Jack was a traitor.

Queenie couldn't be trusted either. She lived lies, on stage and at home. Always acting. Always superior. With those damned eyebrows, she always looked wide-eyed and surprised. He had found her on the beach like that, sprawled on a beach blanket next to the Casanova from her theater.

Cappie got up from the bed, stretched. He didn't sleep well here. The street noises were foreign to him. He needed the lull of water, the motion and sound of lake water. There was nothing to eat in this apartment, and no kitchen, just a hotplate on the windowsill. They were on the fifth floor and the view out the window was drab, all buildings—bricks and cement and windows, blinds half pulled down like eyelids over glazed and unseeing eyes.

*Her eyelids were half open like she was concentrating on her
final overzealous performance: consuming tainted hooch, a
few drops of doom supplied by an import man with red
poppies on his black velvet vest.*

Vaudeville. Burlesque. Any two-bit stage that would pay her to flaunt her
ass and show off her ample assets. Slowly peeling off layers of clothing to
the drumbeat of the music, starting with the long white gloves.

"It's time to quit. You're a mother. You should act like one."
"And live on what? The measly tugboat money?"

Queenie got her drama, like she wanted. But there wasn't anything
distinctive about the way she went, passed out in the hot sun, too wasted to
fight the waves that washed in. When he left with Nattie, Queenie was
very much alive but oblivious, her mouth hanging open, snoring, bugs
crawling on her face. She was too far gone to fight any waves that might
try to pull her and her Casanova over the brink. She'd just tumble away,
trash washed out by the waves.

It would be a tragic mishap with only the lake and liquor to blame. He
would be home with the girl. Who would blame him?

It was a miracle Nattie hadn't drowned. He'd found her by the water's
edge, playing like she was swimming. A wave could have carried her out
to the lake. She wasn't supposed to be at the beach at all. She was
supposed to be with the neighbor children selling newspapers, riding in the
red wagon, but for some reason the plan had changed.

He had been plotting the day for weeks. The woman's audacity had
become too much for him to live with, flaunting her hijinks in his face,
humiliating him in front of the other men on the dock who knew where she
performed. It was time to settle the score. He just needed to give her a tiny
shove. No one forced her to drink the entire bottle. She did it to herself.

But Natalia could have capsized the entire thing. She could have
turned a two-person accident into a tragedy of three. What would he have
done then? If he had lost her—

A fly buzzed past his ear. He swatted at it but missed.

This musty apartment was a haven for flying insects. The first night he was here he must have executed a dozen flies. He rolled up a newspaper. A man needed the proper weapons to go to battle.

Nattie and her friends weren't particularly appreciative of him swatting flies during daylight hours when they were sleeping. He had been ordered to be quiet.

Her roommates weren't happy to have an old captain putting down anchor in their cozy little harbor. Their hostility was as thick as the mucus clogging his lungs. Nattie had tried to smooth it over. He had heard her pleading for patience. "Sure. Alright. No problem," they had said in a chorus of singsong insincerity. The tension was still there.

When they thought he wasn't looking, they made crazy faces and rolled their eyes and stuck their tongues out like deranged psychos.

He wasn't deranged, not completely. He seldom walked around with his tongue hanging out or his eyes all squirrel-buggy. He saved his crazy manifestations for when he was alone. Or on a boat.

He was trying to make light of the situation, dousing his predicament in some sarcastic wit just for fun and, maybe, to prove to himself that his brain was still fully engaged. There was nothing wrong with him that time on the lake wouldn't solve.

Unfortunately, his daughter, together with Jack, had decided he couldn't live on the tug any longer.

He was stuck here for now, a single man cast adrift with four females. What an awkward and dangerous situation—for him, not them. They were messy women and without a regimen. Their lack of discipline and slipshod approach to the care of their quarters was disparaging. The walls were grimy, the linoleum was warped and worn through to the bare wood below. The single window, looking out to Rush Street, was streaked with ancient grease and grime mixed with cigarette smoke and splattered fly guts.

They can thank me for the fly guts.

He picked up one of the film star magazines the girls collected and thumbed through it. He didn't know any of the names or recognize the pictures of starlets. But he scanned the pages, looking for good names for his next tug. *The Hedy Lamarr* had a nice ring to it.

***

Finally, the sun started to slide lower, dipping behind tall buildings, ready to call it quits for the day. The girls woke up, made coffee, complained about this and that, and left for their jobs, one by one, until only Natalia was left.

"I'm sorry, Cappie. I know this is hard for you," she said from the doorway. "But it'll be only another day or so until we can find you a better place to stay." She wore a blue dress. It looked old but decent. She had pinned a piece of overly ornate pawnshop jewelry at the neckline, so less of her fishy-scale tattoos—and less cleavage—showed. She probably did that for him, knowing he didn't like her being immodest.

He didn't say anything, not sure what might set her off again. He didn't want more yelling.

In the few days he'd been here the yelling had become routine. Nattie had so much pent-up outrage, as if she'd been mistreated, not pampered and indulged. How could she see it so differently? None of those musicians or waiters or passengers ever hurt her, really. It was all theater nonsense, all harmless.

He'd never heard her complain back then. She'd had the run of the boat, hadn't she?

> *"Your daughter has been in my office again. A jar of maraschino cherries seems to have spilled on the ledger. She uses my typewriter, uses my pencils and inks, and leaves a mess. How do you let her have the run of this boat?"*

He was tired of it. He tried to look compliant, but that wasn't a trait he knew much about. He pursed his lips, thinking that at least looked childish. Maybe that was what she wanted—her chance to play parent.

"Jack's helping to ask around, see who has a room near the dock. He promised he would find something suitable," she said. She looked like she wanted him to say something. Or do something. But what? What could possibly make her happy?

She stood almost straight, leaning on a cane, letting it take some of her weight off her legs. No one would guess she wore elastic bandages around her lower back and rubbed all kinds of ointments and creams on her legs, magic potions from the nurse that were for circulation, she said.

They owed the nurse a lot. That woman had saved Nattie's life, took care of her while he had his little issues with the law. He didn't know where Nattie would have gone if it wasn't for the Polish nurse.

"She'll stay with me. I'll take her in. That way I can
rejuvenate her.
Get her walking like she should be." The nurse stood in front
of the tall, imposing judge's bench, wearing her starched
uniform.
Margret argued, "But you're not family. All of us on the Lake
Maiden consider her family."
Viola piped in too. "You heard the judge. The court expects
family to step in."
"Well, you all have done a lousy job looking out for her so far,
for Christ's sake. How the Good Lord Almighty ever let you
people put this child in a glass bowl, like she was goldfish, I'll
never know. Now I've got some undoing to work."
Cappie had the last word. "I want the Polish nurse to take her.
Nattie will go with Halina."
The judge, shaking his head at the entire spectacle, pounded
his gavel, and it was done.

Cappie was so proud of Nattie for what she had accomplished. But he couldn't tell her.

Ever since she was a young thing, she had looked at him like she knew what he was: a coward, a pawn of the bootleggers who supplied the boat. She also knew, at some level, what had happened to her mother and that he was to blame. And, no matter what he did to try to return to her good graces, she would never forget it. She would never forgive him. He knew this in his heart. So he didn't even try.

"You look nice," he said. "That's a nice dress. And you're standing almost straight. You look almost normal. That doohickey is a nice touch." He pointed at the brooch.

She gasped like he had punched her in the gut.

"Almost normal?" she said, her face red. "Did you call me ALMOST NORMAL?" She stomped the floor with her cane. "How dare you say I am almost normal. And then comment about this stupid pin. Do you know why I put it here? Because I was ashamed for you to see my tattoos and

302

what little bit of cleavage I have." She tore the pin off and threw it at him.

He ducked his head, but it hit him squarely in the chest—his heart—and the pin fell to the ground.

Her tears started.

Not again.

She sobbed, but it didn't stop the words she spit out. "And you have the audacity to say that's good—it's good I covered up with the little doohickey. When you—*you*—put me in a skimpy little costume with nothing but shells over my little-girl tits for everyone to see. You did that. You put me on display."

She tore open her dress and exposed her white brassiere, looking far too grown-up for his little girl who wasn't a little girl anymore.

"Do you ever think what that did to me? Did you ever once worry if it was right to show me off like I was a thing for your boozy pals to ogle?"

"I wanted you to feel special. Pretty. Enchanted. The mascot of the boat. The star attraction . . ." He fumbled for words, knowing there was nothing he could say that would make her hurt go away.

"And you see this little . . . doohickey, as you call it? Do you know where this is from? I stole it when I was kid on that godforsaken boat. I was a thief. I had a whole clamshell case of jewelry I stole from the dolls and dames that strutted past my tank, feeding me orange slices soaked in whiskey. You turned me into a tramp and a criminal, just like you."

"I'm sorry, Natalia. Don't say such ugly things. You're not a tramp, nor were you ever. You were my beautiful mermaid. My beautiful daughter."

"I am not a mermaid," she said, crumbling in fits of tears. "I am a woman. And I don't think I want to be your daughter any longer."

"Please, Nattie—"

"In the morning, Jack will take you to some other place to live. I have to go to work now. Like *almost normal* women do. I have to go show off my mermaid chest and scales to more men." She gripped the front of her dress closed and slammed the door behind her.

At least that's over.

He got up from his chair, rolled up a newspaper, and stalked the fly buzzing against the window, hitting its head over and over against the filthy glass.

Whap. Cappie got him.

PAM RECORDS

I'm still good for something.

He left the bug-ball on the sill, its legs curled up to its bug belly.

Evidence.

CHAPTER 48

NATTIE zipped her costume over her legs, then unzipped it. Then rezipped it. She sat on the rim of her tank. After the man from Antonio's organization had made his threats about trouble coming, Pat had some men make a wooden cover for the tank. It had a hinged trap door that locked. Pat thought it would make Nattie feel safer, knowing the tank was secured from tampering.

But the top cover didn't protect the air hoses or pump. It had been weeks since she saw the woman dressed in black kicking at the air compressor and the hoses.

This contraption doesn't look safe. I don't trust it, the spirit woman had said.

Nattie had a hard time shaking the creepy feeling. Dread was a heavy weight. It made breathing hard. Fear—on top of all the other pains she was feeling—was taking a toll. She was tired. Her legs felt heavy. She wanted to sleep. Even that nest of pirate sails in the prop room would be comfortable now, or the room Halina had made for her in the big noisy house. There was a jar of dragonfly wings on the windowsill and a jar of milkweed pods and a jar of sand from the beach and a bottle of rain. She got well while living in that room. Halina had filled the aches as best she could.

"Hey kid, you up there, what are you all so droopy about? You sure got a long face," Viola called up to her from the foot of the ladder. "You okay?"

"Oh, Vi—I don't know what's wrong with me. I just don't know what to do anymore." She couldn't hold back the tears.

"Oh, honey, don't do that. You'll mess up the makeup." Viola climbed the ladder. "That crap's not waterproof, you know."

They both looked at the tank of water and realized at the same time how absurd Viola's comment was. They broke out laughing.

Nattie splashed a handful of water at Viola.

"You got me, kid." Viola stretched out on the new platform, smelling like freshly cut wood. "Pass the sun oil and my sunglasses, will you? I'm at the beach."

"It's midnight on this beach, Viola. The stars are out, dear."

"All the better for secrets. So, tell old Viola what's bothering you, honey."

Nattie sighed, closing her eyes, trying to ignore Vi's confidence in her snug, revealing costume.

She finally found some words.

"My father," she said. "Ever since he pulled his little disappearing stunt with Jack's tugboat, I've just been so mad at him. I can't stop yelling at him. You should hear me. I say such awful things."

"To Cappie? Well, baby, he might deserve it. He was always a bit of an inflated ego on the *Lake Maiden*, you know. I suppose he wasn't much of a father, always glad-handing his VIP guests."

"It's more than that. It goes way back," Nattie said, twisting a braid in her hair while she talked. "I remember weird bits of things. My mother was an entertainer, you know. Queen of the Stage. But I don't think she really sang opera, if you know what I mean."

"Who in their right mind would sing opera? God, that high-brow crap is annoying." Viola swatted at Nattie's hand to stop her from twisting her hair.

Nattie plucked at the shells dangling around her neck instead. She thought of the shore, the sand, the waves, her mother lying in the sand with the black-haired man. She had thought they were dancing lying down. She had been so stupid.

"I remember Queenie and a special man friend of hers. They were having a picnic. And some hanky-panky. I saw them rolling around. Can you imagine the horror?" She laughed and raised her eyebrows in mock shock.

"How educational."

"Yeah. Very. Then I saw my mother's face in the sand, mouth hanging open, crawling with ants."

"Oh, disgusting. Stop that." Viola swatted at her face like she felt ants. "This is some lousy beach you got, kid."

"I know. Then Father pawned me off on the neighborhood kids, Anka and her brother. They were stuck looking out for me while he did his tugboat thing."

"Aw, I bet you were a cute little thing. I remember when you came on board. A minnow-sized mermaid, we used to say."

"Pretending to be a magical creature was a fun game, sometimes. Maybe it wasn't all bad. I suppose I can't blame my father for knowing nothing about raising a daughter, especially on a boat with poker, whiskey, and dancing girls. You were all such bad influences, right?"

"Oh, we were terrible. Remember those ruffled little things Margret called spanks? I used to lose mine all the time, on purpose. I hated those britches. Ruffles across my butt like a toddler. Pshaw!"

"You were too glamorous and sophisticated for ruffles! That's why all the fellas fell for you."

"Oh, you attracted attention too. I remember that little red-haired young man that was sweet on you."

"Then he disappeared," Nattie said. She was tired of laughing. Jakub wasn't a joke.

"Poof!" said Viola. "He went up in smoke. Or boiler room steam!"

"I think the beach is closed, Viola. You better get down."

"Ah, kid, don't be mad. I don't mean anything bad. I didn't know you were still sore about that boy. C'mon now."

Nattie pushed Viola toward the ladder. She pushed too hard. Viola caught herself, just grabbing the ladder before she went over the side to the cement below.

"Watch it, kid. You need to be more careful." Viola wasn't laughing anymore, either.

"Accidents happen sometimes," Nattie said, shrugging.

"They're not always accidents, though, are they?" asked Viola.

"Like my mother's death? Like Buster?"

"We all knew Queenie was removed from the picture. Buster was pushed. Those weren't accidents, babydoll. Things that are orchestrated aren't accidents. You better be careful, like I said. Watch it. No one likes troublemakers or being *reminded* of trouble. Let it go, girl."

Nattie watched Viola strut away. Her legs were as perfect as they had been ten years ago, except for the purple veins climbing her calves, hideous, poisonous vines climbing upward, taking hold of her flesh.

Nattie shivered. The water dripping down her back was suddenly ice cold.

If she was trapped in the tank and drowned, they would call it an accident, Nattie knew. There would be no questions. No one would look further than the fish scales on her arms and the sequined tail twisted around her legs.

"She got all tangled in the water and couldn't get out," they would say to each other. "She wanted to be something she wasn't—a tragic delusion."

She knew Pat, Margret, Jack, even Anka and Viola all felt just a little bit sorry for her still. She was still the misfit kid who never outgrew the jokes and the winks. Now she was just a bigger joke in a skimpier costume, a more pathetic excuse for a man-teasing siren, taking after her mother.

She looked down at her costume. When had it become so shabby? When did it become worn and weathered like it had been through a storm? Empty strings dangled down, broken, the sequins lost. The colors were faded. Turquoise was a faint hint of mist blue. Sea green was the color of old, dying grass under snow. Shells were chipped and broken. Ribbons were knotted into nests where pink larvae burrowed into green moss hanging in clumps. She could smell the rot.

She had a show to do. The Tuesday night crowd was thin, not too boisterous, but they still deserved a performance. That was what they came for. No one walked into Anchors Away for the booze or ambiance. These bright-faced young men had one thing on their minds.

She adjusted her top, making sure the shells were covering the right places. How many thousands of times had she gone through the same motions? Over and over and over.

Why bother.

She took it off.

A cold wind crossed her chest. She heard Halina gasp, and an old woman cackled a hideous laugh. Someone slapped Nattie's face. She turned to see who it was, but no one was there.

Her top fell into the water. She covered her chest with her hands, suddenly ashamed. Halina would be furious if she knew. So would her father. And Jakub.

Nattie had told Halina she didn't remember the night of the storm on the *Lake Maiden*, but she did. She remembered everything, including Jakub saying goodbye. He had kissed her cheek. He had touched her hair. He had whispered in her ear in his sweet, gentle voice.

"I gotta go to Canada, Nattie. I gotta stay low for a while. I did something bad. Real bad. Something I can't undo. I wish I could. I won't forget you. You stay who you are. Don't let anyone change you into something you're not. You're perfect as you are."

She wished she could forget him. All these years and she still thought of him and his eyes, blue gray like the lake in January, almost frozen. He had believed in her, so she still believed in him, the last almost-pure thing she knew. She clung to him, a buoy that would save her life one day, as absurd as that seemed.

She tried reaching for her top without falling in. It wasn't showtime yet. She grabbed a towel and covered herself.

Viola came through the curtains, leading a man who was fidgeting with his hands, wringing them, jamming them in his pockets.

"Mermaid Natalia, we have a gentleman patron who's bought a ticket to be Mermaid Mesmerized—in person," said Viola coldly as she led him to the ladder alongside the tank. He looked around at the bizarre scene like he was walking into a house of mirrors: a giant aquarium tank and a mermaid on the ledge. As he got closer, Nattie realized he looked familiar.

Could it be—?

"Jinks!"

"Hi there, Miss Nattie. Look at you, all grown up. A real woman. I knew you'd be a looker when you grew some and blossomed." He grinned. "I knew you would grow into your costume. But looks like you outgrew it." He tried to tug on the towel that tangled down the ladder rungs.

She crossed her arms in front of her. Her face was hot.

He laughed.

She remembered that mocking laugh. All the waiters—

"No need to blush, Miss Nattie. It's just me, Jinks. You know me. I brought you biscuits and maraschino cherries back in the day. Remember?" He started to climb up the ladder.

She flinched and pulled away.

"I should have brought a biscuit to toss you for old times' sake. That would have been funny, huh? Me tossing you a biscuit again, after all this time."

"I don't eat biscuits tossed to me anymore," she snarled at him. "Or fermented fruit. Can't stand the thought of those sickening sweet cherries, either."

"Well, how about that! It's almost showtime," interrupted Viola, trying to usher Jinks back to the audience. Her cold shoulder tone was gone. She was big sis again, trying to get rid of the annoying waiter. "The show must go on, you know." She winked at Nattie.

The wink.

"Wait—I've been looking for you, Jinks," Nattie said, leaning over the ladder, holding the towel tightly. "I've been asking around down by Dukes. I hear you have something of mine."

"Yeah, Nattie, I heard you been asking. I took a few beatings, men trying to get out of me where I was hiding diamonds."

"I didn't mean for you get beat up, Jinks. I just want my things."

"That's why I'm here. I couldn't take that to my grave," said Jinks, as Syd came along and started yanking on the man's scrawny arm.

"Wait, Syd," Nattie said. "Jinks, what did you do with my jewels? Where did my crown go? And how'd you get them? You thief!"

"Me? You shouldn't say that, miss. Wasn't my fault. Margret sent me to your tank to fetch the crown. But I found a whole lot of fancy jewelry in the sand. And I couldn't resist it." He bowed his head like a dog expecting a newspaper swat on his nose.

"So, what did you do with them?"

"Remember those rat-runs? We called them rat-runs, remember?"

"Yes, Jinks. Just out with it. Where did they go?"

"I hid them in the galley level. G8V4. I remember. Eight. Like eight days of the week."

"But there are seven days—"

"Not if you are a waiter on a paddlewheel. We used to joke that the eighth day of the week was our day off."

"G8V4," Nattie repeated. G8V4G8V4.

Hooting and jeering came from the other side of the curtain. The boys in the audience were getting impatient.

"Hey, Nattie, the crowd is waiting," said Viola. "It's showtime. Come back later, Jinks. We have a show to do." She pushed Jinks off to the side. He didn't go far. His face turned blustery, a storm building. A humdinger of a storm . . .

310

The musicians took their places.

Nattie groped in the water but couldn't find her top.

Anka dropped the needle on the phonograph. The music started. Riggs pulled the curtain open, and the spotlight dazzled through the tank water, reflecting from bubbles, bouncing, making starbursts that were pink and blue like dawn on the lake, like the jewels that had sparkled in her hands—until they were gone.

She had loved her jewels and the promise they held. They were hope, and they were stolen from her, like the hope that was dashed on a Rocky Shore made of chicken wire and lies. And now all that was left was hidden on the dry-docked boat. G8.V4.

She fumed, sizzling with bottled-up resentment. She tried to listen for her cue, but her mind was on the *Lake Maiden*. She hated the boat and everything to do with it, including the child that was stupid and blind to the trouble she caused for herself. No one had forced her to become a thief. No one had forced her to flirt with waiters. Maybe she was treated like a harlot because she was one.

She had thought those treasures could be her ticket off the boat. She remembered that crazy plan to leave in an empty barrel. Then what? She had thought she could escape the pretend world she had invented, until she got all tangled in the strings of dangling crap: sequins, ribbons, shells, promises from a boy who wanted to take her sailing into the blue. Then she didn't know which way was up or down.

Here she was. Still confused. The spotlight shining in her eyes was too bright, oddly bright, magnified by the water and tears.

I was so stupid.

The glare made her eyes burn.

She closed them, waiting for the sting to fade or God to grant some hocus-pocus. He didn't. She listened for her cue but didn't hear music, only jeers, men's shouts, unimaginative and simple, like their brains.

"Mermaid! Mermaid! Mermaid!"

She felt vibrations through the platform where she sat, tickling her *dupah.*

Anka and Viola had started their routines. She was off track now, behind. Damn.

She tried to concentrate, but—

No—

Wait—

Hands pushed her into the tank.

> *And then, at thunderclap two, Jakub would push her on stage.*
> *"We'll take your chair out. I'll give you a good push and jump*
> *on the back. We'll go a-flying!"*

The cold water was like a slap. She sank. To the bottom.

Instinct took over. She swam. She made a grand flourish of tail and arms and her hair flowing behind as she made a swirl, rushing to catch up to where she should be in her routine. Bubbles tickled over her bare breasts.

She wasn't embarrassed. She felt free, like a real mermaid. Those fake shells sewn to her top had dragged her down like weights. For the first time she felt what it was like to swim without lies hanging around her neck.

She belonged here. She was at home in the colors, the glimmers, the motions, the ripples, the rhythmic ebb and flow. Her twisted spine and frail legs didn't matter. She was majestic.

Until she opened her eyes. Faces gaped, distorted through the water and glass into hideous monster faces. They shouted and pointed. She felt vibrations and heard muffled sounds.

She suddenly felt ugly. She was vulgar trash, almost naked.

She continued the routine without thinking, trying to cover herself with her arms.

Five, six, seven, eight. Turn, two, three, left, five, six, right, eight. Air, two, three, breathe—

No bubbles. No air.

No. Air.

The hose must be kinked again. She tried yanking it free. Nothing.

She swam to the top, but the enclosure had been pulled down, the trapdoor shut. She pushed it. The door wouldn't move. Between the water surface and the planks across the top, there was a gap of an inch or two if the water was still. She lifted her face, opened her mouth, tried to gulp air. But as she splashed, she made waves. Water covered her face and she breathed it in. She coughed and choked. Water burned her throat.

She banged on the wooden cover. She slapped the glass.

"Help. I need out. Now!"

Now. A rush of electricity pulsed in her arms and her cramped legs. She heard the nurse.

> *"Yelling is good for the blood pressure. Adrenaline pumps through the veins. That's the stuff that makes you want to fight. Defensive.*
> *Determined."*

She wanted to fight. She wanted to breathe.

She heard others pounding on the wooden cover, too. Syd was on top of the tank, messing with the hose, and Davis was trying to open the hatch. It was locked. Anka screamed. Then Viola.

Who the hell locked it while she was inside?

Her mouth was at the top of the tank. There was air. But not enough.

Jinks.

The churning water made it hard to find air pockets. She went under. Deeper, where it was calm and dark and safe. She'd find comfort there.

She saw Queenie instead.

> *"What do you think you are doing, young lady? Get out of that bathtub right now. Enough of this game. You're not a mermaid. Enough already. Stop your splashing."*

She floated back up. She tried to breathe. If only she could slow down her breaths, calm down, there would be enough air . . . until Syd got the door open . . . if she didn't panic.

> *"Air. Pulse. Rhythm is contagious. Runners go further to music, did you know? Our bodies seek rhythms. It's natural. That's why music helps heal."*

Slow breaths. Slooow down, she told herself.

Calm. Like the lake at dawn. Soundless. Silent except for the sound of a cat lapping up milk. Mr. Whiskers rubbed against her face, purring a steady hum of contentment.

She hummed the only song that came to her.

Roll out the barrel, she hummed, slowly, treading water, making slow, small circles with her arms.

Roll out the barrel of fun, Mr. Whiskers purred. A nice slow cat-prance-on-little-paws tempo. Calm.

She let the water hold her up. Mr. Whiskers swam next to her. A catfish. Sweet boy.

One, two. One, two, three.

She could breathe.

One, two. Again.

The cat-purring polka of fun.

Breathe.

The polka of fun.

She drifted into the harbor at dawn. Seagulls flew over her as the sun inched higher in the pink, cloudless sky. She paddled her arms in small motions, not making waves. The water was calm and so was she. The lake carried her and Mr. Whiskers to safety.

Inhale.

She was fine. She was strong. She was smart, independent, and capable. She didn't need a spotlight or a costume, ink on her skin or props.

She saw her future. The old wounds would heal, anger and hurt washed away along with the shadow of her sick mother that had loomed over her for so long. All of it would fall away, like lifeless scales being shed, dropping one by one.

Exhale.

"Get to one side, Nattie. That's it."

She heard a thunderous whack.

Wood splintered. Glass cracked. The entire tank shuddered and rattled. The vibration ran through the water like electricity. The tank broke.

Water gushed out, taking her—

A hand reached through the water and pulled her out.

Jakub!

CHAPTER 49

HALINA took the bus to Jedediah's church on Sunday. She would need to tell Pat something to stop her asking about the stupid coin, and she wanted to make sure Jedediah was on board, in case she needed to drop his name. There was no coin to get back. It was cashed in and the money spent. Ace had come through a long time ago. Now she needed a story with just enough facts to stop a hound dog in its chase.

Jed happily showed her all around the Silas Washington Memorial Chapel after services. He had made good use of the stack of money. The chapel was small and simple but sweet. The singing was good, too; Mabella was still belting out hymns with her big voice, despite her short stature. She wasn't as wide as she used to be. Getting out of the kitchen business had probably been good for her health, saving her life, maybe. There was that to hold on to. She and Jed had tied the knot a few years back. That was good, too. They were both twisted up inside and needed someone else who'd been on the *Lake Maiden* that night to help straighten them out. Who else could understand? Well, they did a whole bunch of God-praying, Halina knew.

Halina had done what she could. She made tonics for a bit and did some doctoring for the congregation. But the money was really all they needed for a new start on land, where the memories weren't so vivid. That and they needed someone to blame.

She supplied both.

She had known Jed would do good with the money; he was that kind of man. And his family was owed. She did feel partly responsible for their loss, but more so, it was the *Lake Maiden*, the whole dang boat and crew, that had let Silas down and caused the waste and suffering.

Jed didn't know the money came from a coin from a bootlegger. A bundle of cash had just appeared in the donation basket one day. It just happened to be a day when Halina had attended services, standing out, as white as mashed potatoes without gravy. She wasn't stupid. She knew she might need a favor from the man one day. It was good to let him suspect she'd played a part in the donation's magical appearance.

315

"The place is looking very nice, Jed. You've done a good job seeing to her, maintaining all this white paint and holiness and heavenly smelling furniture polish on the pews," Halina said, running a gloved hand over the spotless windowsill. Not a bit of grime or a dead fly to be seen. Sun came through tall arched windows and made playful patterns across the floor, fishes and birds flying to heaven on crosses with wings.

"I hope you have plenty of help. You're getting too gray to be hauling buckets and mops."

"Yeah, I just tend to the preaching now. A committee sees to the mopping. They look after the chapel and me and Mabella. We look after our own. Always have, always will."

That got her spine prickling. "What are you getting at, Jed?"

"Nothing, Nurse. Nothing. I'm just saying we're doing fine. We don't need no more handouts, though. Our folks is proud and they don't take to being saved by anyone except Jesus."

"Well, good for them. Good for you. I'm not here to do no rescuing. I'm all out of rope to toss to the drowning. It's my turn to ask for help."

They walked back to the choir room, where Mabella was hanging up the white choir robes, taking her time, like slow was the same thing as somber and holy.

She may not have been as happy to see Halina as Jed had been. She had sort of a pinched sneer on her face like she was constipated or had a fart stuck crosswise. Halina resisted the temptation to inquire. She was working on not being so direct. It wasn't easy. Pussyfooting around wasn't something that came naturally.

They exchanged pleasantries like old friends, because they were in a house of worship and wrestling wouldn't be ladylike. But Halina thought she could take Mabella, if it came to that.

"I came to tell you, Jed, that my sister's asking something of me I can't give. Something big. Something she thinks is owed to her."

"Oh yeah?" Jed stepped back.

Mabella got blustery, huffing out her mouth, her ears, maybe her eyeballs too. Smoke hovered over her head. "You wouldn't be thinking about reclaiming something, would you?"

"Oh Jesus! No. Of course not. Why would you say that? Some things you can't take back, no matter what. Good God, woman."

"What then?" Jed put a protective arm around his wife.

"Well, it's like this. I might need to tell Pat that I did something with her gold coin, something useful, so she'll stop asking for it back. That's all. Just a story she would believe."

"What gold coin?" said Jed. "We don't have no gold coin. This place was built with donations. Green cash money in the donation box."

"Of course you don't have a gold coin. You never did. But if I tell Pat my story like it's a fairy tale, I'm hoping you'll nod if she asks you about it. Just if she does. She might not, you know."

Mabella groaned and stormed off, mumbling and praying and blaspheming all at once. Half the choir robes were still scattered over chairs.

Halina took over hanging them, finishing the task that had been started. She was always stuck doing the finishing.

"You just want me to say you gave us some fancy coin? Then what?"

"You can tell her God gave it to you, for all I care. Just tell her you had it and it's gone. You cashed it in at a pawnshop that has long since packed up and closed."

"God works in mysterious ways, I know. I can say that without lying."

"He sure does, Jed. He sure does. Thank you."

He nodded. "Want some pie before you go? Mabella makes a nice pie. I think there's a slice or two left over. Enough so Mabella can get her friendliness back on."

"Kindness to visitors does a woman good, you know."

"Oh, I know. I'm looking out for her soul, don't you worry, Nurse. You look out for yours. I'll look out for Mabella."

"Good deal."

Jed led her to the entry. They passed through a gathering area, mostly empty now, just a few tables in the corner. Dribbles of music came from somewhere. Musicians were tuning up.

Odd.

She stepped on something. A bedraggled red carnation was on the floor. It had been crushed and smeared about.

"Someone lost their boutonniere, looks like," Halina said, picking up the flower carcass.

"We had a funeral last week," Mabella said, coming out of nowhere. "Put an old friend to rest."

"I see."

317

***

Halina stood on the sidewalk, thinking. Something unfinished ate at her, nagging, insistent, like a dull knife whittling at hard wood.

Determined.

Then the wood snapped. She heard it.

What is that?

"Who is there?"

She was cold, her breath visible, spirit mist.

Stop that. Go away. I'm not listening to you.

She heard a steam kettle screaming, then a man screaming, plummeting from a ledge two stories high. He landed with a horrid thud.

Halina staggered and fell, landing with a thud. Very unladylike. She heard voices through the ground. Vibrations of words came to her as she clenched the dirt, digging with fingernails.

"She knows. That nurse. She's got spirits all up in her hoo-hoo. One of 'em told her."

"Knows what, Mabella? That's crazy talk. We don't need none of that now."

"It ain't crazy. I saw it in her eyes. Buster's been harkening to her."

"Hush, you, woman. No one cares about Buster no more. Except me and God. And we settled up long ago. I did my penance for my part. It needed to be done. God agreed, you know."

"But she had the judgement look on her. Like she might butt her nose into your trespasses. Spread them out in the open."

"You is wrong. She's got more guilt than you and me put together. And she knows it. So, she'll be quiet about my sin. Keep it to herself. Now, you do the same."

"I know you thought were doing good, Jed. I know."

"Amen," said Jed.

"Amen," said Buster.

"Amen," said Silas.

***

318

Halina waited until Monday to visit Pat. She thought she would find her at Anchors Away. She didn't enjoy the thought of stepping foot in that cesspool, but it was the best place to talk to Pat.

She walked up to the building. The neon sign was dark. Boards were nailed across the doors and windows. Something was terribly wrong. What?

She pounded on the door. No one came. There was a *Closed by Order of the City Health Department* notice nailed to the door, but she didn't take the time to read all the mumbo jumbo. She knew it didn't mean anything— could be they just didn't grease the right palm or pay the right inspector their fee. Who could say?

Nattie. I need to see her.

She went around to the back door in the alley, which she remembered opened to the backstage and the big tank. She had watched Nattie dangle her tail in the water many a time, swirling it around, like she was stirring soup with a scaly spoon. She had looked so pretty, all grown up, a gorgeous young woman.

Halina banged on the door. It was locked, but that wasn't much of a challenge. She didn't carry her satchel of supplies anymore, but her handbag had all she needed: a hairpin and some hair cream to loosen the inner workings.

When she pulled the large metal door open, Halina was immediately shocked by the smell.

It was humid, wet, rotting wood, mildew, and mold. The overwhelming smell of stagnant pooling water. She gagged. Then she noticed the nothingness where the tank used to be. It used to be right there. Right? Yes, right there.

The glass was gone, but the wooden ledge was there. Sand was still on the cement base, along with some greenery that used to be alive, once upon a time, maybe. An air tank and hoses and some kind of generator were scattered sloppily around.

The stage curtain was there, closed, hanging like a heavy wool blanket that had been caught in the rain. The bottom four feet were darker than the top half. Wet. So much water.

She went out onto the stage and peeked around the curtain to the main room. Tables were all turned over, tossed; chairs, too, like a giant wave had washed through.

She thought of the *Lake Maiden* taking on water, tossed in the storm.

She felt sick.

Streaks of daylight broke through the boards across the front window, making slants of light beams and sharp angles. They crisscrossed the room the same way light had crossed the chapel yesterday. It was nearly the same pattern, and the same play of light that had crossed the empty shelves in her basement, reminding her of minnows with wings, flying from ocean to sky.

Patterns were repeating, over and over, lessons being beat into her head like Sister Beatrice repeating the multiplication tables, pounding her ruler on her hand in the rhythm of the numbers, and a merciful Lord bestowing multiplying abundance, then dividing and subtracting it again.

Some fates can't be escaped. What's yours is yours.

Chills and spiders ran up her arms.

Baba laughed. Then God. Then Baba told her to get her sister down from the table.

> *"She shouldn't be dancing on the table like that, in your mama's churchgoing shoes."*

At the bar, two stools were upright, occupied by two people, one bottle between them.

> *"Get her down. Take her home. Before something bad happens."*

Pat and Margret sat hunched, cast in long shadows. They didn't bother to look up.

"Did you come to gloat? Or to hand over the coin?" said Pat.

> *She may be older, but you're the smart one*, said Baba in her ear.

"Neither," said Halina.

> *We all have our burdens*, Baba said.

"Well, do you have any tonic in your handbag? Anything for pain?" asked Margret, rubbing her jaw with a chunk of ice in a red scarf with stars. It looked like something from a waitress uniform, or a pirate show.

Family. That's your weight to carry, Halina, like it or not.

"No, I didn't bring anything. Just me."

You can see it as a burden or a privilege. Take your pick.

"I've got two shoulders, though," Halina added. "And bus fare. Enough for the three of us. Why don't you both come home with me?"

CHAPTER 50

RICHARD sat at his desk, plugging away at his plans, listening to the big game between the Bears and the Cardinals on WGN and a transistor turned down low. He was trying to be discreet. A radio wasn't part of approved office protocol, but this was a rare event. Everyone had been talking about the game, taking sides, predicting which Chicago football team would pulverize the other. He had twenty bucks riding on the Bears.

At 1330 hours, WGN broke into its coverage of the game.

He stopped what he was doing to listen. A news reporter spoke breathlessly.

"Hello, NBC. Hello, NBC. This is KTU in Honolulu, Hawaii. I am speaking from the roof of the Advertiser Publishing Company Building. We have witnessed this morning the distant view of a brief, full battle of Pearl Harbor and the severe bombing of Pearl Harbor by enemy planes, undoubtedly Japanese. The city of Honolulu has also been attacked and considerable damage done. It is no joke. It is a real war."

Richard dropped his pen. He had been right. He felt sick. This was what he had been preparing for.

His phone rang. Phones throughout the offices rang.

At 1400 hours the colonel gave a staff briefing in the auditorium, but very little new information was available. Faces up and down the rows of seats were grim, each man and woman deep in thought about the ramifications of the news and what it meant for them.

Along with a few of the other ranking officers, Richard was called to the podium. He wasn't prepared to elaborate, but he assured everyone they would rise to the challenges ahead. Training was their expertise. They would train the new wave of navy sailors. He wasn't particularly fond of speechmaking, but he said what he had to. He said it with conviction. He hoped his confidence in his plan could be seen and heard.

Everyone returned to their desks, on standby, anticipating new orders.

Richard didn't have to wait. He knew what had to be done and what new responsibility he faced. He was ready. Now he would get the funding he needed.

He ran the numbers again.
And again.
He was sure.

CHAPTER 51

NATALIA wasn't sure what to do. The new apartment was so tiny. The walls were closing in. It felt like that tiny old tank on the mezzanine: a few feet of sand, water to her knees, chicken wire and plaster rocks. Nowhere to hide besides her vivid imagination. It was a shame she couldn't escape to some underwater fantasy these days—maybe ride a seahorse off into the sunset. Wouldn't that be nice?

It had been a week since the attack on Pearl Harbor but she still wasn't used to the idea of the country being at war. She and Cappie were both listening to the news on the radio, each about to climb out of their skins, itching with worry, sick with dread. He rolled his wheelchair back and forth in front of the window like he was watching for enemy planes. She paced the tiny kitchenette.

She thought about going to Anchors Away to be with the other girls, even though she had vowed she would never return to that place. She just wanted to see Viola and Anka and Flossie, her family. Would Pat even open the bar? It hardly seemed right to serve beer to sailors when the country was now at war. Was it at war? Was it right to serve beer?

Shouldn't they all be doing something more patriotic? More holy and God-pleading? She wasn't normally a churchgoing woman. Jed's Sunday sermons on the *Lake Maiden* were as close as she came to the gospel. But . . .

Dear God . . .

Nattie had no idea what to say to God or how. She tried to hear Halina's voice and her God talk. Halina's healing had been full of God-fearing warnings about excesses and promises of heavenly bliss for those who ate their vegetables and did their leg stretching exercises as ordered. The Bible according to Halina was also explicit about finding healing in the dangling robe strings and wind-whispers of a God who traveled in fog drifts and sent messages through shadow shapes and the designs of dragonfly wings. The Bible, apparently, was also very against tattoos of fish scales on a person's shoulders. Imagine that. It might have even been a special, lesser-known commandment: thou shalt not be a mermaid in a glass tank with self-inflected ink scales and false fishiness.

Nattie had her own beliefs. They mostly centered on beaches and water and the miracles of nature doled out to the worthy, the innocent, the deserving and respectful. And she believed in justice. The world had a way of making the righteous prevail, eventually. She didn't know if that was God or just the laws of nature, balancing out the bad with the good.

Soaring and sinking. Flying and diving. Living and dying.

She shuddered and rubbed her arms, wishing she could rub off the sudden chill.

Cappie had heard the news about the attack first, that day it happened. He'd been listening to the football game while she made soup. Now they listened to the radio continuously, as the newsmen rambled on and on, speculating and supposing but saying nothing new.

Cappie seemed excited by the prospects of war. An oddly enthusiastic "we'll show 'em" reaction had bubbled up from his wheezing lungs. He was energized. "You know they'll be sorry within two, maybe three months. The Pacific Fleet will wipe 'em out, blow 'em out of the water, damned fools."

His eyes danced, flicking around the room like he was looking for something. His hands fidgeted with a blue hanky in his hand to catch tongue slobbers and eye drool. "I could enlist, contribute to the war effort, you know. I could. I could skipper a supply ship. Or a troop carrier. I would just need a first mate who could follow orders. Not one with a temper, tossing—"

"Oh, Cappie." She was tired of hearing the veiled hints about Jack's poor handling of the *Lake Maiden* during the storm. Sure, Jack was no choir boy. She'd figured out long ago that Jack must have thrown Mr. Whiskers overboard. She forgave him. That was ancient history.

"The navy would be glad to have me."

"I don't think that would be a good idea, Cappie."

"I want to."

> *"I want to go to school."*
> *"You'll be laughed at. I'm protecting you. I deserve a medal for saving you from—"*

PAM RECORDS

"Why won't you let me?"
"You're not able. Maybe later."

"Cappie, let's just eat lunch for now. We'll talk about it later. Maybe later."

She put a bowl of soup in front of him, but he was too agitated to eat. Nattie felt the same. She put the pot of soup on low. Maybe later.

"Let's get this rust bucket moving!"

The radio broadcaster interviewed people walking past the studio. Some were rushing to enlist. People said the lines at recruiting offices spanned blocks, men already signing up, ready to do their part.

They reported Japanese restaurants and businesses being looted and vandalized. Windows broken, doors and walls painted with vulgar, angry sentiments. She worried about her friend Sunny. She was Chinese, not Japanese, but most Chicagoans were ignorant to the distinction, and it seemed anyone with Asian heritage was suspect: Japanese, Chinese, Korean. She tried calling the salon, but there was no answer. She had no idea where Sunny or her brother lived. She thought about going to see—

But she couldn't leave Cappie like this.

He had been in a mopey mood ever since the *Lulu* incident.

Jack was still mad. Cappie was still stuck bunking with Nattie, much to his distaste. She couldn't help the rotten living quarters. It was the best she could do. She just couldn't stay on Rush with the girls any longer. This new place was a dirty, stinking trash heap of grime and rat-infested vacant apartments where past renters had simply left everything and never returned. It was eight stories high, with one elevator that most residents didn't trust. Cappie's roll-chair was useless on the stairs. Her legs weren't up to the challenge, either.

At least the apartment was far from that street. Far from bar after bar. Men. Neon. Noise.

And someone who wants me dead.

She was still unsettled from that horrible night. It had been personal. She could have drowned, or she could have been cut to ribbons by the shattered glass. And then there was the mystery she couldn't put out of her mind. She'd come out of the water looking for him.

"Jakub. Where is he?"
"There's no Jakub here, honey." Syd wrapped a towel around

her bare shoulders, acting like he didn't see her bare chest.
"He pulled me out. I saw him."
"Now, now. You've had a big scare. Maybe you—"
"I saw him. His hand pulled me out. It was him."

Jakub was there, then he wasn't. Syd and Davis had insisted they were the ones who'd broken through the hatch with an axe. She had grabbed hold of the wood decking and hung on, they said. They pulled her up as the water rushed out. That was their version. She was still certain Jakub had saved her. She just didn't know how.

> *"There's no point in asking what for and how come when God is pulling you out of the shit pool." Halina rubbed tingling oils into Nattie's knotted leg muscles. "Don't ask questions. Just hold your breath and kick with all you got until you reach the surface and can breathe again. Doesn't matter how you get out, just that you do."*

Maybe Halina could explain it. She had a way of turning the bizarre into believable, with a side dish of warm "why not." She'd have some theory as made-up as those tonics she carried in her satchel.

Fanciful and miraculous.

It was funny. She realized Halina's mystical miracles and her own mythical costume were cut out of the same gauze-thin frills, see-through and color-shifting, casting spells. She and Halina both jousted with reality.

She suddenly missed swimming. She missed Halina, who had taught her so much. Who had saved her.

It had been weeks since she saw her, and she would really like to talk to her, to hear her reassurances. But she knew Halina was still mad. She wouldn't answer the phone.

When Nattie had changed and packed up her things that night at Anchors Away, she'd sworn she was done swimming in a tank. No more trying to live up to her mother's legacy and her father's vision of her, a freak in the spotlight to be gawked at. She didn't have to fulfill that sick prophecy.

She had left her tail on the sandy floor like it was a skin she had shed, discarded and left to decay.

Except she had no idea what was next for her. Was she done with water or just done performing her ridiculous act?

Nattie shifted in the rickety chair. It wobbled, its seat worn, paint flaking, hardly a throne.

> *"We should carve our initials in it."*
> *"Why would we do that?"*
> *"Because people do that."*
> *"Not people who live on boats."*

Cappie groaned, fighting invisible villains.

She patted his arm. "Shh. Shh. It'll be okay."

She wiped at the ink lines itching on her arms. She felt a breath on the back of her neck where the scales ended. Was it Halina's old woman ghost, Baba? Reminding her to keep kicking until she could breathe again?

Or Queenie exhaling? Taunting? Seeking revenge? After all, Nattie had ruined her stage career by being born.

> *"Some costumes define you, you know. Without them, what would be left?"*

Nattie hummed her humming song, a droning noise to block out Queenie's shrill voice, which nagged and picked at her in lulls of motion and moments of quiet. She'd been louder than usual recently. Insisting on being heard. The Queen of the Stage was annoyed that Nattie was giving up performing. She felt denied and put out, apparently. Nattie wasn't continuing the bloodline.

> *I was a star. I belonged on stage. I was Queen of the Stage.*
> *You ruined it. You ruined everything. Ungrateful.*

The curtain at Anchors Away had been drenched, tables and chairs overturned by the tidal wave of water from the broken tank. Men ran. Yellow-livered, chickenshit, spineless sailors ran like sissy girls. She could have died. Who saved her? A vision? Someone she used to love. And always would.

Cappie rolled from the table to the window and looked out. The chair was awkward in the tiny apartment, the wheels becoming wedged between chairs and walls, caught in doorways not wide enough. It was a giant anchor holding him in place. Who knew where he would wander without it. He was restless, his feet pedaling like he was walking in sand.

She planted her feet firmly on the floor. The soles of her slippers gripped the linoleum. No shifting sand. No water. No waves. No tail to get in the way. No breaking glass. No Jakub.

"Cappie, do you want more coffee?"

He didn't answer. He was at the helm; his hands were on the wheel. He was taking the boat out to the harbor.

Maybe she'd go along for the ride. Couldn't hurt, could it?

CHAPTER 52

HALINA was in the kitchen, chopping vegetables for soup. Her mind wandered. She tried to think her way out from under the heavy weight on her shoulders. She tried lining up the odd-shaped bits of worry floating in her head like the edge pieces in a puzzle. They just didn't want to snap into place. The news on the radio was fragmented. Confusing as hell.

She knew she wasn't very smart. Sister Beatrice had beat that fact into her with a ruler all through school. But Halina knew plenty about war. She knew it was heinous and devastating and the most horrific thing in the world. How God allowed it, she would never understand.

It meant innocent men died. She couldn't do much about that. But other innocent men didn't die; they were hurt. They needed refuge and healing and help finding their way again. And nurses were important for that. She could do something for those men.

As news of the attack sunk in, she became certain she wanted to help the cause. More than anything, she wanted to be useful.

Nattie didn't need her anymore. No one did.

Camel had come home from the war with no hands. He had flippers like a fish. He had been so ashamed to ask for help. He couldn't eat. He couldn't blow his nose. He couldn't wipe his own butt. When his mama departed the earth, Halina took him in. Not everyone had the stomach for it.

> *"Pat, I need help bathing Camel. We can't risk infections."*
>
> *"Oh, Halina, I can't. I can't look under his bandages. What if I gag or—"*

Halina never gagged. She talked sweetness to the man day and night, blubbering, dripping like honey, sickening sweet goodness and sanctuary from bitterness. She lathered him in pure love deep enough to float a ship.

The army had supplied two hooks like he was a pirate. Those were useless except for scratching itches. She had made a leather harness out of belts and screws. She could attach a fork when it was eating time. She fashioned a spoon for scooping, too, and a spatula doohickey for butt wiping, but that, admittedly, had limited success. She tried, though. She did everything she could. And it wasn't enough.

She bought him opium for the pain. Until there wasn't enough opium in all of Chicago to help him.

Then she did what she had to do.

"Goodbye, Camel. I love you. I'll look after Jakub. I'll make sure he stays safe and he grows into a fine young man, like his father."

He didn't thrash. He rubbed his forehead against her forearm, nodding up and down in a rhythm like waves in a lake, like wind in a tree, like mysteries ebbing and flowing from earth to heaven, where she would see him again, someday.

She would volunteer again. This time she wouldn't have to lie about her age and her training.

She needed to see Nattie first, make sure she was okay. She might owe her an apology. And some cash. There was a little left. She'd leave it under her pillow. With a piece of peach tree bark and a ladybug shell. For luck. And love.

CHAPTER 53

NATTIE had never been a breakfast person. The morning rituals that normal people followed were new to her. She was used to sleeping into the afternoon, working all night.

Cappie insisted she start waking up at dawn, when the light first cracked open the day and decided its direction. They had breakfast together. Well, he had eggs. She had coffee.

She read the *Tribune*. The news was mostly bad. Nattie kept as much of it from Cappie as she could. He deserved some protection. When he did catch wind of some news on the radio, he started in on the idea of enlisting in the navy. Yeah. He and Jack could take an aircraft carrier across the Atlantic, or the Pacific. And it could have a paddlewheel and waiters. She could be the mermaid mascot.

Brilliant idea.

This morning she had to read the main article three times to make sure she understood all of it. Not going to school had its disadvantages. But the newspaper seemed to make politics more complicated than they needed to be.

We're in the war now. We need to defend ourselves, plain and simple.

Chicago, as a major producer of steel, was another prime target, some people were saying. It was hard to imagine how enemy planes would get that far inland from the west or the east coast, but there were maps in the newspaper naming cities that would be on a shortlist of targets: Washington DC, of course; then the Virginia shipyards; New York, because of Wall Street; Chicago and Pittsburg for steel; Detroit for factories, the kind that could be retrofitted to make planes and tanks.

Change is coming.

She turned the page and tried to concentrate. More articles about the US response to the attack filled the paper, rows and rows of drifting words.

A picture of a man in uniform was in the center of the page. He looked so familiar . . .

Him! The kind man who had helped her to the deck.

She read the article:

Pilot and Navy Commander Richard F. Whitehead, Aviation Assistant to the Commandant of the Ninth Naval District headquartered at the Great Lakes Naval Training Center in North Chicago, the US Navy's largest training facility, is launching a new Chicago-based training program designed to train pilots and crews for duty on aircraft carriers, floating airbases that can respond to conflicts in both the Atlantic and Pacific theaters of war.

Whitehead, tasked with training more than 10,000 Naval Aviators, has responded with a startling concept. He is stationed 800 miles from the Atlantic but has 22,300 squares miles of water in his backyard: Lake Michigan, the fifth-largest lake in the world. He intends to make the most of this body of water. Safely within the US borders, carriers on Lake Michigan would not need armor, deck guns or escorting destroyers.

This is the inspiration behind his proposal, which has gained approval this week despite several previous rejections, sources have revealed. The training efforts will be backed by local Naval support facilities, including Naval Air Station Glenview and an Aviation Mechanics School, which have been notified to gear up for large-scale training initiatives.

Housing for recruits and classroom facilities as well as feeding, clothing and equipping the influx of soldiers will present supply challenges, some of which are likely to impact Chicago residents. Regular cargo traffic and leisure activities on the lake may be diverted. Mayor Edward Kelly has vowed that all citizens of Chicago will support the war effort, including this important role of training naval pilots.

Chicago was picked as the training site for many reasons. One of Whitehead's biggest challenges was that aircraft carriers are too wide to fit through the Welland Canal, the section of the St. Lawrence Seaway in Ontario that bypasses Niagara Falls to connect the lake to the Atlantic. The solution? Take a vessel already stationed on Lake

*Michigan—specifically, a luxury passenger boat, a coal-fired, steam
driven paddlewheel—and convert it for use in war.*

*Sources would not reveal the name of the ship, its current dock or
where it will be retrofitted, citing security. But all indications are that
the navy will begin retrofitting soon.*

*Tugboat captains willing to volunteer their vessels and time for the
effort are asked to contact the Great Lakes Naval Training Facility.*

There was no doubt in Nattie's mind. It had to be the *Lake Maiden*. She
was the only coal-fired, steam-driven, luxury passenger paddlewheel on
Lake Michigan.

Nattie closed the newspaper and folded it in half, then in half again.
Then she took it to the bedroom.

Cappie could never see it. He would be furious to think of his beloved
Lake Maiden being torn apart and rebuilt, only to be overrun by irritating
navy recruits.

She wished she could burn the article, but the smoke wouldn't be good
for Cappie. He's want to see what she was up to. Plus, she wanted Jack to
see it, Anka too.

Jack would know what to do. Maybe they could stop the *Lake Maiden*
from being chopped up and turned into something horrid to be used in an
ugly war. Planes landing on her beautiful deck, uniformed men stomping
around her elegant ballroom . . . and what about the stage? What would it
be turned into?

Nattie couldn't even see how it would be possible.

Captain-Father's bridge, the three smokestacks, her mezzanine, even
the giant wheel that turned with the powerful grace of a seasoned dancer,
its buckets picking up water to toss over its shoulder, carefree, making
lapping noises that were like music. They would all have to go.

She heard the rhythm. She smelled the water. She felt gauzy fabrics
tightly wound around her legs, locking them together so she could only
hobble, relying on the kindness of passengers to help her up the grand
staircase to the mezzanine.

"In all your splendiferousness . . ."

She remembered the man helping her across the deck when she was looking for Jakub.

Then the kind stranger had helped her get back to her station, that stupid little tank where she sat on a kitchen chair and hid stolen jewelry in the slimy sand.

"There's a crew staircase back this way."
"Ahh, but then the other passengers can't see your
splendiferousness as we go up the stairs."
"Spediferishnose? Is that like seductress?"
"Much better."
"I just wish people would stop calling me names."
He asked directions to the bridge. "I'd like to meet the
captain. Shake his hand. One nautical man to another."

He had not told her he was shopping for a ship. And he didn't say he had intentions to ruin hers. She should have tossed him overboard. Or introduced him to the boiler room boys. They could have fed him to the boilers or stabbed him with a switchblade knife. It would have served him right.

Nattie reached under her bed and pulled out the old clamshell suitcase, now well-worn and scuffed, missing much of its illustrious sparkle. She wasn't sure where the glitter had gone or when. Perhaps the glitter fairies retrieved it one night, repossessing careless glitter applications because of their risks to logic and reason. Or cockroaches nibbled it away, speck by hideous speck.

Halina had saved the suitcase the night of the storm, knowing it was important to Nattie. She'd rescued some money from Father's desk, too, and stashed it in the case for Nattie to use as needed. Miraculously, the stack seemed to replenish itself after every Halina visit.

It had been weeks and weeks since she'd seen Halina. The nurse had been so mad about the tattoos. She was so pigheaded. She wouldn't answer the phone, except once, when she hung up as soon as she heard it was Nattie. Nattie didn't even get a chance to say she was sorry.

It had crushed her.

Now, the money was gone. She had pawned the last of the pearls. There wasn't much left.

Nattie tucked the folded article under the jar of dandelion fluff and the jar of dragonfly wings. The wings looked so fragile, like tiny stained-glass windows that had lost their colors.

She found some of Cappie's fountain pens; a matchbox of bent fishhooks; sugar-sand; a mermaid charm bracelet, not worth much; a watch fob; a lighter; some sequins; and a paper crown.

She sat on the floor with her treasures spread out. She cut shapes from the paper crown. She drew an anchor and fancy curlicues using the fountain pen.

> *In front of her tank, there was a signpost with a small, framed sign.*
> SPECIES: *Mermaid, freshwater variety*
> DIET: *Maraschino cherries, orange slices, and martini olives. Requires mass volumes.*
> NOTE: *Mermaids don't do tricks. So stop asking. And they don't sing either.*

She stitched on some sequins and attached the chain from the watch fob, dangling pearls from the bracelet, and seashell charms. Then she fashioned a pin from the fishhooks. She scraped a bit of sticky glitter from the suitcase's hinges and dabbed it onto her handiwork.

Not too bad.

She took her clever creation to Captain-Father.

"Look what I found! Cappie, look," she said. "A medal for your uniform. Remember the medals you wore? Here's a new medal for you, Captain."

He looked up from his plate, baffled, bits of egg hanging on his whiskered chin.

"That's a medal?" he asked.

"Well, it may not be perfect, but it's something. Here, let me pin it on you."

Carefully, she pinned the medal to the pocket of his coarse blue work shirt and tap-patted it for good luck. The shirt needed to be laundered.

"There! Reporting for duty, sir," she said, saluting him. She stood as straight as she could, hardly bent at all.

He saluted in return. "The helm is yours. Take her out to the harbor, first mate. We need to reach Mackinac before midnight."

"Aye, aye, Captain!"

"Have you seen Mr. Whiskers?" he asked.

"No, Cappie, I haven't seen him today."

"I'll put some of this hash out for him in case he comes out."

"Okay, Cappie."

She put the clamshell suitcase and the treasures, including the newspaper article, back under the bed. She kept one thing out: the gold lighter with the name Alfonzo Salvatore and XXX on the back. Poor Alfonzo had lost his lighter somehow. Thieves were everywhere.

There's got to be a pawnshop in this neighborhood.

"I'm going out for a walk to get some fresh air and sun. Do you want to come?" she called from the closet. "I'll push the chair. I can give you a good shove and ride on the back. We could go a-sailing down the street! What do you think? Might be good for you."

But when she turned back to the table, she saw Captain-Father had fallen asleep, his chin resting on his chest, snoring, a long line of drool making a wet spot on his shirt.

She helped him up and led him to his favorite chair, a wooden rocker padded with handmade pillows. No gold paint, no sprinkles of glitter. She took the hanky in his hand and draped it over the wet spot, like a bib.

She traded her slippers for shoes, put on her hat and gloves, took her cane, and went out into the crisp air and sunshine, the gold lighter in her pocket. The cold hit her. December in Chicago was always brutal, ever since she could remember.

> *They bundled her in blankets and put a hot brick from the oven, wrapped in newspapers, under her legs. The frost on the wheels of the red wagon made a cracking sound as Szymon pulled the wagon over the sidewalk. The wind tore at her ears. "Pa-per! Get your newspaper here."*

It had been weeks since she'd been by the dock. Would the lake have ice sheets? Frozen waves, icicles hanging from the piers, chunks of ice floating like giant ice cubes?

Where would the navy take the *Lake Maiden* to begin retrofitting her? Nattie closed her eyes and tried to listen for her old friend. She might be calling. She might be hurting. She might be lonely and afraid.

I'm coming. I'm coming.

CHAPTER 54

RICHARD Whitehead trudged down the long corridor to his office, the buckles on his galoshes jingling, gray snowy muck falling off as he walked, leaving a trail. The clock said 0600 hours. He had hoped to arrive before his colleagues and hunker down behind a closed door, the office blinds drawn and the phone "accidentally" knocked off its cradle. Maybe he would live to see another day.

He was too late.

The fluorescent lights were already burning on the second floor, home for aviation. The coffeepot was half-empty, and his desk was covered with messages. His aide, James, was taking down another one, phone to his ear. James's face was flushed, and he was perspiring profusely despite the harsh chill in the office. He looked like he had been running interference for hours; a conscientious and capable lad, he must have come in early, too. Too bad his commanding officer, the idiot Captain Whitehead, had made the blunder of the century.

"Good morning, sir," James said, not looking up from his desk in the outer office.

"Is it?"

"No, sir, it is not. Indeed, definitely not."

"I didn't think so."

Richard sat at his desk.

He didn't bother to remove the goloshes. But he took off his hat, mostly because his head was throbbing. Already.

James paused and took a deep breath before he began reciting the events that had transpired so far.

The newspaper article had been out for ten hours. Surely *all* of Chicago, the navy, the armed forces, and the global allies couldn't already know that he had let confidential information out. He had bought a paddlewheel boat. The news had leaked.

"So, the admiral wants to see you."

"Of course he does. What time?"

"Ten minutes ago."

"Fine, I'll turn back the clock."

"Better turn it back to last week when that reporter called. This time tell her—"

"Yeah, I know what I would tell her this time. I know good and well what I should have said to her when she called for confirmation of her story. I should have told her—

"Commander Whitehead!"

He stood and snapped to attention, galoshes flapping around his uniform trousers. "Yes, sir!"

The admiral filled the doorway with his imposing presence, all sharp angles, hard edges, and contrasting colors held together with discipline and something that looked like fury.

"Commander Whitehead, I have one question for you."

"Yes, sir?"

"How the hell can I court-martial you for leaking classified information when I have hundreds of people calling to tell me your idea for training on Lake Michigan is brilliant? The appropriations department is overrun with local businesses offering to make donations to support the cause. Seems Chicago is eager to join the war effort, just like everyone else."

"I don't know, sir. But I didn't leak it. It was a reporter. She was at the auction, saw that the paddlewheel sold. And she put two and two together, I guess."

"Well, it's not like the project won't be out in the open. It'll be out on the lake, right there, where anyone can see the retrofitting going on and then the pilots taking off." The admiral shook his head. "So, not a lot of damage done, I suppose. And the response of the Chicago citizenry is certainly a positive," he added, looking over the stack of messages on Richard's desk.

"Yes, it is positive. Shocking. But good," said Richard, starting to breathe again. "Sort of warms a man's heart to have the backing—"

"Just do it. Don't muck this up, Whitehead. That's an order," the admiral said sharply, pivoting on his heel to turn. "Don't make me come down here again, either."

"Aye, sir."

"And you can take the rest of the calls. What the hell am I supposed to tell all the tugboat captains that have volunteered?"

"I'll be happy to take those calls, sir."

"Whitehead, just do it. Don't muck this up."

"Yes, sir."

The admiral left, and Richard sat down at his desk, letting a long, loud sigh escape. He sounded like an inflatable lifeboat that had sprung a leak.

How fitting for the circumstance.

James came to his desk with one more message in hand. He had obviously heard everything and was relieved as well.

In fact, he seemed to be smirking.

"Well, James, seems we aren't being relieved of duty," Richard said. "But do me a favor. If another reporter calls, hang up."

"Will do. But what if a mermaid calls? I took her number . . ." James raised his eyebrows eagerly.

"Mermaid? What kind of prank—"

"She said she met you on the paddlewheel. She was the mermaid."

"Ahhh, the splendiferous mermaid," he said. "I remember."

She'll be all grown up by now, won't she?

"James, call the mermaid for me. Make sure she's okay, will you? Buy her dinner or something."

"I'm not much for seafood, sir."

"James, just do it," he said in his best admiral's imitation. "Don't muck this up."

CHAPTER 55

SZYMON carried the bag of groceries up five flights of stairs to Anka's apartment on Rush Street. She and the other women from that sleazy bar still lived there, except for Nattie, who was too good for them now. Anka and the others were looking for new jobs. Maybe not looking hard enough, though. Anka had her heart set on marrying Jack. At least that would get her off the stage, finally.

Szymon helped out with groceries when he could. No point in anyone starving.

He knocked. Viola and Flossie both came to the door like they were expecting someone. Their disappointment was obvious.

"Oh, it's you," said Flossie. "Darn."

"Don't mind her," said Viola. "Come in, Szy. But Anka is . . . napping."

"Hey, Anka! Your big bad brother is here!" Flossie shouted. "Better come out before he huffs and puffs and blows the place down."

Szymon put the groceries on the small table, giving Flossie a frown to put her in her place. "I brought a few things," he said, "to help hold everyone over until the job situation improves."

"Oh, don't you know—?" Flossie started, but Viola elbowed her.

"What's all the noise?" Anka said, coming out of the bedroom, tying a short robe at the waist. He wondered why she bothered. It didn't cover much. He looked away but felt his face flush.

"Hi, sis. I just brought some groceries," he said. "I guess I should have brought you a wool sweater, too. Aren't you cold?"

"Don't start, Szymon. Seriously," she grumbled, pulling the robe to her neck. She looked through the grocery bag, pulling out cans of soup, a carton of eggs, a loaf of bread . . .

"You didn't have to do this, you know. Jack bought me dinner. He's been good to me, Szymon. Really. You can stop worrying." Anka started putting cans in the cupboard. "Jack is a good man. He has his own boat, you know! And he takes me out in the harbor in the dark. It's so romantic.

342

And for our honeymoon we might go somewhere enchanting, like Niagara Falls." She spoke in that dreamy voice she got when she talked about Jack. Or any man with two legs.

Her first infatuation was when she was thirteen, he remembered. She had followed the dogcatcher around the streets trying to be his assistant. When she was fourteen, it was the mailman who had smiled at her. By the time she turned sixteen, she had been in love with a barber, grocer, plumber, butcher, and bus driver. Anka wasn't discerning in her dreaming devotions. At least Jack wasn't twice her age, and he had all his teeth and hair. He was a step up from some of her past crushes. Except for his minor indiscretions—bootlegging, scuttling a ship, and being responsible for the deaths of four—maybe five—people. That's all. Small flaws.

"So stop your fussing. Please," she added.

"I don't know if I can stop worrying. It's just what I do."

"Well, pick something else to worry about."

"Or *someone* else!" Flossie butted in, grinning. She leaned toward him and stroked his muscled arm.

He pushed her hand off, shaking his head.

These women . . .

It was getting hot in the small apartment.

"Okay. Okay," he said, wiping his sweaty hands on his pants. He started to leave, but—

Viola was smiling at him, studying him, top to bottom. She was wearing a nice dress, green with stripes. She wore glasses. He had never noticed that before. She hadn't worn them at that stupid tavern. She looked so much more sophisticated with them, didn't she? She could be a librarian.

"Hey, did you see the article?" he asked, pulling the folded page from the *Tribune* out of his pocket.

He was sure it was about the *Lake Maiden*, although it didn't list it by name. It was the only steam-driven, coal-powered paddlewheel he had ever heard of on this lake—or any of the other Great Lakes. He had hated that damned boat for so long, but now, the thought of it being defaced and retrofitted seemed sad. It was just one more thing that would be forever changed—ruined—by this war.

Of course, Anka and Flossie had no idea what article he was talking about. They weren't keen on staying abreast of current events, even such important ones.

Viola, though, seemed to know something. She grabbed the paper from him and read the article aloud, adding commentary, like she was a radio news broadcaster. Then she got to the part he had circled.

The training efforts will be backed by local Naval support facilities, including Naval Air Station Glenview and an Aviation Mechanics School, which have been notified to gear up for large-scale training initiatives.

"Why's this circled, Szymon?" Viola asked, suddenly sounding serious.

He explained how he had wanted to be a pilot until he found out he was color-blind. Aviation mechanics might be as close as he could get to an aircraft.

"Mechanics. That's what I do at the *Tribune.* I keep the big machinery —the presses and such—running. They're not flying machines, but they require precision. Everything needs to align just right, you know."

"Oh, I'm sure it's very important," Viola said.

"And, well, I'm pretty good at it, too. Would be a way to help the war effort, you know. Do my part."

Viola smiled again.

She told him about a group called the USO, a club for servicemen. One was going to open at the railroad station soon. She was helping them get organized and getting some of the other gals she knew to volunteer.

"Since the tank broke at Anchors Away, I've been thinking those sailor boys should have a nice place to go for recreation. You know? Some place not so, so, so . . . well, you know."

"Ol' Vi's getting soft, that's what it is! Look at her, all serious all of a sudden," teased Flossie. "She's turning into a mother hen."

"Great. A big brother and a mother hen. What else do I need?" said Anka, swatting at them both.

"A new robe," Szymon said.

"Ha. Hardy-har-har. You're so funny. I almost forgot to laugh." Anka shook her head. "You just never give up, do you?"

Szymon went to the door, knowing he had better leave. Why risk making Anka mad? But she was right. He didn't like to give up. There was one more thing, another bit of unfinished business that had been eating at him . . .

"Hey, ladies, where did Nattie move to? I still have her mother's trunk. I want to deliver it to her. She might appreciate it. Something from her mother's famous stage era."

> *"Madame Bagda Wiśniewski, Queen of the Enchanted Song and Dance"* was stamped on the trunk in gold ink.
> *"I'm sure Queenie would have wanted her daughter to have her stage mementos, the items she treasured, don't you think?"* The opera house man patted the lid of the trunk like it was a valuable museum piece he was handing over. "There's a journal on top.* The Joys of Motherhood.
> *Lovely. A daughter would want that, don't you think?"*

CHAPTER 56

JACK walked Rush Street late at night. He was restless. He had known he wouldn't be able to sleep, so he went out. He figured he'd have a couple of belts, maybe meet some navy recruits, pump them for information—find out what training was really like.

Were they even taking guys like him? Tug captains with a history? He hadn't been charged with any crimes in the Prohibition scandal, and some even called him a hero for saving Anka as the lower level filled with water. But he had been the first officer, and he had grounded the ship. He knew no other captain could have saved her from being tossed on the rocks. Scuttling her was the best way to save her from more serious tears to the hull. He did the right thing. He was certain.

So how come I replay it over and over in my mind all these years?

Maybe the navy wouldn't want him. Maybe they had some kind of restrictions against men with a background. He did have some battery charges, fights now and then, but nothing that a few dollars under the table couldn't solve. During those years on the *Lake Maiden*, he had met some powerful people, people who could come to his aid anytime he asked. Maybe.

The uncertainty was driving him nuts. He just wanted to ask some of these fellas how close the navy looked at their backgrounds. Should he try using a different name? Or he could have someone from the mayor's office vouch for him.

Who could I get? Who's still around?

Maybe he should try buying some papers, a birth certificate, a driver's license. Just about anything could be bought on these streets. But he had spent most of his money on Anka's ring.

He could get Cappie to back him if he needed to buy his way into the navy. Cappie owed him.

He realized the irony. A history of fighting might be what kept him out of the fighting.

When the draft had started back in 1940, he'd registered, like every

346

other able-bodied man. But he hadn't been called yet. Now, with Pearl Harbor, that could change soon enough. If the draft board called you, you went to the army, more than likely. If he enlisted, he could pick the navy. Or so he had heard.

Nobody knew for certain. It was all so confusing and frustrating. Administrative types who controlled such things could be such idiots. As Jack got older, he got less patient with incompetence. Stupidity was just as annoying as troublemakers. So many fools walked these streets, the uneducated, the illiterate, the men with no jobs and women with no morals. No wonder his temper was always smoldering.

When he was on the *Lake Maiden*, he'd taken care of the troublemakers easily. They either wised up or were told to leave. Sometimes he helped them. Simple.

These days, it wasn't so easy. Land had its own rules, foreign to him in many ways. Plus, he didn't have the backing of Antonio's organization anymore, no more beefy goons he could call on to haul a man off the ship if he tried to interrupt Jack's plans. And, now, he had Anka to worry about. She was a heavy burden. He had been unsure about marriage for several years, putting off the proposal, afraid of being tied down, on land.

He'd rather be on the lake. Or the ocean. To be stationed on an aircraft carrier would be invigorating. A ship slicing through the Atlantic, Wildcat planes on her back. He could almost taste the power.

He walked. He stepped around groups that were loitering, talking, laughing. Some uniformed men stood in a huddle, slapping backs and leaning on each other, deciding where to go next. Another group of five men walked in front of him. They took up the entire width of the sidewalk.

He was alone.

He walked faster. Behind him, some rowdy fellas were shouting nonsense, something about a woman and her anatomy. Disgusting comments.

The cold night air burned his lungs with each breath. His gloves were back on *Lulu*. He jammed his hands in his pocket, making his shoulders hunch up to his ears. He felt bigger. He was ready for anything.

A pair of singing men staggered into his path. Army men. It figured.

"Hey, watch where you're going, assholes," he yelled.

He felt energy pumping like he had gulped down an entire pot of coffee. His ears started ringing. He guessed his blood pressure was ramping up, his ticker on full speed. He was ready to join the navy now, to go off and fight now. He needed to take a swing at something to prove to himself he was able. He wanted to fight for his country. Hell, he just wanted to fight.

The street was crowded and noisy. You would never know the country was at war, he thought. It seemed more like a celebration. Maybe it was a goodbye party or a "look out, we're coming for you" party.

All the bars were hopping, throngs of bright-eyed young navy boys overflowing onto the sidewalks, some with glasses in their hands, some staggering. They looked too young to be training for war, more like they should be selling newspapers or playing baseball, not heading off to be stationed on destroyers and carriers, leaving sweethearts behind.

Women didn't understand. Anka didn't want him to enlist. She was selfish, thinking about the wedding and having a baby, not about what this meant for him. He could work his way up in rank and skipper a boat. He knew he could. He would live his dream.

He just had to get Anka to see it from his point of view. Thank God he had gotten her out of Anchors Away and that nightclub dancing business. She had finally listened. If she wanted to be married, she would have to listen to him from now on. He knew how a navy wife should behave, and that didn't include dancing at bars dressed in those skimpy outfits. He couldn't stand the thought of men looking at his girl.

Anchors Away. It was just up ahead. He had heard it was boarded up, but Anka didn't like to talk about it, Flossie or Viola either. They knew how he hated Anka's old life and got close-lipped about the place.

Men were milling around on the sidewalk at the end of the street. A big man controlled the crowd.

Must be standing room only. A popular place.

He made his way up to the door. The sign hanging over the window was wood, no fancy neon. It was hand painted, fast and sloppy.

PAT'S HIDEAWAY.

Syd was the big man guarding the door. Good old Syd.

They exchanged glares. Syd didn't seem happy to see him, but he let him in. What else was he going to do? Turn him away?

Syd should have. He should have blocked the door. Locked it. Barred it shut with iron gates. That's what it would have taken to save her from the beating she deserved.

Anka was on the stage wearing next to nothing, a string across her bottom and doodads with tassels stuck to her—

She waved a bedraggled fan in front of her, out of step with the music.

She's dancing on the stage half naked.

His head exploded in fury. His vision clouded with red bursts. He heard a roar. She had lied to him. Made a fool of him. Betrayed him. She was without morals and beyond redemption. This wasn't the woman he had loved. This whore needed a lesson, right here, right now, in front of all these people.

Anka posed. A few feathers fluttered on the fan she casually waved. Her high heels were baby blue, like the walls. She smirked coyly at the crowd. Until she saw him.

He charged the stage at full force, like a bull. Rage fueled an intense rush of energy.

"How dare you, Anka! You'll be sorry," he screamed as he swung his fists. "You'll be so sorry you defied me."

CHAPTER 57

PAT sat at her desk writing a letter to Antonio. She crumpled another draft and tossed it to the trash basket, which was already full of crumpled attempts. She couldn't get past the lousy first paragraph. She wasn't sure what she wanted to say. She could convey it in a nasty stink-eye glare or with her fists. But the right words weren't coming.

Since the incident with Nattie and the tank, she had been a nervous wreck, anxious and paranoid. Frazzled.

Opening again as Pat's Hideaway had been a tough decision, but she couldn't go back to Ontario with her tail between her legs. She needed a comeback, even if it was a low-budget, no-frills tavern.

But she also needed to tell Antonio he'd better not mess with her again. She wasn't certain he was behind sabotaging the water tank. But there was a damned good chance he was.

She was about to give up on the letter. Maybe she could telephone him. She considered a trip to Canada and wondered if he was still at the headquarters they had been using. Or had he moved? Had Frenchie moved in with him, hot to trot and call the shots?

Pat heard shouts coming from the main room. The midnight show had just started. Syd could take care of it. She was in no mood to play referee for some drunks and, above all, she didn't want to see the police or the MPs. Those navy boys were so keyed up these days.

The roar cranked up a notch, louder, more shouting.

"Jesus, Syd, can't you get this under control? Davis, what's going on?"

She got up to see what the trouble was about. Was it Antonio's troublemaker again, trying to scare her into producing a coin? What did he expect her to—

She froze, hardly believing what she saw.

"Anka! Oh no . . ."

She was on the stage. Some tall asshole was beating on her relentlessly. Syd was up there too, swinging his fist at the tall guy, trying to pull him off Anka. Her white fan was spattered with red blood. She wasn't moving.

Oh my God.

"Anka!"

Pat pushed through the throng. Syd finally pinned the man's arms back and she saw his wild, snarling face—Jack. The tug man who was courting Anka. What on earth had gotten into him? He beat up his own girl?

"Oh, Anka, look at you, poor thing. Anka. Anka." Pat kneeled beside her. Anka was unconscious, her face bloody, gashes on her neck and arms. Pat shook her and tried to find a pulse in her neck, then her wrist.

She stood and called for Davis. "Call an ambulance. Hurry."

Viola ran over, screaming and crying and making more noise than necessary.

"Viola, shut up. Go get some towels. Clean ones."

Pat had seen her sister do this. She remembered. *Stop the bleeding. We have to stop the bleeding. Make sure her breathing isn't blocked.* She could drown in her own blood.

"Oh, Anka, honey, please hang on. Help is coming."

Viola came with towels.

Pat remembered Halina hovering over her son, Jakub. She remembered her motions, her hands moving so quickly over his small body. And so much blood.

"We have to find where the blood is coming from, so we can stop it."

"Viola, help me."

Anka's entire head was a bloody mess, so finding the source of the blood wasn't easy. There was a gash on her forehead.

"Put pressure here." More blood gushed from the bridge of her nose. "Tilt her up a little." Gurgling came from her nose area. Blood had been pooling. Blood was coming from her mouth, too. "She's drowning. Get the oxygen tank from backstage. Get the air tube."

Davis was there, helping to tilt Anka up, holding her head.

"Clear her mouth so she can get air."

Anka gagged and choked, sputtering blood and vomit.

Pat pulled her jaw open and reached into her mouth, wiping out the mess as best she could. More blood came up, and whiskey and empty heaves.

Davis came with the oxygen and the face mask from the old tank. It didn't look very clean.

"Get that dirty thing away from her," Pat yelled. She heard herself; it wasn't the calm voice that her sister had always managed when there was a crisis. Halina had made it look easy.

> *"We have to take the boy to the hospital."*
> *"He won't live that long. He'll bleed out before we get him there."*
> *"Do something."*

Pat took a deep breath. Then another. This was no time for her own asthma to flare up. She thought of her sister talking air into her lungs.

"Anka, listen to me. We'll breathe together."

She put the oxygen face mask over what used to be a nose. That wouldn't work. It was too mashed, bubbles and gurgles coming out of it. She tried putting the tube in her mouth. That didn't seem to be much better.

Anka was pale, her hands gray blue.

"God, help me," Pat said.

Pat started talking in Anka's ear and tapping her shoulder in a regular rhythm of heartbeats.

> *Settle in God's magnificent lap. Feel his hand. His pulse. Your pulse.*
> *The heartbeats are steady as rain. Hear the whisper . . .*

Pat heard nothing but her sister's voice, her own voice repeating the words in an echo, the same hypnotic drone that had saved her so many times. And had saved her son. Her sister had saved Jakub. Now she would save Anka, too.

> *Air fills your lungs. One, two. Fills your heart. Air and goodness.*
> *Three, four. In with newness and light. One, two. Out with darkness,*
> *damp and dimming.*

Breathe, Anka. One, two. *Padum, dum.* She heard the counts and the rhythm. She heard her sister singing "The Beer Barrel Polka" while Baba picked the burned flesh off her arm when she was just a girl.

Roll out the barrel of fun.

Anka gasped! She took in a gulp of air. She was breathing, inhaling and exhaling. One, two. In with the newness. Nothing existed except voices and healing. Halina, Pat, Anka. The three of them made a triangle like the holy trinity, something God-touched and good.

Then she realized the old woman was there, too. This was a four-sided tent, pumping oxygen, sustaining life. Baba took over the talking. Her voice was clear, uncontaminated with tears.

The police arrived and handcuffed Jack. He blustered with justifications, reasons he said Anka deserved what she got. The ambulance arrived next, and the attendants took over, pushing Pat out of the way, moving Anka to a gurney, carrying her out to the waiting ambulance.

When Pat stood and looked around, she was surprised to see the place nearly empty. The patrons were all gone. Viola and Flossie were huddled off to one side. Davis and Syd were at the doors, keeping nosy bodies from getting in the way.

She felt very alone.

Pat looked down at her hands and her lap where Anka's head had been lying. Her black sequins were red from Anka's blood.

She might as well have punched Anka herself. She was just as guilty. This tavern was a bog of slime, thick with misspent anger and grief. And she had waded in deep, taking these women with her, leaving them to fend for themselves.

God, help me.

CHAPTER 58

NATTIE stood on the pier, as close as she could get to the construction. It felt like miles between her and the center of activity. That was probably a good thing. Any closer and she might dive into the mess and start punching these callous busy bees as they scurried over her boat, destroying it.

Maybe she could hurt one or two before she was stopped.

She plunged her free hand into her pocket and paced, leaning heavily on her cane.

The sky was bright blue today, but the wind was sharp. Here on the water, it felt like knives hurtling at her, slicing away her skin. She turned her back to the water, as if that could help. It didn't.

Didn't matter, either. She wasn't going anywhere.

Other spectators were lined up, too, watching the fascinating choreography. It was a public area, on the lake, not exactly something the navy could hide away, out of view. But new signs had appeared overnight on the way to her usual spot.

Loose lips sink ships.

She wondered if the signs were a warning for her.

We'll let you watch, just don't tell anyone what you see.

Who would she tell? She was alone.

Anka was in the hospital with head trauma, Szymon staying close by her side. Viola was lingering near Szymon, playing at being supportive, his pillar to lean on. It was a new act for her, but she seemed to be pulling it off. At least, Szymon was buying it, and that was all that mattered right now. Maybe they needed each other.

War was doing that. Making odd connections, some rushed, some that had been simmering under the surface for a long time.

Nattie had visited Anka in the hospital twice, but it was awkward. For some reason Szymon blamed her, like it was her fault Anka got into the stage business. Of course, it wasn't really her fault. Was it? She didn't

354

know what to say to him, or to Anka. The poor girl, her head wrapped in bandages, was still mostly out of it, surfacing only for a few minutes at a time, then sliding back under.

Nattie understood. She had been there when she had her concussion the night of the storm. Now Anka was swimming in the same warmwater lagoon.

Pat's Hideaway was shut down once again, the police tired of being called to her tavern to break up trouble. This last incident had involved a half dozen sailors who tried to stop Jack from beating poor Anka to a bloody pulp.

Jack was in jail and probably would be for some time, unless he wanted to enlist. Apparently, that was an option his PD was pursuing. The army wanted men who could fight.

Lulu was docked. Nattie had managed to swipe a set of keys, which she kept hidden in her clamshell suitcase. She thought about taking Lulu out with Cappie. He would get a thrill, being back on the lake. As soon as it warmed up, they would do that. Captain-Father could teach her a few things. They could take up tugboating together. She could be the captain. Wouldn't that be a hoot.

> *Tugs in the harbor made big hoot-hoot bellows, like jumbo sized mama owls calling their owlets for dinner. The owl babies never answered. Maybe they had deformed legs, too, and were ashamed.*

Maybe they return, after all.

Captain Natalia. She could make some doodad medals for her blouse. No, she would need a uniform! A white uniform!

What a thought. But it had an appeal. The idea called to her, a familiar song, a rhythm perfectly matched to her heartbeat and every breath.

Sounds like something Nurse would say.

Nattie leaned on her cane and tried flexing her calves. The muscles were taut like a wash line. She hadn't seen Halina in months and was out of ligament oils and tonics. She hadn't been in water for a long time either, and she could feel her muscles tightening more every week. She feared her back was swaying into its old curve. She wasn't sure what to do about it.

The way Halina had turned on her was a major hurt, like a belly flop into water that knocked the air out. Halina had been her big supporter, the one source of hope she could count on. Then she pulled that away. And over something so petty. Tattoos. Maybe she hadn't really cared about Nattie at all. Maybe Nattie deserved to be shut out and crapped on. She was stupid.

There was no phone in this hellhole where they lived now, and every time she found a payphone and tried calling Halina, there was no answer. The way the wacky woman hated phones was just absurd. Kooky.

Nattie fingered the lighter in her pocket. She hadn't pawned it yet. Something told her to hang on to it, even though they needed the money badly. Their diet of oatmeal and watery soup was getting old.

Cappie was getting weaker. Margret was at the apartment with him now, back in the picture, doting on him like she really did care about him. Imagine that. Margret stayed with him during the day so Nattie could leave. Nattie told them she was looking for work, but every day she was drawn to the pier to watch the dismantling of the *Lake Maiden*.

Today, cranes were placing steel beams, widening and lengthening the deck. A new skeleton was taking shape in front of her. It was like watching God create a new species out of the old.

The paddlewheel was still attached, at least for now. Other navy ships were docked on either side of the *Lake Maiden* with supplies in crates on their decks, hundreds of busy men carrying plans, tools on wheels, and machinery that took six men to move. Welders were focused on the hull, hanging from scaffolding that hardly seemed sturdy enough, like flies dangling from spider webs, swaying in the wind. Sparks flew around them.

She couldn't see what was happening below deck, of course. It seemed all the focus was above water, on the deck where the planes would take off and land. It was so hard to picture.

> *"I'll give you a good shove and jump on the back and we'll go a-flying down the mezzanine."*

"Yoo-hoo, miss, over here!" A sailor at the end of the dock waved to her, his arms making wide circles to get her attention.

She pretended not to hear him. He was probably going to shoo her along, but she had no intention of leaving.

He stopped waving but walked closer, a fast walk with purpose and confidence. She knew a bootlegger who had walked like that, all cocky and smooth. He just powered right up, smooth talking and smiling with enough confidence to knock you to your knees.

> *"I brought you a present, Miss Natalia, something pretty.*
> *Pearl earrings. Lovely, don't you think? Every mermaid*
> *should have pearl earrings. Right on your ear. Near your neck,*
> *where you ought to be kissed and kissed often. See?"*

Her knees buckled.

The navy man caught her.

She slapped him. "Keep your hands to yourself, mister!"

"Yes, miss. Sorry. I thought you might need assistance."

"Well, I don't. And what do you want?" she asked, recovering her senses. "I can stand here, you know. This is a public dock. You can't make me leave."

"I didn't come here to make you leave. You're right. You can stay and watch. Commander Whitehead sent me. I'm his aide, Seaman First Class James Riley, not to be confused with James Whitcomb Riley, the Indiana writer."

"Well, hello, Seaman James Riley. Believe me, I would not have confused you with James Whitcomb Riley. I'm Natalia Wiśniewski. I used to live on that boat, the one you and your friends are defacing."

"I know. The mermaid," he said, giving her a good look-over as if checking for a tail and gills, some shells dangling around her neck and weeds in her hair.

"I left my tail at home," she snipped.

"Certainly. Of course. I see," he mumbled, his ears as red as his blushing face. "The wind sure is brisk out here on the dock, isn't it?" The dope didn't have a hat.

"The navy doesn't issue hats to sailors like you?"

"Well, yes, but I rushed over here. You see, Commander Whitehead saw you and sent me. He's over on the *Liberty*, the ship he's using as a command station."

"I called him when the article came out. He didn't answer."

"I've been trying to telephone you—on his behalf—for days."

"There's no phone in my apartment. It's a bit on the bare side."

"No wonder I couldn't reach you."

"I do have an address, if you had really tried to find me. The mailman knows where to deliver checks. The big *nonexistent* checks from the government that stole my father's boat and defaced it."

"We have been a little busy, making *improvements*, as you can see." He pointed to the construction on the dock.

"Well, I want to talk to Commander Whitehead, the man in charge," she snapped. She had no intention of explaining her need to any lowly minion.

"He asked me to make your acquaintance and reply to your message. He said he remembered meeting you. And he wanted me to thank you—"

"Look, I don't want a message passed to me through a Seaman First Class. I worked at Anchors Away, a hangout for sailors." She didn't even try to hide her disdain. "I've had enough of seaworthy, anchor-dragging, keel-hauling, salty jokes of sailors like you. I want to talk to Commander Whitehead."

"He's busy."

"So am I."

"Didn't look like it a minute ago. Looked like you had a heartache and needed someone to listen to your troubles. At least that was what this keel-hauling navy boy saw. Oh, wait, first I need to pull an anchor out of my ass, it seems."

She raised her hand, ready to slap him again.

He grabbed it. "Hold on, miss. I'll take you to Commander Whitehead. Follow me."

It was a long walk. She leaned heavily on the cane, but soon fell several steps behind the sailor. Her back started clenching, muscles cramping, with yards to go yet.

The sailor finally noticed and waited.

"I'm sorry. I'm not used to walking such distances," she said, feeling stupid and silly and clumsy and worthless all at once, especially since she had just been so harsh to this man. Maybe she should tell him to forget it. Maybe she should hobble home and never come back.

"That's okay. I imagine swimming is more your strength. I should have known," he said. He tried a goofy grin, but he seemed to realize how stupid his comment was.

"Well, I would dive in and swim over to the *Liberty*, but, darn the luck, I forgot my thermal-lined wool tail and waterproof long johns. Water's a little icy for my summer-weight scales. Don't you hate it when that happens?"

"The navy picks out my clothes for me. Makes it easy."

"Except when you forget the wool cap."

He offered an arm for her to lean on. "Nobody's perfect," he said and shrugged. He kept talking, like he was oblivious to her struggle. Maybe he was trying to take her mind off the pain. Or he just didn't care. "Tell me about the *Lake Maiden*. I'd like to know more about her past life, before she enlisted."

Nattie didn't feel like chatting, but she thought this nincompoop should know the boat his stupid navy was ruining. Maybe he'd at least feel guilty, like he should.

"She was enchanting in her heyday. There were formal dances every night on the mezzanine, where my little tank was set up."

"That must have been lovely," he said. "Tell me more."

"Well, let's see . . . I was the mascot, you could say. I had the run of the boat, except, of course, I couldn't run." She pointed to her cane and her ankles, which were swelling from the walking. "But it was just one big playground when I was little. The first few years after my mother disappeared, I was like a doll everyone wanted to hold and play with. The crew sort of adopted me. Bootleggers were always around—ruthless men —but they brought me candy and gifts like pearls. The seamstress made me an elaborate mermaid costume that was quite exquisite, hand-sewn with sequins and shells. I had a shawl of pearls and beads. I had a tank with rocks and sand and a throne. Can you believe it? I thought I was special."

"I'm sure you were special."

> *"You're something special, Miss Natalia, like these pearls. I can make you feel something special, too. Let's go in your dressing room. I have something to show you."* Antonio ran a finger over her bare shoulder.
>
> *"Something surprising. A big surprise. And you can earn your new pearls. Don't you think you should earn gifts?"*

She wanted to slap this sailor. He was being patronizing and stupid. She didn't need his fake sympathy.

"Well, a funny thing happened, Mister Navy. I got too big. I grew up. Then no one knew what to do with me and my smart-alecky sass, flirting with boiler room boys and bartenders. I wanted to be glamorous like the chorus girls. I was sixteen and thought getting drunk on the dribbles left in whiskey glasses was a perfectly normal thing. I thought musicians and bootleggers groping me was a normal day. Go figure." She shrugged.

> *"I like pearls."*
> *"Of course you do. And I like you."*
> *"Do you really? Honest?"*
> *"I'll show you how much."*
> *"Really?"*

He stopped. This time she was the one who walked ahead, enjoying being shocking, like when she used to spit sardine tails over the railing.

"I enjoyed the attention. I let them give me . . . gifts. Then, when a man was stabbed, bleeding all over my wheelchair, I wondered if the fight was over me. I thought men fighting over me was so romantic, you know, like Guinevere with knights fighting over her." She looked over her shoulder to see if he could possibly fathom what she was talking about. He didn't look shocked. He looked . . . starstruck. The idiot. Another stupid sailor.

"Well, one man ended up dead and the other took off to Canada. I had a concussion. I was out of it and pretty mixed up for a few days," she added, as matter-of-factly as possible. Just more cockamamie bullshit in the life of a mermaid.

Her right leg buckled and she stumbled.

He rushed to her side and steadied her. "Maybe we should rest a minute. We have a ways to go to get to Commander Whitehead. Here, let's sit. Do you need my coat?"

She shook her head. She was warm enough, all heated up from her little traipse down memory lane.

He grabbed an old tin pale that had been left on the dock, flipped it over, and offered it to her with a grand gesture, like it was a velvet-covered chair for a queen. She curtseyed and eased herself onto the makeshift stool.

Maybe she was like Guinevere after all.

They were close enough to the *Lake Maiden* that she could smell the iron and fresh wood. The noise of pounding and sawing mingled with lapping water. She could almost reach her boat, but she was just out of reach, like Mr. Whiskers when he would run off and hide. She missed Mr. Whiskers, the silly tabby. Maybe he was still on board, asleep in the galley, waiting for handouts of rock-hard biscuits and green cheese.

"You fellas haven't seen a cat on board, have you?"

He laughed. "No, ma'am, not that I know of. Did you lose a cat? Should we look for him?" He looked at her very seriously, like he believed her. For a navy man, he seemed sincere.

Whitehead had been sincere when she first met him, too. Maybe the navy had a couple of good guys after all.

"No, I don't think Mr. Whiskers would come to you. He's very selective about the company he keeps. He's a master mouser, too. I doubt there will be a single mouse on your boat."

"It seems we should know all about the *Lake Maiden* and her history, to honor what she was before she takes on her new mission training pilots. She really is going to be useful in the war effort, you know. You can be proud of her."

> *"Are you proud of me, Mama?"*
> *"What for? You haven't done anything special."*

"She was a good friend when I didn't have other friends. Can you believe it? I was friends with a boat. Strange, I know."

"It's not so strange. Ships have a way of bringing out the best and worst of men. So it's understandable that the *Lake Maiden* would bring out the best in you and the worst in some of the crew and the rest of the cast of characters."

"I suppose. For a while there I got carried away, took the mermaid thing pretty seriously. Maybe because I didn't have a mother keeping me in line. The waiters used to feed me leftover biscuits and the garnishes from drinks. They got me drunk, for crying out loud." She laughed, but there was still bitterness there, and embarrassment. "I can't believe I'm telling you this. I hardly know you."

"It's perfectly alright, miss. Seeing the *Lake Maiden* like this must be disturbing, stirring up a bunch of memories."

"Yes, well, enough reminiscing. No more talk about it." She pasted on a smile.

"If you say so."

She got up. The rest had eased the ache in her back. She and Seaman First Class went on.

"Could you take me on board?" she asked. "Just for one last look below deck."

"Oh, I don't think so. No. No way that would be allowed. A civilian? And in a construction zone? No. Absolutely not. No way. A top-secret project? I would be court-martialed." Then, more lightly, he added, "I'd be keelhauled. Hung by the yard arms. Fed to the fishes."

"Oh, you saw our pirate show!"

"I wish I had."

"I was crowned the Queen of the Pirates in the last act. I had a crown!"

That crown had been so pretty. Could it really still be below deck? With it, she and Cappie could move out of the hole-in-the-wall apartment.

The rat-runs. Eight days of the week. The galley level. G8.

It had sounded farfetched when Jinks told her he stole the jewelry and crown. Then, after being trapped in the tank, she had put it out of her mind, not wanting to think about that night—or Jinks—ever again. But she needed to know. She needed to get back on board the *Lake Maiden*.

> *"I'm sorry I took your jewels. I hid them one level down, in the first vault. G8V4. I remember. Eight. Like eight days of the week."*

"Seaman Riley, if I told you I knew where some jewels were hidden on the *Lake Maiden*, could you help me retrieve them?"

"I'm sorry to say, Miss Wiśniewski, that anything that was left on the *Lake Maiden* is now property of the US Navy. There's nothing of yours left to retrieve."

"But they're mine. Diamonds. Pearls. A crown. I want them back."

"That's impossible, miss," he said. "I'm sorry."

He didn't look sorry. He looked like a miserable chickenshit coward who followed arbitrary orders and couldn't stand up for what was right. And he didn't have an imagination. And he wouldn't know what to say to a real mermaid if he met one, and she didn't care one stinking iota.

Pucker up and kiss my ass, sailor boy.

CHAPTER 59

JAMES was still cold; his hands on the steering wheel were half-frozen. Sitting next to Miss Ice Queen didn't help. He was driving Miss Wiśniewski to her apartment. She had been reluctant to provide the address, and as he drove through the seedy neighborhood, he realized why. This was a street of derelicts and thieves and prostitutes, immigrants fresh off the boat, vagrants living in lean-to huts, wayward souls wandering with nowhere to go. It made his skin crawl.

The entire street looked like a trash heap. The litter—empty bottles in paper sacks, broken glass, flying newspapers, soup cans, a shoe—created a dismal backdrop. He saw rats in the alley trashcans as big as cats.

She didn't talk the entire drive, only pointed to a place where he could park so she could get out. He insisted on walking her to her door, despite her petulant protests.

He was frustrated. No, he was downright annoyed. Her childish behavior was uncalled for. She was intentionally being difficult because he had refused to help her find some nonsense that she'd left behind on the ship ten years ago. One minute she'd been fine, talking about her days on the *Lake Maiden*, but then, as soon as he said she couldn't go on board, she'd shut down. Her face had collapsed, a balloon deflated.

She fumbled with her keys at the apartment door. Music and a woman's laugh came from inside.

"You can go now, Admiral Riley. Oh wait. You're just Seaman Riley, right? Your mission is accomplished. Package delivered to the right hellhole. You can move along."

He ignored her rudeness, still hoping to make amends.

From behind the apartment door, phonograph music screamed.

"My, it sounds like someone is having an afternoon party!" James said. "You didn't tell me you had a fun roommate."

"It's just my deranged father and his prostitute lover," she answered coldly. She tossed her hair over her shoulder. He eyed the tattoos running up her neck, ending at her delicate ear. She was wearing pearl earrings with a slightly pink hue, like her cheeks. She may have been talking tough, but she was blushing.

"Oh, I would love to meet your father, captain of the *Lake Maiden*," he said. James could play this game. He was good at poker. He saw her bid and raised her. "I can't wait to hear his tales." He was all in on this farce.

She froze in the hallway; her face was the oddest mix of terror and admiration. She obviously hadn't expected him to accept the challenge. He was supposed to run, disgusted.

Not going to work on me, sweetie pie. I can stick. I'm a sailor in the US Navy. We don't run from a challenge. We don't blink, either.

He took the keys from her hand and unlocked the door, pushing it open for her before she could protest.

He rushed in, hand out, ready to shake the hand of a captain. "Hello, Cap—"

The old man was riding a wheelchair in little circles with a woman on the back, squealing with delight. They froze when they saw James and Nattie. The woman jumped off the back of the chair.

Nattie's mouth dropped open.

"Oh my, Nattie, hon, we weren't expecting you this early," the woman said, fumbling to fix her disheveled hair and rebutton a blouse that hung over scrawny shoulders and droopy bare breasts.

"Well, isn't this fun," said the old man. He was wearing an old captain's jacket and white boxers. James saw no sign of his pants. "Would you like some lunch? Biscuits and jam?" the old man asked, quite nonchalantly, like he was caught dilly-dallying with a woman all the time. Routine.

"Sounds lovely. I could use a bite. Strawberry jam, I see. My favorite," James said, helping himself to a rock-hard biscuit and a spoonful of red jelly from the jar on the table. He went at it enthusiastically while introducing himself.

"I'm Seaman James Riley, not to be confused with James Whitcomb Riley."

"This is my father, Captain Wiśniewski," Nattie said. "And Margret. She was in charge of the stage performances on our boat—"

"Ship. She's not a boat. She's a ship in the US Navy," James corrected her. He couldn't stand for the *Wolverine* to be referred to as a mere boat.

"You're late, sailor. Permission to come aboard," the captain said, saluting. James was unsure if the man was kidding, mocking him, or if he seriously thought he was welcoming him on board his ship. He figured he would play along. Seemed both the old man and the daughter had one foot in dark Delusionville. Or was it a happy-go-lucky Wonderland?

James stood and saluted the captain, then the captain's friend, then the captain's daughter. Salutes for everyone, all around.

"Oh, James, I am so embarrassed," Nattie cried, collapsing in a chair. Ice Queen was melting all over the floor, the poor thing. She looked utterly defeated, fighting to hold back tears.

"Hey, no need for that. There's nothing wrong—"

"Yes, there is. I'm so sorry." She hid her face behind her hands.

He felt terrible and stupid. He had been heartless, he realized, trying to be the by-the-books navy man when, really, he was stricken with her and wanted nothing more than to bandage her hurts and reassure her that she was the most beautiful woman he had ever met. Her tattoos and other leftover traces of a mysterious history only made her more enticing.

Wouldn't it be wonderful to get to know her with all her fascinating nuances?

"Oh, Miss Wiśniewski, I'm sorry, too," he said. Would it be appropriate to pat her shoulder? Her hand? He didn't want to risk making her angry again. Maybe he could find a way to cheer her up. Maybe he could help her. What would be the harm?

He found a handkerchief in his pocket. "Here, no more tears!"

The woman, Margret, started helping the captain put his trousers on. She struggled to lift him to his feet.

"Let me," James said, rushing over. He hoisted the man up so she could hike up his britches. He deserved to have some dignity. Respect. A captain deserves respect.

"Up you go!" he said. "All better. Full steam ahead, Captain. Steady as she goes. And look." James winked at Nattie. "I think I saw Mr. Whiskers dart by."

Nattie smiled a pathetic little-girl smile. "Where?"

CHAPTER 60

NATTIE climbed into the taxi, scooting across the rear seat to allow room for James. Being graceful in a dress and heals wasn't something she had mastered. Ever. She hoped she didn't look too klutzy. James barely had time to get situated in the seat before the driver sped off down State Street, darting between cars and lanes. The driver, apparently, was on a mission to cram as many fares into his shift as possible and getting the passengers to their destination in one piece was purely optional.

They should have walked from the restaurant to the movie theater. If she had been any other girl, they would have walked. But James made a big show of insisting on getting a cab for her. Took him over twenty minutes of waving and whistling and jumping out from the curb to finally catch a cab. He was proud of himself, grinning triumphantly, like he had harpooned a whale.

Take that, Captain Ahab.

She pretended to be impressed. Then realized she really was.

Taxis were in high demand on a Saturday night these days, everyone eager to store up good times before. . .

James wasn't one of those overly eager, gung-ho types, all hands and heavy breathing. He was patient. Methodical might even be a word that suited him, although she hadn't known many people who fit that bill. So, maybe she was wrong. Maybe he was just a stuffed shirt. Placid, to a fault. Or had a turd stuck cross-wise, as Halina would say. Maybe he was just going through the motions.

Keep the mermaid busy.

Or, maybe he wasn't really that interested and was content to keep her at a distance, something to watch and study. No groping.

A fish in a fish tank.

It was cold in the cab. She pulled her jacket collar up higher, arranging her hair over her neck in one practiced swoop-cover-hold motion. How many hundreds of times had she done the same motion? Too many. At least she wasn't arranging shells on a string.

367

She fiddled with the pearls on her gloves and dried to brush off dirt from the palm of one. She had grabbed the railing as they left the restaurant. A mistake. Mimi had been right all those years ago. She wasn't a white gloves kind of gal.

But she had been afraid of falling down the stairs of that swanky place. *Splat. Just like Buster.* And had needed something to hang on to. Her knees had been shaking. Still were. Her hands too. A date with a nice young man in the US Navy was something special. Unbelievable. She wasn't quite sure how to behave or what to expect. Was she supposed to be serious or funny or coy or charming or provocative? She knew how to swim in tank full of water, not much else. Seeing there was no tank in the vicinity, she felt a bit out of place.

She didn't remember when she had been this nervous. Maybe the first performance in the big tank. No, that was always effortless.

She risked a quick glance at James. He wore his uniform and a wool coat. His shoes were so shiny they reflected the colors whizzing by. His profile was a silhouette against the neon of shops and theaters and traffic lights along the busy streets. Chicago was bright. The cab was mottled and pulsing, muted underwater colors. If she had music, she could perform. Right here.

She tried to see his eyes but could only see his profile as he focused straight ahead on the street and the traffic. If he was worried about the taxi diver's sharp turns, he didn't show it. James looked blank. He was the sailor-perfect poster of calm, stoic indifference with a stiff upper lip and God-fearing devotion to something. But what? Probably something that floats. He was a navy man, after all.

The cab braked at a traffic light, the driver grumbling about wasting time.

James sighed, obviously relieved. "Some ride, eh?" he said as he leaned toward her.

"You could say that again." She made a silly, OH NO face, like it was the chaotic driving that frightened her. It wasn't.

Their eyes caught. A tautly stretched line connected him and her, her and him. It reverberated with tension. His face wasn't calm and stoic at all. His eyes were wide open, with a deep yearning, the kind she had only seen on a stray dog begging for food.

This man was hungry.

She didn't understand at all. He wanted something, but what?

Me?

Or, he wants out of the car right now?

He took her hand and squeezed.

"Sorry for the reckless driving," James said.

Then he added in a louder voice—so the driver could hear, "I'm sure this fine cabbie is going it take it slower now. We only have another block to go, right?"

The cab driver rolled down the window and spit something out. That was his answer.

"Oh, don't worry about me," Nattie answered, squeezing his hand back. "I love an exciting ride. Gets the adrenaline going. Pulse-thumping, my friend—she's a nurse, well, kind of a nurse, more like a healer—says it's good for healing. Gets the blood juices flowing. And the heart."

She took her glove off, then put her hand back in the warmth of his hand.

She looked up at his face to see if that was an okay thing to do. Or too presumptive? Maybe good girls didn't act so forward. She wasn't sure.

He smiled the most radiant, charming smile, his eyes boring into hers, looking for something. Some affirmation. Was he asking something. From her?

How can he be so desperate when he is so lavishly handsome? He could have all the girlfriends he wanted

She had to look away, confused about his expression, afraid of being sucked into some trap she didn't understand. She felt out of her league.

This is a dangerous man.

"Don't look at me like that," she said. It was more a whisper. She was surprised at how raspy her voice sounded, like she had been running. *Where has all the air gone?*

She pulled her hand away, suddenly cold. She put the glove back on.

"Like what?" he answered. His voice was soft, calm, unphased by her stupidity and fear.

"Like that. Like you're trying to see through me, pick me apart, find parts you like or don't like. I don't know what you're after."

"I can't see through you. You're a mystery to me. But I want to know you. More of you. All of you," he said. He pulled her hand away from her neck. "You fascinate me and I want to spend more time with you. Lots more."

"So you can figure out where the zipper is? Where the scales end and the girl begins? Are you like all the others?"

"Nope. I'm not like anyone you have known. No one else has felt this way about you, I am certain, Natalia."

"That's an awfully big claim," she said, pulling back. He was putting on an awfully big act, like the Amazing Mario over-hyping the next mesmerizing illusion. *An astonishing death-defying feat, shattering the laws of physics and logic.*

"But it's true," he said, pulling her closer, his arm around her shoulder.

"Really?"

"Promise."

She didn't resist. She wasn't cold any longer, a blush of heat rushing from her belly to her face. She could feel his breath on her cheek. Then his lips on hers. He pressed his lips gently, then harder, more urgently probing for a welcoming response from her. He found it.

Her suspicions melted. She melted. She became fluid, edgeless, boundless as he kissed her and she kissed back. Again and again. And the only thing she knew was a longing for more.

And the taxi darted among traffic, back and forth from lanes, like a flowing current of waves, the rhythm of a ship. She didn't want it to stop.

James did. He. Stopped. Abruptly. Pulled his face away. Paused. Thought. Smiled and then he gave the taxi driver a different address. "There's someone I want you to meet," he said.

"Okay."

And he bowed slightly to rest his head on her shoulder. And sighed.

The grand, kind, gentle man put his head on her shoulder and held her trembling, gloved hands.

She sighed, too.

"As long as I'm home in time to help Cappie to bed," she said.

"I don't want you go back there, ever again."

"I have to. He needs me."

"So do I."

"He's my father."

"An obligation? That's all? What could you owe him?"

"I don't know."

I don't know. I don't know.

CHAPTER 61

HALINA answered the telephone after twenty-seven rings. Some stranger was on the line, yammering. He claimed to know her. She didn't see how that was possible. She didn't leave the house much these days. It wasn't a good time to be married to a German man, was it? People talked, all uppity and persnickety with their glares and sideways looks like she had betrayed the whole country and was a lousy traitor or spy. She knew that was what they were saying. So she stayed home.

There was no good reason to go traipsing about anyway. No one to see. Nothing to do. No one needed healing anymore. They had doctors and hospitals and clinics for that. She wasn't needed. She was far from old, but she felt used up, all her goodness and God-loving passion fizzled out, pissed on by a dog with no manners. She could hardly blame the dog, but still, it felt lousy.

She had tried volunteering at the hospital. They'd looked at her last name, Müller, obviously German, and said they didn't need her. She should have used her maiden name. That would never work. That name was even more soiled with bad history.

She told the voice on the phone that she didn't know any Szymon. She slammed the phone down. She hated phones. Why God had invented them, she had no idea.

She had just enough time to make a fresh cup of coffee before the phone started ringing again. This time she held out until ring thirty-three, when she couldn't take the noise any longer.

"What do you want?" she yelled into the telephone. ". . . Nicky's organization? A pawnshop? *That* gold lighter? Why didn't you say so?" She sat down, holding her housecoat tight around her. The kitchen suddenly felt chilly. Had someone left a window open?

The man on the phone tried to explain.

"She had you pawn the lighter? Nicky's people said that? I didn't know Nicky remembered me. So, why are you calling me about a lighter?"

She hadn't thought of the man on the bus—Alfonzo—for ages. Hadn't thought of Szymon either, not since the night of the storm on the *Lake Maiden*. He had struck her as a pushy sort. He was the one who'd insisted she leave Silas in the galley and go tend to Nattie backstage when she fell. He was the reason she left Silas before she was sure he was coming around. Maybe if she had stayed in the galley longer, she could have—

"Hold on, mister. Of course, I know Natalia and care about her. Who do you think got her walking again and got her legs untwisted? Santa Claus? It was me, mister. What's wrong with her? Something wrong with her legs?"

"Well, it's been a few months, I suppose. Not since that big tank of hers in that tavern busted. I heard about it from my sister, who was staying with me for a bit. But Nattie hasn't been by to get more of the lotions for her legs. She was due for some months ago. She needs to keep up with the exercises and the rubdowns for circulation, so she doesn't get clots or bad veins. Or the muscles could contract up again, and then—"

She had even brewed up a new batch of the liniment and the rubbing oil, had it in jars in the basement, hidden under dishtowels, waiting for her.

"What do you mean? How long has this been going on? And you let that happen? You're a bigger fool than I thought you were. Where is she now? . . . How am I supposed to know where she moved to, you doofus? . . . South Harbor? Well, that's not too far. I'll take the bus. . . . No, I don't want you to come and get me."

She thought about the bus and how far she'd have to walk after she got off. She didn't have boots. Gallivanting through snow was hard on shoes.

"Well, I suppose. That might be faster than walking to the bus stop. Everyone has an automobile these days, don't they? You have one that runs respectably? Won't conk out in the middle of the street?"

She gave him the address, the main cross streets, and where to turn. She told him to look for the house with red trim. When she hung up, she realized half the houses on the street had red trim. Polish red.

She wasn't thinking straight.

Nattie, girl. What happened, honey?

She rushed to get dressed. A plain housedress would do, nothing fancy. She wasn't trying to call attention to herself as the healer, called in to save the patient when all else failed. But she had to admit, it felt good to be needed.

Now she had to be able to fix things. A simple bandage wouldn't suffice, that was certain.

Nattie just wasn't herself, the man had said on the phone. She was talking about going out to deep water. Kept saying she was going to dive in where it was safe. She wouldn't eat. Couldn't sleep. Kept talking about a cat with whiskers.

He had asked for an elixir to help her sleep. Maybe she would feel better if she could rest, he said.

What did he know?

Good God Almighty, what had caused this? What threw her into this tailspin? She had been so healthy for so long. Years. What happened?

Halina's satchel was in the back of her closet, out of the way. She wasn't sure what was in it these days. She wasn't even sure what kind of tonics she would need. What could she use? Which of her usual concoctions would help a woman with the Weepies?

She threw in a few basics, items from her windowsill and dresser and walls. Candles, matches, a bottle of rainwater, a Mason jar of dragonfly wings because they were pretty. She emptied hairpins and buttons and traces of face powder from any jar she could find and filled the empty jars with useful elements. Yellow dandelions still on their stems, tied into a chain, the flowers all wrinkly and crunchy. Some bits of willow bark. Yarrow and lavender from last summer, tied in clumps with twine. A book of Psalms. That might be nice. She dropped that in the bag too.

Maybe some rejoicing would be all the girl needed—letting go of the bad, celebrating the good. Baba had always been one to recommend celebrating the good.

That did wonders for most patients. That and—forgiveness.

Thank God Jakub had come into the captain's quarters the night of the storm.

"Jakub!"

"Aunt Halina. What are you doing here?"

"Helping the girl—"

"Is she hurt bad? Is she going to be okay?"

"It's just a bump. She'll be fine."

"Thank goodness. I was so worried when I heard." He touched Nattie's pale hand. *"I would have checked on her sooner, but I've been avoiding a certain first mate. He has it in for me."*

"Why? What happened?"

"It was a stupid fight. Seems I'm always getting the bad end of the deal when it comes to fights, doesn't it?"

"It does." Halina reached out a hand to his chest.

"Well, it ended bad. I came to say goodbye to Nattie. I'm going to Canada."

"Don't go. Are you well? Your heart? I'm so sorry. I know you have jagged scars. I know you aren't strong. I'm so sorry, Jakub. I did my best. I'm sorry—"

"Aunt. You saved my life. You don't have to be sorry. I don't blame you. I love you for what you did when I was a kid. You took care of me, patched me up when no one else wanted me. That was the best thing you could do for me, even better than the doctoring. You cared about me."

And he held her hands, tightly. It was not the grip of a sick boy. He was strong. And plenty handsome; his red hair was coppery in the lantern light, his face stern with conviction.

"You wanted me to live. You fought for me. I owe you my life. Now, take care of my girl. Make sure she's fine. Make sure she knows she's loved. Do that for her. Please."

She put an old babushka in the satchel too, one that had been Baba's, and the wooden Madonna, the one that had been held in the sweaty hands of so many patients, including the boy Jakub, who grew into a fine man, one she was very proud of.

She wrote a note for Theo:

I have some doctoring to do. I don't know when I'll be back.

This is important. Something I have to do.

Then she sat down to wait for Szymon.

CHAPTER 62

SZYMON pressed his back into the corner of the tiny apartment, wishing he was a smaller man so he consumed less space. There wasn't enough to go around. He stayed because he felt responsible. He stayed out of the way because he was scared shitless. The nurse was on some high-horse campaign, yelling and setting them all straight on their errors and wayward ways and lost souls and sins of their mothers and JesusChristMaryandJoseph.

Szymon wasn't sure if she was preaching, doctoring, or inciting a riot. She sure had a way of getting the blood going, though. Nattie, who sat in a kitchen chair, wobbled from stone-faced stoic to a sobbing mess as she listened. Back and forth she bobbed like a boat in a storm.

Funny.

A boat in a storm was the beginning of the story. Here they were in the same predicament. Up and down.

Frantic to survive. Hanging on for dear life.

Nurse was busy while she yelled. She cleaned. She cooked. She was brewing something awful smelling on the hotplate. She alternated between tending to Nattie and tending to Nattie's father, who sat in his wheelchair, humming a made up song. She fed them soup. Then applied ointments, including something rancid-smelling that she dabbed on a sore on Captain's butt from sitting too long in that stupid chair. She called it a bed sore, which was odd since there were only two cots in the room, neither even close to resembling a decent bed.

Nurse had said she could smell the infection as soon as she came in the room. Szymon had thought it was mold in the trash bin. He was wrong, he learned. Wrong about that and a whole bushel-basket full of other things, too. How he managed to live to see twenty-five birthdays without some woman seeing to his upkeep was a miracle, he was informed. That one he believed. He needed a woman.

Viola had been telling him that too. She was almost as subtle as Nurse.

Maybe they're in cahoots, an elaborate plot to get me hitched. Would that be such a horrid thing? Maybe Viola with her new glasses and fresh outlook would make for an interesting life. An intriguing wife.

The nurse poured one concoction into a jar, then started cooking another. Jars of various disgusting colors were lined up on the windowsill; the light passing through them cast odd shape-shadows on the gritty floor. They seemed to move.

I might be crazy. It's contagious. I caught it.

"You!" Nurse shouted at Szymon. "Why are you just standing there? Get to work. We have work to do here."

"Me?"

"Do you see anyone else I'm talking to? I need supplies. You can go buy them. Bleach. Rubbing alcohol. Epson salt. A dishpan. Ivory soap. Witch hazel. Onions. Lard. I need more burners. And pots. White cotton towels. And willow bark."

"You expect me to get all that? Willow bark? Really?"

"And take Cappie with you. He needs to get out of this place. Take an extra blanket. Take this money. Keep his chest warm. Be an hour. No more. Nattie and I need to talk. Girl talk. We don't need you two here to listen to us."

"Why? What—"

"This."

The nurse held up the *Joys of Motherhood* journal by the corner like it was poisonous. In her cleaning, she must have found Queenie's trunk, which Szymon had delivered to Nattie.

Nattie gasped and clutched her belly, bent over, started back in on her muffled wailing.

How does that woman have any tears left in her?

"You just had to deliver this to her, didn't you? Men. You're all idiots. Get out of here. Go get my supplies and take that foolish old man, too."

"I didn't know. I didn't know the journal would say ugly things. I thought it would be good."

"Pfft. There are no joys in motherhood. You fool. You saw the title and thought the woman wrote about her beautiful daughter and the wonder of giving life to her. That's hogwash. She wrote about pain. Disappointment. Fear. Resentment. Anger. Normal garbage a mother feels—even if the child is perfect."

Nattie stood. "She didn't want me. She hated me. She wished I wasn't born," she wailed.

376

"Of course she wrote that, my dear girl," Nurse said, scooping Nattie into her arms. "She wasn't well. Probably hadn't been for a long time."

"She wrote such horrible things about me. I was just a baby and she hated me." Nattie's muscles went slack, and she collapsed onto the nurse.

"I tried so hard to be a good girl. I wanted her to love me. I tried. I always suspected she was ashamed of me. Now I know it."

Nurse led her to the cot in the corner, where sheets were twisted into a nest. They both sat on the rickety thing, testing fate.

Szymon would have bet his left nut that that cot would be on the floor, both women flung to the ground, legs sprawled—

"Umm, excuse me, Nurse. . ." he tried to warn her.

Neither Nurse nor Nattie even knew he was still there. They were deep into stories about mothers who were less than perfect. Szymon couldn't hear all of it. But he got the gist. Life wasn't fair. Sometimes you got stuck with a rotten mother. So what?

She doesn't know the whole story, not even half of it.

He thought about telling her. But the stubborn woman wouldn't even listen to him about the damned cot legs bowing under their weight. He sighed. All the weight was on him. Maybe he was the one who would make everything collapse. Flat as a pancake. Rubble to be picked through. And put back together. Who could do that? Who could put it all back the way it ought to be? Fixed?

Nurse started humming. Some churchgoing hymn he vaguely knew of. She rocked Nattie to the rhythm, tapping her shoulder at the same time, a steady one-two, three-four beat. A-maz-ing grace. Pat, pat. Pat, pat.

What's that tapping about? But as he watched, his revved-up breathing slowed to match the beat. One, two. Singing gave way to talking. Nurse was sputtering some fairy tale, trying to explain how a mother could care more about stripping on a stage than caring for her child.

Apparently, demons can drain a woman of decency, suck up all the selflessness that mothers usually have and turn it sour.

That was an excuse for being vicious? Hurtful to a child? Cruel? He sure as hell didn't think so. But what did he know?

Hell, I was there. I know how it was. Really was. I know the truth— better than anyone.

"Well, Cappie," Szymon said quickly, "are you ready for an outing? Seems you and me need to go to a drug store. I think we better getting going."

Captain looked at him. Their eyes connected, and they both seemed to be fighting the urge to roar and punch a wall, set the nurse straight about Queenie's subtle ruthlessness. But who would understand if they hadn't been there? Queenie had her fans. She was a star.

Finally, Captain said calmly, "Anything to get out of this crap shack. Take me to the lake, will you, son?"

Szymon hesitated, rearranging his hat, his hair, his protective tough-guy shell that was crumbling into little bits as the captain studied him with clouded, watery eyes, huge purple bags hanging under them.

A wheelchair, blanket, lakeshore, distance, weather. It was a lot to manage. Szymon looked out the window. The clouds looked harmless enough, the wind calm. He could do it. He owed the man.

"I suppose we could manage a swing by the lake shore. Just a look-see. No jumping in, mind you," Szymon teased.

"Now, sit there nice, baby, while we sell papers. No jumping up and dancing around in this wagon. No cartwheels, mind you."

"And it seems we need to find a willow tree, too. Any idea where we might find a willow?"

"I know one. You take the wheel, helmsman, and I will navigate." Cappie seemed genuinely enthused. Maybe the nurse was right. Maybe he needed to get out and spend some time with another man, one who had known him in better days. Someone who understood the power he once had—and what he lost. Szymon certainly fit that bill. He'd been there for the rise and fall. Up and down.

"Aye, aye, Captain. Maybe we should put shoes on your feet, though, not slippers? Do you have shoes?"

Cappie shook his head. "I have medals."

"I see. Okay, slippers will do. Slippers for the skipper." Szymon draped a blanket around the man's shoulders and across his chest, where medals used be. "Off we go, sailing into the blue yonder!" He gave the chair a big push and resisted the temptation to jump on the back. He didn't want to break the damned thing.

I've already done enough damage.

"C'mon Cappie. Cast off. Full throttle ahead, or whatever you boat men like to say."

***

378

Szymon took long strides down the sidewalk, eager to get to the corner and turn toward the lake. The wheelchair made clickety sounds over the cracks in the sidewalk. Cappie didn't say anything. He was hunched down, like he didn't want to be seen. What was that about? Szymon didn't ask. He figured the man was entitled to some peace and quiet and a chance to hear himself think.

The block wasn't very quiet, though. A dog barked and another one answered, back and forth, like they were each defending some lousy patch of territory or scrap of food. Traffic added background noise. Old cars, delivery trucks, men on the way to work or home from work or looking for work drove by, engines revving, drivers honking their horns. From one of the windows way up high in the building, a baby started crying. He wondered if someone was hushing the child, picking it up, telling it everything would be alright.

Hush now. Shhh. It will be alright.

He couldn't get Queenie out of his head. He thought of that portrait hanging in the opera hall. He wondered if portraits of other Vaudeville-era entertainers were hanging next to the Royal Highness. Maybe a poster of the man with shoe polish on his face, dressed like a hobo, tap dancing around a cardboard lamp post. Or the man on a unicycle juggling cabbages.

He had seen part of the show a few times, invited by Queenie, who didn't see a thing wrong about inviting a twelve-year-old boy to a burlesque show.

"You'll love it. The show is so educational. And patriotic. You'll be saluting the flag!"

Those were different times. The Great Depression was far from great. Everyone was desperate, afraid of losing even more.

His father had saved all his life to buy the apartment building. Then renters couldn't pay their rent. Some skipped out and went God knows where. Others refused to leave even when they couldn't pay. Father had tried to be kind. But truth was, he had bills to pay too. Like fire insurance.

Szymon had heard the talk. The walls were paper thin. Captain Wiśniewski had friends. Those friends didn't want the Wiśniewski family evicted.

"It would be such a shame to see that family with the little sick girl turned out, wouldn't it? And wouldn't it be a shame to see the whole building go up in flames? Poof?"

Szymon reached the corner. He paused to catch his breath. He was all riled up again, panting and breathing funny, bent out of shape, thinking about old days.

"Well, which way, Cappie? Left or right? Up to you." Maybe there was some chance in hell the old man did know where a willow tree was.

Captain pointed left.

"Okay, left it is, my man. Heading due north. Hang on. Hell, we could go all the way to Canada."

"I've gone that route before. Don't think I'd be stupid enough to do it again." Captain sounded wistful.

There I've done it again. Stuck my foot in my mouth. Saying the wrong thing.

"I'm sorry, Captain, I wasn't thinking—I didn't mean to bring up the storm and bad memories for you. It just came out."

"That's fine, son. It's not your fault."

Szymon pushed the wheelchair, gripping the handles as tight as he could.

He had to hang on to the door handle. It was hot. His hand was sweating, heat climbing his arm. He could feel his face getting red.

The door to the incinerator was heavy. He was supposed to be burning trash. Father had sent him. Chores.

But then he'd heard voices in the basement hallway. Queenie and her man friend, the one with black hair that was slicked back into a wave, like a duck's tail.

"Alfonzo said he'd be there at noon. He'll meet us at the beach. He'll grab her and put her in his truck."

"Then what?"

"He says the fella who wants her doesn't mind about the legs.

Says at least she won't run away."

"But when he gets a look at the scars, he might think differently. Are you sure he wants a cripple? I don't see how a couple could possibly want to raise her . . ."

"There's no couple, baby. Just this fella, Hank. He says he'll take her, take care of her good, teach her all she needs to know."

The incinerator door wanted to slam shut. But then they would hear him and know he was there, listening to them. He had to be quiet so he could hear more.

"Then we can go to New York. Make it big there. They'll love you. We can't take her with us, you know."

"I know. I can't take her. I can't stand to see those bent, scrawny legs, like chicken legs."

"And your sailor boy knows squat about raising a girl. Especially a crippled one. She'd end up fish bait, and you know it. His bootlegger friends—well, she would end up swimming with the fishes."

At the time, Szymon hadn't quite understood all of the conversation. Now he had an idea of what might have been destined for Nattie.

He shuddered thinking of it.

Thank God Cappie had believed him when he told him what he'd heard. Thank God Cappie had intervened. He must have met them at the beach, got there before the Alfonzo fella showed up.

Szymon wasn't sure exactly what happened that day. But when he heard Queenie was found dead on the lake shore, he knew it was no coincidence, no twist of fate. No, Cappie had done something to protect Nattie, of that he was certain.

Szymon had been relieved at the time, but he had also felt responsible. He'd told. What if he had gotten the facts wrong or misunderstood the conversation? They had been whispering and the incinerator had been roaring. Maybe they'd made a harmless plan, something that would be good for Nattie.

Of course not. He knew the score.

All these years, he had felt responsible and wondered if he did the right thing. It was a heavy burden for a young boy, heavy for a young man too.

"Oh, Captain, right you are. Look there. I see a big old willow tree in that school lot. I'll just ask if we can borrow some bark," he said. Then he thought about that conversation. "Come to think of it, they might not understand. Maybe I should just try to break off a bit—"

"You might need this," Captain said, pulling a switchblade out of his back pocket. It had a pearl handle.

"Hmm. What are you doing with this?" Szymon asked, hardly able to hide his surprise. "I suppose it would be useful."

"A man needs to be prepared. All the time. Never know when you'll run into some troublemakers. Or need to steal some tree bark to help your daughter." Captain reached over his shoulder and put his hand on Szymon's hand. "You know I would do *whatever* is needed to help my daughter."

Well, that's an understatement if I ever heard one.

"You understand, son? I did what I had to do. So did you."

"Aye, Captain. I understand."

"Very well. Carry on." And he pointed to the weeping willow tree, its long branches hanging low, brushing over the empty playground pavement.

Children who weren't really there played, sang, and skipped, happy and whole, well and guilt free.

CHAPTER 63

NATTIE sat in front of the mirror in her bedroom, getting prettied up. She had curlers in her hair, and she had bought some new rouge and paint for her nails. The nail paint was called mermaid pink. She couldn't resist; it was a joke only she would be privy to. Sort of personal and private, the way some jokes should be. Well, she might tell Anka when she went to visit her at the Convalescent Center later, after the big bash at the pier.

Her feet were shoe-horned into some new flats. Her legs were less swollen. They had been cooperating, the new exercises helping. But she couldn't help but worry about the presentation. What if she stood up on cue to receive the fancy plague and toppled over, planting her face in the laps of some navy dignitaries?

That would be a lovely spectacle, wouldn't it?

Deep breaths. In, out. One, two. Once, more. Five, six.

She had agreed with Szymon that taking Captain-Father to the christening of the *Wolverine* might be good for him, and good for her, too. She couldn't keep hiding from her father what had become of his prized *Lake Maiden* paddlewheel. And she couldn't keep hiding her father—and his decline—from James.

James was a good man. She was learning to trust him, even if it was challenging at times. He was as unsure how to have a serious relationship as she was. That first night when they kissed in the cab, he gave the cab driver a new address so he could introduce her to someone. It was Max, his dog, an old cocker spaniel. He said her hair reminded him of the wavy fur on Max's long ears. It was supposed to be flattering.

It took her a good week to see it that way. She eventually forgave him for comparing her to a dog. She figured it was a step up from being called fish girl.

James had his quirks. But she was learning to love them. And him.

***

It was almost time to go. Szymon would be picking up Nattie and Cappie in an hour. She hadn't seen him in weeks. He'd been tending to Anka, getting her set up in the Convalescent Center. It was a sullen place, dank and run-down. Anka was improving, but it would be a long road with lots of physical therapy. She was relearning to walk with braces and canes to help her legs hold her weight. Jack had broken both legs with powerful kicks.

Halina was helping when she could, but the bus ride was long and the nurses on the ward didn't appreciate Halina's unique version of help.

> *"Moaning and groaning is only good for the bedroom. Rest of the time, it's annoying. No one wants to hear it."*
> *"I can't do it."*
> *"Well, with that attitude you won't do diddly-squat except wear out your ass, just sitting on it. I expect better from a good Polish girl."*
> *"I'm no good."*
> *"You're good for something. Damned tootin'. Or we wouldn't be here."*

The nurse was good for homespun truisms. Some were definitely Old Country derivatives; others were made up on the spot. And some were pure BS.

Nattie had learned her lesson about skipping her exercise regimen. Since she wasn't swimming anymore, she had to work harder at the exercises and keep flexing her legs and using the ointment and oils if she wanted to improve.

She had been annoyed with Szymon for calling the nurse. She didn't know why he butted his nose in. Well, pawning the gold lighter had really triggered the reunion with Halina. Ace at the pawnshop had called someone named Nicky when he saw Alfonzo's lighter. Alfonzo was one of Nicky's crew, some big-time distributor Halina knew from the neighborhood. Halina might have been sweet on Nicky some time back, seemed like. Nicky knew how to reach the nurse and knew she would want to be informed that her longtime patient was desperate for money.

When Halina had arrived at the apartment, she was full of commotion and noise. She was sure someone had physically hurt Nattie, and she was going to find out who and give them a piece of her mind. She was going to take care of them once and for all and put an end to whatever or whoever was giving her Nattie trouble.

She had called it the Weepies. It was a condition to be taken seriously, not hush-hushed and hand-patted away. She had sensed that Nattie was hurting and in serious pain.

Nurse Halina listened to all of Nattie's ranting, even about the journal her mother had left behind.

She opened the lid of the old trunk.
There was a removable tray with sectioned-off compartments.
A matchbook, six gold buttons of various sizes, a needle and
thread, some red sequins, and one small brown snail
shell, empty.
Under the tray, some costume pieces and a shawl with ornate
beadwork. She ran her fingers over the texture, reading the
ripples like a blind woman reading braille. The story was
moving. There was a pair of long gloves with buttons up the
side. She tried them on. They were awkward, baggy here, tight
there, oddly shaped, like skin that belonged to someone else.
She found a brush and comb set and a mirror, gold. This
wasn't a drugstore set painted gold with glued-on glitter. The
mirror wasn't cracked. She saw herself for what she was: a
young woman taking charge of her own life, finally.
Then she saw the journal with her mother's handwriting.
The Joys of Motherhood, *it said.*
How sweet.
Nattie smiled and rubbed the goosebumps from her arms. She
opened the book and began reading. She quickly lost her
smile. There was nothing sweet and sentimental on these
pages. They were filled with bitterness and resentment.

May 10. She bawled all day. Again.

May 12. I can't stand the wailing. It never ends.

May 20. The burden is killing me. How did this happen to me?

May 22. More crying. Shrieking.

May 23. How can I get rid of her? Who will take her?

June 2. Another snotty nose.

June 4. She won't eat. She won't sleep.

June 12. She is an anchor around my neck.

July 15. She's sucking the life out of me.

July 18. I can't stand it.

July 20. She whimpers. A pathetic cat crying mews. I can't take another day.

Aug. 3. Her legs are twisted. She just wants to be carried.

Aug 15. All she says is Da-Da. Daddy's girl. What am I? The slave maid.

Aug 18. Screaming. More mess. Spewed all over my one nice dress.

Aug 28. Wretched. I'm so tired of piss and shit and baby puke.

Aug 30. Someone help me.

Aug 31. I would rather be dead.

The disjointed, ugly words had jumped out at her from the pages. She was devastated. She was ashamed. She must have been a horrible burden, sickly and ugly, with bowed legs, a disappointment.

I was a child. I couldn't help it.

Halina had an interesting take on the journal. When Nattie had shown it to her, the nurse's reaction was calm, matter-of-fact.

"So what? All this proves is she was a sick woman. Exactly what I've guessed all along."
"Sick? How about cruel and mean?"
"Well, if you want to add that too, go ahead. But she was sick. These aren't the words of a well woman who was cut out for being a mother. She didn't have the fortitude. She was all self-

focused. Obsessed with being Queen of the Stage. Not
motherly material."

"Why did she even have me?"

"Pregnancies aren't always planned, dear." She shrugged.
"Do I need to educate you on that, too? Didn't those floozy
dolls on that boat teach you anything? Do you know how a
man's hooey works? I can draw one . . . Here, get me a
pencil—"

"Stop!"

Halina seemed to understand Nattie's pain, but she refused to let her be defeated by it. She had a way of making her get up off the ground, even when she wanted to wallow there a bit.

She made the calm return. Like the lake at dawn. Soundless.

Nattie looked in her mirror. She pulled out the curlers one by one, slowly. Blond curls bobbed around her shoulders. No strings. No dangles of sequins and braids of weeds. The room was silent except for little cat-lapping-up-milk sounds, water lapping at the metal hull.

Mr. Whiskers wasn't real. She wasn't sure if he ever had been. Maybe a long time ago.

Inhale. Slowly. Breathe. Stay calm. She heard a voice say: You are in charge of you, young lady. No one can tell you who you are or what you are.

She heard it clearly, like a woman was standing next to her, but no one was there.

She floated, drifted into the harbor. Seagulls flew over her as the sun inched higher in the pink, cloudless sky. She paddled her arms in small motions, not wanting to make waves. The water was calm and so was she. It held her up and carried her to safety.

She was fine. Just fine.

I am well. I am whole.

She brushed her hair back from her face, surprised to find her face wet. She dabbed at the dribbles with a hanky and rubbed new rouge on her cheeks. She fixed her curls, brushed her hair, tucked last year's thistle blooms behind her ear.

She rubbed some spit polish on her shoulders so she looked fresh out of the lake, just rescued from the Rocky Shore. Thunderclap two. Her face in the mirror was patched, broken, and put together by a blind man. But that was fine. She was fine.

Breathe. In, out. One, two.

It was time to go now.

Put the past away, Missy. You don't need it anymore. Learn from it and go on, said the voice.

It sounded a lot like an old Polish woman. She smelled like peaches and smoke.

Maybe it was just the wind in the window, blowing the curtains around. Maybe it was the handful of olives and dill pickles she had for lunch, or nerves about going to the ceremony.

Nattie sighed, exhaling old aches, all dried up and dust-like, hardly worth a sneeze. She brushed them over the railing to the main deck one level below, where Jakub was selling tickets, the silly boy.

CHAPTER 64

HALINA carried the washtub of wet laundry to the backyard clothesline. It was only half of the last load, not too heavy. She was taking every precaution possible. She'd even cut back on the cigarettes and hadn't had a whiskey in months, except for when the need for circulation called for it.

She wore her baggy blue sweater, but not because it was chilly. The sun was climbing over the peach tree, which had plenty of white blossoms that would eventually be peaches, at least some of them. Not every bloom ended up a peach in the bushel basket. Nature was picky. God, too. He had his reasons. She needed to trust.

She pinned one corner of a sheet to the clothesline, then pulled the fabric taut and pinned the second corner. The sheet billowed like a sail on a sailboat, rippling in the wind, going somewhere far away.

Not really. Staying in port was good. She liked staying home these days.

She was fixing up the place. She could smell the bleach on the sheets. It was also under her fingernails and in the callouses on her hands from scrubbing and gripping the scrub brush so tightly. For three months now she'd been cleaning the old house, cellar to attic, removing the toxins that had accumulated over the years: deeds gone wrong, vengeful words, selfish acts, unsanctioned mercy. It needed a good cleansing. If the house had been a patient, she would have been administering enemas and purges.

She wasn't sure if the house was feeling better, but she was. The queasy mornings were just about over. That was a good sign. She was past the critical months when God was most apt to change his mind about another chance, another life.

God only gives you what you can manage, Preacher Jedidiah had said on her last visit. He was a good man, far better at comforting and consoling than the priests at St. Florian. Plus, she liked the music in Jed's church and all the singing. The whole congregation welcomed her, eventually, after they saw she meant no harm. Some made jokes, of course, but they were the good-natured ones, not mean.

"Don't you worry. You're welcome. You be like one vanilla cupcake in a bakery full of chocolate frosting, caramel cream, fudge bars, and gooey brownies with walnuts! That's okay, Miss Nurse," said Jed one morning before services began. *"Standing out can be good for the soul. Makes you take stock. Makes you want to be sure your nose is clean, 'cause you know everybody going to be looking at it."*

"Well, thank you, Preacher," she said. *"If that's advice, I'll heed to it. I put a clean hanky in my handbag just in case I was tempted to get snotty. Sometimes snottiness creeps up on a woman like me."*

"That it does!" interrupted Mabella, holding her hand out to Halina to shake. Mabella was sly-grinning, a half insult and half tease. *"But I suppose a white hide deserves preaching and saving just as much as any,"* she added.

"Maybe more."

"We won't hold that against you none," Mabella said, squeezing Halina's hand like she was trying to squeeze blood out of a turnip. *"As long as you done card-cheating. And leave those nether-world spooks at the door. And no more selling that dandelion tonic water at bingo night, mind you. Gave Jed the shits for days."*

"Well, I am focusing on other arts now. At least trying. But I can't help being a lightning rod for spirits with some vengeance left in their bones. I have what some call a colorful personality, you know."

"What you got ain't color, honey. It's hogshit. Plain and simple. And there's no whitewashing that. So don't even try that here, in this house of worship." Mabella straightened her choir robe, white with gold trim.

"Yes, ma'am." Halina knew when it was time to be contrite and humble. Baba knew, too.

The old woman seldom knocked on walls these days. She had dribbled away so gradually Halina didn't notice until it was too late. She really didn't need her advice anymore, though. Halina's skills had far surpassed the original healer's instinctive recipes and actions. But those rudimentary principles had formed a good foundation.

She had been tending to Anka some, helping her regain strength. She would have a long haul ahead. But it was possible, if Anka wanted to heal.

Healing takes work. It doesn't just happen.

Nattie finally understood that. Thank God.

Not everyone figured it out.

***

Chuck hated being called for the tag-and-bag runs in the middle of the night. They were always in the middle of the night, making the spookies even worse. Chuck lost the coin toss meaning Max got to drive and he would be the bagger. He hated bagging women. Especially the old ones. They reminded him of his mother, the ol' dear.

***

Halina picked a pillowcase out of the laundry basket and pinned it to the line. Then another. Then a towel. Then a smaller square of cotton. Then another. Until she had a whole flock of little white diaper squares flapping in the breeze, about to take off.

She was going to be ready. This time was the right time, she was certain.

***

Chuck and Max struggled to get the gurney up the narrow stairs. Always stairs. Always middle of the night. Always a copper standing at the doorway waiting for them with paperwork to sign. Always stink and flies. This flop house had plenty of stink.

"What took you two so long? I've been babysitting this dame an hour," griped the uniform.

"We've been busy," said Max. "I doubt she caused you much trouble, being dearly departed and all. Or is she a looker, giving you ideas, heh?"

"That's a laugh. Good one. Maybe she thought she was a looker. Or was at one time. Take a gander for yourself," said the uniform pointing to the body on the floor, laying in a tangle of dirty bedsheets, clothes, empty cans, old phonograph records scattered about. There was a phonograph player on the floor too, still turning, but only a hum coming from it, the record done.

The uniform shut it off. He could have done that an hour ago. The clod probably couldn't handle the smell.

The woman was either 50 or 90 years old or somewhere in between. She looked worn out, wrinkled, skinny and droopy, her hair silver, like the sparkly dress she wore. It had long fringe and sequins, like those dresses flappers used to wear. She had silver shoes too and legs all purply with bulging veins. And, a funny thing, she had hands that were too small, like they stopped growing when she was a child. Her arms were bruised, too. Track marks. A needle beside her. A card on the floor: Eastern Sun Imports. Seymore Houseman, Proprietor.

"I'll take that," said the uniform. "Maybe Vice can pay Seymore a visit. Too late for her maybe, but—."

"—Better late than never, I suppose," Chuck said, sliding the black bag under her, rolling her into it, arms flopping, a shoe falling off. He tossed the sequined shoe in with her. Symmetry. A woman's gotta have shoes. Two shoes. Wherever she's going. He zipped her up.

***

Halina counted the diapers. Hoping it would be enough. Hoping she could be good enough. She took a deep breath. She could smell peaches and lake air, fresh. She would be a good mother, as good as could be expected, but not perfect. She had bought a tiny little sleeper at a second-hand shop. She had soaked it and scrubbed out the stains. She wanted to be ready. Everything clean and fresh. She hung it on the line. Zipped it up empty. Neat. Tidy.

***

Another zipped bag. This one was for a man pale and scrawny. His eyes were still open, his mouth frozen in a grimace like he been screaming when he croaked. Scared of their own shadows, these junkies get. The driver didn't pay no never mind, nor no hoot, nor holler. Wasn't his job to give a rat's ass. So he didn't. He didn't get paid none for anything but bag, tag, and transport. Who cared about another junkie dead in some garage off Rush Street, where all the drug-crazed cats go to get their nibbles and fix. No one would miss this lowlife, he guessed. He zipped him up good. He wasn't going no place now, not ever again.

***

She would teach the child things, important things, like wellness and healing and the power of faith and heartbeats and pulse rhythms. Tides, dandelions, dragonflies, and mermaids. There's no escaping the burdens of family, but you can rise above it and be better. Good things come to the righteous.

Eventually.

CHAPTER 65

HER heels clicked on the marble floor. Her gray pinstripe suit made swishing sounds as she sashayed down the hall, emphasizing her sway with each step. She liked the feeling. She was a fox: sleek and elegant, but dangerous. She even sniffed the air, like she was hunting for prey, maybe a light snack, maybe a small critter she could roast or a chick she could pluck from a nest and swallow in a gulp. She was hungry.

The savings and loan building doesn't house prey. Only predators, she reminded herself, smiling, knowing she was about to change that. She held all the cards.

She paused at the glass door at the end of the hall, just long enough to check her lipstick in her reflection. It was perfect. Bold. Like her plans for the organization going forward.

You betcha, buddies.

She pulled open the conference room door and saw six eager-eyed bankers sitting around the oval table, drooling over the prospect of financing Salvatore and Son's new Brewery, Distillery, and Distribution. Great Lakes BDD. One out-of-place man slouched at the end of the table. His hair was mostly gray, stringy, hanging down over his eyes, matching a half-ass beard that was supposed to hide his slobbers and sallow complexion.

All that hair couldn't hide the droopiness on the right side of his face. She could see it. So could everyone else. This man had experienced a stroke. The vacant far-off stare was the clincher. This man was in charge of nothing. Not even his bowels, the distinct stink from that side of the room said. That was okay. Mimi could take care of it when she took him back home. Then, she could put him back to bed where he could be watched. Or not. But, first, the signature.

"Well, hello!" she exclaimed as she gushed into the room, hands on her waist, making sure everyone noticed her new silhouette, lean but still curvaceous. Much like a mermaid. Ironic? Just funny.

"I'm here gentlemen! Pat's here. Let's get this transition all sealed up," she said. "Sealed with a kiss, isn't that right, dear Antonio?" she said as she rushed over to the gray-haired man and gave him a wet, luscious kiss on the forehead.

Smack.

She left lipstick. She took a starched hanky out of her purse to dab at the red smear. She came close, nose to nose to the man. "Isn't that right, dear husband? Tony. Aren't you just the cutest man in all of Quebec?" Well, of course Jakub was cuter. The darling boy. Man. The heir.

She made another smooching sound, in the air. And she winked at Mimi, the caregiver and accomplice in the back of the room, on standby with her medical bag, in case her patient had a sudden breathing spell or choked or fell or just stopped breathing. That could happen.

Anytime.

After he signs the papers.

CHAPTER 66

JAMES Riley, not to be confused with James Whitcomb Riley, paced the temporary stage that had been erected on the *Wolverine*'s deck. She was no longer the *Lake Maiden*. He scanned his clipboard of last-minute items for confirmation. All was on schedule, everything going as planned for the christening. The navy specialized in precision and execution of complex endeavors like this one. If they could coordinate fleet maneuvers across two theaters of war in two oceans, they could easily launch a new training program. Simple.

Commander Richard Whitehead made it look simple. The man was a master at planning and logistics. It had been an honor to work under him and see how he pulled off such a plan. So far, *all systems go.*

The hard part came next. The first landings and takeoffs were scheduled for this afternoon, with the flight instructors making the initial runs. There were still some questions about what wind speed they would need for the aircraft to get the necessary lift. James wasn't a pilot, so he wasn't sure what all that talk was about, but he knew some of the officers were nervous.

The runway wasn't as long as an actual aircraft carrier. It was close, but not exact. That had other officers worried, but not Whitehead, who had been a pilot in the last Great War. He was confident. If he had doubts, he hid them well.

Today, James was just worried about the press corps. The public wouldn't normally be privy to navy activity, launches like this. But the transformation of the *Lake Maiden* to the *Wolverine* and the work that would happen here would be right in front of Chicago residents and businesses. They needed to be on board, supportive, indulgent of the noise and chaos the steady stream of aircrafts landing and taking off in their backyards would cause. So, Whitehead had decided, a PR gesture was called for.

The upper brass went along. At this point, they seemed willing to give Whitehead just about anything he wanted. The navy needed his pilots as fast as he could churn them out. Speed was everything these days. Every memo he received had URGENT at the top.

Amid all this, finding time to spend with Nattie had been hard. They'd had dinner a few times. He was awestruck by her calm, peaceful demeanor. So tranquil. He had been stationed at Pearl for a couple years and remembered the Hawaiian beaches at dawn, the tide pools full of exotic creatures that had been trapped by the outgoing tide. She reminded him of a tide pool. She was beautiful in a natural sort of way, like a piece of green sea glass found on the shore, the broken edges polished by the constant churning of sand and water until they were silky to touch.

He had been afraid to touch her, but he'd helped her walk a few times, letting her take his arm as they walked to their table at the restaurant. She'd left her cane at home, she said. She seemed embarrassed about it, but he didn't understand why. There was no shame in needing assistance. A cane or the arm of an admirer were fine things to lean on.

He did admire her. She had survived so much. He wanted to know more about the *Lake Maiden* and what the old paddlewheel was like in its heyday. Her stories of the rat-runs, as she called them, were intriguing. Stories of bootlegger loot that he couldn't quite believe; the memories of a child exaggerated by time or bad dreams.

She had plans for the loot, she said. She needed the money. She had an old friend with medical bills, and her father's medicine wasn't cheap. She was broke.

I could help fix things if she would let me.

Most of the work on the *Lake Maiden* had been on the deck. The lower skeleton was basically left intact, just the extras removed to make her lighter and faster. Furniture, of course, was extracted, along with cosmetic frivolities like the wooden staircase. They kept the auditorium for training lectures. Unlike full-sized carriers, there would be no elevators or deck for aircraft storage. So the lower decks didn't get much attention. She was right: her loot, if it existed, might still be in the walls. A chance.

He was willing to risk his career so she could find out.

Today might be the last chance.

Once the daily routine of qualifying pilots started, getting a civilian on board would be nearly impossible. It was now or never.

***

There she was. She wore a beautiful lavender dress, the collar buttoned all the way up to her neck, hiding her tattoos. She was so sensitive about them. Her dress was longer than most women wore their hemlines today; she was sensitive about her legs, too, it seemed. Someday he would get her to see she was splendid.

Szymon was next to her, acting overbearing and protective, as usual. James had formed a respectful alliance with him, accepting that they each played a role in Nattie's life. Nattie could use a big brother. Szymon had also been helping with the captain as his health faded. The big man was surprisingly good at nurturing, having tended to his sister for so long.

Nattie pushed Captain Wiśniewski in his wheelchair. He seemed frail but alert. He was coping with the loss of his dancer girlfriend well, it seemed. He had been stoic about the loss, Nattie had said.

"She was an old doll, what could you expect?"

James shook his hand, and Captain locked eyes with him, drilling him with questions and making accusations with his steely grimace. Without his oxygen tank, which was tied to home, breathing was difficult for the captain. He wheezed noisily, his chest rattling like it had nuts and bolts banging around.

James was eager to get out of this man's reach. His ice glares looked like they could do some damage. The man had probably done plenty of damage in his day, and prison would have toughened him further.

How can such a cold, harsh man have such a gentle daughter?

It seemed family didn't completely dictate a person's outcome. Thank God.

"You look lovely, Nattie. I'm so glad you're here early. I can show you around—a nickel tour," he said a little too loudly. He wasn't good at acting. But he remembered his lines.

Szymon offered to sit with the captain, waiting for the others to arrive. Szymon knew nothing of the plan. They thought it was best that no one else was involved, in case something went wrong.

"We'll be back soon," James added. They scurried away, James feeling like a kid about to raid his grandmother's cookie jar. Nattie's eyes were wide open, turquoise, bright. She was beautiful.

There were no staircases anymore. They had to go down a metal ladder. He went first so he could catch her if she slipped. He was careful to avoid looking up her dress as she slowly made her way down. But he couldn't help but notice the scars on her legs, as they were right in front of his face. She saw him looking uncomfortable. *Damn.* He should have hidden his face better.

As she stepped down the last step, she folded her dress around her legs, wiped at them, like she could wipe away the scars.

"Don't, Nattie. There's no need to do that," he said.

"You're right." She took a deep breath. "Besides, there's no time." She looked around, did a quick scan, got her bearings. "My tank was here, front and center, with curtains on either side and a small dressing room for me behind my tank. That's where I would wait for the next batch of gawkers—that's what I called passengers," she said in a tour guide's monotone voice. "The tank was glass. It had a throne, some slimy sand, and a few buckets of water Jedediah the janitor-preacher would haul over." She looked at James, asking something with her eyes.

He felt round and soft, damp with compassion—the blubbering, embarrassing kind that was a waste of time. He felt on the verge of erupting and wondered if she could see through the officer façade.

"I'm sure you were beautiful in your costume," he said.

She frowned. Apparently, compliments were not the secret to winning her affection.

Of course not, man. Wise up.

"I hid my treasures in the sand. There were gifts from men: jewelry and pearls. They liked to give me pearls . . ."

"But Nattie, honey, we need to find your treasures," James said, interrupting her. "We have to hurry. Where was the rat-run, Nattie?"

CHAPTER 67

NATTIE'S mind raced. This was all too much. She was on the *Lake Maiden*, a frightened girl in love with a red-haired boy who'd stood her up to go hang out in the boiler room and get in a fight with the tough fellas he wanted to be like. He'd thought he could be one of them. He couldn't be one of them if his life counted on it.

He left her alone. Abandoned her.

"Maybe we'll go a-sailin' Saturday."
"That would be fun."

Had she answered? Or did she just think it? Her tongue got fat and stupid when she thought of him ogling the other girls, especially the galley girl with her braids and flour-dusted, heaving chest.

Jakub liked the biscuit girl.

Nattie's brain got confused, full of static and anger and made-up sounds like underwater creatures living in her ears, like static from the wireless, like her mother yelling for her at the shore.

"Come back from the water. You're too close to the water."
Until she fell asleep in the sand, snoring, with whiskey
slobbers on her face, and the man with black hair slapped her.
And then he smacked at the ants on her face. He wanted to kill
the ants.
Or Queenie?
He yelled at her. She spit in his face. He got blustery, fumed,
sizzled red-hot mad. She said she changed her mind.
He said the deal was made. She couldn't back out. She said
No. He said too bad. He put his hands around her throat. He
choked her and choked her and squeezed harder.

Her eyes were open but they didn't blink. She stared without seeing.

Then Captain-Father came. He pulled Nattie out of the water that was eating her dead legs that couldn't kick fast enough to swim.

But he left Queenie to be washed away. Cleansed by the waves.

Thunderclap one.

"We'll sail down the mezzanine, you and me. I bet those wooden wheels could get going plenty fast with a good shove. That's what I'll do. Give you a big shove."

Thunderclap two.

James poked her arm.

He looked so handsome in his dress whites. Why was he gawking at her like that?

"C'mon James, hurry," she said. "The rat-run was a corridor just for crew so we could bypass passengers. Mostly it was so the whiskey could be hidden if there was a raid." She looked back to see if he was following her. She took his hand to hurry him along.

He's so sweet, innocent looking. How can he survive a war? He'll need a tonic to make him stronger, I bet. I'll have Nurse make him some tonics.

"I loved to play in them, sneaking around, people never knowing where I might pop up. I would just pop up! Surprise, grab a drink or some diamonds, and disappear again," she said, laughing. "It was great fun, like playing hide-and-seek with the entire ship."

There were fun times.

"Father never knew where I was. Mimi and Margret would get so mad. The mermaid wasn't ready for a performance, they thought. Then I'd pop out of the rat-run in the auditorium. Here I am! No wonder they were so annoyed with me." She started feeling along the wall, along the riveted seams held together by a fresh coat of US Navy paint.

"We could access the passageway from behind my tank. There was a button in the wall. Come on, help me look. It should be about here."

She ran her fingers along the walls, listening for vibrations and sounds, whispers from her old friend. The *Lake Maiden* was silent. Angry? Hurt beyond caring.

This is no way to be, boat. Play nice. It's me.

There! "I found it!" A slight bump like a mosquito bite that had been scratched raw. It had been painted over, a pukey shade of green.

The panel slid open. There was the dark walkway, familiar and welcoming.

"G8. For eight days of the week, Jinks told me."

"But there are seven days of—"

"That was the joke. Waiters—and mermaids—got the eighth day of the week off."

"Where are we now?"

"M2. So, down a level and six sections that way. I'm going. You wait here."

He tried arguing, but she didn't listen. She knew this boat and these passages and wasn't going to leave this last game of hide-and-seek to someone else. She needed this.

Even though the door remained open, the light was dim and got dimmer the further she went. The string of lights wasn't much help. Half of the lightbulbs were busted. She felt her way, hands on both sides of the run, stepping carefully so she didn't trip on . . . something.

I just hope there aren't real rats. Alive or dead.

She didn't hear anything. Not even the gurgling of engines or pipes or water lapping at the hull. It was odd. This wasn't the living, breathing *Lake Maiden* she had known. This vessel was stoic and silent. She didn't recognize it.

A few more yards to go, but the passageway was almost totally black now. She couldn't make out any more chalk codes. The air was stuffy, hard to breathe. She took small shallow breaths through her open mouth. Why wasn't there air? She felt like she was suffocating, in a water tank with no bubbling airline.

The other entrances and exits were all shut off. Of course, that was it.

It's only because you're nervous. Stay calm. In, out. One, two.

She counted her steps, trying to keep track of where she was. She pictured the mezzanine and the distance from her tank to the bandstand, the VIP tables with red fringe tablecloths.

This should be G8. There should be another button on the right wall now.

She groped around, palms open, fingers spread wide, fingertips tingling with anticipation.

She choked and gasped. She needed air.

She found the button to vault-four.

The last time it was touched was the night of the storm, when Jinks hid the loot, when Silas died because of a silly fight, when Jakub said goodbye.

It opened.

The vault was closet sized, big enough for a couple kegs of whiskey. There were no barrels, though. She felt along the dark walls and floor. There, in the back corner, on the ground, her fingers found a fabric bundle, lumpy, metal clinking.

Her heart raced.

Through the fabric she recognized the shape. A crown. Her crown! The gift from her father. She never got to wear it on stage, she realized. Other jewels, a necklace, hatpins, diamonds. Gold. Hope.

She turned and stumbled, bumbled, fumbled, dark closing in.

There wasn't enough air. The vault door had closed behind her.

Her chest heaved and gasped, empty.

The hose is kinked.

She couldn't see, couldn't breathe, couldn't swim.

She couldn't give up now. She needed to open the vault, follow the rat-run out. Air. James. A better life. Free of old chains.

Little breaths. One. Two. Three. A polka.

Roll out the barrel. Roll out the beer barrel of fun.

Fingers groped to find the vault door. Where was it? A button? A switch? She pat-patted walls, bricks, the edges, the floor, the gaps, the nothing spaces.

Her legs wobbled, weak. Panic. She fell.

"Get up off the ground. Do want to get your dress dirty?"

It was her mother's voice, shrill with distain.

"I can't help it."

"That's a lousy excuse," the woman in a black sequined gown said, spittle and ants flying off her bright red lips as the spotlight closed in on her hideous face, long dead, long defeated, but still nagging.

"Get up. I'm not going to pick you up, you know."

"I don't need your help," Nattie gasped. "Not anymore." She groped along the vault door. There! She found the trigger. The door slid open.

"Bravo! Bravo!" the Opera House audience cheered.

She stumbled back into the corridor, determined to find her way out.

"Bravo! More!" the *Lake Maiden* audience cheered.

At least there was a light. A dangling light bulb cast odd shapes onto the wall. She brushed at them like they were cobwebs.

"Maybe I need your help. Have you ever thought of that?" the woman whisper-hissed.

"It's too late," answered Nattie

"You can still forgive. Forgive."

The word was like a spray of steam from a boiler.

"Forgiveness," said a gasp of oxygen from a kinked tube.

"Ssss. Shhh. Pleasssse. Sssstop crying, baby," said a desperate voice *"Stop it."*

Nattie shook her head at the pathetic woman.

"I've hated you all these years. I should have pitied you."

"I didn't want your pity," Queenie sobbed.

"*I never wanted anyone's pity,*" Nattie answered.

"You're wrong. Wrong. You were all wrong. It was wrong," Queenie cried, words sluggish and sloppy and hard to understand.

But Nattie understood clearly. With bright clarity.

Escape. She needed out of this passage way. *Out. Now. Air.*

"Follow me," called Jakub.

"March," ordered a soldier with bandaged eyes and mitts for hands.

"Repent!" shouted Jedidah from the mezzanine railing as he pushed Buster and he fell, silently into the abyss.

        She stood straighter.

I

        staggering toward

Didn't

        the opening

Do

        and daylight

Anything

        and air

Wrong.

        and James

She could see daylight at the end of the passage.

I didn't do anything wrong--

Except let go of a cat that was scratching her arm, digging claws into flesh, climbing and dangling and howling, a wicked beast.

And she stole this jewelry from passengers.

The bundle writhed in her hands like a snake. She held it tighter. She couldn't let go. It was the last hope, even if it was ill-got. It was all that was left of the dangerous days she survived. She deserved medals for perseverance.

She reached the entrance. No new scrapes. No seeping old wounds. Just some dirt on her knees she brushed off quickly before James could see.

"Look, James! I found it! Look!"

James was at the opening, waiting for her. And so was Commander Whitehead.

She froze, pulling the bundle of jewels closer, gripping them tighter.

"Miss Wiśniewski, I see you made yourself at home—once again—on board," he said.

She stood taller, making the curve of her spine almost-straight, as best as it could be.

"Of course," she said with the confident fierceness of a captain steering his ship through a storm. "This was my home."

"But now it belongs to me. Well, to the US Navy."

"The US Navy was about to steal my belongings. I just wanted them back. That's all."

"Let me see these belongings. What kind of contraband do we have? We can't have someone removing items that belong to the US Navy . . ."

He grabbed the blue-green scarf that had hung around the dressing room. He untied the knot and undid the twirly twists of fabric that had been wrapped so tightly for years.

He had trouble holding it all. Brooches fell from his hands to the ground. Necklaces dangled; the clumps of pearls wiggled as they uncoiled from their tight imprisonment. Then there was the crown. It hadn't tarnished a bit. It was still bright, polished gold, shiny with stones that sparkled like magic and heaven combined.

Commander Whitehead put the crown on her head. It fit so much better now than when she was sixteen. Maybe she had grown up a little.

The commander adjusted it slightly.

"I see you dropped a little doodad on your way to your seat. It looks fine now," he said.

The commander handed the bundle of other jewels to James.

"Here, Riley. Fix this. Inventory these items and mark them for donation to some worthy cause. The navy has no need for jewelry. What were you thinking?" His words were stern, but his voice was amused. He bent closer to her ear and whispered, "You look splendiferous."

Then he quickly stood straight.

"A woman can't just walk off a US Navy vessel with navy property. Riley, get rid of these things . . . as soon as today's ceremony is over. Understand?"

"Oh, yes, sir. Definitely. Indeed."

Nattie understood, too, and she trusted them. It had been a long time since she'd trusted someone so completely.

The commander nodded and ushered Nattie down the big open space that used to be a mezzanine, letting her lean on him, while James followed, restoring the bundle to a neat package, as ordered.

"So, Miss Wiśniewski, Mermaid Queen. I'm glad you're wearing your crown today. We've arranged for a photographer from the *Tribune*. If he asks, you'll tell him, won't you, that this is your crown, one you've owned for years, certainly *not* one you found on a navy ship." He winked.

She nodded. "Of course," she said. She winked back, but he didn't notice. He was looking straight ahead.

"So, what kind of good cause do you think could use with a hefty donation? I imagine you have an idea, being you are such a clever young woman. The good cause will need to be something worthy of a seaman risking his career over. And a commander taking a gamble, too, if that matters."

She didn't have to think about it. She had known all along what she would do with the money from selling the jewelry and the crown.

"My friend, Anka, needs a place to get better. My father, too. And I know a nurse who needs a place to work, something important to do so she feels useful. I think my old neighborhood, Hegewisch, needs a clinic. A place for healing. It would be good for the people there, the Old Country people who don't trust hospitals. It would have fresh air and music. Dandelion tonic. And maybe a pond, some water with rocks around it. Ducks could swim in it, and we could feed them bread crust and old biscuits."

"No mermaids in this pond?"

"There's no such thing as mermaids, Commander."

He laughed. "Oh, I see."

"Now, dancing pirates . . . that's something else entirely."

"Of course, miss. I never caught your show, I'm afraid. I'm sure it was charming."

"Nope. It was horrid! But those days are all put to rest now. Water under the bridge."

He paused so he could pat her shoulder. "Well, good for you," he said. "I'm glad for you. I'm glad I met you. You gave me this idea, you know. You helped the US Navy immensely."

She didn't know what to say. She looked at Seaman Riley, who was nodding enthusiastically. He had such a handsome smile, didn't he? Her tongue got fat and stupid when he was around, her brain all mushy too, racing in circles.

Good times were ahead for them, she saw. A house. A child who was perfect in every way, head to toe. Running.

"Here, Seaman Riley, escort our guest back to the stage. I think we're about ready to begin. We've got work to get done. No time to waste. There's a war on, son."

Nattie took her place in the front row, next to her father.

She didn't fall into any dignitaries' laps. She didn't fly across the mezzanine, landing in whiskey barrels, making a lovely spectacle of herself so the Chicago and navy bigwigs would get a good chuckle.

She reached into her purse; not big enough to be called a satchel, but it held many healing totems and treasures, including a matchbox of dragonfly wings, a jar of bent fishhooks, and new white gloves bought for the occasion. She had been saving them, waiting until after the rat-run mission so they didn't get dirty. She pulled them on, counting the little white pearls on each wrist. She still loved pearls. No one could take that away from her.

She rummaged in the purse for some hairpins, too, and used them to secure her crown. Maybe she'd keep this stage prop, an insurance policy in case any old bootleggers came around with threats or demands of repayment. She would have something to leverage.

Smart.

She spread out the hem of her dress so it covered most of the seat. She liked to spread out the gauzy-fine fabric so the pretty little floral pattern, roses and daisies, looked like she was fresh from a garden picnic. She might be pretty enough for a five-cent postcard.

And her father looked so proud of her.

She patted his hands in his lap. They were wrinkled and calloused, cupped around something unseen and unreal. But she knew it was trying to skitter away, wanting to slip below deck, out of reach of creepy waiters, storm waves, and angry first mates.

"We'll be fine," she whispered in his ear. "You can let him go now."

Captain-Father didn't say anything. He didn't smile, either. But he opened his hands, and Mr. Whiskers scurried away, faster than a mermaid with a sequin tail.

EPILOGUE

GEORGE was a tall man. The navy didn't have flight suits that fit a tall man well. This one was riding up his behind and needing adjustment, but he wasn't about to reach behind himself and dig his boxers out of his butt while standing at attention on the deck of the *Wolverine*. He had more dignity than that. More smarts. And more fear of being seen. This was no time for stupid indiscretions.

As one of the youngest pilots in this class of naval aviators, he knew extra attention was on him. He was used to pressure and high expectations. Being from a well-connected Connecticut family had a way of putting a spotlight on you. People were watching.

He tried to concentrate on the announcements. The wind was whipping off Lake Michigan so fast that it made a roar in his ears. The flimsy flight helmet hardly helped. The buckles hanging below his chin rattled, a tinkling sound that belonged to some old Christmas memory.

He should have gone to the dentist before enlisting. *Don't think about it*, he told himself. *Concentrate. Do you want to wash out before you even get over there?*

He had a long list of things he should have done before reporting to duty. Many were more important than seeing to his teeth. He tried to keep them from distracting him. But the goodbye kiss from his girl was hard to forget.

They had talked about tying the knot before he enlisted, but she had assured him that they would have plenty of time when he returned. He was going to make sure she was right.

But the world was in a hurry these days, including the navy.

It was hard to believe he was standing on the deck of a ship that only a few months ago had been a paddlewheel. Even more confounding was that they were going to take off and land on this ship. It hardly seemed big enough. But he trusted the men leading this corn belt fleet.

The navy had acquired the paddlewheel and installed a long wooden flight deck, built a new bridge island, installed arresting cables, and rerouted the funnels to the starboard side of the ship. The ship was refitted while still afloat. They learned at the induction briefing that, at the peak of construction, 1,250 men worked round the clock. Forty-five miles of welding and 57,000 bolts with washers and grommets were used. Imagine that. Who was counting? The fella approving the budget, he figured.

The ship was commissioned in August, and she began her new assignment in January '43, stationed in Chicago at the Ninth Naval District Carrier Qualification Training Unit. But they all called it Navy Pier.

The navy training center in Glenview was also a big part of the operation. That's where they bunked. But no one was there long. Three or four days at most. The aircraft were stored there, too, since the *Wolverine* didn't have lifts and lower-deck storage like an actual aircraft carrier would. They took off from Glenview, flew to the *Wolverine*, and landed on her deck. The signal men were all new recruits training, too. So a pilot had to hope to get a crew who knew what they were doing. There wasn't time for talking. As soon as you were down, the next fella was coming in for a landing. They had it down to a fast-moving machine with three landings a minute. Then they'd do takeoffs, too. You'd circle and land again. And do it over. And over.

It took eight successful takeoffs and landings to qualify. If you failed, you likely lost a very expensive aircraft and your life. Ditching in the water meant a high likelihood of drowning. Rescue tugs were stationed around the *Wolverine*, but odds were against recovery, everyone knew. Rumor was there was one tug captained by a woman. After one crash, she dove in the water and pulled a pilot out of the lake. Navy gave her a medal, they said. He wasn't sure that was believable. But who could say what was truth these days? It was a nice story, anyway. Hopeful. Maybe a little bit of fairy tale was good for a pilot about to go to war.

Landing on the *Wolverine* wouldn't be exactly the same as landing on a carrier, but close enough, they said. Of course, everyone knew calm days would be a problem. The carriers needed to generate sufficient speed to meet the wind-over-deck landing minimums. Aircraft like the Hellcats, Corsairs, and Avengers needed speed for lift.

They'd be flying Hellcats tomorrow. He knew that aircraft inside and out. The navy made a fella do his homework. The first day was ground school, the second day was practicing on nearby farm fields, and on the third day, pilots completed qualification flights on the *Wolverine*.

The book learning was the one thing they could control. There was no controlling the lake. And if there wasn't enough wind, they would all be sitting and waiting, doing more book learning to keep them busy.

His class was on the deck getting a briefing about wind speeds. Officers liked to talk. They liked to get a fellow used to the feel of the ship on the water, too. Someone thought it would help you understand the rhythm—the natural up-and-down rocking motion of a ship. Rhythm. He felt it.

He could that see some men in the ranks were looking a bit green. Not him. All those summers at the family vacation home in Maine made him comfortable with boats. He'd been sailing since he was a kid. The navy was for him, there was no doubt. But flying was the greatest excitement that was possible.

His hands itched, ready to get to the controls. He'd accelerate down the runway, gaining speed. Then pull back on the throttle. And take off!

Off toward the horizon, flying high into the great blue sky. He'd be free of all those expectations that got tangled around his throat, choking him. He'd be the man he wanted to be, no rich-kid labels pasted on his forehead.

Here I come.

Great things were ahead, he knew. As soon as this war was won, good times would be back.

And the ship bobbed up and down like it was nodding. Agreeing.

HISTORICAL CONTENT

Launched in 1912, the Seeandbee was a Great Lakes luxury side-wheel steamer cruise ship owned by the Cleveland and Buffalo Transit Company. It traveled between Cleveland, Buffalo, New York, Chicago, and Detroit. With the stock market crash, the paddlewheel business eroded, and the original owners went bankrupt. In 1939 the Seeandbee was purchased by Chicago-based C&B Transit Company, and the ship continued operating until 1941, when it was dry-docked.

Vice Admiral Richard F. Whitehead (then a commander) had the idea of converting a paddlewheel into a training ship. Although the proposal was initially turned down, it was fast-tracked following the attack on Pearl Harbor.

The Seeandbee was acquired by the United States Navy in 1942, renamed USS Wolverine, and converted into a freshwater aircraft carrier. Stationed on Lake Michigan, the ship was used to train naval aviators in carrier takeoffs and landings. Another paddlewheel operating on the Great Lakes, the Greater Buffalo, was also bought and retrofitted, becoming the USS Sable.

From 1943 to 1945 the USS Wolverine and USS Sable, sometimes called the Cornbelt Fleet, were used in the training of 18,000 pilots, landing signal officers, and other navy personnel. One of these trainees was George H. W. Bush, who trained on the USS Sable when he was nineteen years old.

ABOUT THE AUTHOR

Pam Records has been a professional full-time writer for over 40 years, with a background in journalism and a successful career writing about technology and software topics. In 2019 she ventured into historical fiction, loving the genre and atmosphere-rich storytelling. She has two published novels, including the award-winning *Trapped in Glass*. Her third novel, *Tangled in Water*, features a burlesque mermaid, bootleggers, and a mystical Polish healer that readers of the first novels will recognize. Pam and her husband recently uprooted from the Midwest and moved to Savannah, a city rich with history—and inspiration for future novels.

Learn more at PamRecords.com

www.historiumpress.com

www.ingramcontent.com/pod-product-compliance
Ingram Content Group UK Ltd.
Pitfield, Milton Keynes, MK11 3LW, UK
UKHW041816110325
456069UK00001B/72